19. N
30. A

2

ARK LADY'S CHOSEN

23

Ple
To
o

B

DARK LADY'S CHOSEN

Book Four of the
CHRONICLES OF THE NECROMANCER

GAIL Z. MARTIN

SOLARIS

First published 2009 by Solaris
an imprint of Rebellion Publishing Ltd,
Riverside House, Osney Mead,
Oxford, OX1 0ES, UK

www.solarisbooks.com

ISBN: 978 1 844168 30 9

10 9 8 7 6 5 4 3 2 1

A CIP catalogue record for this book is available from the
British Library.

Designed & typeset by Rebellion Publishing
Printed in the UK

For Frances Zehner and Betty Martin, my mother and my "second mother." Their belief in me helped to sustain my vision for the books on the long road to publication.

ACKNOWLEDGEMENTS

Once again, bringing a book to life requires a brotherhood of dedicated people who are bound together for the love of the story. Thanks always to my husband, Larry, who is my first, best editor, and to my kids, Kyrie, Chandler and Cody who have to live with a writer. Thanks also to Christian Dunn, Mark Newton and Vincent Rospond for bringing my dream to life. And of course, thanks to my agent, Ethan Ellenberg, for his support and encouragement. I also want to thank my friends at the Carolina and Arizona Renaissance Festivals, who have allowed me a glimpse into the life of a bard. And of course, thanks to all my readers and to the author and convention friends who make life on a book tour livable.

THE WINTER KINGDOMS

CHRONICLES OF THE NECROMANCER

THE FIRST YEAR *of the reign of King Martris of Margolan, son of Bricen, did not usher in the hoped-for peace. Though Jared the Usurper wore the crown for less than a full year, the damage that he caused brought Margolan to the brink of famine and fractured the centuries-old Truce between mortals and vayash moru. Loyalists to the Usurper King went into hiding, none so defiant as Lord Curane of Lochlanimar, whose granddaughter was forced to bear Jared's bastard son.*

Just after the Feast of the Departed, King Martris Drayke wed Princess Kiara, daughter of King Donelan and successor to the throne of Isencroft. Their wedding, a rare love match, also sealed a covenant made long ago between their two kingdoms. The marriage joins the crowns of Isencroft and Margolan until heirs can be born to place the kingdoms under separate rule once more. Within a month of the wedding, the king and queen announced Kiara's pregnancy. Succession assured, Tris had no choice but to lead his army south to Lochlanimar to lay siege to Curane's stronghold.

On the battlefield, the great energy river called the Flow is violently unstable, making it increasingly dangerous for Tris and his mages to counter Curane's blood magic. The Margolan army is a tattered shadow of its former greatness, hurriedly reformed after Tris took back the throne. Rebels who followed Ban Soterius in the uprising, relatives of the thousands of people who were murdered or disappeared under the Usurper's reign, and willing ghost fighters make up the bulk of the forces, along with a few dozen vayash moru and those mages who have defied the Sisterhood to go to war.

The siege is going badly. Nearly three months into the war, casualties are high, winter storms are fierce, and food is scarce. Plague has broken out among the soldiers, sent by Curane's blood mages. Magic and the Flow pose as great a threat as any of Curane's weapons, and Tris Drayke may lose his life, his kingdom and perhaps his soul if the tide cannot be turned.

Within Shekerishet, a traitor threatens Kiara's life. Several attempts on the new queen's life have barely been averted, and suspicion falls on old friends and trusted supporters. Alone in a foreign land, Kiara must rely on herself for protection. The crowns of two kingdoms depend on her ability to discover the traitor's identity and outmaneuver the dangers before it is too late.

In Isencroft, violent opposition to a joint throne raises the threat of civil war. Cam of Cairnrach, King Donelan's Champion, has been taken as a hostage to force the king's hand. Cam has discovered the identity of a traitor whose actions betray both King Donelan and Tris Drayke, but he may well die before he ever gets the chance send a warning.

Lord Jonmarc Vahanian faces treachery of a different sort in Dark Haven. Rogue vayash moru, led by Malesh of Tremont, have slaughtered mortal villages in an attempt to draw out Jonmarc. Malesh tried to bring Lady Carina across as a strike against Jonmarc, but the Dark Gift warred with her healing magic, leaving her neither mortal nor undead.

In desperation, Jonmarc swore Istra's Bargain, a soldier's vow to trade his soul to the Dark Lady in exchange for the death of his enemy. It is a suicide pact. He and Lord Gabriel of the Blood Council, along with vayash moru loyal to the Truce, have left to battle Malesh, aided by the shapeshifting vyrkin. Destroying Malesh before a cure can be found for Carina may assure her death, because of the strong bond *between maker and fledgling. Malesh's threat to destroy a village every night left Jonmarc no choice, although the price of peace may be Carina's life.*

Tris and Jonmarc thought that taking back the crown of Margolan would return the Winter Kingdoms to peace and prosperity. They were wrong.

DAY 1

CHAPTER ONE

HOOF BEATS THUNDERED in the winter night. The wind was bitter cold. Jonmarc Vahanian pulled his collar up to shield his face. Thirty *vayash moru* rode with him, outfitted for battle. *Vyrkin* loped alongside them, shape-shifters in the form of large wolves. The *vayash moru* were the Dark Haven guard—almost all of its undead members, save the dozen who had remained to guard the manor house. The rest came at the summons of Riqua and Gabriel from their broods. Jonmarc was the only mortal among them. Tonight, anger and grief overrode fear.

They rode to end a war before it could begin. He rode to avenge Carina.

The skin on his chest burned over his heart where he had drawn the sign of the Lady. Jonmarc had made an oath—Istra's Bargain, as soldiers called it. In return for the death of his enemy, Malesh, Jonmarc had bargained with the Dark Lady at the cost of his soul. He didn't expect to return to Dark Haven.

The bond between maker and fledgling is so close that the fledgling dies the maker's death. Gabriel had warned him that destroying Malesh would also kill Carina, giving her less time to recover from Malesh's botched attack. Malesh's challenge to destroy a village every night unless Jonmarc faced him in battle left no other choice. And so they rode. Jonmarc let the battle coldness deaden feeling. He had one mission: to destroy Malesh quickly and painlessly. The truce between *vayash moru* and mortals would be preserved— at the cost of any chance to save Carina. After that—well, he didn't expect there to be an 'after that' for him. That was the bargain.

"Remember what I told you." Laisren, his *vayash moru* weapons master, rode up alongside him. "Fledglings die easy—wood or metal through the heart. Direct sunlight. Decapitation. But if Malesh has older *vayash moru* on his side, it gets tougher. Stabbing through the heart immobilizes, but it won't kill the oldest ones. Sunlight cripples but won't destroy—not if they're more than a few hundred years old. The only sure way to destroy one of the Old Ones is to cut off the head."

Jonmarc glared at him. "How do I know which ones are the Old Ones?"

Laisren's smile was chilling. "When nothing else destroys them."

Months of training with Laisren had honed Jonmarc's legendary sword skills sharp enough to hold his own against a *vayash moru* opponent. Pitched battle against dozens of undead fighters would be something else entirely. Jonmarc had hedged his bet. Underneath his right sleeve was a single crossbow quarrel in a powerful spring-loaded launcher. It was his last resort, useful only when he was close enough for point-blank range. Malesh was young enough in the Dark Gift that a quarrel through the heart might destroy him. If not, it would immobilize him long enough for Jonmarc to strike the fatal blow. Under his left sleeve was a knife sheathed for quick release. A baldric across his chest held more knives, and a crossbow was slung over his shoulder. In his right boot, he had a blade that he could slip forward. It wasn't much, but he hoped it was enough.

A forbidding stand of massive trees stretched between the village and Dark Haven. Local legend held the forest to be haunted, and few hunters would venture into these woods even in dire times. As they rode, Jonmarc sensed the presence of spirits around them as wisps of green light flickered in the distance between the trees. A year on the road with Tris Drayke, Margolan's Summoner king, had made the appearance of ghosts unremarkable to Jonmarc.

The revenants seemed to be waiting, watching their group in anticipation. Ghosts were the least of Jonmarc's worries tonight.

Gabriel, riding beside Jonmarc at the head of the group, reined in his horse and raised his hand to signal the others to slow. They dismounted, and tethered their horses. The road below them sloped downward toward the small village of Crombey, a clearing surrounded on three sides by dense forest. A few dozen homes lay quiet in the moonlight, smoke rising from the chimneys. Just before second bells, the village was still. At the edge of the forest was the Caliggan Crossroads. The main road ran parallel to the woods, and at the crossroads, the road branched, offering a dirt path into the darkness of the forest, or down the hill into the village. The trampled snow made it plain that Jonmarc and his party were the only ones foolhardy enough to take the forest road. Dark stories told of a sharp-toothed crone who would set upon travelers at the crossroads and feast on their hearts. Tonight, the crossroads was empty.

In the distance, bells tolled twice.

As the last tones of the bells faded, dark shapes streaked from the forest, moving fast, gliding above the snow.

"It begins," Gabriel murmured, stepping forward to meet a dark-clad opponent.

Jonmarc drew his sword and stood ready, gripping the hilt two-handed. He struggled against his own mortal fear and the pounding of his heart for the awareness that would let him track the movements of his opponents. He had the fleeting image of a slim, blond man barely out of his teens as the first *vayash moru* struck at him. Jonmarc wheeled, landing a solid Eastmark kick that threw his enemy backward. The black-clad man lunged again, and Jonmarc swung with his sword, connecting hard with the attacker's shoulder and opening a gash that would have felled a mortal. Jonmarc could hear laughter as the man swung his own sword, a pounding blow that made Jonmarc stagger backward as he parried.

Jonmarc could not spare his attention for the fighting around him. Out of the corner of his eye, he saw that a force at least as large as his own was engaged against them. He could hear the clang of steel and the snarls of the *vyrkin*. A second *vayash moru* joined the blond man, circling Jonmarc like a predator.

"Where's Malesh?" Jonmarc shouted. "This was his challenge. I came. Didn't he have the balls to finish what he started?"

"Malesh will come in his own time," the blond man said with a cold smile. There was a blur of motion. Jonmarc let his intuition guide him and reacted more by feel than by sight. He swung hard; his blade connected again. At the edge of his sight, he saw the second *vayash moru* move.

Jonmarc lashed out with his sword and wheeled into a high Eastmark kick. His blade sank deep into the blond man's chest, spilling dark ichor across the snow. The *vayash moru* stepped back, sliding along the blade, and began to tremble. Jonmarc lunged, twisting the sword, and the *vayash moru* arched and screamed. The second man attacked faster than Jonmarc could turn, and he felt the *vayash moru*'s sword slice painfully into his forearm. Before Jonmarc could swing again, there was a rush of air and a large, gray form sprang from the shadows. A huge wolf tackled the *vayash moru*, teeth bared, knocking him backward. Behind them in the snow, the body of the first *vayash moru*, stabbed through the heart, crumbled into dust.

The *vayash moru* slammed the pommel of its sword against the *vyrkin*'s skull as the wolf lunged for its throat. Jonmarc heard the snick of sharp teeth as the *vayash moru* grabbed at the scruff of the wolf's neck. There was madness in the *vyrkin*'s violet eyes as the animal snarled and twisted, pawing at the air for the chance to sink its teeth into its opponent. The *vayash moru* ripped the animal free, throwing it hard against the trunk of a tree and tearing a deep gash through the *vyrkin*'s shoulder.

Jonmarc swung hard, striking for the neck, but the *vayash moru* moved faster, with a kick that knocked Jonmarc's feet out from under him. The *vayash moru* pinned him, bending

Jonmarc's sword arm back painfully and pressing against his rib cage with the heel of his free hand until there was the snap of a rib breaking and Jonmarc twisted in pain. "Malesh said we couldn't kill you," the *vayash moru* said, and Jonmarc could see amusement in his opponent's icy blue eyes. "But he didn't say we couldn't have some fun." The *vayash moru* brought his knee down, hard, on Jonmarc's thigh.

Jonmarc stifled a cry and let the knife in his left arm sheath fall into his hand. He slammed the blade into his attacker's back, sliding it through his ribs and deep into the heart. The *vayash moru* jerked upward, his blue eyes widening, as ichor oozed from the edge of his mouth. In one fluid move, Jonmarc flipped him backward, ignoring his own pain to straddle the *vayash moru* and bring his sword down and through its neck. The head rolled clear in the snow, spurting dark liquid that smelled like old blood. Jonmarc scrambled clear as the body began to disintegrate.

"Behind you!" Gabriel's voice cut through the darkness and Jonmarc staggered to his feet just in time to parry a broadsword's stroke that nearly tore his sword from his grip. His attacker was a woman whose dark hair was caught back in a tight braid. Her eyes glinted with hatred. In the shadows, the wounded *vyrkin* whimpered, but did not rise.

Jonmarc crouched, knife in one hand, sword ready in the other. He did not wait for her attack. With a cry, he charged toward her, bringing his sword down with all his strength as he let his dagger fly. The dagger caught her in the chest as the sword cleaved her from shoulder to hip. Jonmarc snatched his blade free and swung again, slicing clean through her neck. He stopped only long enough to retrieve his knife, rising in a defensive stance.

He felt air move behind him too late to turn. Strong hands seized him from behind by the upper arms, immobilizing him. The strain on his broken ribs made Jonmarc gasp in pain. A dark-haired *vayash moru* with the coloring of a Trevath native advanced on him with a cold smile. The man landed a hard punch below Jonmarc's ribcage that made Jonmarc double over, and then struck him hard enough across the face that Jonmarc's vision swam and he almost blacked out.

"Hail, Lord of Dark Haven," the Trev mocked. Blood flecked Jonmarc's split lip.

"Malesh send you to do his dirty work?" Jonmarc growled, lifting his head defiantly. The Trev swung again with a blow that made Jonmarc's ears ring.

"The rest we kill. You—he wants alive. For now." The Trev stood back, readying for another punch.

Jonmarc bucked backward, counting on his captor behind him to remain solid. He lashed out with his feet, sliding the blade in his boot out and kicking for the Trev's chest. His foot connected hard and the Trev registered a look of shock as a black stain began to spread across his chest from the blade sunk deep in his heart.

There was a howl and a snarl, and Jonmarc felt an impact as the man pinning his arms behind him staggered, loosening his grip enough for Jonmarc to twist out of his hold. The *vyrkin* took the *vayash moru* to the ground, sinking its teeth into his neck and closing its powerful jaws. Beneath the *vyrkin*, the *vayash moru* twisted and bucked, trying to wrest free. There was a crunch as the *vyrkin*'s teeth snapped bone and crushed sinew.

"Get back!" Jonmarc cried, readying his sword. The *vyrkin* sprang free and Jonmarc's sword whistled through the air, severing the *vayash moru*'s head. An acrid smell filled the air as the body crumbled.

Jonmarc looked around him, sword raised and ready. The snow was littered with dark patches of dust. In the moonlight, it was difficult to tell his *vayash moru* allies from their attackers, but Jonmarc thought the majority of his fighters were still moving. A shrill keen split the night air, and as one, the attacking *vayash moru* took flight. Gabriel and the others gave chase, but only as far as the forest's edge.

A whimper close at hand focused Jonmarc's attention. A large male wolf was seated next to a crumpled form near a tree. Jonmarc scanned the horizon once more for danger, and, sword still ready, walked over to where the wolf sat. A second wolf lay in a pool of blood in the snow beneath the tree. The wounded wolf twitched and moaned, then gasped and fell silent, its breath shallow and fast. From the angle of its body, Jonmarc guessed its spine was broken from the force of hitting the tree.

The male wolf nuzzled the fallen one and raised his head to howl. The wolf on the ground relaxed and shuddered one more time. As Jonmarc watched, the body began to shimmer as if the air around it were bending and folding in on itself. The blood-covered body of a woman lay still in the snow. Jonmarc knelt next to Eiria and covered her with his cloak.

One by one, he heard the rest of the *vyrkin* pad up near them until a circle of twelve wolves ringed him. The large male wolf, which Jonmarc knew was Yestin, howled again, and the pack responded. Chilling as a wolf's howl was, never had Jonmarc heard the depth of pain that filled this cry. Jonmarc heard a light crunch in the snow behind him and turned to see Gabriel and Laisren.

"I'm sorry," Jonmarc murmured to the wolf-Yestin. He looked up at Gabriel. "How bad?"

Gabriel's expression was somber. "Five of ours. Ten of theirs. But either Uri lied about the number of *vayash moru* Malesh made, or—and I think this is more likely—he's been joined by others. Malesh is less than a hundred years old. The *vayash moru* he made himself should be much weaker than all of those who fought for Dark Haven. It should have been a rout. It wasn't. I'm afraid the war has already begun." He frowned as he looked at Jonmarc, and ripped a strip of cloth from his shirt as a makeshift bandage. "You're hurt."

Jonmarc stood. He winced as the movement jostled broken ribs. "I'm still alive. That's more than I expected." Blood was running down his forearm. He let Gabriel bandage the wound to stop the bleeding. "Malesh didn't show up."

"He was here," Gabriel said tightly. "I saw him in the woods at a distance—but I was busy fighting two *vayash moru* that definitely weren't new fledges."

Laisren joined them. "I sent scouts into the village. Malesh broke his word. They're all dead, just like Westormere. Probably since sunset."

"Damn." Jonmarc looked from Laisren to Gabriel. "What now? We can't let Malesh keep slaughtering villagers."

Gabriel nodded, looking out along the dark horizon. "Agreed. He's trying to provoke a war and he wants to make a statement by killing you."

"The *vayash moru* I fought were definitely looking for me. They said they had their orders."

Laisren looked from Gabriel to Jonmarc. "There's another village half a candlemark's ride from here. It's the only settlement nearby that would be large enough for anyone to notice. We could set a trap for Malesh there—be waiting for him just after sunset."

"Assuming that Malesh chooses to strike there next," Jonmarc countered.

"Malesh is arrogant," Gabriel replied. "This win will make him even more sure of his abilities. Laisren's right; it's a logical next move. The question is, how many *vayash moru* does Malesh have on his side—and how many of the elders have joined him?"

"Riqua's sent all of her brood she can spare—everyone who's not needed to guard the manor house," Laisren replied. "We don't dare pull anyone from there—it would make it too easy for Malesh to double back and strike."

Gabriel pursed his lips, thinking. "My brood is small. Mikhail is in Margolan, and those who aren't with us tonight are at Dark Haven. There isn't time to find Rafe and Astasia and beg them for help—assuming they'd side with us. We're on our own."

"What about Uri?" Jonmarc asked. "Wasn't he supposed to bring Malesh back under his control?"

Laisren snorted. "If I know Uri, he's fled Principality and he's holed up in a nice, comfortable crypt on the far side of Isencroft by now."

"Malesh isn't going to listen to Uri," Gabriel replied. "It's too late for that. We've got to finish this." He glanced up at the sky. "We need to clean up here and get to safety before dawn. It's less than a candlemark's ride to Wolvenskorn through the forest from here—but we need to hurry."

Jonmarc nodded and turned, reaching down to pick up one of the discarded cloaks from a dead *vayash moru*. He walked over to Eiria's body, and exchanged that cloak for his own, carefully wrapping her in the makeshift shroud. The *vyrkin* still sat guard, and even by moonlight, Jonmarc could see that they also had received injuries in the fight. He lifted Eiria's body into his arms and gasped as it strained his ribs.

"We can bury her in the crypts beneath Wolvenskorn," Gabriel said quietly as Laisren brought up their horses. "Generations of the *vyrkin* rest there." He glanced from Jonmarc to the *vyrkin*. "And we'll see about patching you up."

Laisren swung up to his saddle and reached down to carry Eiria's body. Jonmarc gritted his teeth as he mounted and the movement jolted his ribs. The group set off, leaving the moonlight behind them as the shadows made it too dark for mortal sight. Jonmarc kept his sword in hand. After a long trek, they saw the hulking form of Wolvenskorn outlined in the moonlight.

Wolvenskorn's tall, sharply sloping peaks stood out against the sky, topped by narrow gables. Three levels of wooden and stone wings, one behind the next, rose from the snow. Each level had a deeply slanted roofline. The building was capped by a tall cupola ringed by carved monsters. The oldest wing was daub and wattle, with a sod roof that sloped back into the forest soil.

Grotesques and gargoyles looked down from the roof onto the front courtyard. Between them, intricately carved runes were both decoration and protection. The wooden sections of Wolvenskorn were set with carved panels and the lower halves were covered with overlapping shingles. An ancient circle of stone pillars circled the manor, placed there, Gabriel once told him, over a thousand years ago. Jonmarc hoped that their magic was as strong as Gabriel believed it to be.

Despite the time, servants ran to meet them, taking their horses. Jonmarc entered Wolvenskorn surrounded by the *vayash moru* fighters whose torn clothing told the tale of battle even if their wounds had already healed. The *vyrkin* followed them, some limping, some bleeding from their battle wounds. Two of the *vayash moru* carried dead *vyrkin*, shifted back to human form. A servant motioned to the *vyrkin* and they turned down a corridor. At Gabriel's nod, Jonmarc followed.

A fire blazed in one of the three huge fireplaces, and Jonmarc guessed it was a courtesy to him and to the *vyrkin,* as the *vayash moru* had no need of it. Piles of clothing lay in rows near the fireplace, and the *vyrkin* who were not too badly wounded padded over to them. The air seemed to shimmer and fold onto itself as the wolves shifted shape, their outlines blurring as they became men and women. Servants helped them dress, or wrapped blankets around those too wounded to dress themselves. Eiria's body lay covered with a cloak near the door, and Yestin, now in human form, sat beside the corpse and rested his head in his hands. Jonmarc walked slowly toward his friend and sat down wordlessly beside him.

There's nothing I can say that will help, Jonmarc thought. *And I know too well what he's feeling.*

One of the *vyrkin,* an older man with a trim, gray beard and deep-set eyes, took a large cloth bag from the shadows and laid it on a table. He lifted his hands over the bag and spoke in the language of the *vyrkin,* a clipped, tonal language that seemed to Jonmarc to be the speech of wolves adapted for humans. The man lifted his hands in turn to the four corners, and bowed to the north before carefully loosening the knots which bound the bag. *A vyrkin* shaman, Jonmarc guessed.

From the bag, the shaman withdrew a stole

made of woven hair, set with pieces of bone. Chanting under his breath, the man smudged a dark kohl mark on his forehead, chin and cheekbones. His eyes seemed to glow as he took a scepter set with a carved head of a raging wolf whose eyes were rubies. Two mortal servants came to assist him, bringing clean cloth for bandages and water to mix poultices. The shaman slowly moved through the *vyrkin*, beginning with the most badly injured. As servants prepared the bandages, the medicine man chanted over the injured *vyrkin*, and sprinkled powders or dark liquids into their wounds, taking what he needed from the pouches and vials that hung from his belt. Over those worst injured, the shaman laid his hand on their forehead as he chanted, letting the scepter rise and fall in his other hand. The music was strange to Jonmarc, ancient and decidedly not human. Jonmarc could see the badly injured *vyrkin* relax under the shaman's touch, and saw their breathing come more smoothly.

Finally, the shaman stood in front of Jonmarc. "Will you accept my healing, wolf-brother?"

Jonmarc nodded. The shaman indicated for him to stretch out on the floor, and Jonmarc did so, grimacing as his broken ribs protested. The medicine man put his hand on Jonmarc's forehead, resting thumb and forefingers on his temples, and Jonmarc felt the pain lessen. The shaman frowned, and pulled the throat of

Jonmarc's tunic to the side, exposing the mark of the Lady. A shadow crossed the shaman's face.

"Bloodsworn," he said in heavily-accented Common. He spoke words Jonmarc did not understand, and let his head fall back, raising his arms.

"He's given you a blessing," Yestin said without looking up. "He's asked the Wolf Father to heed your oath and deliver your enemy into your hand. You're fortunate. Such things are not granted to those outside the pack."

"Thank you," Jonmarc murmured as the medicine man returned his attention to Jonmarc's badly cut arm. He felt the tingle of magic as the wound closed under the shaman's touch, but it felt completely different from Carina's healing. The shaman laid his hands on Jonmarc's broken ribs, and Jonmarc could feel the warmth of his magic binding the broken bone together.

When the shaman had finished his healing, he turned to Yestin and laid his hand on the top of his head. In a quiet baritone voice, the shaman began to sing, and although Jonmarc did not understand the language, he knew it to be a dirge. He listened closely, and strange, wondrous images filled his mind, of thick forests and deep snow and the speed and power of the ultimate predator, of the solidarity of the pack and the warmth of the den. When the song was over, Yestin looked up, his eyes bright with tears, and nodded, unable to speak.

The shaman carefully put away his things, murmuring prayers or incantations as each item was placed in his bag. He left the room, accompanied by several of the uninjured *vyrkin*. Servants brought out food—platters of raw meat for the *vyrkin* and a plate of cheese and dried meat for Jonmarc, along with a glass of brandy.

When they had eaten, the shaman appeared in the doorway. He wore a long cape stitched with runes that seemed to shift and move as Jonmarc looked at them. Around his neck on a broad strap hung four disks of silver. The first was a waxing moon, and the second round disk was the full moon. The third was a waning moon, and the fourth was a ring, symbolizing the new moon. Two streaks of dark red paint had been added to the markings on his face. At his appearance, the *vyrkin* stood and gathered up their dead, filing from the room in silence. Gabriel touched Jonmarc's shoulder, approaching so soundlessly that Jonmarc jumped. Without a word, Gabriel indicated for Jonmarc to come with him.

They followed the silent procession down flights of stairs hewn into the rock of Wolvenskorn's foundation. Through torch lit, narrow corridors, they moved steadily lower, and the air grew colder. After many turns, the passage opened on a huge room. Torches in sconces set the room in flickering light. Large smooth stones seemed to rise from the bedrock and disappear into the ceiling, and Jonmarc wondered if they were the same ancient pillars that ringed Wolvenskorn. On the walls of the cave, stories unfolded in detailed paintings made onto the rock itself. And in the center of the room a large slab had been pulled back to open a shared crypt. Laid out in front of the crypt were three shrouded bodies, each wearing a single silver disk on a thin leather strip around their necks. From their outlines, Jonmarc guessed that two of the bodies were male. And he was certain that the third, smaller body was Eiria.

The *vyrkin* ringed the crypt, while Gabriel and Jonmarc stood behind them. Jonmarc saw Yestin, black-clad like the others, standing near Eiria's body. The shaman stood in the front, between two large torches. When the room was quiet, the shaman began to sing, and his voice echoed from the rocks in the yips, growls and clicks of the *vyrkin* language. He began a slow dance as he sang, and Jonmarc guessed that it was a story in movement, although he had no idea of what was being told. Even without full understanding, the ritual was moving, and Jonmarc fought to keep control, to keep his thoughts away from his last sight of Carina, lying still and pale back at Dark Haven.

The shaman ended his song, and three of the

vyrkin men stepped forward, gently lifting the bodies into their arms. Yestin sagged to his knees and made a cry of complete desolation as the bodies were lowered into the crypt and the heavy stone lid ground into place. The two men standing next to Yestin helped him to his feet, although it seemed to Jonmarc that Yestin leaned heavily on them for support as the group filed soundlessly from the chamber and back up the stairs to Wolvenskorn. Once back within the lower level of the manor, the *vyrkin* headed away down a corridor, and Gabriel laid a hand on Jonmarc's arm, shaking his head to keep him from following.

When the *vyrkin* were gone, Jonmarc turned to Gabriel. "Now what?"

"We rest. When we rise, we'll see if we can intercept Malesh at the next village."

"What if we're wrong?"

Gabriel looked solemn. "Malesh wants to be found. He intends to confront you. I suspect that he knows how fiercely we'll protect you, and his goal is to reduce our numbers before he attacks you."

Jonmarc wandered into an empty bedroom. Beyond the mullioned window, the first streaks of dawn lit the sky. "I thought you had to be at rest before dawn."

Gabriel stepped up beside him. "Four hundred years allows me to see a glimpse of sunrise and sunset. I've missed them." He paused.

"As Laisren told you, our strength grows over lifetimes. For those of us who survive this long, a few moments in full sun will burn us, but not beyond what can be healed. Much as if you thrust your arm into a fire. At first, the damage is reversible. After a point, no healing can restore what's been consumed. I don't fear death, but I'm no fonder of pain than I was when I was alive. As you saw on the battlefield tonight, there are better ways to die."

Jonmarc looked at the glow above the mountains in silence for a moment. "I expected Malesh to be at the battle. I thought we'd fight, and it would be over."

Gabriel regarded him, as if guessing his thoughts. "Perhaps Riqua and the others will find a way to bring Carina back. It's not impossible—it just hasn't been done before. There's still hope."

Jonmarc did not turn. "Personally, I've never had much luck with hope."

CHAPTER TWO

"THAT WENT WELL, don't you think?" Malesh of Tremont stretched out on the divan. Although he'd observed the night's battle from a distance, killing the Caliggan Crossroads villagers had more than sated his thirst.

"An excellent start," Senan replied. "Any particular reason you watched from the forest while the rest of us did the fighting?"

"For the same reason generals don't fight on the front lines. I wanted to see the way the forces aligned. See what Gabriel and Riqua could bring against us. And I wanted to see how Jonmarc Vahanian would handle true battle against *vayash moru*."

"And?" Berenn asked. Senan and Berenn were two of Malesh's inner circle, young nobles near his own age whom he had brought across to make existence within Uri's brood more tolerable. Tonight, they took shelter together in one of Malesh's safe places, the remnants of a family crypt beneath the ruins of an old manor house. It was one of the many such places Malesh had prepared for the night when battle would begin. Comfortably outfitted with chairs and beds, stocked with a supply of bottled goat's blood and lanterns, this safe place and the others like it had room enough for Malesh and his coterie.

"Our strategy is sound. Send the volunteers from the other broods against the Old Ones defending Vahanian. Pick off his best defenders."

"Vahanian killed three *vayash moru* himself," Senan countered. "I've never seen a mortal fight like that."

"Another reason to let the newer fledges find his weak points for us," Malesh replied.

"Can we expect reinforcements? What of Rafe's and Astasia's broods?" Berenn asked.

Malesh smiled. "Neither Rafe nor Astasia want to take sides. By not opposing us, they support us. Their broods are free to decide for themselves—and some of them are joining our ranks."

"This must end."

Malesh and the others looked sharply toward the corridor. Uri stood in the doorway. For once, Uri was completely lacking the golden chains and jeweled rings that were his signature. Gone, too, were his elaborate waistcoat and his frilled shirt. Dressed in black without ornamentation, Uri looked more like a mourner than a lord.

"End?" Malesh questioned, languorously swinging his legs down so that he sat up to face Uri. "We're only getting started." He fingered the talisman around his throat, the blood magic charm that shielded his thoughts from his maker. "What's the matter, Uri? Hurt that we didn't invite you to the party?"

Uri's dark eyes glinted with anger. "Riqua and Gabriel are bloodsworn against us—not just your fledges, but against all of my house. Tresa and Calthian are dead—killed as a warning and left at Scothnaran's doorstep. I've sent the rest into hiding."

"Some may be hiding—but the rest came to me. If they didn't want to fight before, seeing Tresa and Calthian murdered made them ready to see my point of view."

Uri stepped into the room. "You've destroyed two villages. How long until King Staden sends his troops against you? Even if you kill Vahanian—and it's going to be harder than you think—Staden can't let you succeed. Once the burnings start, the mortals won't be worried about 'good' *vayash moru* and 'bad' *vayash moru*. They'll burn us all."

Malesh looked away, pointedly toying with the gold chain at his wrist. "Then we will unite against a common enemy and take what is rightfully ours. That's what you're afraid of, isn't it, Uri? Burning?" He stood and faced Uri. "Do you know what I fear? I fear an eternity pretending to be less than I am. Playing the servant when I'm born to be the master. We deserve to rule over the mortals. You said so yourself. We deserve to rule with the Goddess because we are gods ourselves."

Uri's move toward Malesh was blocked by half a dozen *vayash moru*. "This isn't the way to do it. Mortals outnumber us. We can't make fledges as quickly as they breed. Even if they die by the hundreds, by the thousands, there are more of them left to hunt us." Uri looked around the impassive faces of Malesh's circle. "I remember being hunted in Trevath." He swept aside a crystal pitcher with his arm; it shattered on the floor, spraying blood across the room.

"You think you're safe in your hiding places. The mortals can track you if they want to badly enough. There are Hunters out there; Trevath and Nargi have never stopped using them. There are mortals just looking for provocation to send out the Hunters, and you're giving them exactly what they need to turn others against us."

"All these years you've protested the Truce— it was just empty bluster," Malesh goaded.

"We rule best from the shadows, behind the throne."

"That didn't work too well for Arontala."

"He pushed too hard—and he was a traitor to

our kind. Many mortals want what we have—eternal life, eternal youth, beauty. They're willing puppets to gain us what we want—a say in how the kingdoms are run, power over our own destiny."

"I don't care to rule from the shadows," Malesh said disdainfully. "War's coming—a war that will sweep up the mortals of the Winter Kingdoms. When it comes, we'll feast on blood, and we'll be the only ones strong enough to rebuild from the wreckage. The mortals will turn to us to save them."

"This is madness. You have to end it—now."

"No." Malesh swept his arm to indicate the room and the half-dozen *vayash moru* in it. "Your time is past. We rule now."

Uri moved before Malesh could stop him, crushing Senan's throat and tossing him aside. Berenn rushed toward Uri, and Uri dodged him, faster on his feet than Malesh expected, swinging around to strike again. Berenn maneuvered Uri into position with his back toward Malesh as Malesh withdrew a shiv from under his sleeve. As the *vayash moru* circled Uri, Malesh dove, sinking the shiv through the back of Uri's coat and into his heart. Uri sputtered blood and dropped to the ground, immobilized.

Malesh smiled. "I had it on good authority that the Old Ones don't die from a strike through the heart—at least, without other, magical weapons. My blood charms may not let me destroy you, but I can keep you from getting in my way. We're creating what you've always wanted—a world where the strongest rules." His smile faded. "My sources were a bit unclear as to how long I can keep you like this. The guesses ranged from a few days to... forever." He signaled to his group to move toward the door. "Enjoy your rest while we fight your battle—the battle you never had the balls to start."

CHAPTER THREE

"SHE's MOVING. LET's see if she comes around."

The voices were distant, dream-like. The darkness was so complete it seemed to have mass, a smothering dark liquid instead of nothingness. She fought her way through it with a desperation close to panic. The darkness impeded her, making every motion an act of will. She focused her waning energy for a final push, and burst through the barrier that kept her in darkness.

Lady Carina Vahanian opened her eyes. The room around her was dark, its heavy curtains pulled tightly shut. Candles glowed dimly, enough for Carina to make out the forms of people standing around her bedside, and the luminous form of Raen, the ghost girl, in the shadows. One of the forms moved closer.

"Welcome back," Sister Taru said with a tired smile.

Another feeling washed over Carina, a new sensation of ravening hunger. She felt as if she had been climbing mountains for days, pushed beyond endurance.

"Drink this." It was Riqua who spoke, holding out a glass of liquid. Carina was too famished to question, and gulped the liquid down before she finally registered the strange taste as she drained the glass. It tasted, she thought with revulsion, of milk and blood.

"Have I been brought across?" Carina's voice was scratchy and faint.

"Not exactly." Royster the Librarian moved up beside her on the left and sat on the edge of the bed. "That's the problem."

Lisette, Carina's *vayash moru* lady in waiting, stepped closer to help Carina sit, supported by pillows. Carina could see the worry in Lisette's face, and saw echoes of that same concern in the dimly lit faces of the others.

"What do you remember?" Taru asked gently.

Carina closed her eyes and grimaced. "I went to Westormere," Carina said quietly. "To heal the people with fever." Her eyes darkened. "We were attacked by *vayash moru*. They killed... everyone. I fought, but Malesh was stronger." Her right hand rose to her throat, finding the two fresh punctures that were not yet healed.

"He forced me to let him drink… and then he made me take his blood. He meant to bring me across."

Taru's eyes were sad as she took Carina's hand. "Malesh is young in the Dark Gift. He didn't know that a healer can't be brought across—not with the healing powers intact, anyhow. The healing magic wars with the Dark Gift."

"Right now, you're stuck between," Riqua finished. "You're not living, but you're not *vayash moru*, and you're certainly not dead."

Carina closed her eyes, sensing her healer's magic within her own body. After a moment, she looked at Taru. "I can't stay this way. I can feel the strain. What now?"

"Now, we try to find a way to heal you— or bring you across fully," Royster answered. Carina turned to look at the elderly scholar. Royster's white hair was even wilder than usual, as if he'd been running his hands through it. He and Taru looked tired and rumpled, and she wondered how long they had been keeping their vigil and whether they had slept. Even Riqua looked worried.

Carina looked to Taru. "Where's Jonmarc?"

Taru and the others exchanged glances. "Malesh challenged Jonmarc for the title of Lord of Dark Haven. Jonmarc, Gabriel, and most of the *vayash moru* guard left at sunset yesterday. They haven't returned, and the sun has just set again."

"How long do we have, to find a cure?" Carina asked.

Taru spoke, her voice unusually gentle. "We're not sure. There's no record of something like this happening before. But you're right—it's putting a tremendous strain on your body. We think that we have about six days to find an answer before your body burns out."

"There is another complication." They all looked at Riqua. "Malesh wasn't successful in bringing you across, but he brought you far enough that you're somewhere in-between. We don't know how strong the bond is between the two of you. Normally, the bond between maker and fledgling is strong enough for the first several lifetimes that to destroy the maker destroys his fledges. They die his death."

The horror of Riqua's statement dawned slowly on Carina. "So if Jonmarc kills Malesh before we find a way to cure me, there's a good chance that it will kill me, too? That I'll feel what Malesh feels?"

Riqua nodded.

"Did Jonmarc know?"

Pain flickered in Riqua's eyes. "He knew. But Malesh said he'd slaughter a village every night that Jonmarc delayed."

Carina swallowed hard. "Sweet Mother and Childe." She shut her eyes for a moment, trying to forget Malesh's boast about destroying Jonmarc. Instead, one of the dreams that had haunted her in the darkness returned vividly, taking on a dangerous new meaning. Carina opened her eyes and looked up at Taru. "I had a dream. At least, I thought it was a dream. Now, I'm not so sure. I saw a clearing in the forest, and a crossroads. There was a small village. The forest was dark. And I saw *vayash moru* fighting in the moonlight. But it was if I was seeing it from a distance. It wasn't a long dream—just a glimpse. I didn't see how the fight ended." Her gaze searched their faces. "Could I have been seeing it through Malesh—through the bond?"

Riqua's expression was somber. "This complicates matters." She turned away. "They were headed for the Caliggan Crossroads. That village is much as you describe." Riqua began to pace. "It answers our question about whether or not Malesh created a bond."

Taru looked at Riqua. "Does the bond go both ways? Can the maker see through the fledgling?"

Riqua shrugged ill-humoredly, as if Carina's revelation had thrown off her assumptions. "It depends. I wouldn't expect Malesh to be powerful enough to form so strong a bond. Perhaps it's a fluke because of Carina's magic. What we're doing now, trying to heal Carina, shouldn't be dangerous even if he were to know it through the bond. It might even work in our favor," she said slowly, thinking as she spoke,

"if it distracts him from going after Jonmarc."
She sighed. "There's no helping it. We'll work
around it."

"If what I saw wasn't a dream, if it was
something I glimpsed through the bond with
Malesh, then for some reason, Jonmarc hasn't
fought Malesh yet." Carina said. *I'm assuming
that in a fight, Jonmarc would win and Malesh
would be destroyed, which would kill me*, she
thought. *But if they fought, and Malesh won...*
Carina squeezed her eyes shut tightly against
the rest of that thought.

"It would appear so," Royster answered
neutrally. If the corollary occurred to him, he
did not say it aloud.

Carina set her jaw. "I'll help you search the
records. I can't stay in-between like this. And
if we can reverse what Malesh did, before
Jonmarc destroys him..."

"We must act quickly," Riqua agreed. "Lisette
can help you dress. We'll be in the sitting room.
It's become our study. Royster has some ideas,
things he's found in some of the old records.
They may be worth a try."

Riqua, Taru and Royster filed from the room,
leaving only Lisette and Raen. The ghost girl
watched from a distance as Lisette helped
Carina change and offered her another glass of
the blood and milk mixture. Carina regarded it
with distaste.

"I know what you're thinking," Lisette said

with a sad smile. "But it was the best we could come up with. Riqua didn't think that… as you are now… you could digest solid food. The bit of the Dark Gift you possess hungers for blood. You must keep your strength up." She offered the glass. Carina took it without looking closely and forced herself to drink the mixture, struggling not to gag. She handed the glass back to Lisette.

Raen dared to draw closer and knelt in front of Carina, reaching for Carina's hand with her own ghostly touch. Although Raen did not speak, her concern was clear in her face. "Thank you," Carina said raggedly to both Lisette and Raen. "I suspect you kept vigil with the others, too."

"We'll do whatever you need us to do, m'lady," Lisette said, and Raen nodded. "The whole manor is awaiting word."

"There's too much to be done for me to stay in bed." Carina tried to stand and wavered, as Lisette rushed to steady her.

"You need more time to rest, m'lady."

Carina shook her head. "If Riqua's right, I'll be dead in less than a week unless we find a way to reverse what Malesh did. So I'd better get up and start helping, or I'll have eternity to rest— and I wasn't counting on that just yet."

Carina stood by sheer willpower and managed to stay on her feet. Lisette drew her gently to the window, pulling back the heavy curtains to reveal the courtyard below. It was nighttime, and the courtyard was lit with torches. "Look there," Lisette said quietly.

In the center of the courtyard, a group of perhaps twenty people stood singing in the snow. Near them was a pile of objects Carina could not quite make out at this distance.

"As soon as word got out about what Malesh did, they started coming," Lisette said. "This morning, there were only ten of them. More come every time I look. They're the villagers, the people you healed, the townsfolk who believe in what Lord Jonmarc is doing to restore Dark Haven. Those things in the snow—they're charms and other gifts. The townspeople brought them. They stand there and they sing, they pray, they chant. Neirin offered them shelter, but they refused. They say they will stay until you're healed."

Carina watched a moment more, overwhelmed. She clasped Lisette's hand, and Lisette let the curtains fall closed. "It's a lot to take in at once," Carina confessed.

Lisette squeezed her hand comfortingly, and Raen stepped closer. "We're here for you, m'lady," Lisette repeated. "Whatever you need—just ask."

Carina slipped in to the sitting room a few minutes later. Riqua, Royster and Taru were hunched over a huge book that lay open on the table, and Royster was translating from a language Carina could not identify. They looked up as Carina entered, and Taru stepped to the side to make room for her around the table.

"Royster brought the books that he could from Westmarch," Taru explained. "You have to understand—Gabriel sent messengers to us two nights ago. We had very little time to prepare, but we each brought what we could. Kolin and Jess have made another trip to the Citadel and to Westmarch to bring more things, now that we have a better idea of what we need. Thank the Lady that *vayash moru* can move with speed!"

"To know how to heal you, we have to understand what happened to bring you to where you are," Royster said in a professorial voice that might have been explaining the lifecycle of a crustacean. "The thing is—no one has ever really looked at the Dark Gift that way before. We know how people are brought across, but we don't know why it changes them, or how the change happens.

"We're certain that there's magic involved— very old magic. And we think that it works—at least in part—like the shapeshifting magic of the *vyrkin*, only instead of shape, the *vayash moru* magic changes the way the body functions. It's all just conjecture at this point," Royster concluded with a sigh. "But it's a fascinating study!"

Taru looked at Royster with affectionate

annoyance. "Leave it to the scholar to get lost in his books," she said, but her eyes softened her tone. "If Malesh had been able to bring you across completely, there'd be no changing it. The transformation would be permanent. But you're in the middle—and that's why we think there's a chance to reverse it."

Riqua met Carina's eyes. "There is another option. We may find that it's easier to complete the transformation than to undo it."

"But you said that it was my healing magic that made it impossible to receive the Dark Gift."

Riqua nodded. "There are stories... old stories... that tell of a mage losing his magic, or having it taken away. If we could find a way to extinguish the magic, we think the transformation would proceed on its own."

Carina's eyes widened. "But I wouldn't be a healer anymore."

"That's right."

Carina sat down in a chair near the fire. She looked down at her hands, and turned them palm up. "When being a healer cost me my family, when my father banished Cam and me, I don't think even then I would have given it up if I could have. It's too much a part of me. I don't think that existing without it would be possible." She knew her pain was clear in her face, although she found that she could not cry. "Goddess help me! I'd rather die."

"That's what Jonmarc thought you'd say," Taru said. "That's why we've focused all our efforts on trying to reverse what Malesh did. But you deserved to know all the options." She paused. "We do have a couple of ideas on how to attempt a healing. Royster is convinced that the Flow has something to do with this. Lisette told us about how the Flow reached out to you at Winterstide, and how Raen led you down to the chamber below Dark Haven to try to heal the Flow."

Carina nodded, remembering. The Flow was a great river of power that ran from the far north underneath Dark Haven and through the southern plains of Margolan and beyond. It had been damaged eleven years before, when the dark mage Foor Arontala tore the Soulcatcher orb, the prison of the Obsidian King's spirit, from where it had been secured within the power of the Flow. That damage affected the magic that drew on the Flow's power, gradually making it more unstable, aiding blood magic and impeding light magic. Of late, the Flow had become volatile, and Carina had seen the effects of that volatility on her own magic. "What do you have in mind?"

Taru took a deep breath. "Curing what Malesh did is beyond the normal scope of my healing. But if you're willing, I want to try to tap into the Flow and channel it to magnify the healing energy." She took a deep breath. "I don't know what will happen. The Flow has been violently unstable. But I think Royster's instincts are correct—the Flow is part of this, somehow."

Carina met Taru's eyes. "I'll do whatever it takes. When do you want to start?"

A few minutes later, Carina sat in a chair facing Taru. Riqua, Royster and Lisette stood at a distance, watching closely. Taru took Carina's hands in hers and closed her eyes, concentrating. Carina did the same, focusing her healing power on the bond Taru opened between them. Taru reached out her magic, opening herself to the Flow.

Carina felt the familiar tingle of the Flow's power. It grew stronger, until the air around them crackled with strong magic. Carina fought down fear. She could feel the fluctuations in the Flow, random surges and drops that would make drawing on its power very unpredictable. Carina focused her concentration on Taru, who was weaving her magic to the very core of Carina's being, seeking to find and heal the tendrils of Malesh's pollution. Taru's power increased, and Carina stiffened, barely keeping herself from crying out as Taru probed at the changes that made Carina neither living nor dead.

A blinding flash of light crackled through the room, and with it, along the channels of magic, a searing blast. Carina heard a scream. The power of the blast threw her from her chair, knocking her across the room. Her head swam as if she had slammed against a rock, and the pathways of magic ached from the recoil. Carina opened her eyes as Royster bent over her.

"Are you all right?"

Carina nodded weakly, struggling against a throbbing reaction headache. Royster helped her sit. On the other side of the room, Riqua and Lisette knelt beside Taru, who lay sprawled near the broken pieces of her chair. With Royster's help, Carina made her way to Taru's side.

"She's breathing," Riqua said. She looked at Carina. "The Flow?"

Carina nodded, and wished she hadn't as her head throbbed. "It's as wild as when I went down to the catacombs. Healing magic doesn't usually draw directly from the Flow the way other magic does. If it's this difficult to manage healing, how is Tris fighting a war in Margolan?"

Riqua shook her head. "With great difficulty, I assume. Taru says that a number of Sisters have gone rogue and followed him as battle mages. He'll need all the luck we can wish for him." Taru stirred, and they turned their attention to her. Lisette lifted Taru easily and carried her to the divan.

"Not exactly what I planned," Taru said with a weak smile. Carina clasped her hand.

"I'm sorry that you got hurt."

Taru shrugged. "Not the first time I've paid a price for magic. Can you tell—did it make a difference?"

Carina closed her eyes and searched her power. The strange sense of floating within her own body that she had noticed when she first awoke remained strong as ever. "I don't think so." She managed a wan smile. "We could wait for daylight and see what happens if I open the curtains."

Riqua frowned. "That's not a good idea." She looked at Royster. "If the Flow plays a role in this—and I agree that's likely—we need to find a better way to channel it."

Royster had a faraway look. "I have an idea. Come on. I want to check something I thought I saw in one of the old healing scrolls."

They huddled around Royster and his books and scrolls until late into the night. Taru joined them, although she remained seated and looked pale. Carina realized that Taru and Royster had reversed their days and nights for her benefit and Riqua's. Still, she could see the fatigue on their faces. Time wore on, with Taru compiling a list of books and scrolls for Kolin or Jess to bring from Westmarch or from the Citadel of the Sisterhood. Although Carina listened as the others argued, she still felt too overwhelmed to do more than answer when asked a direct question.

Finally, the fifth bells rang. Royster began to

put away his books, and Taru stretched. Carina thought that even Riqua looked tired. "Riqua needs to take her rest," Taru said. "And Royster and I must eat." She looked with concern at Carina. "You shouldn't push your strength too far, Carina. After a short break, Royster and I'll come back and resume the work. You should rest."

Carina watched them go, and moved to follow.

"I thought you were going to rest?" Lisette had entered from the sitting room so quietly that Carina had not heard her approach.

Carina gave a wan smile. "I will. But my head is so full right now, I thought I might go to the chapel to think."

Lisette nodded. "We've kept you out of the sunlight as a precaution. Please, m'lady, stick to the inner corridors. Sunlight burns terribly when you're newly brought across."

Carina nodded. "You need to rest, also. I'll be all right," she reassured Lisette.

Carina let herself out of the room and made her way through Dark Haven's protected inner corridors down the steep steps to the chapel of the Dark Lady. Banks of candles ringed the room, and the torchlight behind the huge stained glass depiction of the Dark Lady made the figure seem to sway. As usual, the chapel was empty. Carina had never even glimpsed the *vayash moru* caretaker who kept the candles burning and tended the torches that lit the stained glass here in an underground sanctuary where daylight never reached.

Born in Isencroft, Carina had been raised to the Aspect of Chenne, the Warrior. As she and Cam hired on with the mercenaries of Principality and Eastmark, Carina had learned the ways of most of the other Aspects, and found that, as a healer, her heart was drawn most to Margolan's dual allegiance to the Mother and Childe. But alone in the chapel, Carina could not take her eyes from the glowing face of Istra, the Dark Lady, in the magnificent stained glass at the front of the chapel.

Wild, black hair framed Istra's darkly beautiful face. Red lips were pulled back to reveal sharp eye teeth beneath. But the expression was that of refuge, not of threat, and Carina found herself drawn to the glowing amber eyes, eyes that seemed to follow her as the torchlight gave the entire stained glass image the illusion of motion.

She had ventured to the chapel with the vague hope that she might find comfort. Now that she was here, she felt at a loss. She had no idea how followers of the Dark Lady made their offerings, or whether Istra might take offense if an offering were made to her in the manner of one of the other Aspects. Carina made the sign of the Lady and bowed low, and murmured the words of a half-remembered prayer from her childhood.

"In the dark places, I call to You. In the barren places, I seek Your face. Comfort me in the night, for I have no consolation. Lead, and I will follow."

A slight breeze slipped past Carina, enough to make the candle flames tremble and to ripple the surface of the reflecting pool that lay in front of the largest statute. It was a magnificent depiction of Istra, her protective cloak spread wide, lifting the broken body of one of her *vayash moru* children toward the sky, her features twisted with grief.

Just as Carina was about to leave, she saw a small bundle near the foot of the statue. She walked over, and reached down to pick up a stylus and a bottle of ink. Carina sank down to her knees, recognizing the intent that brought the items to the altar.

"Jonmarc's made Istra's Bargain," Carina murmured aloud. *Riqua was right. He knew what it would cost to destroy Malesh. He's not coming back.* She hugged her knees and rested her forehead against them, finding that tears were denied her. A glow lit the air next to her, and Raen's form gradually grew more solid. The ghost girl laid an insubstantial hand on Carina's shoulder in comfort, and sat beside her in silence as Carina rocked back and forth, inconsolable.

CHAPTER FOUR

M Y DEAREST TRIS
There's been no word of how the siege
is going, and my imagination is inventing all
kinds of reasons that I haven't heard from you.
Please send some note to ease my mind. I miss
you terribly.

I'm doing well and the baby is beginning to
show. Perhaps now I can keep some food down.
Cerise says the stomach problems will go away,
but not soon enough for me. Crevan means to
keep me safe, but I'm not used to staying in my
rooms all day with a guard at my door. Harrtuck
has gone with some guardsmen to put down a
problem in the hill country, and it seems as if one
by one, old friends slip out of reach.

There's so much I want to tell you, but I don't
dare trust it in a letter. When you return, so

*many things will be set right. Until then, we're
doing our best to carry on.*

*I pray the siege will be short and that you can
come back soon. Stay safe, and send word.*

With love, Kiara

Kiara sighed and slipped the note into an
envelope, then sealed it with hot wax and
pressed her signet, marking the wax with the
crest of Margolan's queen. She handed the letter
to Crevan, the seneschal.

"You're certain my letters are included in
the packets that you send to the front?" Kiara
probed.

The thin man fidgeted, reminding Kiara of a
long-legged bird. "Yes, my queen. But the snows
are deep, and even documents that require the
king's signature are not returning quickly. Some
have not come back at all. It takes most of a
week to reach where the army is camped—and
that's when the roads are passable and there are
no brigands. I fear the king has other matters
on his mind." Crevan smiled. "I'm sure your
letters to him are a comfort, even if he's not able
to respond. I have another messenger leaving
tomorrow with the supplies."

"Thank you," Kiara murmured.

"Begging your pardon, m'lady, but you look
tired. Perhaps you should rest."

Kiara sighed. "I will. I just need to slow my
thoughts."

"As you wish, m'lady. Shall I have some tea and cakes sent up?"

Kiara shook her head. "Thank you, no. Macaria brought up some mulled cider. I'll have some later."

"Sleep well, m'lady."

Kiara turned away as she shut the door. "I'm worried, Cerise." Tonight, she sat up late in Cerise's room, since the healer stayed up later than either Alle or Macaria. "It's been almost three months since the army left and I haven't received any notes at all from Tris. That's not like him." She set the letter aside. Beyond the frost-covered windows, the bells in the bailey tower chimed midnight. Jae, her small gyregon, lay as close to the fire as he dared, curled up to stay warm. Tris's three dogs, two wolfhounds and the mastiff, sprawled near the fire as well.

"There are all kinds of reasons why," Cerise said gently. "The war may give him very little time for personal luxuries. The king may hesitate to send so personal a message through uncertain hands. Your mother fretted for all the same reasons when your father was away on campaign."

"I wish Tris were here, Cerise," Kiara said quietly. "So many things have happened since the army left. Malae's death. Mikhail and Bian locked up. Harrtuck sent away with the troops. And the attacks..." Her voice drifted off. "I don't want to tell him about what's happened—

he has enough on his mind. But I know that if he were here, we'd get to the bottom of it." Her hand fell to the slight curve at her belly. "Staying locked up in my rooms seems like a poor way to manage my first months as queen!"

Cerise laid a hand on her shoulder. "Until we know who's behind the attacks, there's no choice." She smiled. "It's late. Crevan's right; you should rest."

Kiara nodded and stood, stretching. "If I don't hear from Tris soon, I'm going to scry. What good is the regent magic if I never use it?" Cerise always kept the windows open at night, and a cold breeze fluttered the parchment on the desk, making Kiara shift to move out of the chill.

Cerise frowned. "Carroway told me how dangerous it was when you tried to scry on your journey."

"That was because of the Obsidian King and Foor Arontala. They're gone now."

"There are still dark things that seek you—and your child—on the nether plains. Please Kiara, reconsider."

Kiara nodded tiredly. "All right. For now. Good night, Cerise."

Carrying her candle, Kiara moved to the doorway that separated her rooms from Cerise's. Jae and the dogs stirred from their spot near the fire to follow her. Kiara opened the door, and saw that Alle had taken up a spot for the night in a chair near the fire, and that Macaria had fallen asleep at the table, with her head on her music and her flute beside her on the floor. Kiara smiled and walked over to gently shake Macaria. When she didn't wake, Kiara set the candlestick on the table and used both hands to shake Macaria by the shoulders.

"Wake up, sleepyhead! You'll have a cramp in your neck."

Macaria did not rouse. Kiara turned toward where Alle was sprawled in her chair. "Alle, wake up!"

Alle did not move, but Cerise came to the doorway. "What's wrong, Kiara?"

"They won't wake up!"

Cerise closed her eyes and sniffed the air, extending one hand as she used her healer's magic. Her eyes opened wide. "Bad air. Open the windows wide—hurry!"

Kiara ran to open the mullioned windows and threw both sets open as far as the heavy leaded panes would go. She helped Cerise drag Macaria and Alle close to the cold, fresh air, and fanned them as Cerise went for cold water and her healer's pack.

"Can we open the balcony doors in the king's room?" Cerise asked. Kiara used her key to open the double doors that separated her sitting room from Tris's bedchamber, while Cerise went to fetch the guards. Ammond and Hothan, two of Kiara's favorites among the guards, came quickly, lifting Macaria and Alle easily and following Kiara into Tris's chamber. Kiara flung the doors to the snow-covered balcony open. The winter wind blew the curtains wide and wisps of snow drifted onto the Noorish carpet. Ammond and Hothan held the two unconscious women so that the cold wind would blow squarely in their faces, while Cerise daubed their skin with snow.

"Lay them down," Cerise ordered, and Ammond and Hothan complied. Cerise took a vial of green liquid from the pouch at her belt and forced Alle's mouth open, carefully dropping the sharp-smelling liquid onto her tongue. She did the same for Macaria.

"None of us has felt well today," Kiara said, helping Cerise administer drops of a second liquid.

"How did you feel?" Cerise asked tersely as Macaria began to stir. In a moment, Alle groaned and grimaced.

"Alle's had a headache since this morning, and my stomach's been worse than usual," Kiara replied. "Macaria was complaining of being terribly tired. She perked up some after she went down to practice with the bards for a while, but when she came back this evening, she tired easily." She looked at Cerise. "Do you know what it is?"

Cerise nodded, tight-lipped. Alle opened her eyes. "Why am I lying in the snow?"

"What's the last thing you remember?"

Cerise asked, letting her hand move from Alle's forehead down her neck and chest, stretching out with her healing magic.

"I had a horrible headache, and I thought that if I just closed my eyes for a while, that it might be better," Alle replied. "What happened?"

Macaria caught her breath sharply, and Cerise motioned for Hothan to help her sit. She opened her eyes, and shivered. "Where am I?"

Kiara knelt beside her. "Safe. We're trying to figure out why you and Alle got sick."

"It's not sickness," Cerise said in a clipped voice as she finished running her hand over Macaria's forehead. "As soon as I came into your room, my magic told me the air was bad. I've seen this before. Fire sends off bad vapors as well as heat. If something blocks the flue, the bad air fills the room. You're lucky that you were in my room instead of going to bed early. All three of you might have died."

Kiara and Cerise exchanged a glance. Kiara realized Cerise shared her suspicions. They said nothing as Hothan and Ammond helped Alle and Macaria walk back into the bedchamber, and Kiara secured the balcony doors behind them. Cerise motioned for them to come to her rooms, and made sure the door to Kiara's chambers was shut tightly with blankets sealing the gap beneath it. They opened the windows wide.

"Tomorrow morning, I want you to check my chimney personally," Kiara instructed Hothan.

"If anyone asks, tell them I complained because of the soot. Take a long stick and see if you can find something stuck in there. Once the air clears, we can try the same thing from the bottom."

"Shall I inform Master Crevan?" Hothan asked.

Kiara shook her head. "Not yet. Let's see what we find."

THEY SLEPT FITFULLY, huddled together and covered with layers of blankets, as the fire in Cerise's fireplace was no match for the winter wind that blew through the open windows. Jae slept at Kiara's feet, huddled next to Tris's dogs. As soon as it was light, Hothan left his post at the door for the dangerous climb to the palace roof.

They ate breakfast in Cerise's room and dressed in Tris's chambers, to give the guard time to check the chimney. After another candlemark, Kiara returned to her own rooms, which were freezing cold. The fire had gone out, and the open windows had cleared the air.

Wrapping her cloak around her, Kiara motioned for Cerise to bring her a lantern and grabbed a poker from near the hearth. Kiara shoveled the embers into the fireplace bucket, and laid a heavy mat over the still-warm hearthstone as she lifted the lantern and twisted into position to see. Gingerly, she poked upward with the iron bar. The bar struck something hard. Kiara handed Cerise the lantern, and poked harder, using both hands. The metal bar rang out against stone.

"There's something wedged in there, just beyond where I can reach," Kiara said. "It's got the chimney partially blocked."

"But not beyond the reach of a man," Cerise mused.

Just then, Hothan returned. His face was red with cold and he was rubbing his hands together. "You're right, m'lady. There was a rock wedged in near the top of the chimney—fit well enough to let the smoke out, but covered enough to keep the bad air in. I was able to pry it loose, but I probably broke a brick or two doing it."

Kiara dusted herself off and motioned for Hothan to take her place at the hearth. "Thank you. There's something stuck at this end, too. Please, try your luck." She handed him the poker. After a few minutes, Hothan gave a hard push and bits of rock fell to the ground. Kiara bent down and picked up one of the bits, turning it in her hands.

"That's strange," she mused. She looked at Hothan. "You're quite sure the thing jammed in up above was a rock?"

Hothan nodded. "More like a shaped rock, from a building. It had been chiseled."

Kiara looked at Cerise and the others. "This is the same—look at the tool marks."

"Someone meant for the chimney to be plugged. They meant for us to suffocate," Alle said quietly.

The seventh bells tolled outside. Macaria jumped up. "I'm due to meet with Carroway and the bards," she said, rushing into Cerise's room to change clothes. "I'll find out if they've heard anything—or seen anyone around the rooftop. And I promise to bring back fresh pastries if cook hasn't sent some up by then." Macaria slipped past the guards and into the hallway.

"What now?" Alle asked. "One of us has been in the rooms at all times."

Kiara took the rock and dropped it down the garderobe. "Who came near the fireplace?"

Alle frowned. "When I've been in the rooms, only the servants who deliver the firewood. Macaria and I take turns leaving for meals, but it's usually the same two men who bring the wood and set the fire morning and evening."

"Did you notice anything different? Did they spend longer than usual or do anything out of the ordinary?" Cerise asked.

Alle thought for a moment, and then shook her head. "I have to admit—so long as they came in and went straight to the fireplace and left without touching anything, I didn't hover over them. I don't remember them acting oddly."

"To most of us, servants are nearly invisible,"

Cerise said quietly. "That makes them the perfect spies—and the perfect assassins."

"No one asked to enter your rooms except for the fire starters, and the kitchen servant who brought up your supper," Ammond said. "I agree with Lady Alle. It was the same two men who usually come, and there was nothing about it that stood out in my mind."

Kiara looked to Ammond. "See if you can find the servants who brought the wood yesterday— morning and evening. Say that the logs were too green and didn't burn well. Or you might say I didn't like the way the fire was set. Anything to give you an excuse to see if the two regular fire starters made the rounds yesterday and whether anyone is acting suspiciously. We probably can't prove who did this, but perhaps we'll flush out some information."

"Done, m'lady," Ammond said with a bow, quickly leaving the room.

"Now, we wait," Kiara said, glancing at Alle, who nodded. "Whoever did this will know something went wrong once it's clear we're not dead. If we're lucky, he or she will double back to figure out what happened. And if we're not lucky… maybe whoever's behind this will wait a while before trying something else."

Ammond returned within a candlemark. "I found one of the fire starters," he reported. "Caught up with him when he came back to the woodshed for another load. His name is Lasset, and he's been at the palace all his life, except for when he ran away last year to hide from Jared. He's an older man, and he was most distressed that m'lady was unhappy with her fire," Ammond said. "Once I got him to stop apologizing, he mentioned that he hadn't seen Sarrey—that's his partner—since last night. Seems Sarrey missed making the rounds this morning, and left Lasset with the whole job. He says he doesn't do your rooms until after tenth bells in case m'lady wants to sleep late."

"What about Sarrey?" Kiara asked.

"That's the interesting part. As I was coming back from the woodshed, there were guards out behind the stables. I went over to see what the excitement was about, and it seems that someone put a knife in Sarrey's back sometime last night." He grimaced. "And since it's a sure bet that Sarrey didn't stab himself, that means someone didn't want him answering any questions."

"Thank you," Kiara said quietly, sitting down. "That will be all. Say nothing of this to anyone." Ammond and Hothan bowed low and went back to their post in the hallway. "Damn! We still don't know whether we're up against one plotter or more than one—or even what they hope to gain."

Alle smiled conspiratorially. "Let's try to get our minds off what happened. At least until we know what's behind it. I suggest something far more fun—like taking bets on how long it will be until Carroway and Macaria finally admit they're in love."

Kiara chuckled. "All last year while we were on the road, Carroway kept writing ballads and dedicating them to her. Honestly, he's moon struck over her whenever she's not around, and when she comes near, he pretends that he's all business!"

Cerise built a new fire with fresh kindling and wood from the pile next to the hearth. "I've never seen two people so attracted to each other make everything so complicated. It doesn't take a seer to know the girl's head over heels for him. If he's worried about getting involved with her while he's her patron, then why not find her another patron—like Lady Eadoin? 'Tis what many a lord of the manor has done when a pretty young ward has stolen his heart."

Despite everything, Kiara chuckled. "Or Macaria could take a lesson from Tris and me and combine falling in love with being outlaw vagabonds!"

Just then the door opened. Macaria entered and set the basket of breads on the table, turning away quickly. Even so, it was obvious that she had been crying.

Alle exchanged concerned glances with Kiara and took a step toward Macaria. "What's wrong? What happened?"

Macaria stifled a sob and turned back toward

them. "They've sent him away!" she said, struggling to maintain her composure. "Crevan's banished Carroway from Shekerishet."

"Why?" Kiara gasped.

Alle moved to offer Macaria a glass of water, but Macaria waved her away. She began to pace. "It's all over the palace. You know how careful Carroway was to never be alone with the queen. One or more of us were always, always here if he came to the suite, and he didn't come often. But the old rumors, about him and his patronesses, they just won't go away. Someone at court spun a new story. They're saying that he seduced the queen, that with the king gone, they've been lovers—"

Kiara paled. "Neither of us would ever betray Tris like that."

Macaria wiped her eyes with the back of her hand. "Most folks don't let facts get in the way of a good story. Paiva and Bandele, two of our closest minstrel friends, think it's being put around by Lady Guarov. She's got a mean tongue, and she was a friend of Lady Nadine." The others took her meaning. Nadine was the noblewoman King Bricen banished years before for forcing Carroway into an affair when he was barely in his teens.

"Where's Carroway?" Alle asked, as Cerise laid a hand in comfort on Kiara's shoulder.

Macaria drew a ragged breath. "He's under house arrest at the Dragon's Rage Inn, until the king returns. If it weren't for Carroway's friendship with the king, Crevan would have probably put him in the dungeon. As it is, he's forbidden from returning to court or being in the presence of the queen, on pain of death." She looked from Kiara to Alle to Cerise. "What are we going to do? He'll be charged with high treason."

Kiara drew a deep breath. Her heart was racing. *If the gossips believe the rumors, then only two courses are possible—that we conspired together or that he forced me. The penalty for either is death or exile. There's no doubt about the paternity of the baby, thank goodness, but after the birth...*

"Unfortunately, there's nothing we dare do," Cerise said quietly. "The charges may be against Carroway, but they implicate the queen. She can't lift a finger to help him without seeming to confirm the rumors." She shook her head. "We knew there were nobles here who lost their chance at power when Tris took an outland bride. There are Margolan interests that benefit from disgracing Kiara. And then there are Curane's spies and Jared's loyalists who stand to gain if there were any question about the suitability of the child to take the crown. Lady Nadine has a powerful motive for revenge. There are too many suspects, and we don't even know if we're fighting one or all of them."

"Aunt Eadoin will know what to do," Alle

said. "I'll find out what she's heard. She'll know all the players. I'd been thinking of asking her if we could come to stay at her manor for a while to get you away from the palace and out of danger. Brightmoor is small and all of her servants have been with her forever. It would be so much easier to spot an intruder or an outsider."

Kiara nodded, and met Alle's eyes. "Go to her. We need all the help we can get on this. Damn them! One by one, all our friends become targets. We've got to figure out who's behind this, or Tris could win the battle to find his court fighting amongst itself.

"The more we stay secluded in our rooms—trying to thwart the assassin—the freer the gossips are to talk," Kiara said, trying to still her own emotions. "But if we let it be known about the attacks—assuming anyone would believe us now—it undermines Tris's authority. He'll look unable to control his own court or assure my safety. If either of the rumors makes it back to Isencroft, father will be outraged, and the nobles will push him to save face. He's already in a precarious position with the divisionists. This could force him into two losing choices—to do nothing and appear weak, or to break the treaty and declare hostilities. Isencroft can't afford a war—and neither can Margolan."

UPSTAIRS AT THE Dragon's Rage Inn, Master Bard Riordan Carroway paced the small, spare room. Outside, the two guards who had escorted him at sword's point from Shekerishet kept watch. Carroway ran a hand back through his long, blue-black hair. His stomach had been knotted since Crevan told him what the rumors alleged. Nothing Carroway had said moved Crevan to change his pronouncement of banishment, and in the absence of the king, the seneschal's word was law.

A servant arrived within a few candlemarks after Carroway was imprisoned in his room. The servant brought the contents of Carroway's room at the palace, confirmation that the banishment was expected to be permanent. His instruments were propped carefully against one wall. Clothing spilled from a large trunk. A smaller trunk held sundry personal belongings. On the table, dinner sat untouched.

Carroway looked up sharply as the door opened, half expecting to see soldiers come to move him to the dungeon. Macaria slipped into the room, lowering the hood of her cloak. She looked drawn and her eyes were red-rimmed from crying.

"Oh, Carroway!" she cried, flinging her arms around him. "I came as soon as I could. Are you all right?"

Carroway gave a bitter smile. "For someone accused of high treason, tolerably well."

"But it's not true. We all know it's not. King Martris will believe you. You're his best friend."

Carroway sighed. "I'd like to believe that. But I've also heard enough stories about the kings of the Winter Kingdoms to know that more than one was betrayed by his best friend and his queen." He sank into a chair, his long-fingered hands clasped tightly together. "Besides, the damage is done. It's not just the charges against me. Everything that's being said also hurts Kiara. Margolan can find a new master bard easier than it can a new queen." He avoided meeting her eyes. "If I were chivalrous, I imagine I'd write a flowery note protesting my innocence and then have the good manners to hang myself, saving Tris the trouble. It might even make a good ballad."

"Don't joke about things like that."

Carroway shrugged. "It's one of the better options."

"What do you mean?"

Carroway looked at her with a pained expression. "The usual penalty for high treason is hanging, or if the king feels theatrical, beheading. Throw in adultery with the queen, and there's precedent for being drawn and quartered." Impelled to move, he stood and began to pace once more. "If Tris decides to spare my life, the next possibility is confinement in one of the citadels of the Sisterhood, forced to take vows to the Lady, that sort of thing. If I were to be locked away at Westmarch, I might not mind too much—they had some Keepers there who were fine musicians—except that confinement traditionally includes castration, to make the point." He grimaced. "Not a pleasant thought."

Carroway turned away from Macaria, unable to watch the expression on her face. "Exile has its own set of complications. It would depend on how clearly the king let his displeasure be known. Out of the seven kingdoms, Tris is related by blood, marriage or alliance to five of them. Nargi and Trevath are hardly prospects," he said distastefully. "No other court would welcome me if it would sour relationships with Margolan. Neither would the most powerful nobles. That would leave the lesser houses, the ones that would be unlikely to be noticed by the crown, or the inns. I'd be playing for dinner and a place in the stable, but I might keep body and soul together."

There was another option, one he would not speak aloud. *While they might not offer me a bard's position, there'd be more than a few of the nobility who would welcome me via the back entrance, trading shelter for... favors. Lady Nadine wasn't the first to offer, just the most aggressive. It would keep a roof over my head—at least while my looks last. Sweet Chenne! Am I reduced to whoring already?*

Macaria slipped up behind him and put her arms around him. Carroway stiffened at her touch. "We've talked about it, the others and I.

Paiva, Bandele, Tadghe and Halik all agree that if you're exiled, we'll go with you. We stand a better chance together." She rested her cheek against his back, and Carroway closed his eyes. *Please don't say you love me. Not now. I don't think I could bear it.* He used all of his acting skill to keep his face neutral as he turned, gently disengaging from her embrace.

"What would that serve? Without me, you all get promoted," he said, although his smile was lopsided. "You have the talent to become the new master bard. Your music has real magic. And now, you've become the queen's protector. It's the access and the position you've always wanted. I'll manage."

"Kiara thinks it's a plot," Macaria blurted. Carroway listened intently as Macaria told him about the most recent attack. "There's no doubt that blocking the flue was intended to kill. And it might have succeeded, if Kiara hadn't sat up late with Cerise in Cerise's rooms. Cerise always sleeps with the windows open—must have ice for blood," Macaria chuckled, although her eyes were bright with tears.

"I'm glad you're all right."

"Alle's going to see about inviting Kiara to Lady Eadoin's manor for a while. She says it might be easier to protect her there."

"That's an excellent idea. Eadoin might also be able to find out who's behind the rumors."

"Alle's already working on it," Macaria replied.

Carroway took her hand. "That's your first priority: protect Kiara and the heir. Compared to that, nothing else matters—certainly not a bard, in the grand scheme of history."

"Since I first came to court, I've heard you talk about Tris... King Martris," Macaria said evenly. "And since he took the throne, you've told us all how fair he is, how important justice is to him, what a good king he is. If all that's true, then I can't believe he'll just toss you away. You saved his life when the coup happened, and you protected him time and again on the road."

Carroway smiled sadly. "That's what you do for your king," he said quietly. "And, friendship aside, I was honored to do it. The sacrifices usually don't work the other way around."

Macaria set her jaw and her eyes flashed. "He slipped into Nargi to rescue Jonmarc Vahanian."

Carroway sighed. "Tris wasn't king then. Now, the kingdom is depending on him. There are risks he can't afford to take." Although he longed to take her in his arms and hold her until his fears calmed, banishment placed that choice even further out of reach. "You'd better be getting back to the palace," he said. "And while I like the company, please be careful. You don't want people to say you're carrying messages from the queen to her imprisoned lover."

Macaria swallowed hard and nodded. "I thought about that. I'll be careful. I promise. But I had to come."

"I'm glad you did. Thank the others for me. And please, send my deepest apologies to Kiara. I'd never do anything to harm her, or Tris."

"She knows. We all know that." Macaria threw her arms around him, squeezing him tightly. He let the moment sear into his memory, recalling the press of her body against his, the scent of her hair, the feel of her hands on his back. "There has to be a way out of this," she whispered. "There just has to be."

Gently, Carroway disentangled himself before his composure crumbled. "Maybe. But there's a reason so many of the true ballads have sad endings." He shook his head before she could say anything. "You'd better be getting back," he repeated, surprised that his voice was steady. "It means a lot that you came."

Macaria nodded. She grabbed her cloak and wrapped it around herself, pausing to look back at him, before she slipped out of the door. Carroway poured himself a glass of brandy from the bottle that was sent with his dinner, and was not surprised that his hands were shaking. *Dying young and tragically is the surest way to eternal fame,* he thought. *Maybe I'll be remembered after all.*

CHAPTER FIVE

KIARA, MY LOVE.
I *worry because there's been no word
from you. I search Crevan's packages, and
find only the dull documents that require my
signature. Sadly, even my magic can't reach as far
as Shekerishet, or I'd ask the ghosts for news of
how you fare. I'm worried that you're not well,
that the pregnancy has made you sick. And, if
the king dare admit it, I'm terribly homesick.
Please ease my mind and send just a short letter.
Any news from home would be happier than
what surrounds me on the battlefield.*

*I don't dare tell you all I would like to share.
We've made gains, but there have been costly
setbacks. Ban's been badly wounded. Tarq
betrayed us. Progress is slow. Because of the
damage to the Flow, magic is more wild and*

brittle than I've ever seen it. I've never held much with charms and offerings for luck, but if you're so inclined, the men and I would be grateful. Senne tells me all this is to be expected from a siege. I hate this war, and long for it to be over, so that we can all, by the Lady's grace, return home.

I await your letters more than you can imagine.

Love, Tris

King Martris Drayke of Margolan shivered, wrapping his cloak tightly around him. Outside, the winter wind howled, whipping against the sides of the campaign tent so that a flurry of snow burst from beneath the tent flap. Coalan, the king's valet, added more fuel to the small brazier that struggled to warm the tent. Tris noticed that Coalan was wearing all of the clothing he owned, plus several new pieces he had scrounged from the camp. Even so, his nose and cheeks were red with cold.

"You're sure there were no other packets from Crevan than this?" Tris asked, shaking the pouch for the fifth time, only to find it empty.

Coalan shook his head. "Nothing."

Tris sighed. It was cold enough that he needed to warm the ink to keep it from congealing before he could sign the stack of petitions and proclamations his seneschal had sent with the supply wagon. Most of them were meaningless outside of the court's bureaucracy. Here in the field, early in the third month of a winter siege, little of the pomp and intrigue of court held any meaning. Tris signed the documents and replaced them in the courier pouch along with the sealed letter. "I can hope," Tris murmured.

"Perhaps something was lost when the brigands attacked," Coalan suggested. "I heard that two wagons were destroyed in the fighting."

Tris shook his head. "Doubtful. But thanks for the suggestion." Coalan managed a wan smile. Ban Soterius's nephew was only six years younger than the king. He looked exhausted. Tris glanced toward the still form bundled on a cot near the fire. "How's Ban doing?"

"Sister Fallon says he's not bleeding anymore. That's something. He doesn't have much blood left to lose," Coalan said tiredly. "His fever's down, but the storm isn't helping. It's too damn cold."

"Has he come around?"

Coalan stared at the fire and sighed. "Not yet."

Tris walked over to where Soterius lay. Even without a healer's magic, Tris could see how pale and drawn his friend looked, the aftermath of narrowly escaping an assassin's attack. Tris laid his hand gently on Soterius's forehead and let his summoning magic reach out in the darkness. He did not try to draw on the wild energy of the Flow that surged around them. Instead, he drew from his own life force, a limited but stable supply. He could sense the glow of the blue-white life thread that anchored Soterius's soul. And while that glow burned more brightly than it had the day before, Tris knew that it was far from the strength it should be for Soterius to be out of danger.

"Begging your royal pardon, but you don't look much better than Uncle Ban," Coalan said. The young man's lifelong friendship with Tris made him the perfect valet—unquestionably loyal, refreshingly honest and a link to a shared past that could never be reclaimed.

"I know. But we've got to strike Curane again before his people regroup."

"I'm not afraid to take my place on the line," Coalan said, raising his face with a hint of defiance. "I fought before, with Uncle Ban and the troops he raised. I could help protect you when you use your magic."

Tris's smile was sad. "Ban would never forgive me," he said. "Although it may come to that, if we lose more men. Right now, you serve me best by protecting Ban and seeing that he's well tended. You've already done what my soldiers didn't—protect me from an assassin."

Coalan blushed. "My honor to do so."

Tris laid a hand on his shoulder. "Then you do me another service, by letting me sleep safely." *When the dreams and the visions allow*, Tris added silently. Tris turned toward the door. "Right now, I need to meet with Senne and Palinn for the next attacks."

"So soon?"

"We don't dare let the blood mages regroup. The damage to the Flow aids them at our expense. Although after the last battle, I'm not sure the Flow isn't a danger to all of us."

Four *vayash moru* guards fell in step beside Tris as he emerged from his tent, leaving two mortals behind to guard his quarters. Tris looked out over the snow-covered plains, dotted with row upon row of tents and rutted by war machines. At the far edge of the camp, torches burned, and Tris could see the silhouette of the large cairn built over their fallen soldiers. He had gone to the siege with over four thousand men at arms. In less than three full months, battle and disease had killed a third of those troops, and the ranks of the injured grew with every battle.

He turned to look at the brooding outline of Lochlanimar, dark against the sunset. The outer wall was broken in many places, scorched by fire and pounded by trebuchets, catapults and magic. The tower on one corner was collapsed in a heap of rubble. Lochlanimar's defenders still posed enough of a threat that a direct assault was likely to be a disaster. Time was running out, Tris knew. For him and for Curane. *And nothing's worse than an enemy with his back to the wall.*

Now, the army mobilized for battle just days after tending its wounded from the last encounter. Tris scanned the ranks. Without fresh troops, victory would depend on cunning. Since Margolan's tattered army had no more soldiers to send without risking the palace and the northern roads, cleverness would have to do.

"Is everything in place?" Tris hailed General Senne, who inclined his head in deference on Tris's approach.

"Preparations are nearly complete, Your Majesty," Senne said. General Palinn hurried over, and with him, Tris recognized Sister Fallon.

"The pulse strategy—you can do it?"

Senne motioned for Tris to follow him. "Here's the weapon I told you about." Tris looked down at the contraption and frowned. Mounted on a crank, a three-sided pyramid covered with hollow tubes sat at the front of a massive bow on a solid, heavy cart. Tris looked down the line at dozens of the devices.

"Wivvers is my best engineer," Senne said with pride. "The man's a genius. You really should consider giving him a title when this is all said and done. He came up with these to treble our archer fire. We'll have three ranks of longbows, each firing in sequence for a steady hail. But we don't have enough archers to maintain that fire on all sides. Each machine," Senne said, laying a hand proudly on the contraption, "can fire off three rounds of two dozen arrows. Any soldier can operate it, so long as he can aim. It's not magic," Senne said with a sly smile. "But it's close."

Behind the rows of archers, drummer-and -pipers in armor prepared to raise a war chant to strike fear into the besieged village. This night, the drumming would not end until the battle was over. Two staggered rows of trebuchets ringed Curane's fortress, salvaged from the pieces that survived the last battle. Soldiers stood ready to relay rocks and battle debris into the slings of the trebuchets to keep up a steady barrage.

"The mages are in place," Sister Fallon reported. "We have one on each side to help you in the frontal assault. The mages each have hourglasses, timed for the half-candlemark. They're instructed to pulse clockwise, then counterclockwise, then front-to-back and side-to-side. We'll strike with the element we best control—land, water or air. Or in your case—the spirits. The *vayash moru* are in place, ready to strike when you give the signal."

"I've summoned the ghosts of our own battle dead, and ghosts from the crypts below the fortress," Tris said. "There've also been quite a few defectors from among the spirits of those killed by Curane's plague inside the walls. If the mages can strike against the wardings, the *vayash moru* and the ghosts will break through and cause whatever damage they can before the wardings can be raised once more."

"In theory," Fallon said, meeting Tris's eyes, "that should keep Curane's people hopping while our folks get a break."

"In theory," Tris said. "The mages know to avoid the Flow?"

Fallon nodded. "That's the tricky part. If we're pulling on our own personal reserves, none of us can last long. We might not burn up in the Flow, but we could burn out quickly and be useless for days—or dead."

Tris nodded. "Agreed. Then the pulse will have to work." Fallon nodded in farewell and moved quickly to take her place. This time, Tris opted for the bed of a horse-drawn cart rather than a platform, to keep his position easily mobile and less quickly targeted.

He looked to Senne. "Give the word."

At Senne's signal, the pipes and drums erupted in a fearsome racket, with a wild rhythm of chant and drumbeat that echoed from the walls of Lochlanimar. Torches flared into brightness, illuminating the plain. The first hail of arrows filled the night sky, blotting out the moon. In ranks among the archers, shield bearers carried large, rectangular shields, raising them to provide cover for the archers against the returning volley of arrows from the keep's defenders.

The second and third round of arrows launched, and down the line, Tris could hear the creaking of the trebuchets as they were winched back into position, and the thud of their release, each sending rocks and huge, solid balls of ice into the air, to crash a few moments later against the beleaguered walls.

Tris cleared his mind, letting his generals see to the physical needs of battle. Carefully drawing on his own power without touching the raging torrent of the Flow's power, Tris could see three warded places in the front quadrant of the castle. To counter the wardings, his magic would require surgical precision, not great blasts of power, to avoid drawing on the Flow for support. Tris took a deep breath and let his power stretch out, concentrating his effort and his magic in a focused burst against the weakest of the charms. It was badly set, and the warding shattered under the assault.

Now. Go. Along the Plains of Spirit, Tris sent the order to the waiting ghosts. Without the extra power of the Flow, Tris couldn't spare the extra magic to make the ghosts visible. Those that could show themselves in their own power winked into sight as other revenants began to wail, adding an eerie descant to the sound of the war pipes. Poltergeists assaulted the soldiers on the walls from behind, as *vayash moru* easily dodged the arrows to pick off hapless guards like large birds of prey.

Curane's forces had watched the battle preparations from within their walls. They were ready. Catapults sent rocks and shrapnel flying back through the hail of arrows. Tris heard a rumble from the eastern end of the castle, where Fallon's land magic tumbled the rocks from a portion of the outer wall. The battle raged on, and the magic shifted. From the west, Vira's water magic swirled deep snow into icy spikes and hurled them toward the guards, as deadly and accurate as the arrows. More time passed, and Tris heard a sound like thunder as Beyral's land magic focused a tremor within the walls, sending a portion of the building to the ground with a crash.

Tris felt the blood magic rising even as the Flow seemed to awaken, bucking and heaving along the paths of power. In the last battle, such an upheaval killed one of the mages and badly injured the rest. Then, Tris and the others had been drawing on the Flow's energy, vulnerable when that power suddenly rose against them. Now, without that link, Tris felt the power surge painfully along the channels of magic, but distantly, without the power to cripple or kill.

The Flow was wilder than ever, and Tris knew why. A mighty surge of blood magic broke from all four corners of Lochlanimar at once. The fabric of the night seemed to open up like a curtain ripped top to bottom, and through that gap from the blackness of the Abyss poured a dozen creatures that were the stuff of nightmares. Tall as a man, but misshapen, with corpse-gray skin, the creatures looked about with bulbous heads hung with sharp-toothed, lantern jaws. The things hit the ground running, ripping into the front line of soldiers with long clawed arms. The pikemen held their ground against the beasts, valiantly trying to guard the longbowmen, who kept up their assault as the wail of the pipes was lost among the screams of soldiers and the howls of the beasts.

"Light the arrows!" Tris shouted, and realized that his voice was lost amid the fray. Gathering his magic, he sent a burst of fire along the volley of arrows just sprung from their bows, turning them into flaming missiles. Down the line, the archers adjusted their aim and torch men lit the batting wrapped behind the arrowheads. Tris could hear the creaking and groaning of the trebuchets as they shifted behind him. Then, bright as comets, fiery balls launched through the air, over the heads of the archers, to land not against the castle walls but among the attacking beasts.

The line held, as the fire drove back the beasts and well-aimed flaming missiles found their mark. But even as the flames held one enemy at bay, Tris felt the Flow stir again, and a second surge of blood magic swelled and burst.

With the sound of an explosion, the newly built cairn behind the camp burst open. Rising from the rows in which their bodies had been buried, the corpses of fallen Margolan soldiers lurched to their feet. The corpses staggered forward toward the camp. Some, missing limbs, dragged themselves through the snow. A cry went up from the rear guard as the troops reacted in horror.

"Hold your positions! Remain firing!" Tris could hear Palinn, Senne and Rallan shouting down the line. At Senne's word, two ranks of the rear guard turned, charging back into the camp.

"These are not your comrades," Tris could hear Senne bellowing above the fray. "Those bastards are using your comrades' bodies as weapons. Your friends are dead. Help their bodies rest in peace!"

Tris struggled against the horror of the sight to find his center. *Like the corpses from the moat—blood magic, not true spirit magic,* he thought. *Puppets, not reanimated dead.* He set his jaw, angered by the desecration. *Strike the puppet master, and the strings will be cut.*

Tris closed his eyes and sent his magic along the Plains of Spirit. *You wished to serve. Now is the time,* he called to the spirits of the soldiers lost in battle. He drew more heavily on his own power and lent the spirits the energy to make themselves seen and solid enough to fight. The spirits of the dead men raised a battle cry as they leapt forward, cutting down their own lifeless bodies. Tris felt their emotions surge across his link with them. Unlike their mortal comrades, there was no fear. Anger surged hot at the enemy's use of their bodies as weapons against their own side. While even the most intrepid of Tris's mortal soldiers hesitated at the thought of hacking down the bodies of their dead brothers-in-arms, the ghost fighters lunged into combat. Their swords, given power by Tris's magic, cut through the rotting corpses and the frozen bodies, which fell like severed marionettes.

Carried on the current of their rage, Tris turned his magic to find the source of the abomination. He could feel the Flow undulating around them like a wild sea, waves of power rising and falling like a storm. Tris drew more heavily on his own power, knowing that he could not sustain the draw for long. He found the trail of magic that led him back from the vanquished corpses, and prepared to answer it with a blast of his own.

The night around him opened once again. Before Tris could shift his magic, overwhelming force pulled him in as the sky closed behind him.

Tris fell through total darkness. He landed hard enough to knock the breath out of him, and bit back a cry of pain as his left arm snapped with the force of the fall. *Well, that answers whether or not I'm here in body or in spirit. The question is: Where?*

Before he could adjust his wardings, unbearable pain washed over him, burning along every nerve like fire. Tris stiffened and arched, fighting back a scream as he formed the counterspell. In the instant's reprieve it afforded him, his wardings rose around him, and he climbed warily to his feet.

"Show yourselves!"

Torchlight flared around a circular chamber. Three red-robed figures stood facing him, one to the front and one at each side. Their faces were lost in shadow. At each figure's throat glowed a fire-lit gem.

Avatars, Tris thought. *Just like I fought in the Citadel during my training. Each a conduit for its master's power. I'll bet the chamber isn't real, either. If they've pulled me into the Nether and projected themselves, they've got to be burning energy fast. Still, it's three to one.* To his mage senses, the chamber stank of blood magic. Tris could feel the power of a death warding and knew it was set to his life force. No way out alive.

Tris struck first, sending a barrage of mage lightning streaking from his fingers at the opponent to his right. The lightning bounced off the mage's shields. From his left, a wave of fire enveloped him, straining his wardings. An answering barrage of red lightning added to the onslaught, and Tris could feel the drain of dangerous magic against his wardings as the third mage sent a blast of power Tris knew was spelled to kill.

His shields held - barely.

Before he could respond, the blood magic surged again, and for an instant his shields wavered, enough that pain shot through him as if his head might burst, almost sufficient to black him out. Strong magic sent another wave of fire, and this time, it burned along his skin and caught at his clothes and hair, blistering instantly. He struggled to raise his shields as another blast of power slammed against him like a body blow, hard enough that his vision swam. Wave after wave of power hit him, driving him to his knees as blows pounded like sledgehammers.

Tris pulled hard from his life force to send more power to his wardings, snapping them back into place. The battle outside had already taken a toll on his reserves. He sent a blast of energy back along the channels of power, focusing his attention on the tormentor in front of him, the author of the pain spell. His lips moved as he chanted the counterspell, reversing the blast that had been meant for him. He added to it, so that the magic seared along the path of power in the avatar's glowing gem, outside the Nether chamber, back to the blood mage himself. Sweating with the effort, struggling against a blinding reaction headache, Tris kept his focus until the magic felled his opponent in a blur of fear and pain.

And in that instant, Tris knew what he had to do. *Lady of the Four Faces, forgive me.*

Around them, the Flow had become a storm. Not far beyond the dark walls of the place between realms where they fought, Tris could feel the Flow's power rising and falling like an angry sea. Whipped to gale strength by the blood magic that imprisoned him, the Flow seemed to be howling in rage.

Tris dove down through the link with the blood mage until he found the mage's thin blue life thread. Knowing the other two opponents would counterstrike at any second, Tris spoke the words of binding that twined his own life thread with the downed mage's and pulled hard.

He heard a piercing scream that crossed between the outside world and the Nether. There was a wrenching lurch, and Tris felt the mage's life force pull free of the man's body, felt the soul tear loose of its moorings, and let himself draw in the life energy that was rapidly dimming from the severed thread. Strengthened, Tris let his wardings fall. Simultaneously, he struck both left and right, concentrating his power on the amulets at the avatars' throats. His magic sought one goal: the life force of the mages. Tris envisioned himself grasping the glowing threads in each hand, closing his fists around them and ripping them free with all his might. The screams of the dying mages echoed in his mind as he drew their life energy to him, strengthening his own failing glow.

Still, the death warding held.

Tris took a deep breath. He focused on the glow of his own life thread, grown stronger now with the stolen energy. And then, he drew that glow into pure spirit, watching as his body fell to the ground and the thread within winked out.

The wild winds of the Flow howled around Tris. Time meant nothing. The old tales told of creation, when Nameless and Her horde rode across the winds of chaos, cleaving light from darkness. Buffeted in the storm of the Flow, Tris felt that primordial chaos close around him, as if the energies of all eight Aspects of the Lady were voices on the storm, calling him to rest or judgment. The Flow mirrored his own pain and fear.

In the darkness, the death warding fell.

The night ripped open, and the light of a starry sky was blinding. With the last of his power, Tris sent his waning spirit back to the limp and battered body that tumbled from the rift between realms. Gasping for breath, he landed hard on his broken arm. Pain flared so strongly that he thought the tormentor's spell had followed him. He lay face down, his heart pounding, senses on full alert. Footsteps sounded near him, and his power lashed out reflexively, sending a torrent of fire in the direction of the sound. *If I've been pulled within Lochlanimar, Goddess help me. I can't hold them all off, but I can take them with me.* He mustered the power that remained within his grasp for one final salvo.

Powerful shielding glowed brightly around him before he could strike. A voice sounded with compulsion in his mind. "Safe. Home."

Tris fought the shielding and the voice. His blood was high for the fight; his magic reacted for survival. The shielding shattered. As he spoke the words of power, a crush of spirits enveloped him, pressing from every direction, absorbing the brunt of the magic. Charged with the power of a Summoner, the magic burned, and Tris heard the ghosts' screams as they threw themselves as a barrier between his wild magic and those beyond the circle.

"Safe. Home." The voice—no, voices—sounded again in his mind, with a compulsion that he no longer had the energy to fight. Wardings snapped up around him once more and the press of spirits was a cacophony within his mind. Completely spent, he knew that his life thread was flickering dangerously. *If this is a trick, if I've been captured, it's over. We've lost.*

"Let me through the warding."

"It's too dangerous."

"Let me in!"

"We don't know if he's sane."

"Dammit, let me in!"

The voices were distant, too garbled to identify, as if he were listening through water. Tris still lay where he had fallen, acutely aware that his heartbeat was growing more erratic by the moment. He felt the wardings waver, just long enough for someone to step inside, and then they snapped back into place, but whether the wardings formed a prison or a haven, he did not know. Whoever was inside did not move closer.

"Tris?" A voice sounded at a distance. "It's me. Coalan. You don't have to fight anymore. You're safe. You're home. The *vayash moru* have been trying to send that to you, but they can't get through. Fallon doesn't dare drop the shields until you give us a sign. Please, Tris. You're hurt bad."

Tris let his body relax, willing the fighting energy to drain out of him. He opened his fists and turned them palm up in a gesture of surrender. As the wardings fell, Tris heard bootsteps rushing toward him. Coalan was the first to reach him, and gentled him onto his back. Fallon knelt next to him. Around them, Tris could hear the thud of the trebuchets and the zip of arrows.

"Can we get him off the field?" Tris struggled to place the voice. Trefor, one of the *vayash moru* who had brought back Soterius from the caves, joined them.

"Not alive," Fallon said. Already, Tris could feel Fallon's healing magic warring with the pain. The pain was winning. "We don't have a choice. There isn't time to move him. Cover us."

"Done, m'lady."

"Sweet Lady of Darkness," Coalan breathed. "Where did they take him? How did he get burned like that?"

"If he wakes up, you can ask him. Will you let me draw from you? He's dying."

"Yes. Yes. Take my life if you need to."

"I hope that won't be necessary."

Tris faded in and out of consciousness as Fallon worked. Around him, the spirits of the dead kept vigil, and beyond them, faint but much too close, Tris could hear the soulsong of the Lady. The touch of snow against his burned and blistered skin was agonizing. His broken left arm had bent under him when he had fallen. The channels of magic felt too painful for the slightest mental touch, and the throbbing in his head pulsed with the beat of his heart.

"Stay with us." Trefor's voice sounded in his mind, and Tris knew that for the *vayash moru* to be able to use compulsion, his own shielding must be totally spent. The voice was an anchor in the darkness.

If I die now, my soul is forfeit, Tris thought. *I used my power to steal from the life force of another. Forbidden. Unforgivable.*

"Stay with us."

Finally, Fallon sighed and lifted her hands from the healing. "That's all I can do out here. Let's get him behind the lines."

Tris groaned as Trefor lifted him from the ground. The *vayash moru* moved with immortal speed and the rush of air across Tris's skin felt like a hail of broken glass. When they reached his tent, Trefor did his best to make

Tris comfortable on his cot, and stood guard until Fallon and Coalan arrived, breathless, minutes later.

"Will he live?" It was Coalan's voice.

"If he makes it through the night, he should be all right. It's not the injuries—although Goddess knows, they don't help. He's badly drained. The energy you gave me helped. I'll need more to sustain him, and I don't dare draw further from you."

"Shall I ask for volunteers?"

"Send me whoever can be spared from the fight. Mind that they're not sick or injured. I don't know how many I'll need."

"Done."

"If you have no more need of me, I should return to the lines," Trefor said.

"Yes. Of course. Thank you."

When they were gone, Fallon leaned close to Tris's ear. "Don't you dare let go, Tris. Do you hear me? Hang on. I'll do my best to ease the pain. Just don't let go."

CHAPTER SIX

"REPORT!" LORD CURANE struggled to his feet. Rock dust filled the air. Books and vials littered the floor, thrown from shelves by a well-aimed catapult strike. In the center of the room, the scrying ball that until moments ago had been the center of their attention was blackened and cracked, as if it had been struck by lightning.

Cadoc leaned against the wall for support. Dust made his short red hair grayish-white. Blood streaked down one dusty arm. Dirmed also shakily regained his footing. Three bodies near the broken scrying ball did not move. Sayer, Jortham and Ruari lay still and staring on the floor. General Drostan pushed his way through the debris to lend Curane a hand.

"Report?" Cadoc questioned. "On which part?

The someone-hit-our-tower-with-a-boulder part or the three-of-my-mages-are-dead part?"

"Why are they dead?"

Cadoc fixed Curane with an angry look. "They're dead because Martris Drayke killed them. I told you that we didn't know the limits of his power. We succeeded in pulling him into the Nether. We damaged him—badly."

"Is he dead? You told me you were going to set death wards."

Cadoc reached up to touch his forehead and grimaced when his fingers came away bloody. He sat on the edge of an overturned table and daubed at the cut on his temple with the edge of his long sleeve. "We set the wards."

"Then if you were able to return from the working, he must be dead."

"It's not quite so simple with a Summoner," Dirmed replied.

"Stop talking in riddles!"

Cadoc stalked toward Curane, furious. "You didn't feel Drayke send his power back along the magic to snuff out the souls of the mages he could reach. The only reason Dirmed and I are still alive is that we didn't engage him at that instant. Drayke's body collapsed. But a Summoner of his strength can enter and leave his own body at will. He 'died' long enough to bring down the wardings. That doesn't mean he's really dead."

"If you knew that why did you give him that chance?"

Cadoc stood toe-to-toe with Curane, shaking with anger. "I know it now. I didn't know it when we planned the strike. I wouldn't have put my mages at risk if I'd known it, although you wouldn't have had any such constraint."

"My goal is to win this siege," Curane shouted, dusting himself off. "Your mages have been a disappointment."

Only the null magic charm that hung on a strap around Curane's throat stopped Cadoc from answering with a burst of power. "Disappointment! My mages and apprentices have died for your siege. You wanted a plague we could use to sicken Margolan's army. We created a pox that is doing just that—and you can see from the size of the cairn they've built that it's working. We've struck at them with fire, sent the beasts through the Nether, and sent *ashtenerath* against them."

"It hasn't worked."

"Every single strike 'worked,'" Cadoc shot back. "But a dozen mages alone can't break an army. And apparently, neither can your soldiers."

"I'm amazed you're not blaming your failure on the Flow."

Cadoc's face became nearly as red as his short-cropped hair. "Just because you can't feel the Flow doesn't make it imaginary. You can't work magic, but you believe in its power. It's only because of the Flow's instability that we were able to open up the portal to the Nether to bring the beasts across and to trap Drayke. Dirmed and I won't be able to do any kind of working for several days until we recover from the drain. We're lucky to be alive."

"This squabbling is pointless." Drostan's voice silenced both Curane and Cadoc. "We have a war to win. Martris Drayke may still be alive—but Cadoc believes he was badly hurt. Whether he recuperates and how long that takes may be decisive. His mages must also be exhausted. Even with their supply lines, food is scarce. Whoever lasts the next few weeks is likely to be the victor. What do we have left that's in our favor?"

Cadoc retreated with a glare. Curane shook the last of the dust from his hair and kicked at a bit of broken stone. "Cadoc and I are two of the strongest mages—and while we're drained, we'll recover," Dirmed ventured. "Martris Drayke is just one man. With him down, the camp is vulnerable—none of their other mages are nearly so strong. We may not be able to strike them magically, but whatever our army can do will meet less resistance until Drayke recovers."

Drostan nodded. "I agree. And while I'm not a mage, the instability in this Flow of yours may be a dangerous ally to count on. How long until the magic becomes too wild even for the blood mages to tame?"

Cadoc glanced from Drostan to Dirmed. "We don't know. But we *are* sure what it looks like when the magic becomes uncontrollable. It destroys everyone and everything around it. The last time it happened was at the end of the Mage Wars. The Blasted Lands were the result."

"Are you telling me that we could win this siege and be flattened by magic?" Curane's voice raised a note in his anger.

"It's possible."

"You are here to help us avoid certain 'possibilities' and create others."

Cadoc rounded on Curane. "We can't 'fix' the Flow. Drayke and his mages can't do it either, or they would have fixed it by now. Mages have tried—and died—without result. Blood magic makes the damage worse. It comes at a cost—to the mages who work it, to the victims we draw from, and from the Flow itself. It's meant to be a last resort—not an ongoing practice."

Drostan's voice was a measure of strained patience. "All right then. What can you and your mages do without making the Flow any more brittle?"

Cadoc looked to Dirmed. "We can draw on our own power instead of the Flow as much as possible. Before the strike, I'm sure that's what Drayke and his mages were doing, to keep from being hurt by the Flow. It will limit how much magic we can work at a time; without the Flow, we tire more easily. On the other hand, it should keep us from being knocked cold—or worse."

"I just received a message by pigeon last

night," Curane replied. "The latest attempt on the new queen of Margolan failed—but barely. My man assures me he has a final plan in place—one that will end that problem permanently. He knows the consequences if he fails. I haven't had word from Isencroft in a week or so, but Ruggs seemed to have things moving nicely there—Donelan is far too distracted fighting the divisionists to bother with Margolan."

"Then we must plan our next strike carefully to make it the last," Drostan said. "Our supplies are running low. Even with the deaths in the village, we can't make the food or firewood last until Spring. We'll cull the ranks for the worst of the lot and send them into the ginnels to pack up corpses into barrels we can launch toward the Margolan camp. That should also silence the complainers." He glanced at Cadoc. "If you've been saving back an idea for a last strike, it would be a good time to get it ready. I suspect that when Drayke does recover, he'll do the same. We both have one solid hit left, and the first one to move is likely to win."

CHAPTER SEVEN

CAM OF CAIRNRACH, Champion of King Donelan of Isencroft, rolled over in his makeshift cell and threw up. His captors hadn't bothered to bind his ankles or tie his wrists. Leather John and his divisionists had counted on Cam's broken leg to keep him in his cell. It was doing a good job, Cam thought, sprawling onto his back. The food he'd been given was putrid, and the water brackish. His survival was obviously not one of Leather John's top concerns.

Think like Jonmarc, Cam challenged himself. *Jonmarc wouldn't have gotten himself captured. Not so easily. He would have made it more expensive for them, that's for sure.* Cam pulled himself upright, taking care not to jostle his left hand. He'd managed to bind up the stub of his severed finger with a strip of cloth from his shirt, but his hand still left a bloody mark on the floor. No matter how he moved, the pain from his wounded hand or his shattered leg was agonizing. And although only one night had passed since his capture, Cam knew that without treatment, blood poisoning was a likely outcome. Already, his hand felt warm and swollen.

The first duty of a prisoner is to escape. Gritting his teeth against the pain, Cam looked around his cell. From what he'd been able to make out by moonlight the night before, he'd been brought to an abandoned fuller's mill at least a candlemark's wagon ride from the palace city. The mill stank of urine and pig dung, the fuller's tools of the trade. He'd glimpsed the heavy hammers of the fulling stocks by lantern light when his captors had interrogated him. The details were blurry; a consequence of slipping in and out of consciousness.

His "cell" looked like a storage room. The floor was littered with bits of wood and discarded rags, left behind when the mill's owners departed. What light entered filtered through the gaps between the boards in the wall. A continual draft brought cold air from the back of the small, cramped room. It was the only fresh air, barely counterbalancing the stink from the dung pit. Unfortunately, the mills' owners hadn't bothered to lime their pit or dump their urine cistern. Combined, the smells were enough to sting Cam's eyes.

Cam saw what he was looking for—a short board and a broken broom handle. Painfully dragging himself across the filthy floor, he gathered up the pieces along with a fistful of rags. Grimacing, Cam stretched out his broken leg as best he could. *See if I learned anything after watching Carina all my life.* Cam bit his lip to stifle a cry as he bent forward, stretching to place the wood on either side of his leg and tie it tightly with rags, as good a splint as he could manage.

From the light that slipped between the boards, Cam guessed it was mid-morning. By now, Donelan was sure to have received Leather John's message—a "gift" of Cam's severed ring finger, complete with the signet of the King's Champion. Cam was equally certain that though Donelan's vengeance would eventually catch up with the divisionists, no soldiers would be riding out to parley for his release. *If anything's going to happen, I'll have to make it happen.*

Cam wriggled close enough to the wall to brace against it with his uninjured leg. He gasped as he pushed up, using his damaged hand for balance as his right hand steadied his broken leg. He turned so that the wall supported his bum leg, and slowly made his way around the room, looking for anything in the refuse he might make into a weapon. It took him nearly half a candlemark to limp around the room's perimeter, and his search netted him a handful of rags, two blocks of wood the size of his fists, and a handful of rusted tenterhooks.

Satisfied and exhausted, Cam returned to his original place, making sure to cover his splint with his cloak. He worked until the light failed, twisting the cloth into a rope the length of his arm. Using a few of the tenterhooks, he secured the makeshift rope to each of the blocks, and hammered the hooks into the blocks as best he could by slamming them against the floor. The result was an ugly but serviceable bolo, which Cam fastened around his waist below his shirt.

For a while, Cam thought the divisionists had gone. As the light outside grew dim and the night wind picked up, Cam heard footsteps shuffle beyond the door.

"You're sure Donelan received the package?" It was Ruggs's voice.

"Cohnnar tied a brick to a kerchief with the ring and the finger and pitched it through the guardhouse window. Damn near got him caught. Yeah, I'd say they received it," Leather John replied.

"Good. Did he leave enough of a trail to bring them here?"

"I s'pose. Don't make no sense to me—why lead them to us?"

"Donelan's patience is wearing thin. He's sure to send a garrison after us—maybe ride out himself to make a point. Ice's too thin on the river for them to ford it, so they'll have to take the bridge. That'll slow them down, make them cross in pairs. Our archers can attack from the forest at the valley's edge, pick them off as they cross. Pritcher and Kobs weakened the bridge. All that weight, men and horses, will go right into the river. We score a victory, and Donelan looks like a fool. We might even get in a lucky shot if he comes himself."

Leather John did not reply immediately. "The guy in there," and Cam assumed Leather John meant him, "he knows about Curane."

"Does he now."

"Are you sure of him, Curane that is?" Leather John's voice lacked the bluster it had held the night before. "I don't trust him. He's not Isencroft. Maybe Curane's using us."

"What a fine revolutionary you are!" Ruggs mocked. "Interrogate one prisoner, and you start spouting his lies. I don't dare have you question him again—you'd be signing up for the king's guard."

"You know that's a lie. I just want to know why you're so sure Curane's being straight with us."

There was a long pause, as if Ruggs were considering his next words. "Curane's got the Margolan army—and their king—bottled up in a siege. He thinks his hocuses can magic up a way to kill King Martris, and he's got a solution to your traitor princess and her mixed-blood bastard."

"Oh?"

"Curane's got a man on the inside of Drayke's palace. Well-placed. Wouldn't tell me who. While Drayke's off to war, Curane's man's to make sure your princess doesn't live long enough to birth the brat. He's almost gotten her a couple of times, but she's been lucky. Just had a courier from Margolan a few nights back. Said the court is feeling less friendly these days toward their new queen. Imagine," Ruggs said with relish. "Murder the princess, and we solve a host of problems. No heir. No joint kingdom. Donelan will have no choice except to break the alliance."

"Curane gets the Margolan throne for Jared's son and we get what we want. That's what I wanted to hear."

Cam could hear scraping sounds, as if something large and heavy were being moved in the outer room. "Now if you're through with your questions," Ruggs said. "I have some questions of my own for your prisoner."

The light in the storage cell had grown quite dim. Cam took out his bolo and waited for the door to open. *I can't run and I can't fight, but I might get in a lucky shot.* The door opened, and Cam saw a short, powerfully-built man silhouetted against the light. He let the bolo fly with all his might, swinging his good hand with full force. The unwieldy blocks sailed through the air, smashing into the doorpost as Ruggs ducked out of the way.

"Bring him out."

Two guards hurried into the makeshift cell, each grabbing Cam roughly under the arms. They dragged him out and forced him onto a wooden table, securing his wrists above his head and his legs to the bottom with a rope across his ankles. At Ruggs's signal, the guards threw the table up on one end, so that Cam hung upside down, with his head beneath one of the sluices that once carried water from the river into the mill.

"I want to know what Donelan knows about us," Ruggs said, stepping into the light where Cam could see him. He had the look of a man from Southcroft, with a broad face and a shock of dirty red hair.

"Go to the Crone."

"Leather John tells me you've been spying on us for a while. Pity about the boy. I don't much like informers."

"Go screw the Dark Lady."

Ruggs nodded, and one of the guards stepped forward with a large bundle of rags. He wrapped them around Cam's head and stuffed them into his mouth. Cam heard the groan of old wood being pried free, and heard the distant sound of gears turning. A gush of ice-cold water covered his face, soaking into the rags and filling his nose and mouth. Cam twisted and jerked against the ropes that held him.

"All I want to know is—what does Donelan know about us?"

The icy water knocked the breath from Cam, and the flood across his face made it impossible for him to breathe. Instinct took over and Cam bucked against his bonds, arching and straining. Desperate for air, he sucked in water, gagging from the force of the torrent. His vision grew red and his head swam.

"Give him a chance to speak."

The water stopped. Cam sputtered and retched, gasping for air.

"Nothing to say? Pity." The water started once more. Cam jerked hard enough he felt his shoulder dislocate. His heart was racing and his lungs burned as if he'd swallowed coals. Every nerve seemed to be on fire, every sense screaming for air. Ruggs punched him hard in the stomach and Cam lurched forward, taking in a full mouthful of water. He began to shake uncontrollably. The water stopped again.

"What does Donelan know?"

Cam groaned. Someone yanked the sodden gag from his mouth. "Abyss take you," he managed.

The water began again. Cam jerked against the ropes hard enough that blood started down his wrists. The shaking turned to spasms as his body fought for life. The freezing water poured over him, choking and smothering him as it filled his nose and mouth. Ruggs landed another blow to his gut and a second to his side. Cam lifted off the table straining against the ropes, enough that water filled his lungs, squeezing out air. He opened his mouth to gasp for breath and water filled it, too. This time, the water did not stop until light and darkness seemed to blend together, as if consciousness were a flickering candle. Cam's heart hammered, blood pounding in his ears.

Ruggs bent down near his ear. "Give me a number. Just a number. I'll make it stop. Tell me how many of us Donelan thinks there are."

"Four… hundred." Cam's voice was a hoarse whisper. Drops fell from the sluice and Cam flinched.

Ruggs straightened. "There. He can be reasonable."

"Should I start the water again?"

Cam waited to die.

"Not today."

Ruggs jerked away the rags. Soldiers turned the table roughly on its side. Cam puked water and blood, violently expelling both from his nose and mouth. It was another minute until the shaking stopped. The soldiers cut him down, and Cam tumbled to the floor, falling hard on his broken leg. He lay still in a pool of vomit. Ruggs's boots came into view.

"You may not be as expendable as I first thought. Funny about the water cure. After the first time, it goes much faster."

Soldiers jerked Cam to his knees, barely managing to drag him across the floor. He lost consciousness as they descended a rough stone staircase into the lower level of the mill. When he awoke, his sodden shirt was stuck to his skin and he was shivering with cold in the darkness. The floor was made of stone, and no light filtered in. The air was colder here, and the stench of pig dung heavy. Cam sucked in great gulps of air despite the stink.

I broke. No matter that I lied. They broke me. And if they do it again, I won't be able to hold out.

"Good to know you're alive. It's been a while since they threw you in here," a voice said. "Thought they tossed in a corpse."

"They nearly did." Cam's voice was rough, strange to his own ears. "Where am I?"

"Near as I can tell, we're in what used to be one of the dung pools. It's a round stone room with one door that's locked."

"Who are you?"

"I was unlucky enough to be squatting here when the brigands came. They threw me in here and forgot to kill me, I guess. Or perhaps they meant to let me starve. It's been two days and no food. There's a trickle of water comes down that wall—it's probably all we'll get." The voice was quiet. "Caught a glimpse of you when they threw you in here. From the way they worked you over, I'm guessing you're a bit more important than a squatter."

"Just a soldier in the wrong place at the wrong time." *I wasn't important before I knew their plan. Now, they can't afford to let me go. Donelan's spy in Margolan is a traitor. Kiara's in grave danger. Curane's behind it all. And I'm the only one who knows.*

DAY 2

CHAPTER EIGHT

"I'M NOT CERTAIN I understand you, Lord Vahanian." The village elder stood. "We have lived in peace with our *vayash moru* neighbors for generations. Why should we fear now?"

Jonmarc took a deep breath. "There's a small group of *vayash moru*—led by Malesh of Tremont, one of Lord Uri's brood—who have broken the Truce. They want to provoke a war. They've already destroyed Westormere and Crombey. Our best guess is that your village is next."

"How can we stand against *vayash moru*?" The speaker was a man a dozen years or so older than Jonmarc, a merchant by his clothing.

"The other two villages weren't prepared. They had no idea they'd be attacked. I have a force of *vayash moru* and *vyrkin* who want to defeat the rogues and preserve the Truce.

They can't move until sundown—and neither can Malesh. We'll just need to defend ourselves until Lord Gabriel and the Dark Haven guard can arrive."

"How is that possible?"

Laisren was right. This is crazy. I'm supposed to be the defender of vayash moru, not showing mortals how to destroy them. What choice is there? I'm also sworn to defend Dark Haven's mortals.

"You don't have to fight them. All we have to do is hold them off. At most, it will be a matter of minutes before Lord Gabriel and my guard can get here. But in those minutes, Malesh's brood could wipe out a village the size of yours—if you aren't prepared."

Jonmarc paced as the council deliberated. Mead's Ferry was a tiny village, notable as a target only because it was the closest grouping of more than a few families. They were herders and farmers, with a few merchants who scratched out a living selling to the traders and travelers who passed by on the road. The sun was already low in the sky. There was barely enough time to prepare, even if the council ruled in his favor. *Gabriel told me I was wasting my time. I should have slept longer, saved my strength for the battle tonight. But I had to try.*

"Lord Vahanian." The village elder walked toward him. "We've reached a decision. We'll prepare as you advise."

"We don't have much time. Let's get started."

Jonmarc knew too well what kind of weapons the villagers might have. Mead's Ferry was much like the village where he had grown up. Knives and slings, handy for hunting game, were plentiful, but of limited use against this enemy. Few men owned swords, and none were trained to use them. Bows, torches and bonfires were the only weapons sure to keep Malesh and his brood at bay, but fire posed as great a threat to the villagers as it offered protection.

The villagers set a ring of bonfires around the green in the center of the town. Inside the ring, Jonmarc and the villagers stacked as many torches and arrows as they could find. Women and children tipped the arrows with cloth or soaked new reed torches in oil. Jonmarc kept an eye on the sun. He carried a crossbow, and had a full quiver of quarrels on his back. On his left arm was a single arrow in a hand-made launcher, his close-range, last-chance weapon.

"Light the fires," he ordered.

The winter evening quickly became warm as summer as the bonfires caught and blazed into light. The bonfires formed a burning fence around the perimeter of the green, quickly melting the snow. "That should keep Malesh's crew from getting in on the ground," Jonmarc said. He signaled the archers. "Watch the sky. We can't make the flames high enough to keep out the *vayash moru* without roasting ourselves."

From the woods came a distant cry, more chilling than a wolf and wilder than a loon. Outside the bonfires, shadows began to move. Every villager old enough to hold a bow was armed, arrows drawn, ready to shoot. In the center of the green, the children clustered, whimpering with fear. Clouds moved across the moon, but fleeting dark shapes moved more quickly, and Jonmarc brought down his arm to signal the archers.

"Fire!"

Bows twanged as arrows flew. Most disappeared into the night, but one of the shadows fell, plummeting into the fire. A blazing figure stood among the flames, screaming. Flames burned away flesh and clothing like paper, and the rest seemed to melt as if made from wax.

"Again!"

Another hail of arrows launched skyward. One of the shadows fell in the darkness beyond the ring of bonfires.

"C'mon Gabriel. Where are you?" Jonmarc muttered as he readied his crossbow.

"What's that?" a woman screamed from the back of the green. Barely visible beyond the fires, the night seemed to have grown darker. Shadows blurred, and a wind rose, heaping snow onto the bonfires that sputtered and hissed. In the moment the archers were distracted, dark shapes dove from overhead, swooping into the crowd and snatching half a dozen villagers into the sky.

"Hold your ground!" Jonmarc shouted above the chaos. Just beyond arrows' range, the shadows hovered, holding aloft their terrified prisoners. The sky became a stage, lit by the wind-whipped flames. The shadowed shapes held their screaming captives aloft, dropping and catching them to heighten the terror and gain the attention of the crowd below. Swiftly, the dark shapes drew their victims to them, and the cries halted abruptly. As the captives jerked and grew still, the attackers twisted the bodies in their grasp, ripping off limbs and severing heads, spattering the screaming villagers below with gore before letting the mangled bodies fall to ground.

A crash from behind them made Jonmarc turn, crossbow leveled. Three wagons, hurled with inhuman strength, barreled through the waning bonfires, scattering people and burning brands across the trampled green. "Look out!"

Jonmarc dove out of the way of the careening wagons, but not fast enough. One of the wagons rolled straight for him, taking him off his feet. He rolled across it, falling hard, bleeding from gashes along his left arm and leg. He scrambled up, weapon ready.

"Weapons out! Charge!" Jonmarc shouted, anger silencing his fear. Half of the villagers surged forward with him, armed with torches, sickles and bows. The others fled in terror as the dark shapes dove and dodged through the crowd.

Abruptly, the attackers drew back. Jonmarc

leapt across the scattered remains of the bonfire, and glimpsed Gabriel and Laisren across the broad village street, each battling two of the rogue *vayash moru*. His crossbow found its mark, picking off one of Laisren's opponents before Jonmarc had to dive beneath a wagon to avoid one of the black-clad attackers.

In the moonlight, Jonmarc made out a single figure near the edge of the fray. *Malesh.* Jonmarc scrambled from cover and ran toward his quarry, crossbow ready.

Malesh disappeared from sight down a narrow path between two daub and wattle homes. Jonmarc ran after him, dodging the washtubs and laundry lines that littered the alleyway. Even in the cold, the dank passage smelled of chamber pots and spoiled meat. Jonmarc caught a glimpse of Malesh in the distance and doubled his speed, although the bitter cold made his lungs ache. He burst from the alley with his crossbow notched, only to find himself alone in a brick courtyard. By the smell, the building in front of him was a tannery. *That explains why I haven't seen any rats,* Jonmarc thought, forcing down the urge to retch. Three fetid clay pits sat beneath a slanted roof, filled with the tanners' vile liquid. He blinked, and Malesh stood in the shadows behind the pits, holding a small child in front of him.

Malesh sauntered forward. The child, a dark-haired young girl, whimpered in his grip.

"Parley?"

Jonmarc kept his crossbow leveled. "Let the girl go."

Malesh smiled. "And lose my shield? I don't doubt that you're good with that bow. No, I think I'll keep her here where she can be useful."

"I didn't come to talk."

"I have an offer for you."

"Your head on a stake?"

Malesh gave an exaggerated sigh. "Nothing quite so dramatic. But you can end the slaughter."

"How?"

"Your fighting skills are every bit as good as Uri said—better. Imagine what they'd be enhanced by the Dark Gift. I can give you that," Malesh said, meeting Jonmarc's eyes. "Speed. Agility. No more pain, no getting old. Forever strong, young, invincible. Let me bring you across and I'll end the attacks on the villages. You're a lord now—you could be a god."

Would you be a slave again? Jonmarc remembered Gabriel's words when he had asked his friend to bring him across to join Carina.

"Your slave, until I grew strong enough to destroy you," Jonmarc countered.

"You'd be with your lady. That's why I brought her across—to offer you an... incentive... to join me."

Jonmarc's finger tightened on the trigger. The girl squirmed in Malesh's hold, and the *vayash moru* tightened his grip until she cried out. "Careful. By the time your arrow cuts through her, I'll be gone."

"Carina can't be brought across. She's a healer."

"What was I thinking?" Malesh said, feigning surprise. "Oh yes. The incentive. Destroy me, and you destroy her. We have a bond, you know. Make me suffer, and so does she."

"I'm not planning on taking my time."

"Gabriel won't offer you immortality. I will. There are ways to destroy the healing gift. Old books tell of it. Blood charms. Rule with me, with your lady beside you. We're both predators. You mastered the Games in Nargi. You killed to survive, for their sport. Once we're established, the killing can stop. You've as much blood on your hands as I do. Why not rule like a god while you can? Eventually, the Crone comes for us all."

"Because I'm not you."

Malesh shifted, just slightly, enough for Jonmarc to take his shot. The arrow struck Malesh in the chest, piercing through his waistcoat and emerging from the back. There was a blur of movement. Malesh threw the child aside and shot upward, dripping black ichor as he soared into the night. Jonmarc raced toward the girl, who lay in a heap on the snow. Her skin was cold to his touch, and two bloody punctures in her throat confirmed his fears. He gathered the girl into his arms. Her breathing was shallow and ragged. "Hold on," he whispered. "I'll find a healer for you." She stiffened and gasped, then fell silent. Jonmarc bowed his head.

How many people have to die because of me? When does it end?

"Jonmarc!"

Jonmarc turned, still holding the girl's body. Gabriel and Laisren emerged from the alley. Judging from their torn and stained clothing, Jonmarc was sure the fighting had been vicious.

"What were you thinking, going after Malesh by yourself?" Laisren looked more angry than Jonmarc had ever seen him.

"We saw you, but we couldn't get free from the fight to follow." Gabriel looked from Jonmarc to the girl. "You confronted him?"

Jonmarc nodded. "He was waiting for me. He used the girl as a shield. I didn't know she was nearly dead." Laisren moved to take the body from him, but Jonmarc refused. "I got off a clean shot—it hit him in the chest. Then he flew away."

"If he could fly, he's not destroyed." Gabriel looked up into the empty night sky. "He's too young in the Gift. But a near miss ought to make him think twice."

"How bad is it—out there?" Jonmarc asked with a nod toward the center of the village.

"Malesh's brood didn't stay long once we showed up, although from the looks of it, he's recruited more *vayash moru* to his side. I don't think they meant to fight us tonight—they intended to destroy the village and provoke their war." Laisren's voice was tight. "As it is, about of a third of the villagers are dead, and the fire's spread to a few of the buildings. Your strategy to hold off Malesh was sound—not bad considering what you had to work with."

"What now?"

"We'll patrol here for the rest of the night, although I don't think Malesh would dare return. Laisren and I will make sure you get back to Wolvenskorn."

"How do we make sure Malesh doesn't come back tomorrow night and finish the job?" Jonmarc looked down at the dead girl in his arms. He rose and led them out of the tanner's courtyard, back through the winding alley to the center of the village. One of the townsmen spotted them and cried out, running to meet them. He took the girl's body from Jonmarc and looked darkly at the two *vayash moru* before hurrying off toward a group of women who huddled together down the street. When he reached them, the women keened in mourning.

"I can offer to move the villagers to another town but there's no way to be sure where Malesh will strike." Gabriel's expression was grim.

"I'm not so sure." Jonmarc looked from Laisren to Gabriel. "Malesh kept talking about ruling 'as gods.' Isn't there a legend about the

Lady taking her consorts on a certain day of the year?"

"Candles Night," Gabriel replied. "On the cross-quarters, between the solstice and the equinox. That's only a few days from now."

"The old stories say that the Lady's suitors wooed her with blood offerings to show their prowess," Laisren said. "It might be possible to see the villages Malesh has destroyed as an offering."

"Can we regroup, meet him at the temple with everything we've got? Would the *vyrkin* join us? Send a messenger to Rafe and Astasia—they have to see the danger."

"Uri is missing." Gabriel shrugged at Jonmarc's surprise. "No one's seen him in two nights. He was due to make his report—he swore to us he'd bring Malesh to heel."

"Obviously he didn't."

"Uri wasn't among the ones who fought tonight. If Malesh is using blood magic to shield his thoughts, he may be bold enough to try to free himself of Uri's control altogether."

"Could he survive destroying Uri?"

"Malesh is at least a century old in the Dark Gift. Uri's not the strongest of the Council. Perhaps. He may have found other ways to defy Uri. Time will tell."

Jonmarc glanced up at the sky. The night was passing quickly. "I know this isn't going to be a popular suggestion, but do you have any idea where Malesh might be going to ground? We're not close enough for him to get back to Scothnaran quickly, and if Uri really is opposing Malesh, Malesh might not be welcome there."

"You mean to go after Malesh by daylight?" Laisren asked.

Jonmarc spread his hands to indicate the ruined village around them. He knew that even in the light of the waning fires, Laisren and Gabriel could see his tattered cloak and fresh battle wounds. "By night, I'm at a disadvantage. I wouldn't have to go alone—I'm sure the men of the village would go with me. It might help to release their anger—against an appropriate target."

"The Lord of Dark Haven, leading mortals to a day crypt. Do I have to tell you what I think of it?" Laisren's expression made his distaste clear.

"I would willingly do the same if the killers were mortal. Does that make me a traitor to my kind?" Jonmarc snapped. "I'm tired of the killing. The sooner we end it, the more likely it is that we can stop this war of Malesh's from happening. Look around. We can't keep what happened tonight quiet. We've got to bring Malesh down."

Gabriel met Jonmarc's eyes, and in that gaze, Jonmarc knew that Gabriel understood completely what the suggestion cost him. "You, of all mortals, would do that?"

Jonmarc swallowed hard. Even now, eleven years later, the fires of Chauvrenne still haunted his dreams. "What choice is there? If we don't stop Malesh, these villagers won't be the only ones who want vengeance. And when that starts, they won't be choosy about who burns."

Laisren nodded reluctantly. "I'm sorry. I think I know where some of Malesh's brood have taken shelter. We don't usually share day crypts, so whoever's there belongs to him. But be careful—unless you can flood the room with daylight, you're at a disadvantage. You can't win in the dark."

By the time Laisren and Gabriel had given Jonmarc all they knew about Malesh's day crypts, funeral drums had begun a somber beat. "We'd best be on our way—dawn's not far off."

"I'm going to stay," Jonmarc said, following the funeral procession with his gaze. "I'll organize a hunting party—we'll go out when the sun is high. After what's happened here tonight, these men aren't going to frighten easily."

"Do what you must," Gabriel replied. "When you're finished, come by day to Wolvenskorn. My servants will watch for you. Laisren and I will organize the *vayash moru* and the *vyrkin*, and see if there's help to be had from Rafe and Astasia. If you aren't successful in finding Malesh, I think your hunch about the temple of the Lady may be correct. It would be nice to put Malesh on the defensive. And if you're there—odds are, he'll come."

"That's exactly what I'm counting on," Jonmarc replied.

"I DIDN'T EXPECT to find you in here." Lisette's voice was mildly reproving. Carina stirred from where she slept, stretched across Jonmarc's bed. Dimly, she recalled returning from the chapel and letting herself into Jonmarc's room rather than her own. His swords and armor were missing, along with the collection of weapons he stored above the mantle. Carina took comfort in the lingering scent of leather and brandy that clung to the room. Hungry for any semblance of his touch, Carina had curled up on his bed until exhaustion won out over grief and she slept.

Her dreams had been dark. Images flashed in her mind of flame and blood. Distantly, she could hear the screaming of children and the battle shouts of men. She searched for Jonmarc, but did not find him. Sounds of fighting closed in around her against a night lit by bonfires. Shadows flitted along the edge of the fires, cold as the night itself.

The images shifted. Darkness gave way to coruscating light. The light was distant, dim, as if seen from a long way off. A moment before, she had felt the dread of shadows. Now, she feared the light that searched for her. She recognized it from its place deep beneath Dark Haven, and even at a distance, she could feel its pain. It enveloped her as she ran from it, and a torrent of thoughts pressed into her mind. These images were far from Dark Haven, on a windswept plain. Most flashed by too quickly to grasp, but she saw the snap of teeth in the maw of a gray-skinned magicked beast and lumbering corpses dragging their mangled bodies across blood-tinged snow. The light took on the same red tint, bucking and writhing like a thing in pain. It made its entreaty without words, but Carina knew, as the light faded, that it sought her for a reason, for the healing magic that denied her sanctuary in the Dark Gift.

Carina startled awake to find Lisette bending over her worriedly.

"Is it morning—I mean, sunset, already?"

Lisette nodded. She handed Carina a robe, which Carina gratefully accepted. "And although you don't care for the mixture, you need to eat to keep your strength up." She managed a smile. "It wouldn't do for Lady Riqua and the others to work so hard just for you to starve yourself." She paused. "You look sad, m'lady."

"Jonmarc's made Istra's Bargain."

Lisette gasped. "Surely you're mistaken!"

Carina shook her head. "I found ink and a stylus down in the chapel." She looked away. "At first, I thought that I was dreaming before you first awakened me, after Malesh attacked. Now, I realize I was able to hear what was going on around me, but I couldn't respond. Jonmarc came to sit beside me. He said things... things that made sense if he was saying goodbye. And then he kissed me and told me to wait for him, that he'd come for me." She met Lisette's gaze. "I thought he meant Dark Haven, but he had already made up his mind. He meant the arms of the Lady."

Denied tears by the Dark Gift, Lisette's face showed her turmoil. "Laisren went with him, and Lord Gabriel. If there's a way to stop Malesh from killing mortals and save Lord Jonmarc, I know they'll find it. But, m'lady, Lord Jonmarc will never forgive us if we don't save you."

"I saw the Flow again in my dreams," Carina said. "We have to make another attempt to reach it. The things I saw—I know it had to be the war in Margolan. Raen was right. The Flow wants to be healed. And maybe, by healing it, we can find an answer for me."

Lisette looked skeptical. "Even Sister Taru couldn't control the Flow."

Carina struggled to walk without leaning on Lisette as they made their way back to her rooms. It was taking all of her will to muster the energy to keep moving, spurred by the knowledge that time was growing short. Taru and Royster looked up as they crossed the parlor, and their expressions let Carina know that they guessed how much the effort cost her. Riqua emerged from Carina's room carrying a glass of the hated mixture. Carina was grateful that Riqua had at least chosen a tall pottery mug, sparing her the sight of the mingled blood and milk. She readied herself, and then drank it down as quickly as possibly, unable to avoid grimacing. Carina handed the mug back to Lisette and turned to face the others, gratefully accepting a chair which Royster pushed behind her.

"I want to try to connect with the Flow again," Carina said. "But this time, I want to be the conduit—and let Taru's magic amplify mine."

"Too risky," Riqua replied with a dismissive gesture. "We were just lucky that neither of you were killed the last time."

"It reached out to me again last night," Carina said, wondering whether the others could hear the strain in her voice. "You don't understand— my dreams aren't my own anymore. I'm sure I glimpsed another battle through Malesh's eyes. I looked for Jonmarc, but all I saw was fire and shadow." She recounted the vision she had seen of the Flow, and the images of blood magic. "Please," she said, looking from one to another. "I have to try."

Taru nodded. "I'm willing." Royster nodded his assent.

This time, Carina sat in a chair in the middle of the room. Taru stood behind her with her hands on Carina's shoulders. Riqua stepped back, joining Lisette near the wall. Royster looked up from the old books that lay open in front of him. Raen glowed dimly in the shadows, watching somberly.

Carina closed her eyes and focused on slowing the rapid beating of her own heart. She grew calm, breathing deeply and rhythmically, clearing her mind of anything except her memory of the light. She could feel Taru's magic in the touch of her hands. As she did when drawing energy from a helper with a healing, Carina created a bond, enabling her to pull from Taru's power.

She stretched out her right hand in entreaty, mentally reaching out to the roiling energy beneath Dark Haven. Light flared around her, flaming red through her closed lids. Willing herself to remain calm, Carina opened herself to the light, seeking a way to connect so that she could begin the healing.

Power sparked, throwing Taru clear. Carina heard the others cry out and opened her eyes. She threw up her arm to shield her face. A white wind swirled violently around her, sparkling as if made of powdered glass. The wind rose from nowhere, cutting her off from the others, and Carina gasped as the Flow connected to her healing magic, drawing from her as it had done in the caves below the manor house. Carina slid from the chair onto her knees. She could hear voices shouting as if at a great distance, but within the wind, there was nothing except the howl of the Flow, hungering for the warmth of the magic she bore.

A blinding flash of blue light flared, and powerful arms seized Carina, lifting her from the Flow. The blue light moved with them, straining against the buffeting crystal wind. They moved only a few feet before the blue light faded, replaced by an amber glow Carina knew to be Taru's warding. Behind them, the crystal wind vanished as quickly as it had come. Carina collapsed onto the Noorish rug, utterly spent. Thin lines like bloody lace traced across her hands and arms. Though a fire burned on the hearth, she shivered violently. The crystal wind had gone, but in her mind, Carina could feel its lingering touch, and the sense that for the moment, her magic blunted its pain.

Taru lowered her shielding and the others rushed to Carina's side. "You're just lucky Raen and Riqua could reach you," Taru fussed. She laid a hand over Carina's heart and Carina felt Taru's healing magic restoring the energy the Flow had stolen, healing the tracery of cuts.

"I made a difference," Carina whispered as Lisette lifted her gently and placed her on a couch. "I could feel the healing. But it wasn't enough…"

"This is getting us nowhere," Riqua fretted. "If the Flow needs healing so badly, it's hardly going to have the power to heal you."

"Not now. Not until it's healed."

"That's too late if it's destroyed you."

Carina shook her head stubbornly. "We have to try. It's not about healing me. Maybe that's not possible. But if we can heal the Flow, then the blood magic loses its power. I can feel what it's doing to the Flow. It showed me... what Curane's mages have done. I don't think Tris can win his war like this—with the magic broken and out of reach. There's too much at stake. I need to try again—at the source of the Flow."

"No mage has ever survived that," Taru warned. "Many have tried."

Royster looked up sharply, as if he had only just begun to listen. "But never a Summoner."

Taru frowned. "Carina isn't a Summoner. Tris Drayke's the only Summoner of power—and he's down on the Southern Plains."

Royster's face was alight with inspiration. "Do you remember how Tris kept Jonmarc alive after the assassin's attack at Staden's palace? How he anchored Jonmarc's soul with his power? If Tris and Carina worked together—Carina could open herself completely to the healing, and Tris could tether her soul, replenishing her energy. No one's ever tried it. The magic hadn't gotten so badly out of balance when Bava K'aa was still alive—and since she's died, there's been no Summoner for things like this. Yes," he said, rubbing his hands together. "It just might work."

"It would take weeks for Tris to come to Dark Haven—assuming he could ride away from the front lines of a war!" Riqua protested. "Carina doesn't have weeks to wait."

"Maybe he doesn't have to," Taru said quietly. They turned to her expectantly. "We know that this particular branch of the Flow runs from below the Northern Sea down through southern Margolan and beyond. The Sisterhood warned Tris that the Flow runs right beneath Curane's holdings, that it would make the blood mages more powerful because of that." She turned suddenly to Riqua. "How fast could your people reach the Margolan plains?"

Riqua frowned. "At top speed—which we can't sustain forever—three nights."

Taru looked to Carina. "I'll help you write a letter. We'll explain what's happened, and what you mean to do. From the visions you've seen, it doesn't sound as if the war is going well for Tris. He may be as desperate for options as we are. We'll set a time on the fourth night— seventh bells—and ask him to link his magic to the Flow and search for you. He knows your soul's imprint; he must, you've healed together so often. You'll know if he touches you across the Flow. If he can anchor you and hold on before you step into the Flow, we just might have a chance."

"This is madness." Riqua began to pace. "Three nights is a guess. We don't generally move so far so fast. I'd have to use *vayash moru* in relays. The *vayash moru* who reaches Tris won't be anyone he knows. Why should Tris believe him?"

"Trefor is one of your brood, isn't he? And there were others—both from your family and from Gabriel's. Would they recognize one of their own?"

Slowly, Riqua nodded. "Of course."

"Then Trefor and the others could vouch for the messenger—and he'll have Carina's letter, with your seal. I can add the mark of my power, for good measure."

Riqua's gaze was troubled. "I don't like it. But I can't think of anything else and we're all running out of time." She looked to Carina. "If we're wrong about Tris's magic being able to reach across the distance through the Flow, there won't be a way to rescue you. I've seen mages die in that power. It consumes them." She shuddered. "I don't wish to witness that again."

Taru helped Carina to take Royster's place at the desk. Carina thought for a few moments, and then began to write. The others waited as she told the story of Malesh's betrayal and the end of the Truce, of the slaughter of the villagers and her own encounter with Malesh. She wrote of the war that Jonmarc and Gabriel were trying to prevent and the way the Flow reached out to her for healing.

The words seemed almost too fantastic for her to believe as the ink streamed behind her pen. *He'll think I've gone mad,* Carina thought as she finished her plea, folding the letter closed.

Riqua held wax to the candle flame, dripping a red pool to seal the parchment pages together, and pressed her ornate signet ring into the warm wax. Carina added her signet imprint as well. Taru touched the parchment with her fingers, adding the signature of her own magic, warding the note against any reader except Tris.

Riqua looked to Lisette. "Call for Temis. He must leave tonight. Bring him to me."

Lisette left, to return moments later with a tall man whose lank, dark hair was drawn back in a queue. Temis listened intently as Riqua shared his mission, glancing frequently to Carina as they talked. Riqua slipped the sealed parchment into a leather pouch and handed it to Temis. "Nothing is more important than that this letter reaches King Martris by the third night," she said, folding her hands around Temis's. "We know that Malesh is using blood magic to elude Uri and Gabriel. Break that power, and we may save the Truce. Curane is using blood magic to defeat the Margolan army. If Jared's bastard takes the throne, he's sure to resume hunting our kind, as his father did. This may be the salvation of our people as well as the Winter Kingdoms. May the Dark Lady guide you."

Temis gave a deep bow in respect and slipped from the room. Riqua stared after him before turning to the others. "Now, we wait."

The night was far spent by the time they were finished. Carina was exhausted, but the fear of sleeping and the terror of her dreams forced her awake. Riqua and Lisette had already sought their day crypts. Royster dozed in a chair by the fire in the parlor. Carina stood near the window, protected from the first light of dawn by heavy curtains.

If I believed Jonmarc would return, I'd have a reason to care more whether or not I survived. But he's sworn the Bargain. We'll be together. One way or another.

Taru stepped up behind her, laying a hand on her shoulder. Carina knew that Taru could feel the tightness in her neck and that Taru's healing magic could easily read her tension. "I don't think healing is what you're after, is it?"

Carina swallowed hard and shook her head. Tears refused to come. "Too many people have died, Taru. We thought that if we took back Margolan's throne from Jared that it would stop, but it didn't. From what I've glimpsed in the Flow, the war's not going well for Tris. How could it, when magic won't work properly? Now Malesh, breaking the Truce. He wants a war because he thinks the *vayash moru* will win. And Jonmarc—"

"I've never believed that mortals can bargain with the Lady," Taru said.

"But I've seen men make the Bargain, when Cam and I were with the mercs. They never came back." Carina's voice was just above a whisper.

"Men can accomplish the impossible when they no longer care about their own safety," Taru observed. "Many efforts fail because our desire to survive makes us falter at the last moment. If we no longer want to live, and desire only death with meaning, the unthinkable becomes possible."

"Are you talking to me, or about Jonmarc?"

"What do you think?"

Carina sighed. "I don't know anymore. Maybe you're right. Maybe it wasn't the Lady who gave those soldiers their victory. Maybe they were able to kill their enemies because they weren't afraid of death anymore, and they didn't come back because they didn't want to. But Jonmarc knows that destroying Malesh destroys me. He's lost so much. If it comes to that—will he choose to come back?

"I can feel myself dying, Taru. I can feel the magics at war inside me, burning each other out—like this damned war in Margolan, or the war over the Truce. No one wins if everyone is dead."

"Did you tell Jonmarc about the bond?"

Carina was silent for a moment. Far beyond the mountains, a faint pink haze lit the winter sky. "After a fashion."

"After a fashion?"

"Did I tell him that over time, healers become bonded to our mates? That we weaken and die when we lose a lifemate? Not in so many words. I think he suspects. It was his idea for us to make a ritual wedding. He knows what happened with Ric. Does he know the bond is one-sided? That it only affects the healer? No." She shook her head. "It's too much in his nature to put himself where the danger is. I didn't want him to be afraid of risking me. It would cost him his edge, and he needs that." She paused. "I didn't tell him because I wanted him, Taru. I've never loved anyone the way I love him, Lady forgive me, not even Ric."

She turned away. "Goddess, we've made a mess of things! Even if you're right, even if Istra's Bargain is just a soldiers' legend, I'm afraid Jonmarc doesn't care about living through this fight. He's got a score to settle, and no reason to believe that I'll survive."

She faced Taru, knowing that the mage could see the struggle in her face. "There's one chance of something good coming out of this. If I can heal the Flow, that gives Tris a fighting chance in Margolan, and it might make Malesh vulnerable. If Jared's bastard gains the throne, the kingdoms could be at war for a generation. And if Malesh destroys the Truce, the mortals and the *vayash moru* will keep on fighting until they destroy each other." Carina met her eyes. "If I can't survive this war, then at least I can play my part."

"We don't know what will happen if Tris can anchor you. No one's ever done that before. The Flow is the source for all our power. Even healers. It needs your healing, but it may be able to offer you something in return. There is a chance it could help you heal."

Carina looked away. *The Flow might heal the damage Malesh did to me. But unless we figure this out before Jonmarc kills Malesh, it doesn't matter. Malesh's death will kill me anyhow. I don't know whether Jonmarc and I have been together long enough for the bond between us to affect me. But if it does, and he dies destroying Malesh, then I'll die, too.* Worse was the alternative, that she might survive without Jonmarc.

"That's what I'm afraid of."

CHAPTER NINE

"I DON'T THINK this is a good idea, Kiara."
Cerise folded her arms across her chest.
"Scrying drains you at the best of times."

"Carroway told me that scrying didn't go so
well for you on the road," Macaria put in. "Are
you sure it's safe?"

Kiara thumped her fist against the tall back
of a chair in frustration. "Things are different
now. Arontala was hunting us then. He used
the scrying ball to find us, followed my magic
back to find me."

"Arontala and the Obsidian King may be
gone, but Curane still has dark mages. You
must be careful."

"Just a glimpse. Please help me do this. I have
to see how Tris is doing."

Cerise sighed. "I know that tone in your voice.

It hasn't changed since you were a little girl. You're going to do this, whether we like it or not. Very well then. I'll help."

Alle and Macaria nodded their assent. Kiara withdrew a light blue scrying ball from deep within a trunk and set it carefully in its holder on the table.

"That's Viata's ball. I'd know the color anywhere."

Kiara nodded. "I brought it from Isencroft. Mine was... lost... on the journey."

Cerise fixed Kiara with a glare that made it clear the healer was skeptical about the circumstances under which the last scrying ball disappeared. "Viata never could scry well on her own, but she had some gifted seers who helped her watch over your father whenever he left on campaign."

"Then why discourage me from trying?"

Cerise looked away. "What the ball shows us isn't always true. The future is always changing. We might see what has been—or what might be, but never with certainty what *is*. Viata learned that the hard way. One night, when Donelan had been on campaign for a long time against the Western raiders, Viata scryed for him. She saw images from a battle, and saw Donelan hit in the chest by an arrow. It was just a few seconds, but long enough to see him fall from his horse." Cerise's voice shook. "Viata was inconsolable. Nothing Malae or I could say helped. In her grief, she almost threw herself from the window." A sad smile crossed Cerise's face. "Goddess forgive me—but if I hadn't brought her to her knees with a blinding headache, we might not have been able to keep her safe. She was as fine a warrior in the Eastmark ways as you are, my dear."

"And father?"

"When he returned, we learned that he narrowly avoided an arrow, but that it missed him—his horse shied just as the arrow came his way. So the ball showed what might have been, but not what was."

"I understand. And I promise that I won't try to throw myself out the window. But I have to try."

"Very well."

The four women took their places around the ball, holding hands. Kiara drew on a small measure of regent magic to ward their working and bring the power of the scrying ball to life. "Powers that be, hear me! Goddess of Light, attend!" Kiara began, her eyes closed in concentration. "We gather to invoke the ancient Powers. Spirits of the Land, hear me!" she recited. "Winds of the North, obey! Waters of the Southlands, bend your course. Fires of the Eastern Sun, be bound by my command. Land of our fathers under the sun of the West, I compel you by the right of the heirs of Isencroft to reveal what is hidden and find what is dear. Let it be so!"

Alle and Macaria were holding their breath. Kiara opened her eyes as the scrying ball flared and from within, a mist began to swirl. Still holding hands, they stepped closer as Kiara peered at the image. Hazy, as if seen from a distance, an image grew more solid. Kiara could make out the outline of a large stone fortress. Fire lit up the night sky. She glimpsed two figures on horseback and recognized one immediately as Tris.

"There he is!"

The scene shifted without warning, to another night view. The battle for the keep raged, but there was panic in the soldiers' movements, and at the edge of the vision, Kiara glimpsed a gray-skinned beast like she and Tris had fought on the road to Westmarch. "Look there!"

The night opened as if split like a curtain, and Kiara watched in horror as a man's body tumbled out of thin air. Blond hair matted with blood, cloak torn and burned, the body landed in the snow and lay still. The image flickered and disappeared.

"Break the warding!" Cerise whispered as Kiara stood unmoving, staring in horror at the now-dark scrying ball. "Kiara, break the warding!"

Kiara mumbled the words to dispel the magic and the wardings around them fell. Cerise guided her to a chair as Kiara wavered on her feet, and Macaria and Alle clustered around her. "You can't be certain that what you saw really happened," Alle said, taking the cup of tea Macaria poured and pressing it into Kiara's shaking hands. "We never saw the man's face. We don't know for certain who it was."

Macaria slipped away, only to return with her flute. Wordlessly, she began to play a calming melody, but it took several minutes before its magic quieted Kiara enough for her to speak.

"You were right, Cerise. I shouldn't have scryed. We know nothing more than we did before—nothing certain—but I'm more worried now than ever."

Cerise laid a hand on Kiara's shoulder. "Tris is a powerful Summoner. You made a ritual vow to each other. If anything were to happen to him, he would come to you. He has that power. Barring that, you know that he's alive. And from your own stories of his training and the battle against the Obsidian King, he's withstood the worst that battle can do. Take comfort in that, and trust the Lady."

A knock at the door interrupted anything else Cerise might have said. Alle went to answer it, and found a courier standing in the hallway. "M'lady. A message for you, from Lady Eadoin."

Alle thanked him and closed the door, then ripped the envelope open. She scanned down the lines of Eadoin's spidery handwriting, then looked up at the others, who were watching expectantly. "Aunt Eadoin says that there's been an outbreak of fever among the servants. She's got her hands full with the manor, and she's not feeling well herself. She begs your pardon," Alle said with a nod toward Kiara, "but she thinks it best if she stays at Brightmoor until she's well, so as not to put you and the baby at risk." She paused. "That answers our question about taking you to stay there," she said and glanced at the paper once more, then frowned. "That's odd. She also said to thank the queen for the lovely gift of linens. They arrived last week and she had the servants put them out on the beds."

Alle read on, and frowned deeply. "This worries me. Aunt Eadoin enclosed a second sheet. It's very formal. She's made me her proxy, to act in her stead as if I were she."

"Lady Eadoin is up in years," Macaria said gently. "Perhaps it's just a precaution."

"Perhaps. Or maybe she's sicker with the fever than she's letting on." Alle lowered the letter with a sigh. "I was counting on her help to deal with the rumors about you and Carroway. Aunt Eadoin's always been a voice of reason in the Margolan court—even the troublemakers listen to her. I'm afraid we'll have to wait."

"I'm sorry to hear that Eadoin's not well," Kiara replied. "And I'm completely at a loss about the gift. I didn't send anything. Perhaps Crevan sent something in my name out of protocol."

Urgent knocking cut off anything more she might have said. The dogs jumped to their feet at the noise, and even Jae raised his head from where he slept on the hearth. Alle opened the door again, to find Crevan framed in the doorway. The little man looked exhausted and disheveled, as if he had been up all night. He bowed low and stepped inside at Kiara's gesture, carefully shutting the door behind him.

"Crevan, what's wrong?"

"I'm sorry to bear this news, Your Majesty. Please understand, I had nothing to do with it."

"What happened, Crevan?"

Crevan twisted his thin hands. "The Council of Nobles has convened, at the request of Lord Guarov. Not even so much as a by-your-leave, mind you, except that they ordered me to find them a room where they wouldn't be disturbed, and send up their meals with plenty of warmed wine." He looked plaintively at Kiara. "A thousand pardons, m'lady, but they've sent me with a summons to request your testimony. They meet to discuss the rumors that allege you and Master Bard Carroway have committed adultery and betrayed King Martris. It's in their power, in the absence of the king, to find you both guilty of high treason."

Kiara caught her breath. "But the rumors are lies! Nothing improper in the slightest has ever happened. Neither of us would ever betray Tris."

"I believe you, m'lady. But it was for your sake that I sent Carroway away from court. I had hoped to stop the rumors before the talk reached this stage. Now—" Crevan turned his hands palms-up and shrugged.

"Can they do this?" Kiara asked, looking to Crevan and Alle. "Summon the queen? Is it within their power?"

After a moment's thought, both nodded. "In extreme measures, yes," Crevan replied.

"I'm afraid so," Alle said.

"They've sent for you at first bells," Crevan added. "Please, m'lady, I urge you to be prompt. The nobles do not like to be kept waiting, even by the king. It sours their mood."

"Thank you, Crevan. That will be all." Kiara watched the door close behind the seneschal in silence.

"This is bad," Alle said, beginning to pace. "If Aunt Eadoin were here, she could sway the Council. Even Lord Guarov treats her with respect. Before the coup, the Lord of Huntwood—Ban Soterius's father—was also on the Council. He was one of Bricen's staunchest supporters. Some of the others we could have counted on for support died under the Usurper's rule—Lord Alton, Lord Montbane, Lord Theiroth—all dead."

"Who's left?" Kiara asked, forcing down her own panic and willing herself into the coolness that came in preparation for battle.

"Lord Guarov—we know he's trouble," Alle replied. "Lord Acton—he's the elderly gent you met at the wedding. Don't count him out—he's a spitfire for his age. King Martris brought some of the *vayash moru* lords into the gathering, but they left court when the king did—I think they're afraid."

"Mikhail could represent Lord Gabriel—if he weren't locked up in the dungeon," Macaria added darkly. "And Carroway is heir to his family's title—but he's not going to be much help either."

"It's not impossible," Alle said, pursing her lips as she thought. "If they're convening at Guarov's request, it doesn't mean they all agree. There are four others on the Council. Lord Dravan, Lady Casset, Count Suphie and Dame Nuray. Nuray is trouble—there've been rumors for years that she's a spy for Trevath. The others are wild cards. It's been said that they all have ties to other kingdoms. Dravan's reputed to have ties in Dhasson—which might not be a bad thing, since King Harrol is Tris's uncle."

"We'd heard that Lady Casset feeds information to King Staden," Macaria put in. "And that Suphie is Eastmark's puppet."

"Suphie is a troubling man," Alle said. "He's not of Eastmark, but he does a lot of business there, supplying weapons and mercenaries. They say he's not a forgiving person."

"And we still don't know who father's spy is," Kiara added. "Or whether he or she could be of any help. Goddess! The last thing we need is word of the rumors getting back to Isencroft."

"One problem at a time," Cerise counseled. "First bells isn't far away. You need to eat, my dear, to replenish your strength. Then you must dress for high court, and remind them that not only are you Margolan's queen and mother to its heir, but heir to the Isencroft crown as well." She laid a hand on Kiara's arm comfortingly. "I have no doubt that you can face down this enemy as confidently as you've ridden into battle—although perhaps it might be best to leave your sword behind this time!"

The time to meet with the Council of Nobles came far too quickly. Alle accompanied her. Cerise followed, resolute that she must be in attendance as a precaution, although Kiara suspected it was to make certain that the Council never forgot that the queen they sought to judge also carried the heir to the throne. Crevan led them through the narrow hallways of Shekerishet. Ammond and Hothan, Kiara's regular guards, followed and two new guardsmen, the men who had accompanied Crevan, joined them.

Kiara drew herself up to her full height. Though she hated the discomfort of formal court regalia, she understood its power. Her dress was heavy with brocade and velvet, sewn with pearls and gold thread. Its high bodice accentuated her gently swelling belly. The neckline was modest—almost matronly by court fashion. At her throat hung a pendant nearly the size of her palm, the four-headed dragon seal of the heir to the Isencroft throne. The crown of the queen of Margolan glittered in Kiara's auburn hair. She said a silent prayer to the Lady, as she did before going into battle, and found herself wishing for the clean demarcations of a war fought with weapons instead of words.

Six nobles stood as Crevan opened the door to the meeting chamber. They made perfunctory bows in greeting as a servant ran to pull out a chair for Kiara, which she refused.

"Why have you summoned me?" Kiara's voice had an edge to it, the same tone she had often heard King Donelan use when he wished to remind an errant noble of his station. A glance around the table confirmed Alle's guess at the nobles in attendance. White-haired Lord Acton Kiara recalled from the wedding, and Lord Guarov, with his features coldly impassive, was equally memorable. Dame Nuray's looks hinted at Trevath blood, making her easy to identify.

A blond woman sat stiffly to Nuray's right, with an expression that might have been impatience or boredom; Kiara guessed her to be Lady Casset. Of the remaining two men, one had a rough manner, as if he were more at home on the front lines of a battle than with the pleasantries of court. *Count Suphie?* If so, Kiara's hopes of persuading him on the basis of her kinship to King Kalcen died. Suphie was an older man, easily Donelan's age, meaning that he would have been a supporter of her grandfather, King Radomar, and likely to have shared his disdain for Viata's outland marriage. The last man, Lord Dravan, looked old enough to be her grandfather, but his light blue eyes were sharp and his angular features bespoke intelligence. Wild cards all of them.

"There is no way to put this delicately," Lord Guarov said, although nothing in his manner suggested he was prone to doing so, regardless. Guarov was a slim man with hawk-like features and long-fingered, soft hands that made it clear he had never toiled. He had dark eyes that seemed to constantly scan the horizon for potential threats, and the punctiliousness of a bookkeeper. "Credible rumors allege great impropriety, Your Majesty. It is said widely at court that you and Master Bard Carroway have betrayed the king's trust, and your wedding vows. To do so is treason."

Kiara glanced around the table. Dravan and Casset looked clearly uncomfortable. Nuray leaned forward intently, as if watching a drama. Suphie crossed his arms and leaned back, scowling. Acton's anger was clear in his face. *They may be obligated to go along with this, but some of them don't like it*, Kiara thought.

"Is Margolan governed by rumors?" Kiara replied. "In Isencroft, such serious charges require witnesses. Pray tell, have you any to your charge?" One hand rose to finger the crest at her throat, a reminder, in case any there had forgotten, of her own rank. The other hand fell to rest on her belly, silently underscoring her status as the mother of the heir.

"On more than one occasion, Bard Carroway has been seen to enter the queen's rooms," Guarov replied, with a tone as if that settled the matter.

"And did your 'witnesses' bother to tell you than on both occasions, Lady Alle, my healer Cerise, and Macaria, my personal bard, were already in the room and remained there until Carroway left? We were never alone, at any time."

"The rumors do not allege that you were alone, m'lady, but rather that you engaged in treasonous conduct."

Kiara felt her cheeks redden with anger at the implication. "Is it your intention to call the heir to the Isencroft throne a whore who performs for an audience?" She could see the others wince at her plainspokenness.

"I did not use that word, m'lady."

"You didn't need to."

"The fact remains—"

"You have no facts," Kiara cut him off. "Only lies and rumors. Show your 'witness.'"

"I've promised him protection."

"To make accusations without risk?" Kiara's voice was scornful. "This isn't Nargi, where an angry scullery maid can concoct a charge of magery and have even a high priest burned alive."

"It's the charge of this Council to protect the interests of the king."

"I rode beside Martris Drayke to take back the throne from the Usurper," Kiara said coldly. "I fought beside him against Foor Arontala and the Obsidian King. Bard Carroway also risked his life to put Tris Drayke on the throne. Our loyalty is absolute."

"Or opportune." Heads swiveled toward Count Suphie. "After all, you were betrothed from birth to that same usurper, and broke that covenant to become his brother's lover. So *technically*, this is the second instance of adultery."

Kiara fixed Count Suphie with a hard glare. "The betrothal contract averted war between Eastmark and Isencroft. My uncle, King Kalcen, rescinded the charges against my mother when he took the throne. *Technically*," she said, emphasizing the word through gritted teeth, "that dissolved the reason for the covenant with Jared."

"We're willing to accept that it is not your fault, m'lady," Guarov said in a placating tone. "You're new in our land, and our ways may be different to you. Bard Carroway, on the other hand, has a…. reputation… of which you might not have been aware. Don't be ashamed to tell us that he forced you, and we'll have the means to clear your name."

"Old scandals reach even new ears," Kiara replied disdainfully. "Your friend Lady Nadine preyed on the bard as a boy, earning her Bricen's banishment. Now you offer me a bargain that is no bargain at all—to admit guilt and sacrifice the king's loyal friend. Was this what you meant by having your servants send a shroud and burial oil as a gift for the child I carry?"

"A woman is never so tempted to betrayal as when she is pregnant—it's well known liaisons can be made without the… inconvenience… of an unexpected 'souvenir.'"

"Guarov, that is enough!" Lord Acton rose to his feet, leaning heavily on the table for support. "I came to this table reluctantly, and only because I feared you might make a spectacle like this. By the Lady! Stand down and let this pass."

"What do you propose, Guarov? She carries the heir to the throne. Would you hang her— ere the king returns from battle? Pray, what is the hurry? 'Tis not the first time the court has feasted on vicious talk—nor the last, I'm sure." Lady Casset's fine-boned fingers twitched as she spoke, and the carefully studied expression of indifference betrayed a hint of disdain, as if she condescended to speak to one below her station. Everything about her spoke of old aristocracy, from her speech to the antique and expensive jewelry on her porcelain-white throat.

"Nothing so drastic, m'lady." The speaker was Dame Nuray. Kiara regarded her closely. Nuray was old enough to have been a friend of Bricen's first wife, Eldra, a Trevath princess and mother to Jared. Even in her short time in Margolan, Kiara had heard it said that few without Trevath ties tolerated Eldra's black moods and vicious tempers. "Hang the bard, if you have certain proof. And to prevent another 'forcing,' double m'lady's guards—for her own protection."

"I will not be party to this." Lord Dravan slammed his palm down on the table. His voice shook with anger. "I brokered Bard Carroway's fostering here, when he was just a lad. Many's the hunt I shared with Lord Carroway and King Bricen in days long gone." He fixed Guarov with an angry glare. "And I remember Bricen's rage when Lady Nadine badly used the boy and drove him to desperation. If this is your revenge, Guarov, I will have none of it."

"Shall we put it to vote then?" Guarov said smoothly. "Those who believe we should take action to preserve the purity of the crown, please vote." Dame Nuray and Count Suphie added their raised hands to Guarov's vote. Kiara held her breath. Three for, three against.

"In the event of a tied vote on such a matter, I am empowered to appoint a proxy for our missing member," said Guarov.

"None is needed." Alle stepped forward from where she watched the proceedings. She withdrew the parchment from Eadoin. "This arrived today, by courier, from Lady Eadoin. I'm her brother's child, and at his death, became her ward and only heir." She handed the paper to Acton, not to Guarov, who examined it and showed it first to Dravan and Lady Casset. Acton presented it to Guarov, at a distance that enabled the angry lord to read its message but not touch the parchment itself.

"Why was I not informed?" Guarov raged.

"Because Lady Eadoin did not feel obliged to inform you," Alle replied smoothly. Kiara glanced at Alle. During the revolution Alle might have passed herself off as a barmaid, but here in the Council Chamber, her true pedigree showed clearly. "I assure you, fever-stricken though she is, Eadoin will be here by carriage within a candlemark for such a vote if you don't accept my proxy. And when she's done voting, she's likely to have choice words for those who disturbed her sickbed."

Acton's tightly pressed lips seemed to suppress a snicker. A glint of approval glinted in Lady Casset's eyes. Dravan did not make an effort to hide his pleasure. "Mother and Childe, she has you, Guarov. Eadoin's likely to do just that— and enjoy seeing you come down with the pox for good measure. Put an end to this sham. The vote supports the queen."

"One moment." Dame Nuray raised a hand. "I can't see harm in maintaining the bard's banishment. Deserved or not," she added acidly, "his reputation casts dangerous shadows on the queen at court. I'm told he rests comfortably at the Dragon's Rage Inn. Leave him there until the king returns—and see if the king's friendship is as... tolerant... as this council."

"By the Crone's tits," Acton grumbled. "You could damn the Lady herself with the accusations between your words. Yes, for his own protection, leave the bard under arrest. It will protect him from the likes of you."

Acton turned toward Kiara and gave a deep bow. "My queen. Please accept my personal apologies at this embarrassment. As I pledged once to Bricen and then to King Martris, you have my sword and my allegiance."

Kiara inclined her head in acceptance, and grasped Acton's gnarled hand in both of hers. "Accepted, m'lord, with gratitude."

Kiara and Alle turned to leave as Crevan stood out of the way. "Guards," Lord Guarov called, "Please see the queen to her quarters—for her own safety," he said when Kiara's sharp glance questioned his intent.

They began to make their way through the narrow halls of Shekerishet. The four guards closed ranks around Kiara and Alle, crowding through the empty walkway. Ahead, servant's stairs opened into the wall. As they reached the opening, the guard to Kiara's right threw his full weight against her, knocking Kiara off balance and into the stairwell. Arms flailing, Kiara began to fall backward. She slammed hard against the wall, grasping for a handhold. She tumbled once, crying out in pain.

"Death to traitors!" the guard shouted, starting after her. The other guards grabbed for the man as Alle's hand flicked in her skirt. A red stain spread across the astonished guard's face from the knife buried hilt-deep in his chest.

Before Alle could reach the entrance to the stairway, the corridor around Kiara began to glow eerily. Dim shapes appeared in the shadows of the stairwell, breaking her fall and steadying her down the last few steps to the landing. In the glowing mist, Kiara glimpsed the ghostly protectors—Comar Hassad, Ula the nursemaid, and Seanna. Ula and Seanna gentled Kiara to sit as Comar Hassad's spirit raised his ghostly sword in warning, watching the stairs. Alle clamored down the stairs, paying no heed to the frantic shouts from the corridor.

"Kiara! Are you all right?" Alle reached Kiara first, noting with concern the growing bruise on her temple where she had slammed against the rock wall on one side of the stairwell.

Cerise reached them a moment later. "Your aim is good, Alle. The guard is dead—saved him from hanging, although now we won't know who sent him."

Alle snorted. "Do you need to ask? Want to bet he was Guarov's insurance?"

Sounds of a heated argument came from the hallway above. Kiara could dimly make out Lord Dravan's angry voice, shouting down Guarov and Dame Nuray. Any comment was preempted by a sharp pain in her belly that made her double up. She grabbed for Cerise's hand, alarmed.

Cerise's concern showed in her eyes. "We need to get you up the stairs and back to your rooms," she said, laying a hand on Kiara's belly to ease the sudden contractions. Slowly, the three women made it up the stairs where Ammond and Hothan waited, weapons drawn. Crevan was doing his best to lead the arguing nobles away from the area, but by the sound of the shouts that reached them, Dravan and Acton were intent on blaming Guarov for the incident and disinclined to move from where they were until the matter was settled.

The voices stilled as the three women emerged from the stairwell and Kiara stumbled, leaning heavily on Cerise and Alle. Hothan reached Kiara as she slumped, and the last things she remembered were Lady Casset's scream and Hothan catching her just before she hit the floor.

* * *

KIARA AWOKE IN her own bed. Cerise and Alle sat vigil in chairs on either side. In the shadows near the fireplace, she glimpsed Ula and Seanna, barely visible as faint blue images, keeping watch. Macaria lowered her flute, ending the quiet song she had been playing, and came closer, worry clear in her eyes.

"The contractions have stopped," Cerise said, patting Kiara's hand in response to her worried expression. "A bit of vettor root under your tongue took care of that. The gash on your forehead is healed, although some of the deep bruising from your fall may be sore for a while. From the bruises, I'd guess you rolled into a ball when you fell, which means the baby was well protected, although at your expense."

Alle helped Kiara sit and propped pillows behind her, handing her a warm cup of tea.

"Thank you," she said to Alle. "I wasn't sure how that damned Council meeting would end."

Alle gave a tired smile. "I suspect Aunt Eadoin got wind of Guarov's plans. Who knows— perhaps he's the one who sent the linens, and the fever along with them. I've heard of people catching pox from blankets. I wouldn't put it past him."

"I pray to the Lady that Eadoin gets well," Cerise said, checking Kiara's bruised cheek again. "But her illness keeps us from taking Kiara somewhere easier to guard than Shekerishet. It's quite clear that we can't keep her safe here."

Jae left his place by the hearth to waddle over toward the bed and gave a quick flap of his leathery wings to land on the foot of it. Satisfied, he curled up at her feet. Tris's dogs padded over as well, and the gray wolfhound nudged at her hand, insisting to be petted, while the other two lay down on either side of the bed.

"What about the lodge?" Kiara asked. "Tris took me there after the wedding. It's not fancy, but it was built for winter hunts, so it's warm enough. Crevan kept it well provisioned, and it's large enough for us all to stay. There's a guardhouse, so Ammond and Hothan can still watch over us. After today, they're the only ones I'd trust."

"We're not going anywhere until tomorrow," Cerise said firmly. "I want to make sure that you're all right. And riding there on horseback is out of the question for you. Even a carriage ride could be too rough—I don't like moving you."

Kiara squeezed Cerise's hand. "I'm tougher than I look. I feel much better. And if the pains are brought on by worry, then it should be better moving me away from Shekerishet, at least for a little while."

"We can send for a sleigh," Alle suggested. "And a sledge for our provisions. The dogs and Jae can come with us. Kiara's right—the lodge is smaller, and there will be fewer people to worry about. I'll choose the servants myself that go with us—two or three should suffice, so long as one of them is a good cook!"

"If we can move you without danger, then I'm all for putting some distance between us and Shekerishet, at least for a while," Cerise relented.

"I'll go find Crevan and start the preparations," Alle said, standing up and smoothing her skirts. "We'll keep it as quiet as we can, and perhaps we'll throw the troublemakers off the scent."

"I saw the look on Crevan's face when you pegged the guard who shoved Kiara," Cerise observed wryly. "You may want to approach him with both hands in view, so as not to make his heart fail!"

"I know you'll have to make some preparations," Kiara said, looking pointedly at Macaria. "Cerise and Alle and I will be fine if you to want take leave until tomorrow morning."

Macaria nodded, taking Kiara's intent clearly. "Thank you, m'lady. I would be grateful." She headed for the door when Kiara called after her.

"Be careful, Macaria. It's clear we still don't know all the players in this game."

"Aye, m'lady. I'll take care."

ALONE IN HIS room at the Dragon's Rage Inn, Carroway pushed aside his half-eaten dinner. The innkeeper, out of long friendship, sent up a full meal. It was plain but filling tavern fare— far better, Carroway knew, than he might hope for had Crevan confined him in a cell beneath

Shekerishet. Outside, the winter wind banged against the shutters, howling beneath the eaves. He sipped at his brandy and took up the lute he had laid aside.

Since his confinement, there was little to pass the time except for card games and his music. For the first time since his miserable early days as a fosterling at court long ago, Carroway played until his fingers bled. But the solace he usually found in the music did not come. It was better when Paiva, Halik, Bandele and Tadghe came by. Alone, the time passed slowly.

He hadn't seen Macaria since the day Crevan had pronounced banishment. Carroway felt her absence most keenly. While he'd accepted the fact that he was in love with Macaria, he knew that as her patron, he couldn't act on his feelings. The memory of what Lady Nadine had done still hurt too much for him to ever misuse his own power. And yet, he suspected that Macaria actually loved him. He'd been planning to ask Eadoin if she would become Macaria's patron. Such a change would have removed the barriers, making it acceptable for him to woo Macaria openly. Banishment changed all of that.

Carroway stood as he heard the knob turn. His hand fell to the throwing daggers hidden beneath the sleeve of his tunic, daggers the guards had failed to find in the lining of his trunk when they brought his things from the palace. To his relief, Macaria slipped into the room, gesturing for him to close the shutters as she lowered her cowl. She shook off the snow and stamped her feet.

"It's a bad night to be about," Carroway said, knowing his pleasure in seeing her was clear in his face. "But I'll never turn down the company." One look at Macaria's distraught expression, and he sobered quickly. "What's wrong?"

He listened intently as Macaria's story tumbled out. When she finished, Carroway stood, running his hand back through his long hair and pacing in front of the fire. "So I came a hair's breadth from hanging tonight and didn't even know it? Please thank Alle for me."

"I know how close you are to Lady Eadoin. I'm sorry," Macaria said quietly.

Carroway nodded. "She and Queen Serae took me in when my family died. Eadoin's been like a grandmother to me. I'll never forgive Guarov if he was behind something that caused her sickness."

"We don't know that," Macaria said quickly. "And with all that's happened, there's been no time to question Crevan. All we do know is that somebody sent linens to Eadoin right before she took sick—and said the linens were from the queen."

Carroway turned. "Please tell Kiara how sorry I am to have brought this on her." He swallowed hard. "I swore to Tris that I would lay down my life for him when we fled Jared's coup. And while I'm fond of living, I would die for Kiara if it's the only way to clear her honor."

"She would never ask that!"

Carroway sighed. "As you've seen, circumstances may take that decision out of her control." Macaria left her seat and joined him near the fire, warming her hands at the hearth. "I hesitate to ask, but is there other news from the palace?"

Macaria nodded. "Tomorrow, we're taking Kiara to the lodge. She thinks it might be safer there—fewer people, away from court." She swallowed hard. "It means leaving the city." Macaria turned toward him.

"By the time we get back, the king will have returned. Decisions will be made." Macaria drew a deep breath. "I didn't want to go away like this. Not without telling you that I love you."

Carroway caught his breath, silenced for a moment. He spread his hands, palms up. "I have nothing to offer you," he said, his voice catching. "No patronage. No access to court. My lands and title are worthless. When the king returns, I'll be a beggar or a corpse."

Macaria's gaze was intense, but he could not look away. "Then maybe you'll finally believe that I wanted any of those things. You've been so noble, keeping your distance. Now I know why. That doesn't matter to me. I love you, Riordan Carroway, and your music." Her voice grew quiet. "I always have."

Carroway reached out to draw her to him, slowly, as if moving might break the spell of the moment. Macaria threw her arms around him, burying her face in his chest, as his fingers smoothed her fine dark hair. "I don't want to hurt you," he said quietly, pressing his check against the top of her head. "I have no future."

Macaria pushed back far enough to see his face, and she lifted one hand to touch his cheek. He closed his eyes, relishing the touch. "M'lady gave me leave until the dawn," she murmured. "We have tonight."

Carroway's throat tightened at her words. *It's what I've dreamed of hearing her say. But not now.* "You don't know how much that means to me," he whispered. But he shook his head as she tried to draw him toward the bed. "It's too dangerous. If they caught us together, you'd lose everything. I can't let that happen." He tipped her chin up until she met his eyes. "I do love you, Macaria. Enough that I won't see you hurt because of me." He wiped a tear from her eye with the side of his hand. "There now. At least all's been said. No more pretending." He managed a wan smile. "That's something, I guess."

"Not enough," Macaria said, standing up on tiptoe to kiss him. "Not nearly enough."

CHAPTER TEN

"HOLD STILL."

Cam grimaced as his cellmate tied off the rags he'd wound around Cam's broken leg to stabilize it. Cam groaned with the effort to sit. "There. It's the best I can do, given the circumstances, but it might brace that leg a little bit."

"Thank you. What's your name?"

"Rhistiart."

"Well, Rhistiart, I'm sorry you got mixed up in this. It's not going to go well."

"I'd figured that much already."

Only a dim shaft of light came from around the heavy door to their prison. Cam could barely make out Rhistiart's outline; a hint of dirty blond hair and a thin, finely featured profile. "How did you get mixed up with these guys?"

Rhistiart shrugged and sat back down, fading into the darkness. "I'm a bit down on my luck. I was the silversmith's apprentice in the town not far from here. He died suddenly from a fever. I'd been with him for fifteen years; he had no son. But his widow intended to give the shop to her lover, and she drove me out, with a tale that I'd stolen silver. I had nothing. This mill's been empty all season—the fuller died last winter and he had no kin. It was a roof over my head, and I needed a place to stay.

"Two days ago, your 'friends' arrived. I tried to hide, but they found me and threw me in here. I've no doubt that they're brigands. How bad is this trouble that we're in?"

Although he could not see Rhistiart's face, Cam smiled at the man's easy manner and his casual extension of friendship and shared fate. *He could be one of Ruggs's men, sent as a plant to get me to talk. On the other hand, there's nothing to lose. I'm already going to die.*

"About as bad as it gets," Cam replied. "Leather John and his men are divisionists. They mean to topple the king if need be to stop Isencroft and Margolan from joining. Ruggs is even worse."

"By the Whore! And here I'm thinking you might have Trevved out on a bet." Rhistiart paused. "Can't say I'm a fan of seeing Isencroft get mixed up with the Margs. Especially after their last sorry king, the Demon take his soul."

"Tris Drayke is a good man: nothing like Jared. He'll take good care of Kiara—and Isencroft."

Rhistiart gave a sharp laugh. "Chummy with the royals, aren't we! And how would you know this?"

Ruggs and Leather John know who I am. There's hardly a reason to lie. "Because I know both of them. I'm King Donelan's champion. And as you put it, I'm a bit down on my luck."

"Aye, that you are. And your name?"

"Cam of Cairnrach."

"Well, Cam of Cairnrach, we're goddess-screwed in this shit hole. Just in case you didn't know."

"I'd figured that much out already." Cam bit back a curse as he dragged himself to the wall and slowly began to work his way around the room.

"What are you doing?"

"Looking for a way out."

"Already tried it."

"And?"

"I'm still here, aren't I?"

"Maybe you're just not creative."

Rhistiart laughed. "I've been over the walls from floor to as tall as I can reach. My uncle was a fuller. I'd say we're in an empty dung pit." He jerked his head toward the wall behind him. "There's the door you came in through. Solid and tight, with the hinges on the other side. And there's a square of wood just above the floor on that side, maybe square as my forearm, where they probably sent the shit in through a chute. Boarded up tight."

"How big are you?"

"Beggin' your pardon?"

"Shoulders. Can't see you in this light."

"I haven't grown a whit since I was sixteen, more's the pity. A pox-faced actor tried once to recruit me to run away with a traveling company, but it was only to play strumpets, and I wasn't sure it was all by the script, if you know what I mean."

"Then Rhistiart, I have a bargain for you." Cam found the wooden panel and thumped on it with his fist. "Help me find a bit of metal to pry this loose, and if you'll carry a message for me, I'll get you out of here before Ruggs kills the both of us."

Rhistiart's voice was skeptical. "What about you?"

Cam snorted. "You bound up my leg. Was it thicker than yours?"

"Thicker than my waist, to tell you the truth."

"I'll never fit, and even if I did, I can't crawl back to the city."

"What kind of message do you want me to carry?"

"A message to the king's guard."

"The king's guard! Do you think I'm fevered? My master's wife turned me in for thieving silver. I'll be hanged long before they'll take a message to the king from the likes of me."

"I'll tell you what to say—you'll have to memorize it, word for word. And I'll give you the clasp off my tunic. Donelan will know it on sight. I'd give you my ring," Cam said ruefully, "but it's on the finger they borrowed."

"I noticed that."

"Here's the Lady's own truth, Rhistiart. Ruggs is working for a very bad man who wants to put King Jared's bastard on the Margolan throne. Only it won't just be Margolan this time—it'll be Isencroft, too. Donelan doesn't know there's a traitor, and he doesn't know Ruggs has a plot to kill him. If you save the king, I'd warrant they'd forget the silver."

"Biter's blood! Me, save the king?"

"There isn't anybody else, Rhistiart. I'm not going to get out of here in one piece."

Rhistiart was quiet for a long time. "Right then," he said finally. "A bit of metal. Will this do?" Cam heard the clatter of heavy objects near his hand.

"Silver?"

Rhistiart laughed. "Hardly. They're my tools—what I had in my pockets when the brigands threw me in here. And a piece of flint. Will they do?"

"We've no other way to pass the time. They'll do."

Cam and Rhistiart took turns working at the panel. It had been secured with nails driven through the board and into the stone. After breaking two tools, they discovered a combination of chiseling away at the wood and wiggling loose the nails, careful to make as little noise as possible. In the darkness, there was no way to know how much time had passed, and no assurance their captors would not return at any moment. Finally, the board gave way, and a blast of fresh, frigid air swept down the chute.

"Might not be the cleanest way out, but if it's getting that kind of draft, they haven't plugged up the far end with stones," Cam said with satisfaction.

"Well, then. Now what?"

"Now you get your ass up that chute as quickly as you can. Hide if it's daylight. If it's night, get as far as you can and mind you don't leave a trail in the snow. You have my clasp?

"Pinned to my shirt."

"And the message?"

Rhistiart cleared his throat. "I've got a message from Cam of Cairnrach, Champion of King Donelan, and his clasp as surety. Ruggs plans an attack on the king. Crevan betrayed you. Attack the old fuller's mill."

"Good. And you can give directions to get them here?"

"If I'm not hanging by my neck." Rhistiart paused. "What happens to you, if the army sacks this place?"

"The same thing that happens if they don't. I die."

"Good to know you, Cam of Cairnrach."

"Lady bless, Rhistiart. Now get out of here, and run like there's a *dimonn* behind you."

DAY 3

CHAPTER ELEVEN

JONMARC STOOD SOBERLY at the back of the
funeral gathering. If the villagers noticed his
presence, they said nothing, neither welcoming
nor shunning him. Fifteen bodies were wrapped
in shrouds and laid on the village green, awaiting
the full light of day to afford protection to
those who would bury them. Most of the dead
were women and children—easy prey, Jonmarc
thought angrily, remembering the *vayash moru*
who had swooped from the sky like falcons that
had caught the scent of a rabbit. Not until the
bright streaks of a red dawn lit the sky did the
frightened mourners begin to return to their
homes. Jonmarc spotted the same village elder
he had approached before the battle.

"Magistrate," Jonmarc hailed the man.

The old man turned. He looked to be over

sixty winters old, white haired but not stoop-shouldered, and by his build, he had been a strong man in his youth. "Lord Vahanian. I guess I should thank you. Without your warning, we wouldn't have stood a chance."

"I'm sorry I was right." Jonmarc looked down. "And I'm sorry about your loss."

The elder nodded. "Aye. It cuts deeply."

"I think I know where the rogue *vayash moru* have taken shelter from the day. If they're in their day crypt, they're vulnerable. We could punish the ones who did this."

The elder drew a deep breath and looked past Jonmarc at the rising sun. "I saw that Lord Gabriel was here—and I know they helped drive off the biters that attacked us."

"Gabriel and Laisren are angry about what Malesh is doing. They're bloodsworn to stop him—as is Lady Riqua. But they can't move against Malesh by day. We can."

The elder still looked to the sunrise. "No one has hunted *vayash moru* by day in these lands for many, many years. We have honored the Truce."

"Honorable *vayash moru* still respect the Truce. Malesh is a bad seed. He's betrayed his own kind. There's still a chance to stop this before it becomes a war. If this goes on, and King Staden has to get involved—"

The elder nodded, and turned to meet Jonmarc's gaze. "Yes, I know. The price will be high. Too high. We will go with you. May the Dark Lady forgive us."

Later that night, Jonmarc's dreams gave him little sleep. The years faded, and once again, he was in Eastmark. He was tied to the back of a wagon, his wrists chained and his ankles hobbled with ropes. The soldiers hadn't bothered to give him a shirt or cloak when they pulled him from General Alcion's brig. He was shivering with cold, which only made the pain worse. Alcion hadn't been content with forcing him to watch while the men under Jonmarc's command were hanged for refusing the order to burn down a village that could not afford to pay its taxes.

It wasn't enough that the hangmen deliberately made the nooses short, so that his soldiers twisted and convulsed while they gasped for air. Nor was it sufficient to force him at sword's point to watch as Alcion's troops made bayonet practice with their dying bodies. Alcion and his blood mage, Foor Arontala, wanted to make an example of the captain who dared defy them. He had been beaten, whipped, and branded. Arontala had made sure Jonmarc was denied the solace of unconsciousness or shock until Alcion was through with him. Arontala, the same Fireclan mage who had sent magicked beasts to his own village two years before, the beasts that had killed his wife.

When the soldiers dragged him from his cell, Jonmarc expected to see a stake in the courtyard. Death by fire was Alcion's preferred mode of execution for ranking officers who disappointed him. But Alcion's plans were larger. Jonmarc lifted his head defiantly to look at the man on horseback who sat at a safe distance, watching the preparations. Alcion's long black hair framed a face dark as night. That alone told of his pure Eastmark blood. The intricate tattooed markings on his left cheek made it clear that he was also of royal blood. Third in line for the throne, Jonmarc knew, behind King Radomar's oldest son, Kalcen. Lately, Jonmarc had begun to wonder whether Alcion and Arontala had other plans for the succession. Whatever their plans, Jonmarc knew he wouldn't live to worry about it.

Two of the soldiers dragged Jonmarc from the wagon. He stumbled and fell, hobbled by the ropes. He heard the whistle of a sword's blade and tensed, expecting to die. Instead, the blade sliced through the rope binding his ankles, and cut painfully into his left calf. "On your feet," the soldier commanded, dragging Jonmarc to stand.

The other soldier pushed the crossbow against Jonmarc's back. "We have a little surprise planned for you—and your friends."

Yesterday, the soldiers had herded all of the villagers into a barn before the executions began. Women, children, old and young. Now, soldiers pitched hay around the barn. More dragged branches from the woodpile. Behind them stood their captain, a man in the uniform Jonmarc had worn until just a few weeks before.

Next to him were three barrels. Jonmarc had no doubt about the barrels' contents. Oil.

"Nice night for a bonfire," the soldier who held the crossbow against Jonmarc's back murmured. "You chose these villagers over your oath as a soldier. Now, you can die with them."

Soldiers opened the barn door far enough to push Jonmarc through. Inside, Jonmarc saw Sahila, one of the village elders. Sahila met his eyes, and Jonmarc saw that Sahila understood. They were going to burn.

The soldiers kept their crossbows trained on the barn doorway until the massive doors were shut and barred. Jonmarc looked to Sahila. "Any other ways out of here?"

"Nothing they haven't sealed."

Inside the barn, the only light came in slivers between the old siding planks. Night was falling, and soon even that would be gone. Dust floated in the air, making it difficult to breathe. Dust that would make the barn burn that much faster, once the flames came. Jonmarc looked around, desperate for inspiration. He spied a large iron ring in the floor.

"What's down there?"

"Grain bins and root cellars."

"How many?"

"Not enough."

"Get everyone you can below ground," Jonmarc said.

"Those bins could become an oven."

"Up here, we don't stand a chance."

Sahila nodded. Jonmarc watched him disappear into the throng. He walked the perimeter as quickly as his painfully bruised muscles would allow, but Sahila was correct. All the doors were sealed. And even if they found an opening, soldiers on the other side would shoot them down before they could get far.

Smoke was beginning to waft through the small gaps between the boards of the barn walls. Outside, flames began to lick at the old boards, lighting the inside of the barn with eerie, dancing shadows. Jonmarc turned, and was startled to see Sahila advancing toward him with an axe.

"Hold still."

"Like hell."

"You want to die chained like an animal? Put your wrists on that beam, and close your eyes."

Jonmarc flinched as the heavy axe whistled through the air and clanged against his chains, severing them. He looked around. Sahila had gotten at most a third of the villagers into the bins, but the rest huddled in frightened groups. Outside, the flames burned higher.

"Is there anything else below the barn? Even a dung pit is better than being in here when those rafters start falling."

Sahila thought for a moment. "Come with me." Slinging the axe over his shoulder, he led Jonmarc to a place in the center of the hard-packed dirt floor. He flung his axe, and it landed on its blade in the dirt, but it seemed to Jonmarc that the floor beneath their feet shook, just a bit. "Here. Dig here." Sahila motioned for several nearby men to join them. Jonmarc gritted his teeth against the pain as he grabbed a shovel and began to dig. A hand's depth beneath the dirt, they hit wood.

It was growing warmer inside the barn. Jonmarc eyed the rising flames. They were running out of time.

Hacking with their tools and kicking with their combined strength, the men worked until the old wood splintered. Moist, cold air rose out of the darkness. "Caves. They run all through this area. Can't barely plant a field without someone falling into one. No idea what's down there or where it goes. Just remembered my father showing me where they'd closed over one when they built the barn."

"Anywhere's better than here. Let's get them inside."

The cave mouth was narrow, allowing only one person at a time to enter. One by one, the villagers descended, as the flames spread up the walls and to the barn roof. By the time the last of the villagers was down, bits of burning wood were falling around them. "Get in," Jonmarc said to Sahila.

"What about you?"

"I'll come. Just get in."

The roof creaked ominously as Sahila shimmied down into the cave. "Hurry."

Jonmarc needed no urging. He jumped into the hole, banging from side to side as he fell, as overhead, the roof gave way. A shower of sparks and a hail of burning wood followed him down the shaft, burning into his back. The heat took his breath away. He landed hard, and his leg folded painfully under him.

"There's no way out," Sahila said, helping him to his feet. "There are shafts—that's why we've got air. But not even the children could fit through them."

The cave was damp, helping to resist the blistering heat that seared down from above. In the distance, Jonmarc could hear screaming. Around him, babies wailed and women sobbed. A few voices chanted in prayer, begging the favor of the Lover. Men cursed under their breath. They waited.

It took a long time for the fire to burn itself out. Hungry, thirsty and cramped, they waited in the darkness until a night and a day passed, afraid that soldiers might be standing guard over the wreckage, waiting to shoot survivors. When Jonmarc finally climbed up the shaft, it took all his strength to shove aside a fallen beam that was still hot enough to burn his palms. Cautiously, he looked around, expecting to feel a crossbow bolt at any moment. He scrambled out and scanned the horizon. No soldiers awaited them. From the wreckage of the barn, the soldiers had felt assured there were no survivors.

Little of the barn remained standing. Charred timber covered the old barn floor. Sahila joined him and together they ran to free the others who had taken refuge in the bins, throwing aside the wood that pinned the bin doors shut. Silence met them as they pulled back the doors. The odor of burning hair and roasting meat met them. Huddled together, the bodies of the villagers were covered by ash. No one moved. No sound came. Sahila cursed potently. Jonmarc fell to his knees, unable to look away from the carnage. From the cries of the men around them as they freed the other bins, Jonmarc knew there were no survivors.

"Eastmark's not safe for you," Sahila said. "You've got to run."

"What about them?" Jonmarc said, with a glance toward the survivors.

"We have kin in the other villages. We'll slip away, in small numbers so that the guards don't track us. We'll survive."

"I'm so sorry. I brought this on you."

"Would you have spared us by following your orders? We would all be dead. And you've paid dearly for your honor. We're grateful. But we can't protect you. If the soldiers didn't loot my home, I may be able to get you a cloak and a bit of food. Get out of Eastmark. You're Margolan born. Go home where you'll be safe."

Safe. Nowhere is safe.

Jonmarc jerked awake, sitting up in his bed. He was bathed in sweat and his hair hung in his eyes. He looked around wildly, unable to place this unfamiliar room. "You're safe," a man's voice said from the doorway. It took a moment for Jonmarc to recognize the deep, raspy sound of the Magistrate's voice. The man lit a lantern and came into the room.

"Did I cry out?"

"No. I heard your dreams."

Jonmarc was amazed, but the Magistrate's eyes assured him of the truth of his statement. The dreams had never left him, not in the long years since he'd fled Eastmark. The burning was only one of many memories that haunted him, making sleep elusive. Carina was able to trance with him, blunting some of the force of the memories. It had been a long time since he'd fought his way out of the bedclothes, ready for battle. But even she could not make the scars and memories completely disappear.

"Are you a mind healer?"

The Magistrate shook his head. "No. A truth senser—and a dream reader. It explains why I was chosen for my role—and why I never married."

"Sorry I woke you."

The Magistrate looked at him with a gaze that seemed to see far too much. "You know what it is to burn."

"Yes."

"And yet, you would lead us to the day crypts."

"What choice do we have? If we don't punish the guilty, innocent *vayash moru* will be destroyed. It's only a matter of time before the burnings start again. I swore an oath to Staden to be the protector of living and undead. And if that means I stand between them, so be it."

The Magistrate nodded. "You would do this, although *vayash moru* took both your wives from you."

"And if Arontala and Malesh were mortal, what should I do? Pledge to destroy all mortals in vengeance?" Jonmarc took a deep breath, passing his hand back through his hair to brush it from his eyes. "I do what I'm good at. I fight. I try to be on the side of the good guys. When I can tell which side that is. As for the rest, well, I've been cursed since I was fifteen. Don't know why or by whom, but cursed, nonetheless."

The Magistrate's gaze fell to the mark of the Lady that was drawn on Jonmarc's chest. "You swore the Bargain."

"I wanted some insurance. I have rotten luck."

The Magistrate frowned and extended his hand, palm first, toward the mark, stopping just above the skin. His eyes lost focus. "No. Not cursed. Chosen."

"From where I sit, they look a lot alike."

"She won't release you, you know. Not until you've completed the task She has for you."

"Who?"

"Istra."

"I made the Bargain to destroy Malesh and stop this war from starting. That task is over when he dies—and so do I."

The Magistrate's gaze was far away. "Perhaps. Then again, damnation is in the details. You pledged your life and soul to Her, didn't you? But it's up to Her when she claims what belongs to Her. She's chosen champions before. That's what the legends say. I'd ask Lord Gabriel, if I were you. Remember where you are, son. Death doesn't end things here." He seemed to come back to himself. His smile was weary. "You've passed one test."

"Oh?"

"I have my own dreams, you know. The Lady warned me of fire and fire bringers. She said to only trust the burned man." He gestured toward the old scar on Jonmarc's shoulder, where one of the burning beams in the Eastmark barn had caught him. Only then did the Magistrate reveal the dagger sheathed beneath his sleeve.

"You really think you could take me—with that?"

The Magistrate met his eyes. "It's poisoned. I think you know the kind."

Jonmarc repressed a shiver, remembering the poisoned blade that nearly killed him last

Winterstide in Staden's court, the blade meant for Tris. "Well enough."

The Magistrate stood. "There are candlemarks left before daylight. Sleep well."

Yeah, right.

COME MORNING, JONMARC left the village with a raiding party of twenty men. The villagers carried whatever weapons had been salvaged from the ruins of the night before, plus an ample supply of reed torches, tinder and oil. In addition to the day crypts Gabriel and Laisren had told Jonmarc about, the Magistrate suggested several more hiding places.

"What makes you think you know where Malesh and his brood rest by day?" Jonmarc asked the magistrate as they rode through the deep snow.

"I chose the dread places," the Magistrate replied. He had a thick Principality accent and a face weathered from hard outdoor work. "The places that the legends warn us about. Oh, the tales don't speak of biters. Just of men who entered and never returned, or travelers snatched from the road, or children gone missing. Places with strange lights and shadows, where a cold fear takes your heart and tells you that a wise man would turn tail and run."

"How did you narrow the list?"

The Magistrate shrugged. "We need to be home before dark. We know they can attack the village, but I'll still feel safer there than near one of these Crone-damned places."

A crossroads came into view. As at Crombey, one road bordered thick forest. Beside the crossroads was a shabby shrine, its ribbons tattered and faded with age. Someone seasons ago had piled up eight stones to the Lady as a small altar. Stubs of weathered candles sat among the stones, some recent and some dirty with time.

The Magistrate held up a hand and the group reined in their horses, tethering them lightly to the saplings at the edge of the forest. Jonmarc and the Magistrate led the group into the trees, where the branches blocked the light. Jonmarc's crossbow was notched and ready. Beside him, the Magistrate carried a broadsword; he was the only man in the village who seemed to actually have an idea of how to use one. Some of the other men had bows while the rest brought scythes or newly sharpened pikes. Two men carried bundles of wood on their backs, while another carefully brought a large pitcher of oil. A young man carried a wooden cage with a large cat in it. The hedge witch had forced them to bring it, swearing that the cat could sense *vayash moru* and would alert them to the presence of undead. Jonmarc noted the group's uneasiness as a sign they were in the right place. From the looks on the faces of the men around him, they were fighting against something that bordered on sheer terror. As they moved into the forest, the cat yowled.

"Shut that thing up!" Jonmarc snapped. The dreams had left him tired and irritable. His mood got worse the closer they came to the task. It might be unavoidable, but he didn't have to like it.

Jonmarc spotted their destination. A small family cemetery lay long abandoned among the trees. In the Black Mountains of Principality, villagers gave their shrouded dead final rest in the high treetops and in the rocky ledges, making it easier, legend said, for their souls to embrace the Lover. But here in the lowlands, people were more likely to bury their dead. Bits of glass and metal hung from the lower branches of trees to ward away dark spirits. A few worn monuments stood tilted in the frozen ground. In the center of the plot, a stairway descended into another shrine.

The boy with the cat ventured closer. Before he was ten paces from the stairway, the cat reared up and hissed, crying out like a baby and clawing at its cage. Jonmarc waved the boy back and three men brought the bundles of dried wood and kindling. Jonmarc and the archers covered the men as they went as far down the stairs as they dared before setting the fire. They overturned the pitcher so that the oil ran down the stairs and into the shrine, and then one of the men struck flint to steel. The bundles burst into flame, and the fire roared up, as flames followed the trail of oil deeper into the shadows. Jonmarc set his jaw, forcing down old panic that triggered at the smell of burning oil as his heart thudded wildly, wanting to be anywhere but here.

Behind them, the cat yowled like a crazed thing, hissing and spitting in terror.

"Get ready," Jonmarc murmured.

From the depths of the shrine came an ear-splitting wail. A blur of flame rushed toward them up the stairs.

"Fire!" Jonmarc shouted, loosing his quarrel.

Two fiery shapes burst from the shrine entrance. Jonmarc glimpsed faces contorted in agony as the flames consumed the two men and the arrows found their mark. Forced into the sunlight, the *vayash morus*'s outlines flared. Their skin grew translucent, as if the flames glowed beneath it, and then fire shot from their eyes and mouths, rapidly cindering the two forms, which fell in a charred heap in the snow. The smell of burned flesh woke old memories, and he fought the urge to retch. Warily, Jonmarc and the Magistrate approached, but there was no movement, and as one of the men poked at the heap with his pike, it was clear that little remained beyond charred bone.

"Were they the ones we sought?" the magistrate asked.

Jonmarc nodded, feeling sick. "I recognized both from the battle. If there were others who used this site, they'll keep their distance now. Let's move on."

The Magistrate led them to another site at the edge of the forest. It was clear that long ago, a substantial home stood here, although only ruins remained. By the look of it, the home had burned. Before the group could get within fifty feet of the ruined building, the cat began to throw itself against its cage, claws reaching between the bars as if it were trying to run for its life. Jonmarc had always prided himself on not being a superstitious man. Yet as the group approached the burned foundation, he felt the hairs on the back of his neck stand on end. It wasn't just a sense of *vayash moru* presence, Jonmarc thought. It was a shadow that even the bright sunlight did not dispel. He remembered the last time he had felt that coldness: in the presence of the Obsidian King.

"This is an evil place," the Magistrate said. "It burned a generation ago. My grandfather told me about it. Servants disappearing. Errand boys never seen again. They say the lady of the house was mad, and that she murdered the lord and then slept beside his shriveled corpse. Some said that she wanted blood to bring him back to life, but my grandfather thought she bathed in it."

Weapons ready, the group moved warily forward, leaving the crazed cat behind in its cage. They picked their way across the fallen rocks and past the remnants of walls. At the western corner of the foundations lay what remained of a private chapel. The feeling of uneasiness was oppressive here, and Jonmarc knew they had found the right place. He looked around for an opening.

"There," the Magistrate said, pointing to a cracked marble altar. Jonmarc summoned two of the village men, and together they slid the altar a few feet across the snow-covered floor. The air that rushed up from the darkness beneath smelled of decay.

"Do you want the brands?"

Jonmarc shook his head. "I'd bet this goes deeper than the last one." He smiled ruefully. "I've had the privilege to sleep in quite a few places like this with Lord Gabriel's folks, under emergency circumstances." He motioned for one of the men to hand him a torch and headed down the stairs warily, crossbow ready. As he expected, the stairs went deep. As several of the other men descended, their torches lit the small antechamber at the bottom. Six other doorways opened from the main room. Pairs of men, weapons at the ready, brandished their torches as they searched, finding only the bones of the dead. Many of the skeletons were missing their skulls, Jonmarc noted; proof that they were not the first hunters to come this way.

The sixth room had a heavy wooden door. Jonmarc approached it carefully, expecting an ambush. Here below the ground, if the *vayash moru* could extinguish their torches, they were vulnerable in the dark. He jerked back hard on the door, and stumbled as it gave way unexpectedly. When he thrust his torch into the room, he found a comfortably appointed sitting room, filled with furniture to suit a fashionable salon. The room was empty, save for one shape on the floor curled into a fetal position. As Jonmarc held the torch aloft and his bow at the ready, a pikeman poled the shape over.

Uri lay on his side, a shiv in his back through his heart. His body was immobile, but his eyes snapped open at the intrusion, and his gaze locked on Jonmarc.

"Hold your fire!" Jonmarc commanded. "Let's get him closer to daylight—mind that you don't dislodge that shiv."

As Jonmarc kept his crossbow trained on Uri's chest, two of the village men handed off their torches and weapons to pick up the immobilized *vayash moru* by the shoulders and legs, moving him gingerly with their eyes fixed on the shiv sunk hilt-deep in his back and the large stain of black ichor surrounding it. They retreated until they reached the step just below where the daylight reached. The sun was now high overhead, and after the gloom of the crypt, the forest seemed glaringly bright.

"All right, Uri. Riqua bet you'd burn without too much effort, so I want to make you a very clear offer. I'm going to keep my crossbow against your chest while my friend pulls out the shiv. These two gents are going to hold you on your feet. Any move—any move at all—and I put a bolt through your chest and they let you fall into the sun. You know I'd welcome the excuse. Blink if you understand me."

Uri blinked once.

"I want to know where Malesh is. Get in my way and I won't wait for Riqua to watch you burn. Are we clear?"

Uri blinked.

Slowly, the Magistrate withdrew the shiv, as Jonmarc pressed the crossbow against Uri's chest. When the blade was out, Uri remained still, although his features lost their frozen appearance.

"Talk—but don't move."

"Malesh was here. I came to confront him. I told him the attacks must end. I was right about the blood magic. It cancels out my link to him."

"Where is he?"

"I don't know. I told you. I can't read him."

"I should put this bolt through you, for what you've done," Jonmarc said quietly. None of the other men around them mattered to him just then; he and Uri might as well have been alone.

"I can be of use to you."

"How?"

"I do have control over most of my brood. I can feel them. They're afraid of what Malesh's done. I can call them to fight. Or if they won't fight, I can command them to stay out of the way."

"That didn't work too well the last time."

"Even we learn."

"Riqua and Gabriel are still bloodsworn."

Jonmarc saw loss in Uri's eyes. "I know. And they have exacted their price from a score of my children. I have lost enough. I will do what I can, in my own way, to end this war."

Outside, the wind caught the trees and for a moment, sunlight blazed deeper into the crypt, catching Uri on the cheek. The pale skin reddened immediately and began to char, but Uri did not flinch, mindful of the bow pressed against his chest.

"If you want your revenge, then you have it sevenfold as my children die. If we are gods, then we are most vulnerable gods."

Jonmarc hesitated, his finger on the trigger of the crossbow. *No one would fault me. Riqua and Gabriel are bloodsworn. I could claim their oath.* After a moment, he drew a deep breath. "Turn him around," Jonmarc ordered the guards. They turned Uri so that Jonmarc and the mortal fighters had their backs to the sun, able to step into its glare. One of the villagers picked up the shiv, and Jonmarc slipped it into his belt.

"I didn't make an oath with Gabriel and Riqua, so I'll do it now. Do what you can to stop Malesh. But betray my trust, and I'll not only shiv your heart, I'll saw through your neck and tie you in the sun. Is that clear?"

"Bright as day," Uri said as Jonmarc signaled the guards to let him go. He disappeared into the shadows, and Jonmarc and the guards retreated hastily into the sunlight.

"M'lord? What now?"

"We continue the hunt."

THEY BURNED OUT six tombs before the afternoon shadows began to lengthen. The revulsion Jonmarc felt hardened into coldness, and the memories were pushed away to allow him the clarity he needed to fight. He would pay a price for that, later. They routed a dozen *vayash moru*, and every time, it took all of his willpower not to flinch at the smell of their burning flesh and the human terror in their death cries. Uri had said Malesh only had at most two dozen fledges. That meant others had joined Malesh, because given the *vayash moru* who had fallen in battle, Malesh should be out of fighters. Jonmarc doubted very much that was the case.

It was too late to ride for Wolvenskorn. Given the day's activities, Jonmarc had no desire to chance riding by himself after dark. By the time they returned to the village, bonfires circled the town square. Huddled under rough woolen blankets, the villagers slept under makeshift shelters, too afraid to spend the night in their own houses.

"How long can you do that before you've burned all the wood for the winter?" Jonmarc asked as they rode back.

"Not long." The Magistrate sighed. "As you put it, what's the choice? Be murdered now or die of cold later?"

"Not much of a choice at all, is it?" *For any of us.*

Late that night, Jonmarc sat near one of the bonfires, his cloak drawn around him. There was no pretending that he was going to get any sleep. Not after today. Not after the dreams. With Malesh still at large, he didn't dare take the edge off his fighting skills, although he longed for a brandy to blunt the memories that were more difficult than usual to push away.

Eleven years, and you still want to throw up when you smell burning meat. Would they still consider you the Lady's Champion if they knew that the bottom drops out of your stomach every time you hear a gallows door spring open?

He pushed away the mocking voice in his head, and it pushed back. *Maybe you really have found your true home in Dark Haven. Everyone you care about dies. Easier to handle if they're already dead when you meet them.*

But that wasn't really true. The casualties among the *vyrkin* and Gabriel's *vayash moru* were mourned just as deeply by the undead as they would have been by the living. Dead was one thing; destroyed, Jonmarc had come to understand, was entirely different.

Worse, the Magistrate's words rang in his ears. *It's up to Her when She claims what belongs to Her*, he'd said of Jonmarc making Istra's Bargain. The thought of living chilled him much more than any dread of death. Dark Haven without Carina would be unbearable. There had been many years when every night was a battle with himself over whether or not to see dawn. Guiding Tris and the others to safety last year had stopped that. He'd hoped that with Carina in his life, that battle was won—permanently. Now, those dark thoughts returned. But what he'd seen of the restless dead in his year with Tris made him less certain that death actually ended pain. And while Tris could make his passage to the Lady, Jonmarc was not at all sure he was in any hurry to find out which Aspect would come for him. *So much for suicide.*

"I thought I'd find you here."

Jonmarc looked up to see the Magistrate. The older man was smoking a pipe, and the sweet smell of the leaves was a wisp of normalcy amid chaos.

"Was anyone looking?"

The Magistrate shrugged and took a seat next to him. "I wanted to thank you. I know what it cost you to do what you did today." He met Jonmarc's eyes, and Jonmarc knew that, with the Magistrate's truth sensing, the older man really did know.

"Had to be done."

"You're not going to sleep?"

Jonmarc shrugged ill-humoredly, knowing the other could guess his reasons.

"I imagine that asking for a mind-healer's help is out of the question."

"They aren't something I come upon every day. I'm used to it by now." *Carina had hoped to become a mind-healer someday. Someday.*

"I suppose you'll leave in the morning?"

Jonmarc nodded. "Gabriel's waiting for me at Wolvenskorn. We think Malesh may make his next move at the Lady's Temple. It's as good a place as any to make our stand."

The Magistrate looked at him for a moment in silence, and the far-away look in his eyes made a chill run down Jonmarc's back that had nothing to do with the bitter wind. "Shadows and fire," the Magistrate murmured. "And an arrow without a bow. Your place is between the living and the dead."

"COME AWAY FROM the window, Carina."

Reluctantly, Carina turned away from the window at Taru's prodding. Beyond Dark Haven's courtyard, the night was too black to see anything except the stars. "I can't help hoping that I'll glance out and see Jonmarc and the others returning safely."

"You have the scout's report. At least we know something of what's going on."

Carina sighed and moved toward the fire. As if she needed further evidence that she balanced between living and undead, the fire did not warm her, just as the noxious mixture of blood and milk that kept her alive never seemed to sate her hunger. "We know that the village at Caliggan Crossroads was destroyed. We think there was a battle there, but we didn't find any *vayash moru* remains. And the scout said everything was at least a day old. Not much to go on."

"I've sent Kolin to Wolvenskorn. If Gabriel's headquartered there, we may know more soon," Riqua said.

"I know it's too early for your messengers to reach Tris, but the waiting is awful." Carina's voice was quiet. "I'm getting weaker."

"If our relay is working, this will be the second night. Your letter should reach Tris tomorrow night. We can hold the working the next day."

"Assuming the messenger is able to get through. Assuming that Tris isn't so thick in the midst of battle that he can't do the working." *Assuming I'm still alive by the time the letter reaches him.*

Whatever Riqua might have responded was cut short as the door opened and Kolin stepped into the room. "M'ladies," he said with a perfunctory bow. One look at his appearance elicited a gasp. Kolin's straw-blond hair was singed on one side, and his cloak and left sleeve were burned. A seeping burn was healing on his face, and his hands and cheek showed new, deep scratches that were just beginning to fade.

"What happened?" Carina asked, taking his hand in hers out of reflex before remembering that she couldn't heal.

Kolin's blue eyes showed more fear than Carina had ever seen in a *vayash moru*'s gaze. "I'm late coming from Wolvenskorn," he apologized, with a gesture toward his disheveled appearance. At second glance, Carina could see that his pants were torn and wet with snow. "Looks like Jonmarc wasn't able to keep word about Westormere from getting out. There've been two more attacks since then—you've heard about the Caliggan Crossroads. Malesh hit a third village yesterday, but Jonmarc and Gabriel were waiting for him. He got away, but they were able to save most of the villagers."

"Most," Carina repeated quietly. "How many is most?"

Kolin met her eyes. "Gabriel said it was bad." He looked back to the others. "Jonmarc stayed behind in the village today, hoping to find Malesh's day crypts and run him down. Gabriel didn't know how that went, and Jonmarc isn't due back in Wolvenskorn until tomorrow."

"Burning day crypts," Riqua whispered. "Sweet Istra. It's come to that."

"Gabriel and Laisren didn't like it, but they had to agree it was one way to contain Malesh. Oh, and Uri's gone missing."

"There's a surprise."

"So Jonmarc's alive—at least, he was yesterday?" Carina asked.

Kolin kissed the back of her hand before releasing it. "Yes, m'lady. Gabriel said that Jonmarc hoped if he led the villagers to where Malesh's brood slept by day that they might stop other villagers from harming innocent *vayash moru*." He grimaced. "Unfortunately, that part didn't work so well. He's not the only one to realize that we're not fond of fire."

"You were attacked?" Lisette exclaimed.

Kolin nodded. "I wasn't being careful. But Lady True! It's been so long since we had to worry, here of all places. I stopped hiding from mortals a century ago." He glanced down at his scratched hands and burned clothing. "I'm out of practice."

"Tell me what happened." Although Riqua's voice was steady, Carina could hear the controlled anger beneath her words.

"I left Wolvenskorn and I was riding back. There didn't seem to be a need for quicker travel," he said with a glance toward Riqua. "When I rounded a bend in the road, I could sense mortals in the forest ahead. I figured them for brigands—and desperate ones, to be about by night in these times. Brigands they were, but not seeking human prey. The next thing I knew, a ring of fire sprang up around me, and burning arrows were shooting from every side. They'd placed hay bales soaked in oil just beyond the trees on either side, and then sealed front and back when they lit the torch."

The burn on his face was nearly healed, and the scratches on his hands were fading. But Carina knew by Kolin's eyes that the memories would take much longer to go away. "They were amateurs, thank the Lady. I lost my horse to them, but I was above their arrow range before they knew it. Without knowing how many there were, I didn't fancy a fight. Even so, I'm worse for the wear."

"Have you checked on the others?" Riqua's anger was clear in her voice.

Kolin nodded. "Our places are empty. From what Gabriel's said, all of our brood who aren't here guarding Dark Haven are with him, at Wolvenskorn. That's the real news. Malesh isn't acting alone, and it's not only his own fledges. Either Uri lied or Malesh really was able to keep him out of his thoughts. Gabriel says that there were *vayash moru* older than Malesh in the battle at the Caliggan Crossroads. That means he's not only drawing in *vayash moru* from Uri's brood, but some of Astasia's as well—and maybe from Rafe's, too."

"Damn. Then the war has begun."

"I'm sure if Gabriel knew there were hunters out looking for us, he would have warned me. That may not be widespread—yet. But every village Malesh destroys makes it more certain others will take revenge," Kolin said quietly.

"Gabriel hasn't been idle. The *vyrkin* are massing at Wolvenskorn. They hold common cause with us. It seems that Yestin can be quite persuasive." Kolin looked down. "Eiria is dead. She was killed in the first battle."

Lisette covered her mouth with her hands. "I'm so sorry," Carina said.

"Gabriel says that they think Malesh is planning something on Candles Night at *Naithe Dorzhet Bene*," Kolin added. He looked to Carina. "The temple of the Dark Lady."

Riqua looked up sharply. "Even Malesh can't be mad enough to think himself fit to be consort to the Lady."

Kolin shrugged. "The timing fits. Candles Night is only two days away. The old legends say that Her consorts wooed Her with blood."

"Those tales are corrupted," Riqua snapped, more upset than Carina had ever seen her. "The Dark Lady doesn't want blood sacrifice. Only Nameless ever demanded blood, and even then, it was in the ancient stories."

"Still, Gabriel has a point. If Malesh is mad enough to think himself fit to be the Lady's consort, then all this may be an offering to prove his worthiness. In the old stories—"

"The old stories are lies." Riqua's eyes flashed dangerously.

"Not completely." They turned to see Royster in the doorway. "One of my colleagues at Westmarch spent her life researching the Old

Ways, before the worship of the Lady. Only fragments from those days remain. Peyhta, the Soul Eater, is a story from those times. So is Shanthadura."

"We do not speak that name." Riqua made a warding sign. "Those days are gone."

"Perhaps not." Royster seemed completely oblivious to Riqua's dark mood, pursuing the topic with a scholar's fervor. "My colleague found that in the high country, back in the remote villages, the villagers used the names of the Eight Faces of the Goddess, but the practice at the shrines and the murals in the temple were of Peyhta and Sh—" Royster caught himself. "The Destroyer."

"According to my friend the Keeper, Peyhta and... the Destroyer were two of the three death goddesses," Royster continued excitedly. "Konost is the third. She guided the souls of the dead. They are the bringers of plague, famine and war. Together, they are the Shrouded Ones."

"I don't see what this has to do with—"

"It all makes sense," Royster bubbled, eyes wide. "If Malesh knows the old tales, then he's heard that every year at Candles Night, in the old stories, a young warrior was offered to the Shrouded Ones in the sacred place. The three light goddesses sent their champion to kill the warrior before he could join with the Shrouded Ones. Two goddesses judged the battle—Fate and Ohainne, the goddess of the undead. If the champion prevailed, plague, famine and war would still occur, but only for a season, and then the land would be healed. But if the warrior won..." Royster's voice drifted off.

"What then?" Carina found that she had been holding her breath.

Royster's excitement sobered. "Then the Shrouded Ones would be loosed upon the land for a generation."

"Superstitious rubbish, all of it!" Riqua's voice was strident. "Listen to you! A scholar, telling fish wives' tales."

"You remember those days, don't you." Kolin's comment stopped Riqua mid-stride.

Riqua stiffened, and then nodded. "You don't understand how it was, in those days mortals don't want to remember and we Elders can't forget," she said quietly. "How we feared the spirits in every tree and barrow. How many were sacrificed to bring the rains, or assure the harvest, or end the pox." She turned to Carina and Royster, and for the first time, Carina saw old pain in Riqua's eyes. "When I was six years old, they took my older sister to the bogs. They weighted her down and let her sink. They said it would end the famine. But her ghost came to me every harvest, and I knew that it was a lie. When the Shipmen came across the Northern Sea and the Riders invaded from the East, it was a terrible time—war that seemed to go on forever. But they stayed long enough that we heard the stories of their goddesses, and gradually, the old ways blended and changed.

"Even the Crone and Nameless are not as fearsome as the Old Ones," Riqua said. "Those ways should remain buried."

"If it's true that Malesh used blood magic to hide from Uri, then maybe he is trying to become a consort," Kolin mused. "After all, Uri's told his brood often enough that the *vayash moru* are like gods."

"And right now, the Flow favors blood magic," Carina added. "It's wounded, and the blood magic tears at it. First Arontala, and now Curane's mages, and whoever is supplying Malesh with his charms."

"There are always blood mages," Taru said. "Not always mages of real strength, thank the Lady, but dabblers who still can do harm. The Sisterhood has known that blood magic was being practiced, but the blood mages are good at hiding. Foor Arontala was also *vayash moru*— perhaps old enough to remember some of what Riqua recalls. The Obsidian King claimed to be the consort of the Shrouded Ones. Perhaps that was part of Arontala's interest in becoming the vessel for the Obsidian King's spirit."

"And now Malesh is going to offer himself for the honor?" Lisette said, aghast. She made the sign of the Lady and turned to spit on the ground, warding against evil.

"None of this makes any difference," Riqua

said sternly. "Maybe Malesh is mad enough to believe in old superstitions. It doesn't matter why he's going to the Dark Lady's temple, only that Jonmarc and the others find him and stop him."

Carina turned slowly to look at Riqua. "Gabriel sought out Jonmarc. He told Jonmarc that the Dark Lady came to him in a dream. He called Jonmarc Her 'chosen.' Jonmarc makes two blood sacrifices of his own to fight Malesh, doesn't he? My life—and his own."

Riqua and Kolin exchanged glances. "Gabriel is one of the Elders. He's older than I am, and more... observant. My faith was buried with my mortality. Only fear remains. But Gabriel has always been a mystic. He says very little about those days, but his family had the Sight. When Gabriel told the Blood Council about his dreams, we saw no reason to stop him from finding Jonmarc, although privately, some of us had our doubts. When we saw Jonmarc's capabilities, Gabriel's vision seemed possible. Now, I no longer know what to think."

CHAPTER TWELVE

TRIS GROANED AND opened his eyes. His left arm ached to the bone. The pain from the mage's spells was gone, but it left him feeling completely drained. He raised a hand to his face, expecting to feel blistered skin. The blisters were gone, but the new skin was tender to the touch.

"Esme, he moved."

Coalan moved into Tris's field of vision. The young man smiled, and Tris could see relief in his eyes. "Welcome back."

"Thank you." Tris remembered little of what happened after he returned from his battle with the mages, but the image of Coalan braving his blind rage was clear in his mind.

Coalan shrugged uncomfortably. "You weren't in the mood for conversation. I thought a voice you remembered from the old days might do the trick."

The old days. Just over a year ago, when Bricen ruled and Tris's mother and Kait still lived. When he had been just a spare prince happy to be as far from the palace as he could get. When Margolan was prosperous and at peace. A time that seemed so far away as to be in children's stories of long ago.

"The battle?"

"A stalemate." The voice was Senne's. "Fallon told me that you would be waking up, and she guessed you'd want a report."

Tris managed a weak smile. "How bad was it?"

He heard resignation in Senne's voice. "Bad. Palinn's dead. That leaves Rallan and I until you're up and about. We lost several hundred men in the battle—the monster you fought wasn't the only one they turned loose on us. But we've hurt them. Wivvers' infernal machine worked better than we hoped. Our *vayash moru* couldn't get too close with all the fire flying around, but from what we could see, everything that could burn inside Lochlanimar is gone. We took quite a few men off their walls as well."

Tris knew from Senne's pause that there was more, something else the man was loath to add. "And?"

"We've got another five hundred men dead or dying from that damned plague Curane's blood mages sent us. And it's spread beyond the camp. I sent men on a scouting trip and they came back with the report that the two closest villages were full of corpses when they went to barter for wood and food. There'd been some contact—beggars, camp followers, even some merchants desperate for a bit of coin. But it's gone beyond the ranks, so it's anyone's guess whether there were villagers who fled before the sickness took them. And if they did, they've most likely carried it with them."

Plague. The word chilled Tris. He'd heard his grandmother's stories of the last great plague, back when she was a young girl. How disease and death had stalked across the Winter Kingdoms, relentless in its grip. No one could number how many died in that last horror. With this year's scanty harvest, a new plague would find its prey weak and vulnerable. And now that it had escaped the battlefield, the pestilence wouldn't stop until it burned itself out.

"What about Soterius?"

"I'm here. And believe it or not, I'm in better shape than you are."

Tris turned his head at his friend's voice, and despite the way his body ached, he smiled broadly. Soterius was sitting up in a chair facing him. He looked drawn and haggard, but he was alive. "It's good to see you up and around."

Soterius looked chagrined. "'Up' is a relative statement. If you mean, 'not flat on my back,'

then yes. If you mean 'ready to fight,' then no.
I went out into the daylight just to make sure I
wasn't undead, and I didn't catch on fire. So I'm
alive, thanks to you and Trefor."

Tris tried to shift his weight and pain flashed
through his left arm. He grimaced.

"Your arm's healing, but it's going to be
painful for some time," Esme said. "You broke
it when you fell. I've set it and splinted it, but
it's still going to require time."

Tris remembered Jonmarc's convalescence
after the battle with the Obsidian King. "At least
it's not my sword arm," he said, allowing Fallon
to help him sit. He turned back to Senne and
Soterius. "How many more strikes do you think
Curane can take? And more to the point—how
long do you think we can keep up the siege?"

Senne was silent for a moment. "When you're
up to it, I think you should call Tabok and the
ghosts from Lochlanimar. Our *vayash moru*
have made a few reconnaissance forays, and
the situation is grim. The commoners are dead
with plague or weak with hunger. Curane may
have access to food and water inside his keep,
but the villagers are hungry. We've given his
forces a pounding, between the bombardments
and the havoc that your ghosts have caused. The
vayash moru have run night raids when they
can. That Curane's troops haven't countered
more effectively tells me that he's running out
of things to burn to hold the *vayash moru* off."

"And our side?"

Senne cursed. "Unfortunately, we're not much better off. It's the coldest month of the year, and this year seems to be colder than usual. Firewood is scarce. We've run out of rocks to make cairns for the dead, but the ground's too cold to dig. The mages have helped us make ice mounds over the corpses to keep out the carrion-eaters and stave off more sickness." He paused. "We can sustain an encampment longer than we can effectively bombard Lochlanimar. We're low on munitions, except for swords and pikes, which don't help when the other side's behind a stone wall. I stopped counting how many times our trebuchets and theirs just hurl the same rocks back and forth. Whoever built that wall built it well. It's taken a pounding. We've breached it in a few places, but not the inner walls. And our army is in no shape for a frontal assault."

"Food and supplies?"

"Erratic." Senne shrugged. "I took the liberty of handling the packet that came from Crevan while you were indisposed. There was nothing of a personal nature," he hurried to add at the look Tris gave him. "Crevan did say that the quartermaster was finding it difficult to stock the requests—seems things are tighter than usual even in the palace city. Of course, that letter was over a week old by the time it made it here, given the bad storms and the way the roads are. He may have more shipments on the way since then."

"Or there may be even less for the next wagons," Tris supplied, trying to hide his disappointment that no message had come from Kiara.

"The scouts have stripped the land bare between here and the caravan road," Senne said. "What our side didn't take, Curane had already looted, preparing for the siege. I've even sent men south toward the Trevath border looking for supplies. Goddess help us; everything's scarce this year."

That meant famine, Tris knew. Famine and plague together, on top of the damage Jared caused, would be bad. But if his army failed to destroy Curane's rebels, the prospect of war with Trevath might be enough to break what remained of Margolan's forces. And that, he knew, would draw the rest of the Winter Kingdoms into a conflict that could destabilize everything.

For the first time, Tris saw Fallon standing at the back of his tent. "Ask the mages to come. I'd like Beyral to scry again. We need to prepare for another strike. If I've recovered, then any damage I did to Curane's mages is likely to be undone. The battle may go to whoever makes the next move."

Tris turned back to Senne. "See if you can get a final count on our readiness. Men, weapons, anything Wivvers has up his sleeve. I need to know what we've got to go up against Curane again. And if you've been holding back any brilliant strategies for a dramatic finish, now would be a good time to put them on the table."

Senne gave a tight-lipped smile that did not reach his eyes. "I'll see if I can find one, Your Majesty." He gave a perfunctory bow and ducked from the tent.

Esme eyed Tris critically. "I had hoped you'd have the good sense to rest before pushing yourself like this."

"We don't have time. If we win, there'll be time to rest later. And if we don't—well, I can rest when I'm dead."

"Cheery, aren't we?" Esme shook her head. "I'd tell you to take it easy for a day, but I know you won't. Pity I don't have time to stand guard and enforce that request, but I'm due to visit the infirmary and see what I can do to keep the sickness from spreading." The tent flap flared in the wind behind her as she exited.

Tris avoided Fallon's eyes. Now that the heat of battle was behind him, the horror of what he had done filled him with guilt. *It's forbidden to draw on the souls of the living for power. Goddess help me! I won't repeat Lemuel's folly, excusing myself the unforgivable because it was expedient. What I did is no better than the blood mages. I've tainted my soul, maybe risked the wrath of the Lady against Margolan. And I have no idea how to make atonement, or if I even can.*

"It's the potion I gave you that's making you functional right now," Fallon said tartly. "Push too far too fast, and even my remedies won't get you on your feet." Her tone softened. "You have a few candlemarks until Senne returns. We would all benefit if you would rest."

Tris sighed and let her help him lie down again. Soterius stood and clapped a hand on Tris's shoulder. "I may not be in full fighting shape, but I can help Senne with his report, and it might do the troops some good to see that I'm up and around. I want to see the shape of things for myself. Perhaps I can make a suggestion or two that's worth something for the next strike." He slipped from the tent, leaving Tris alone with Fallon.

"I'm not a mind healer like Taru, but it doesn't take one to know that something's wrong. What happened when you disappeared?"

Fighting down his shame, Tris recounted the battle in the Nether. He slowed as he came to the final confrontation. "I knew I couldn't hold out against all three of them much longer," Tris said quietly, refusing to meet Fallon's eyes. "And I knew that with the death wards set, my only hope of getting out was to have enough of my power left to leave my body and be able to return to it." He swallowed, knowing that none of his excuses made his actions acceptable. "I snapped their life threads and drew on their souls' energy," he said quietly. "I've broken my vows as a light mage. Dark Lady take my soul, I know what happened to Lemuel. I won't bring that horror down on Margolan." He knew she could hear the self-reproach that was thick in his voice. "I failed."

Fallon was silent for a moment, regarding him. "Do you judge the *vayash moru*, when they drink the blood of the enemy in battle?"

"Of course not."

"Do you believe there's a *vayash moru* in existence who hasn't—at least once—drained an innocent, by accident or in hunger?"

"Probably not."

"You know what's at stake in this war. And you know that Margolan can't afford to lose you as king. The war to govern the succession would tear it apart—and with it, the Winter Kingdoms. Like the *vayash moru*, you used your defenses. There was no good choice."

"I did something unforgivable."

Fallon's expression softened, and she laid a hand on his arm. "Every soldier who kills snaps a life thread. They just can't see it happening the way you do. Every death in battle makes the victor stronger at the expense of the loser. You didn't make the first strike. You were defending yourself. It was three against one."

"It was wrong."

Fallon took a deep breath. "Running a man through the heart with a sword is wrong, too. But it's what happens on a battlefield.

Margolan needs you as its king, Tris. You have to survive. Curane's mages left you no choice. In that situation, you had to use every weapon available to you—including the full scope of your powers. What makes you different from the blood mages, from Lemuel, is what you do with your magic off the battlefield. At the end, with the Obsidian King in control of his body, Lemuel routinely fed from souls outside of battle. In as much as the Lady can ever forgive any of the pain we cause in war, I don't think that you've compromised your magic—or your soul."

Tris closed his eyes, wishing he could believe her. "The more I learn about my magic, the more I fear the choices Grandfather had to make. I see how easy it is to lie to yourself about why you do what you do, and what a dangerous thing this power really is."

"Men who understand that are rarely the ones who become monsters," she said quietly. "Now—before I have to heal you again, rest. It's not long before the meeting."

Tris wanted to argue, but he could feel his newly healed body protesting. If he were to have any hope of actually being part of the battle, he knew he needed to regain his strength. He accepted a fresh dose of pain medicine, and let himself drift into a few candlemarks of uneasy sleep.

SHEER WILLPOWER ENABLED Tris to be dressed and seated at the campaign table in his tent before the generals and the mages arrived. Only Coalan knew how difficult it had been for Tris to manage, and Tris was certain Coalan would keep the secret that right now, Margolan's king could barely stand. Soterius was back in uniform, although by the way he carried himself, Tris was certain that his friend's injuries still pained him. Senne, Soterius and Rallan were already seated when Fallon entered the tent. Behind her were Vira and Beyral, who quickly took their seats. Trefor joined them a few moments later.

Tris raised his hands, palms out, and closed his eyes, summoning the last members to the table. The air inside the tent grew even colder than it had been on this winter night, and a faint green glow gradually solidified. Tabok and two other ghosts stood before them, almost solid enough to touch.

Senne repeated the report he had given to Tris. The others listened in silence as Esme gave an update on the number of sick, injured and battle-ready troops. Less than two-thirds of his original army remained in any shape to fight. The group looked to Trefor for his reconnaissance update.

"The *vayash moru* managed six missions by air over the last few days since the battle," Trefor said. "We never got close enough to strike, although my men were prepared had the opportunity presented itself. Although we weren't able to do more damage, we did get a look inside the walls. Most of the small structures—homes, storage buildings, shops—are in ruins. Some parts of the town inside the walls seemed completely empty, and we saw corpses in the snow, unburied. The survivors are living in lean-tos or out in the open. There were very few fires lit, although you know how cold it's been. The only ones who had fires were the soldiers, and even theirs were small.

"The buildings inside the keep were in better shape, relatively speaking. Those are the barracks and the armory. We have a feeling that any supplies that remain are being hoarded there. The roofs are made of stone and the walls are thick. Those buildings have held up against the bombardment better than the outer walls.

"The outer walls could be breached. But Curane's men have piled the rubble in tall rows. Any force that tries to enter through the broken places in the walls will be easy pickings for archers as they try to scale one row of rubble after another. And the inner walls are still solid. Any troops that did manage to get past the archers would be trapped between the inner walls and the rubble. It would be slaughter."

Tris nodded. "How many *vayash moru* remain?"

A flash of pain crossed Trefor's features. "Eight. We lost Ilar last night. They caught him with one of the flaming arrows. He was young in the Dark Gift. The flames took him."

Proportionately, the mages and the *vayash moru* had more casualties than any other group. Among the rogue mages who had defied the Sisterhood to follow him into battle, Latt and Ana were dead. Two dozen *vayash moru* had begun the battle, with more joining them after the army camped. They had not been completely welcome among the mortal soldiers, who regarded them with a combination of fear and suspicion.

Senne and Soterius had told Tris about the taunts the *vayash moru* had endured from some of the soldiers, conduct the generals hastened to discipline. But even when the cruel words stopped, no authority could remove the suspicion from the eyes of the soldiers who came from villages whose slaughter Jared had blamed on the *vayash moru*. Trefor and his fellows had kept to themselves, asking no favors and going out of their way to avoid incidents. They tended their own goats, assuring a ready supply of suitable blood, and fed from humans only during battle. And now, only eight remained.

"We are honored to serve Margolan and its rightful king," Trefor said.

"We're grateful for your sacrifice." Tris turned to Tabok, and enabled the spirit to appear nearly solid. "And what of your men, within the walls?"

Tabok stepped forward. "After the last battle, Cadoc and his mages couldn't keep their wardings in place. We were able to get into the tower rooms. There's a girl and a baby locked in there, but they're not Curane's granddaughter and her child. They're gone."

"Damn. How did they get out?"

"I suspect Curane slipped them out of the castle before the army arrived. In the days before your army camped, there were several carriages that left along the southern road under heavy guard."

"Curane knows how to hedge his bets." Senne replied. "The question is, if they fled to Trevath, did King Nikolaj know? Curane and Lord Monteith could be hoping to force Nikolaj's hand. Goddess knows, I don't trust the Trevath king further than I could throw him, but so far, he's been content to wait and watch how things unfold. Playing host to Jared's bastard may be more than he bargained for."

"We're hardly in a position to attack Trevath right now, regardless of what Nikolaj thinks of Curane," Tris said. He turned back to Tabok. "What of Curane himself?"

"We glimpsed him through the arrow slits. He looks like he's lost weight—even among the troops, food is rationed, but Curane is alive and still inside the walls." Tabok smiled. "Mohr has the ability to move objects, although he can't be seen. He played havoc with the mage's workshop, breaking everything that would shatter when he pushed it off the table. They replaced the wardings the next day, but we think that we can breach them again if you need us to."

"Hold off until the assault," Tris said. "If we can, we'll help you. Tell Mohr he can throw as many pots, pans and candlesticks as he likes once the fighting starts."

"As far as Curane's mages go, he has only two left of any strength. Cadoc and Dirmed. They have some apprentices, but from what we've seen, they're not good for much aside from starting fires without a flint." Tabok frowned. "There may only be two left, but it's the worst of the lot. Cadoc and Dirmed were the ones who created the sickness that's killed so many down in the ginnels. They don't care who they kill. Alone, they may not be a match for you," he said with a nod toward Tris. "Together, they are dangerous."

"What of Tarq?" Although Soterius's voice was level, he pronounced the name like a curse.

"The traitor is with Curane. He led the catapult assault in the last battle."

Senne muttered a powerful oath. "Can your ghosts reach him? Tarq knows our weaknesses—and he's fought alongside Rallan and me long enough to anticipate us. That explains why their strikes caused more damage in the last battle." Senne leaned forward, looking earnestly from

Tabok to Trefor. "Assassinate Tarq, and I'll pay gold from my own pocket to your nearest living relative. I want that bastard down."

"No gold is necessary," Trefor replied. "We'll make it our mission."

"As will we," Tabok replied, with a bow.

Tris looked to Fallon. "When Curane's mages pulled me into the Nether, I could feel the Flow. It's worse than ever. It seemed to be coming apart all around me. I tried to fight without drawing on the Flow, and the drain nearly killed me. Is there any way we can use magic to counter what Cadoc and Dirmed will throw at us—without dying from the Flow or burning ourselves out?"

Fallon exchanged glances with the other mages. "Twice, we've felt a surge in the Flow over the last few days. We've argued before over whether or not it's sentient. I believe it is—and it's searching for something. It's wilder than I've ever seen it. Vira tried a minor working and the energies blacked her out. We tried to combine our power to scry the inside of Lochlanimar, and barely got clear before the ball exploded."

Tris winced, remembering all too well how much damage an exploding scrying ball could do from his battle with the Obsidian King.

"If we try to harness the Flow as it is right now, we won't survive. And if we pull from our own reserves, like we did in the last battle, then we'd better have a good plan, because I don't think we'll survive that, either. One way or another, magic is likely to fail us."

Tris looked to Beyral. "What do your runes tell you?"

Beyral nodded, and took a pouch from her belt. Carefully, she spilled out pieces of bone and ivory into her palm. Tris watched as the sigils pulsed with fire. Beyral cupped her hands around the runes and closed her eyes, lifting them to each of the four directions in turn before raising her hands to her lips and breathing onto the pieces in her hands. Then she let the runes fall to the table. The sigils on the ivory pieces landed face down. Blue handfire lines traced a circle and spokes onto the table.

Beyral let out a low hiss as she surveyed the pieces. "Once again, only bone speaks. The ivory is silent. They fall at the cross-quarters, differently this time. *Aneh* and *Tisel* face each other." Beyral's finger pointed to the two runes. "The Formless One wars with the Dark Lady. *Aneh* speaks for chaos. *Tisel* lies upside down. You will be betrayed again, by someone very close to you." She paused. "Two new runes speak. *Sai* is the death rune. The price of battle will be high. It lies beside *Katen*, the rune of life. Together, they speak of Those Who Walk The Night." She frowned. "*Dorzhet* is a powerful rune, the symbol of the Lady, and for the powers of the Nether. When it falls with *Sai* and *Katen*, it speaks of fate and destiny, and of the shadowed places." She looked at Tris. "The runes hide as much as they show. At best, it's a warning."

"Thank you," Tris said quietly. He looked at the group around him, mindful of the members they had lost. Every person, living or dead, showed the strain of battle in their features. "When do we strike?"

Soterius leaned forward. "We can't allow Curane's troops to regroup. But right now, we're not in any shape for another assault. I think we can be ready in two days."

"Candles Night," Senne said quietly. "In the old days, it was sacred to the Shrouded Ones— the blood Aspects who harvested the souls from the battlefields. Fitting, don't you think?"

Tris found that he could not take his eyes from the *Dorzhet* rune. The fire of the sigil throbbed like a living thing, imprisoned within the bone. "May the Dark Lady protect us."

CHAPTER THIRTEEN

"I THINK YOU two have totally lost your minds!" Kiara shook her head, hands on hips, as she watched Alle take a piece of charcoal from the fire and smudge a rune on the mantle of the doors and windows of the hunting lodge.

Alle stopped long enough to turn and look at Kiara over her shoulder. "What, Isencroft is too sophisticated for wardings?"

Cerise gave a sharp laugh, and joined them, depositing four small, smooth stones on the window ledge.

"Not you, too!"

Cerise dusted off her hands and shrugged. "Your mother said an Eastmark warding over your crib every night. Viata disguised a Markian holy woman and spirited her into the palace to say the elements over you when you were born." She chuckled. "Your father and mother rarely fought—at least where I could hear them, but Lady True! What a row they had over that. Donelan was hardly devout, but he didn't want the gossips to get a hold of anything they could use against your mother. Viata wouldn't be moved. She knew she had to give you up to making offerings to Chenne in public, but at home, in a hundred little ways you never realized, she taught you the ways of the Lover."

Kiara raised her hands in a gesture of surrender. "All right, you fish wives. Tell me what I need to do so we can get back inside before we catch our deaths from cold."

"It's pretty simple, really," Macaria replied. "Everyone in my village made wardings around their house on the bright quarters, and strengthened them at the cross quarters."

Alle laughed. "I learned more from my year in exile then I ever learned at court about blessing and cursing! Between the whores at the inn and the hedge witch in the village, they could curse an unfaithful man a dozen ways—and that was before they really got going!"

"Something from each of the elements, for each of the Aspects, my dear," Cerise replied. "Pine boughs to keep away ill humours, and rock to anchor our souls. Those are from the land. Charcoal from the fire, to banish the dark spirits. Pine in the fire works for that as well, and the pine smoke clears away bad air. Water, four times blessed, dripped from a leather bucket to circle the house."

"If you knew these things, why didn't you work them around our rooms at Shekerishet?"

Cerise shrugged. "We tried. But we couldn't ward the whole palace—it was much too large. And as you've said yourself, the king warned you that Jared left dark energies behind."

Kiara helped Macaria gather up fresh pine branches while Alle finished marking the windows. They watched in silence as Cerise made a slow circle around the lodge, lips moving with the blessing, dipping her hand into a small leather bucket and splashing water out of her palm as if sowing seed.

"Can we go inside now? I'm frozen through!" Kiara said, rubbing her hands up and down her arms underneath her thick cloak. Inside, Macaria placed four boughs of pine in the fireplace, and a smaller sprig on the inside sill of every window. Alle withdrew a rough piece of rose quartz from her satchel and placed it on the mantel, and another piece over the door.

"And these will keep us safe?" Kiara asked skeptically as the scent of fresh pine filled the room.

Cerise made the sign of the Lady facing the four quarters and drew a deep breath. "It can't hurt. They say that, properly warded, the only evil that can enter is what is carried within or invited inside."

"I shudder to think what Hothan and Ammond made of all this," Kiara said. Down the lane, she could see her guards on patrol.

"Ha! Who do you think found me the rose quartz?" Alle said triumphantly. "And before you start to worry that the servants will think we've gone dotty, I spotted them not half a candlemark ago making bakers' wardings over the wine and the flour."

"Since I seem to be outvoted, I surrender," Kiara laughed. The trip to Bricen's old hunting lodge lifted her spirits more than she dared to hope. Although the candlemark-long trip by sleigh was cold, it was the first time since Tris left for war that she had felt her spirits rise.

"*Skrivven* for your thoughts," Alle said, seeing Kiara's expression.

Kiara smiled. "I was just thinking about how happy Tris was when he brought me here after the wedding. This was one place Jared left untouched. The dogs stayed safe here, and I think they're glad to be back. Although it's hardly the 'small country place' that Tris described to me!" As if on cue, Tris's dogs came loping up. Jae flew behind them, landing on Kiara's shoulder. The wolfhounds bumped Kiara's hand shamelessly, begging for attention. Jae hissed and kneaded her shoulder with his scaled feet before settling down. The large black mastiff eyed the others and then circled to lie down at her feet.

Bricen's lodge was built of stone, a one-story building with high oak beams and walls covered with the skins of bear and deer. It was small only in comparison with Shekerishet, but larger by far than the homes of all but the nobility. There were three guest bedrooms and a servants' room, with a large common room for feasting and relaxing by the fire after a long day's hunt. Outside was the kitchen and pantry, and cut out of the ground beneath the servants' room was a cellar for keeping roots and wine. A few paces outside the door sat a small stone building that served both as gatehouse and guards' quarters.

Kiara had brought only two servants with them—a cook and a maid whom Alle could vouch for. The lodge was well provisioned with food, wine and firewood. Alle had overseen the provisioning herself, and had promised to share a few of the recipes she had learned during her year with the innkeeper during the rebellion. Cerise had brought an ample supply of powders, roots and medicines, and Macaria saw to the diversion, making sure they would lack no entertainment during the long winter evenings with a supply of cards and dice, and a warning that no one should expect to beat her at *tarle* or *contre*. Her lyre and flute came with her as well, and a small pennywhistle. Free from the stifling scrutiny of the Margolan court, Kiara found herself actually looking forward to their stay.

"Who knows? Cerise might actually teach me to embroider something," Kiara said, dropping into a chair near the fire.

Cerise laughed loudly. "That will be the day, my dear. Not unless you can embroider with the point of a sword. Viata never had the patience for it, either, much to her father's chagrin. It's still considered to be part of the finishing of a well-born lady, you know."

Alle gave an unladylike snort. "It wasn't my stitching that vexed my tutors. My stitches are neat and regular. But once my tutor realized that I'd woven the curses I heard the stable hands say into the design, she made me tear out every stitch!"

Kiara snickered. "Now I'm sure I know why Soterius fell in love with you. Although really, I've never heard anyone curse as creatively as Carroway."

Macaria's expression darkened and she turned away. Kiara exchanged glances with Alle, immediately regretting her comment. "Macaria, I'm sorry. I know you're worried about him."

Macaria shrugged. "No harm done, m'lady. But news of how he fares won't be easy to get out here. I have to hope that Crevan will leave matters as they are until the king returns."

"Speaking of Crevan, aren't you expecting him?" Alle asked.

Kiara nodded. "He promised to come along

with the wagon-load of supplies and bring any news that may have come from the troops."

Alle frowned. "He's coming himself?"

"He said that, given the attacks at the palace, the fewer people who came to the lodge, the better. Goddess bless! What I wouldn't give for there to be a note from Tris in the packet this time."

"Has Crevan told you anything of how the war goes?"

Kiara shook her head. "Very little. He claims that he doesn't know, but I think he's coddling me. I'd asked Comar Hassad, but he said that the ghosts of Shekerishet can't go beyond the bridge. And with Mikhail imprisoned, I hear nothing from the *vayash moru*." She twisted her belt between her fingers. "All I get are dreams, and they're dark."

Cerise looked at her closely. "What do you see?"

Kiara looked away. "Fire. Glimpses of battle. Monsters, like the one that attacked at the wedding. Sometimes, it's the same things I saw in the scrying ball. Other times, I see snatches of things, too little to understand the meaning." She avoided looking at Alle as she spoke. Last night, in her dreams, she'd seen Ban Soterius fall, the hilt of a knife deep in his back. He hadn't gotten up, and she feared for him almost as greatly as she feared for Tris.

"Keep heart, Kiara," Cerise said quietly, patting her hand. "Your young man is full of surprises."

Kiara forced herself to smile, but her heart ached. The biggest surprise had been that in the nearly three months Tris had been at war, there had been no news from him. None at all. *I shouldn't doubt. I know what he did, when we fought the Obsidian King. I've seen his soul. What he felt for me was real—at least it was, then. I had hoped he would miss me.*

But deeper than her disappointment lay a larger fear. *Has Crevan told him about the Council of Nobles? About the gossip? Sweet Chenne, will he believe that Carroway and I betrayed him? Is there anything either of us can ever say to prove our loyalty?*

Cerise squeezed her hand, drawing her out of her thoughts as if she could guess the course they took. "The king has a good head on his shoulders, my dear. Trust him to make the right decisions."

Kiara bit her lip, forcing back tears and nodded. *Dammit! I should blame this on being pregnant, but I'm supposed to be a warrior and I'm acting like a farm girl. If I were in the salle back in Isencroft, Derry would tell me I needed some steel in my spine. Tris expects better from me. I expect better.* But the reality remained. Nothing was unfolding as expected.

CHAPTER FOURTEEN

CARROWAY SAT CLOSER than usual to the fire in his room at the Dragon's Rage Inn. Outside, the winter wind banged the shutters against the inn's walls, and the draft that came from the windows made even the upstairs cold. He'd been grateful for tonight's meal of cheese soup, sherry and a hunk of warm bread. There were many worse places to be imprisoned.

Bandele had brought him a stack of books, knowing that the worst part of his solitude lay in passing the time. A book dealer in the city was one of the minstrels' favorite patrons, and Carroway guessed Bandele had told him about the situation. Carroway sighed and flexed his hands. The books, which told of the earliest times in the Winter Kingdoms, were good fodder for the songs he was writing. If he were to be exiled, those new ballads might tempt a patron into overlooking his tarnished reputation. And if he were executed... well, Carroway thought, leaning back to stretch, at least the songs would be a legacy.

Carroway turned a page. The smell of ink and parchment filled the air. He'd been reading tales of long ago, when the lands that would someday become the Winter Kingdoms were ruled by warlords and tribes, long before the first of the Lady's followers brought their new beliefs to a wild and brutal place. A carefully drawn illustration of a ceremonial dagger impaling two hearts caught his eye. Carroway looked more closely. The dagger had a *damashqi* blade that showed the many folds and swirls of the steel used in its forging. He frowned as he read further, trying to make out the cramped handwriting of the historian who had written the book.

Before the time of King Hadenrul and the ways of the sacred Lady, the Birth Moon and the Hunger Moon were the times of vicious raids between warring tribes, he read. *Raids were carried out early in the Birth Moon, not just for scarce food, but to seize the wife of the rival chieftain. The kidnapped woman, if she was not already pregnant, would be given as a bride to the most feared warrior, who had one month to impregnate her. On the second day of the Hunger Moon, the prisoner would be sacrificed by the chieftain, who lit a bonfire and then plunged a ceremonial damashqi dagger through her abdomen, allowing the blood to anoint the snow. The ceremonial shedding of two lives was thought to bring renewal to the land, but some believe that the true purpose of the ceremony was to gain magical control of the great rivers of energy through blood magic. Others say it was an offering to Shanthadura. When the ways of the Sacred Lady came to the lands in the days of Hadenrul the Great, the practice of human sacrifice ended, substituting the ritual slaughter of a pregnant ewe. Over the years, the bonfires became torches and then candles, believed to be why this eve is now called Candles Night.*

Carroway pushed the book aside, deep in thought. Absently, he sipped at the sherry as he watched the fire dance on the hearth, whipped by the winds that found their way down the chimney. Candles Night was only two days hence, and while it was a minor holiday with almost no sacred overtones in Margolan, he'd always looked forward to the evening of midwinter cheer with its banks of lit candles and a traditional feast of roast lamb and red wine. After what he'd just read, Carroway doubted he could ever enjoy the holiday in quite the same manner again.

Absently, he reached for the pendant at his throat, a gift from Macaria. It was woven from strands of green and indigo thread and her own dark hair. Copper beads marked with runes were tied into the design. She had assured him that the hedge witch promised the amulet would protect him from harm. He discounted the talisman's protection, but he treasured the gift. It was a comfort to know that she shared his feelings, but bittersweet. His future held only death or banishment.

A quiet rap at the door roused him from his thoughts. Paiva, Bandele, Tadghe and Halik slipped into the room, shaking off the snow that clung to their cloaks and shoes.

"I was beginning to think the storm kept you from coming," Carroway said, accepting hugs from Paiva and Bandele and backslaps from Tadghe and Halik. From beneath their cloaks, Tadghe and Halik withdrew bottles of wine and held them aloft.

"Spirits for the imprisoned!" Tadghe pronounced. Paiva and Bandele put down their well-wrapped instruments and withdrew pouches of dried figs, and a small crockery bowl with honeycomb, cheese and flatbread from their bags.

"We had to bring extra, to bribe the guards," Paiva said impishly. "But we feed them well and leave two bottles of river rum for them around back in the snow by the steps, so they're quite willing for us to visit."

"Bless you!" Carroway exclaimed, motioning for them to sit. Halik opened a bottle of the wine and filled cups for all of them as Paiva and Bandele caught Carroway up on the trivialities of the court.

"What of Kiara—and Macaria?"

"They left by sleigh this morning, very early," Bandele replied. "Crevan seemed to be doing his best to make their departure quiet. He may be the only one going back and forth with supplies, so getting word is going to be difficult." She sighed. "The only tidbit that I did hear from Macaria was that Kiara's terribly worried about the king. Seems she hasn't received a letter from him since he left for war."

Carroway glanced at her sharply. "That's not like Tris. He wrote to her several times a week when she went back to Isencroft after the coronation. Almost drove the couriers crazy. That's not like him at all."

"Perhaps he's too busy with the war," Halik replied. "I heard some of the men talking after the wagons came back from running supplies to the army. They said the war's not going well. The men are hungry. A lot of soldiers have died. And there's fever in the camp."

Carroway swore. "Tris needs to win this. Margolan's in a lot of trouble if he doesn't."

"I don't have any news from the queen," Tadghe said, clearing his throat. "But Halik and I have been able to slip down to see Mikhail."

"How is he? I'd imagine Shekerishet's dungeons are miserable, even for a *vayash moru*."

Tadghe nodded. "He's not one to complain, but he didn't mind that we brought him a flask of fresh goat's blood and some dry clothing. The guards thought we'd lost our minds to ask to be let in to see a *vayash moru* in a dark cell, and if it were anyone besides Mikhail, I might have agreed. But he's had time to think in there by himself, and he had a message for you."

"For me?"

Tadghe nodded. "Mikhail said that he's been thinking about the murders, the ones everyone seems to think he committed. He said that he got a good look at one of the bodies when the guards marched him past it. And he's sure that whatever the marks were on its neck, they weren't made by a *vayash moru*."

Carroway frowned. "Come to think of it, I didn't get a close look myself. But I remember there were two punctures, and a lot of blood."

"That's right. But Mikhail says that even if a *vayash moru* doesn't drain a victim, they can kill without leaving that much of a mess."

"Maybe whoever did this intended to make a statement with all the blood."

"Or maybe," Halik put in, "we were intended to look at the blood and not at the punctures."

"What happened to the bodies?"

Halik shook his head. "That's where it gets even more interesting. No one seems to know. I spoke to old Hadric—he's been the court's undertaker for years. Normally, he takes the body if someone dies at Shekerishet and the family doesn't want them to be shipped home for burial. He buries the servants who die, too. But Crevan told him that the bodies were being studied as evidence. Hadric never buried them."

"So where are they?"

Halik met his eyes. "Makes you wonder, doesn't it? You know Bonday? He's the one who fetches the firewood for the kitchens. He told me that the day after Mikhail was accused, Crevan told him to set up for a bonfire in the middle of the night. Said it had to be ready by morning so that they could have the fire right at sunrise. Only in the middle of setting up the bonfire, Bonday says he was called away for half a candlemark. When he came back, he thought the wood was stacked up further than he remembered it. Says he also remembers seeing a bit of cloth fluttering in the wind, but he was behind on his work, so he didn't bother with it." Halik leaned forward. "Here's the kicker. When Bonday lit the fire, he says that there was an awful smell for the first couple of candlemarks."

"So you think someone got rid of the bodies in the bonfire? But why? And who?"

Tadghe crossed his arms and leaned back. "Why? To keep anyone from looking too closely at them, that's why. Despite the gossip about Mikhail, the *vayash moru* still have friends at court. Someone wasn't taking the chance that the bite marks might be questioned."

"I remember the bonfire that next night," Carroway said, thinking. "And at the time, I was surprised. I usually know all about plans like that, but I hadn't heard anything about a bonfire." He paused. "Halik, are you suggesting that Crevan deliberately asked for the bonfire in order to destroy the bodies?"

Halik shrugged. "Doesn't seem like ol' tightbritches, does it? Maybe someone talked him into it. But after we came back from seeing Mikhail, I paid a couple of *skrivven* to the butcher's boy to keep an eye on Crevan without being seen. And I've found out some strange things."

"Like?"

"Like he's keeping a messenger pigeon up on the roof, near Kait's old mews. The falcons put up a squabble when he goes up there, but he throws them some meat to calm them down. The boy saw him take a message off the bird's leg and then replace it and send the bird out."

Carroway shook his head. "For all we know, it might be a message to Tris. It's nearly a week's ride to the Southern Plains. Maybe Crevan had to send an urgent message."

"Aye, the boy said the bird flew south. But if it were a message to the king, why would Crevan go alone in the middle of the night?"

"Maybe it couldn't wait until morning."

"Maybe. But if Crevan's communicating with the king, why is everything at the palace such a mess? Macaria told you about the Council of Nobles. That's just the beginning. I've heard that Crevan keeps putting off paying the merchants, saying that the king hasn't returned the documents he's sent. Yet every week, a messenger comes from the front lines with a thick packet for Crevan, and Crevan sends a new one in its place."

"Crevan was never supposed to be full seneschal," Carroway said, taking another drink of his sherry. "Zachar could have run the palace in his sleep. Crevan was just the assistant."

"Interesting that Zachar died right after the king left, isn't it?" Tadghe said quietly. "I've been wondering about that. Here's a guy who might have been up in years, but he was tough enough to shinny down a garderobe and escape from Jared, and he just dies in his sleep?"

"It happens."

Tadghe leaned forward. "Yeah, but do you know that Crevan wouldn't allow the Sisterhood to prepare Zachar's body for burial? It was his right, as advisor to the king, to be buried with full honors. Crevan refused to let them have the body—said he wanted to do it himself, as a sign of respect."

"I'm not sure I understand—"

"What if Zachar didn't die from a brain bleed? You've told us how that poisoned dagger worked on Jonmarc Vahanian when the assassin struck last Winterstide. A nick with a bad blade, and Zachar's heart stops. And who would know, except a mage, who might just pick up on the poison?"

Despite the warmth of the fire, Carroway felt a chill. "I really don't like what you're suggesting."

"There's more. Paiva and I went to see Bian," Bandele added. "She's not doing well. The cold down in the dungeon has her crippled up with gout. And unlike Mikhail, she's frightened by the darkness. She had an awful cough when we saw her. I'm worried that she might not live long enough for the king to hear her case." She paused. "But Bian wanted to see us badly enough that she managed to get the servant who brings her food to slip me a note. She said she was afraid for the queen's safety."

Carroway winced, remembering the kindness of the old cook. "What did she tell you?"

"Do you remember when Malae died? We know there was poison in the *kesthrie* cakes— the Isencroft pastries. They blamed Bian for that. But Bian told me that it was Crevan who requested the cakes. She says she was too afraid to mention it before, but she thinks she's dying and she wanted someone to know. She also said that Crevan called her out of the kitchen right before the cakes were ready to take up—and that the cakes were alone in the kitchen for several minutes while she answered questions on something trivial. At the time, she thought Crevan was just in a dither because he was new to his role. But Bian's had time to think it over, and she's sure there was time for someone to slip into the kitchen and taint the cakes while Crevan kept her busy in the other room."

Carroway shook his head. "This sounds like the kind of story you hear from some down-and-out drunk soldier. The kind of guy who thinks everything's a conspiracy. No one's actually seen Crevan do anything except send off a pigeon. So answer me this—why? Why would he betray the king? Why would he try to kill Kiara?"

Paiva cocked her head to look at him. "Do you remember when we were trying to identify all of the spies? And we could never figure out who was Isencroft's man?"

"There was one more thing Mikhail told us," Tadghe said. "The night he was arrested, he'd been doing the books up in the exchequer's office. He says he found Isencroft gold that doesn't match what's in the ledger. It was in a bag off in a corner, as if someone wanted it safe but not noticed. Mikhail wonders whether whoever framed him wanted to make sure no one else was watching the books. And the only one who had access to the exchequer's books, besides Mikhail and Zachar, was Crevan."

"Which might explain why Crevan turned down our requests to visit Mikhail," Halik added. "The only way we got in was through those *vayash moru* family connections. I happened to know that both the guards last night have *vayash moru* kin. They went off to 'investigate suspicious noises' right before we came and left."

Carroway ran a hand back through his hair. "I'll grant you that a pile of Isencroft gold is pretty suspicious. But why would King Donelan's spy be trying to kill Kiara?"

"Maybe Crevan's playing a double game," Tadghe said. "I've been talking with the traders who come down through Isencroft from the Northern Sea. They said that they won't make another trip on that route until Donelan gets the divisionists under control. To hear them tell it, Isencroft's on the brink of civil war over the idea of a joint kingdom when Donelan dies."

"That doesn't make any sense! Crevan was born in Isencroft, but Zachar told me he grew up in Margolan."

"Suppose Crevan was loyal to Isencroft— enough so that Donelan made him his spy," Halik said. "Someone that loyal to Isencroft might not want to see the crown divided. I've heard what passes for logic among people who wrap themselves tightly in their flag," he added, dropping his voice. "If Kiara and the baby die and Jared's bastard were to take the throne, Isencroft would surely declare war. And at least for Donelan's lifetime, the crown would be secure—and independent."

Carroway stared at Halik in horror. "We need proof," he said, his voice not altogether steady. "Kiara's on shaky ground as it is. We can't go to her with accusations like this. Eadoin's too sick to help. The lords on the Council who supported Kiara might listen to Eadoin, but who'll believe a bunch of bards? They'll say you've fabricated the whole thing to save me. And right now, we have no proof at all."

"How do we get that proof?" Bandele asked.

"Keep watching Crevan. But you've got to be careful. If you're right, you could be in danger if he suspects anything. And if you're wrong, he could still throw you out of the palace if you get on his bad side." Carroway shook his head. "I wish Harrtuck were here. I'd feel better knowing someone I trust is looking after Kiara."

CHAPTER FIFTEEN

"WHERE IS HE?" Ruggs's voice was deafening, shouting next to Cam's ear. For emphasis, Ruggs grabbed a fistful of Cam's curly dark hair and thrust Cam's head into a large tub of icy water. Cam writhed, both from the struggle to breathe and from the pain of being forced to kneel on his broken leg. Ruggs kept him below the surface until pinpricks of light began to crowd out Cam's vision and his lungs ached for air. Ruggs yanked him back, and Cam gasped, his heart thudding.

"Where's the other man?"

"I don't know."

Ruggs plunged Cam beneath the surface once again, holding him down so long that Cam threw up. When Ruggs pulled him up, Cam's ears were ringing and his head felt as if it would explode as darkness crowded his vision. "Next time I let you die. Where is he?"

Cam spat puke and water at Ruggs. "I passed out. When I came around, he was gone. Took my cloak pin and my last two coins. A whore-spawned thief."

Ruggs looked at him, and Cam knew the other man was debating whether or not to finish him. *Go ahead. It would be a kindness.*

"Ruggs, we've got a problem." It was Leather John's voice behind them. Cam was still pinned over the tub, with Ruggs's hand painfully gripping his hair. "The king's men got Dolancey. They mean to hang him at dawn as retribution for this one. Seems the king did get your message."

"Dolancey was stupid. He gets what he deserves." Ruggs jerked back on Cam's hair, eliciting a groan. "How best to send Donelan my next message, I wonder? He's got your finger. Shall I send him the hand to go with it? Leave the pieces of the puzzle for him to find and reassemble?" Ruggs laughed at his own joke. "I just might—but I think Donelan's fool enough to come after you. I'm betting that he just might take this personally. Isencroft's hot-tempered king, never content to let someone else do his fighting for him. No, you're still worth something as bait." Ruggs stood, tearing his hand loose from Cam's hair.

"I think we'll move you from where your 'thief' mysteriously disappeared," Ruggs said.

"And just in case you've got any other ideas, let me give you something for the pain." Without warning, his boot lashed out, catching Cam on the side of the head and sending him into darkness.

Images filled the darkness. The gates of Brunnfen, Cam's family's manor, stretched high against a gray sky. Never before had the walls seemed so high, or the gates so solid. But never before had Cam been shut out, with those solid doors barred behind him. Carina brought her horse next to his, and the animal snuffled in the cold. Carina was huddled in her cloak, but Cam squared his shoulders, sitting up tall on his horse. Only fourteen, he was as big as most grown men. That just might save them, now that their father had disowned them and driven them from his lands. If they were lucky, they might find an inn that would take on a healer and a hired hand, or a merc group that would accept Cam's word about his age. If not, they would be beggars.

"Don't waste a look back." Carina's voice was quiet against the wind. Cam raised his face defiantly. His father stood on the walk above the gates, and next to him was their eldest brother, Alvior. Alvior's arms were crossed, and his face was set in a hard expression. Alvior, the one who had betrayed Carina's healing to their father, knowing what would happen.

"You can't let them go!" It was Renn, their

younger brother. Without even a cloak, the boy ran across the walkway. "Father, no! Please, no!" He ran at Lord Asmarr, but their father turned away.

"Go away, Renn. This isn't your concern."

"You did this! It's all your fault!" Renn threw himself at Alvior hard enough that Alvior staggered back, despite the fact that Alvior was a man of twenty and Renn was only nine years old. Renn beat against Alvior's chest with his fists, until Alvior backhanded him hard enough that the boy fell.

"Carina! Cam! Come back!"

Cam could hear Renn sobbing, but the guards at the gate remained expressionless, barring them from entry. Carina laid a hand on Cam's arm and used her magic to nudge their horses into motion. She said nothing, but Cam saw the tears that ran down her face. They could hear Renn calling out to them until Brunnfen disappeared on the horizon. *Is she crying for Renn or for us?* Cam wondered. *Renn has to survive living with Father and Alvior, but we're on our own now. Goddess help us.*

Renn's voice rang in Cam's mind as he felt himself struggle out of unconsciousness. He awoke to the squeaking of rats. A cold draft filtered up through the floorboards. The room was half filled with the bales of fulled wool, and dust hung heavy in the air. Faint light illuminated the edge of the door and slipped up through the cracks between the floorboards. Soaked from his interrogation, Cam shivered. His left eye was swollen closed from where Ruggs had kicked him, and his head throbbed. Cam curled into a ball, trying to stay warm. His broken leg ached and his left hand, where Ruggs had cut off his finger, was hot and swollen. He gritted his teeth against the pain.

I wonder how Carina's doing in Dark Haven, he thought, trying to distract himself. *I don't imagine she and Jonmarc will waste time. By spring, I wouldn't be surprised if there's a baby on the way. She's better off out of Isencroft. Jonmarc will keep her safe.*

His throat was still raw from the near-drowning, and his chest hurt from the water he'd swallowed. *At least I know Rhistiart got away. Ruggs wouldn't have been so angry if they'd caught him. But will he take the message to the guards? And will anyone believe him?*

Worse, he thought, might be Rhistiart's success. Ruggs was right; Donelan had a reputation for reckless stunts in battle. They made his reputation as a fierce warrior in his youth. But that was decades ago. Cam did not want to be Ruggs's bait.

He forced himself to sit and look around his new prison. Bales of fulled wool as high as his waist filled most of the room. Dust filled the air, floating in the faint shafts of light. Cam could smell the vile liquid the fullers used in their craft, meaning that the pits where they mixed water, manure and urine were not far away. There was only one door and no windows. Cam guessed he was imprisoned in a storage room.

He shifted, and felt something move in his pocket. With his left hand, he dug down until he found the flint and a bit of broken steel left from Rhistiart's tools. Cam smiled as a plan began to form. He might not be able to escape, but he just might manage to alert Donelan to the danger.

Exhausted, Cam dragged himself closer to the warmth of the baled wool and tried to find a position that was both warm and not too painful. His sleep was fitful. He dreamed of Rhosyn, the brewer's daughter. Plump, well endowed and quick with a laugh, she was everything Cam had ever hoped to find in a girl. Her father, the head of the brewers' guild, might not be noble, but he was a man of standing in the city and well-regarded. Cam had hoped to ask for her hand come springtime. In his dream, Rhosyn welcomed him with a mug of ale and a shameless kiss on the lips.

His dreams shifted to a cold hillside. Cam watched helplessly from where he lay as the slavers torched the caravan camp. Too far away to see what became of the captives, he only knew that when the fires died and the camp was silent, Carina did not come looking for him. That meant she was among the dead—or the captives. Blood soaked his tunic from a deep sword wound. He lay on the mossy ground and waited to die.

"There he is!"

"I see him, but can we lift him, that's the question."

Cam dimly remembered Soterius and Harrtuck dragging him onto a makeshift travois. He awoke in a healer's hut. There had been voices in the darkness, just outside where he lay.

"Why do you want to see him?" It was Soterius's voice, skeptical and challenging.

"The Sisterhood sent me. The healer asked for our help. Stand aside, if you want your friend to live."

Cam recalled an outline of a woman in the doorway, her face lost in shadow. "Hail, Cam of Cairnrach," the stranger said. "What you seek is almost within your grasp." She'd healed him then, with a touch as powerful as Carina's. When the Sister finished, Cam was exhausted, but the pain was gone and a thin pink scar replaced the gaping sword wound.

"Our Sisters told us that you and your twin might seek our help," the woman said. Her face was shadowed beneath her cowl. "We have the elixir you've been searching for."

"Will it heal Donelan?"

"Nothing will heal him until the mage who sent the sickness is destroyed. But the elixir will give him the strength to endure, although it will not be pleasant."

"The slavers took my twin, Carina. They've got Tris Drayke, too. I have to go after them."

"Choose, Cam of Cairnrach. You cannot save them all."

"I've never failed her."

"Then keep your oath to your king and you will not fail her now."

Later, he'd heard Soterius and Harrtuck in a shouting match with the Sister just outside his doorway. "Like hell. We're going after them." It was Soterius's voice, and he was as angry as Cam had ever heard him.

"The battle is already decided. We've felt it in the currents of magic. Your friend's power is greater than we imagined. He has tamed the spirits of the Ruune Vidaya. You will do best by meeting them in Principality."

"Lady, they're not going to Principality," Harrtuck argued. "They're going to Dhasson."

"Martris Drayke can't reach Dhasson alive. The border has been spelled against him. He will go to Principality. You can rejoin him if you leave now."

"And if we don't?"

"The runes were cast. You will die, and Tris Drayke may not regain the throne."

New voices intruded on Cam's dreams. Angry voices, arguing just outside his prison. Groggy, he dragged himself to sit. The voices belonged to Leather John and Ruggs.

"We've got to move. We've stayed in one place too long," Leather John argued. "Maybe you relish a fight against the king's guard, but I don't."

"We stay until I say differently. No one knows we're here."

"No one except the thief who escaped."

"You worry about a pickpocket? He's long gone by now. What's he going to tell anyone? And who would believe him?"

"I don't like it."

"I'm not asking you to like it. I'm telling you to do it."

"And what about Donelan?"

"If we're right and Donelan rides out with the troops next time, we'll have some surprises waiting for him. Curane's man sent gold—Isencroft gold—enough to buy all the weapons we need. There's only one way into this mill, and that's through that valley out there and across the bridge. If they come in after us, we can pick them off from the hillsides. If they try to make a stand on the flatland beyond the valley, we can attack from the forest. The old witch who gave me the spelled dagger assured me that it would fly true and deadly to the person I named in the curse. And if the witch's blood magic doesn't work, well, I have some other ideas on how to kill a king."

"I don't like this. We joined up with you to save Isencroft, not to kill Donelan."

"Donelan's betrayed you. He's sold Isencroft's future to the Margolenses. The princess is whoring her birthright and her claim to the throne. How many times has Margolan tried to invade Isencroft? Three? Six? A dozen? And every time, our people drove them back. Now Donelan wants to hand the crown over to them without a whimper. And for that, he deserves to die."

They moved off, and Cam could no longer make out their words. His hand reached into his pocket, reassuring himself that the flint and steel were still there. He looked at the dry bales of wool around him. He might not be in any shape to fight, but starting fires was something he'd always been good at. For now, he'd bide his time. And then, Cam decided, he would do Donelan one final service.

DAY FOUR

CHAPTER SIXTEEN

Jonmarc Vahanian set out for Wolvenskorn as
soon as the sun was bright in the early morning
sky. He guessed by the looks the villagers chanced
in his direction that they were as happy to see
him leave as he was to go. Jonmarc was ready to
move on. There was work to be done.

The snow was deep and the road lay untouched.
Alongside the road was the forest, a dark, silent
presence even in the daylight. Jonmarc squinted
as the sun glistened off the snow. Just off the
road, near the forest's edge, the snow had been
disturbed. Even at a distance he could see dark
shapes lying still and the broader stain of blood.

Warily, he rode closer. Three large wolves lay
dead in the snow. No, not wolves. *Vyrkin*. The
animals' staring, violet eyes made that plain. He
cursed as he swung down from his horse, sword

drawn. It was clear from the snow that there had been quite a fight. It was equally clear, Jonmarc thought with disgust, that whoever had done this had been hunting *vyrkin*. The nearest body was shot through the heart with a crossbow quarrel and stabbed through the belly as well. He frowned as he knelt beside the other two bodies. In their necks, nearly hidden by the thick fur, were darts. The *vyrkin* had been drugged, stabbed and eviscerated.

A whimper drew his attention. He looked up, and saw a fourth wolf lying further away in the snow. Drugged like the others, this one was still alive, although from the snow beneath it, Jonmarc could see the *vyrkin* had lost a lot of blood. Blood matted its dark gray fur, and a trickle of blood ran from the corner of its mouth. The *vyrkin* raised its head, opening its eyes, and Jonmarc was startled by the pattern of its markings. *Yestin*.

Jonmarc took a blanket from his saddlebags and gentled the injured *vyrkin* onto it. He did the best he could with rags torn from a shirt in his bags to bind up the wolf's wounds, then he drew out the dart and tossed it far from them into the snow. Carefully, he lifted the *vyrkin* into his arms, not surprised to find that it was as heavy as a man. As gently as he could, he secured it behind his saddle. He met the wolf's eyes.

"Looks like you ran into some trouble," he said, not sure Yestin could hear him. The wolf blinked, and Jonmarc took that as a sign.

"I'm sorry about your friends. I'll get you back to Wolvenskorn, and your shaman can patch you up. Hang on. It'll be slow going in this snow."

The wolf-Yestin closed his eyes and slumped. Jonmarc wasn't sure whether the wolf was resigned to the pain of travel or whether Yestin had lost consciousness.

Just as he led his horse back to the road, he saw a group of six men emerging from the forest. He slipped his sword hand behind his cloak to conceal his drawn blade. The men were armed with bows and the man in front carried a sword and wore a collection of daggers in the baldric across his chest. But what drew Jonmarc's attention and fueled his rage was the man's wolf-pelt cloak.

"Making off with our prize?" The lead man shouted as the group neared. Their weapons were raised, and Jonmarc had no doubt they were spoiling for a fight.

"You have no business here. Put down your weapons and go home."

The man with the wolf cloak gave a bitter laugh. "Who do you think you are? Lord Vahanian?"

"Yes."

At that, the group's leader's arrogance was tempered, and he gave a curt hand signal for the others to lower their weapons. He touched his forelock in acknowledgement.

"Beggin' your pardon, m'lord. We've been looking to join up with you. The word's out that you've been to war against the biters that have been tearing up the villagers. We've come to join your army."

Jonmarc's teeth were clenched tightly enough that he could feel a muscle twitch in his jaw. "The truce has been broken by a few rogue *vayash moru*. The *vyrkin* are on our side, trying to protect the humans. So are most of the *vayash moru*."

"On our side?" the wolf-cloaked man repeated incredulously. "My cousins were ripped apart along with their sheep by *vayash moru*. You told us to say nothing. You said you'd take care of it. Well you didn't save Westormere, and you didn't save Crombey. Now you don't want us to fight? Just whose side *are* you on, Lord Vahanian?"

"Malesh of Tremont is trying to start a war. It's a war neither side can win."

The wolf-cloaked man laughed. "Oh, we can win all right. Biters burn and the man-dogs bleed. There are more of us than there are of them. What I want to know is, why do you defend them? They said you were some great hero. I don't see a hero. All I see is a traitor."

"See what you want. Go home now, and you won't get hurt."

The man in the wolf cloak gave an incredulous snort. "Won't get hurt? My cousins are dead—

and they'll stay dead, unlike the biter scum. My mother had kin in Westormere, and they're all dead—every single one of them. I don't give a damn about getting hurt, your *lordship*," he spat. "I want revenge."

"And I want you to get the hell out of my way and go home before you regret it."

"Go screw the Goddess." With that, the wolf-cloaked leader raised his sword and launched himself at Jonmarc. Out of the corner of his eye, Jonmarc saw one of the bowmen level his bow. Jonmarc parried the leader's wild swing and a dagger flicked from his left hand, pegging the lead bowman in the forearm so that he dropped his bow. Another quarrel zinged past, narrowly missing Jonmarc's shoulder. He pulled a short sword into his left hand, pressing the leader back as his two swords scythed dangerously. He pivoted, holding off the leader's press as he swung into an Eastmark kick, slamming one of the other bowmen to the ground before he had a chance to notch his bow. The leader's attention was broken momentarily, giving Jonmarc the opportunity he needed. He ran the man through, barely turning fast enough to parry the crazed attack of two more of the rogue hunters as they came at him with a sickle and an axe. Jonmarc dove and rolled, coming up quickly enough to slice into the side of the axeman, who fell with a scream, blood bubbling from his lips.

A quarrel ripped into Jonmarc's left shoulder and he staggered, barely dodging a lethal swing from the scythe. It missed his belly, but opened up a gash along his chest. The pain numbed his arm and he dropped his short sword. The man with the scythe laughed, brandishing his weapon. Jonmarc heard the archer reload. He charged at the scythe wielder, dodging aside at the last moment as he heard the quarrel launch. The arrow skimmed above his back, catching the scythe man full in the chest. The man fell with an astonished look on his face as blood stained the wolf pelts around his cloak red and he sagged face forward into the snow.

Jonmarc rolled to his feet and came up behind the bowman. In one movement he brought the heel of his left hand against the bowman's back, launching his hidden arrow. It cut through the man's cloak and buried itself quills-deep into his back.

A biting pain struck Jonmarc in the neck. He reached up to feel a dart just below his ear. The sixth man was laughing as he pulled a long axe from a sheath on his back, advancing slowly toward Jonmarc, swinging his blade.

Jonmarc could feel the same drug that had tranquilized the *vyrkin* begin to flow through his veins. The image of his attacker blurred, and Jonmarc stumbled, grasping his sword two-handed. Jonmarc struggled for breath as he shook his head to clear his vision. The axeman was in no hurry, content to let the drug do its work. "We brought the axe to finish off biters," the man leered. "But it works just as well on traitors."

The axe swung, painfully slicing into Jonmarc's wounded left shoulder, but he dodged the worst of it. The swinging axe put its wielder momentarily off balance, and Jonmarc seized his advantage, scoring a slice that opened a bloody gash from shoulder to hip, though not deep enough to kill. The axe man screamed in rage and set about with his weapon, swinging with his full might. Jonmarc dove to the ground and kicked, sending a shower of blinding snow into the axeman's face. Jonmarc rolled, neatly slicing the axe wielder's hamstrings. The man crumpled to the ground, blood turning the snow into a red slush. Jonmarc staggered to his feet, reclaiming his short sword from the ground with the numbed fingers of his left hand.

"I should leave you for the wolves and the bear to find," he said, hoping he could fight off the drug long enough to reach Wolvenskorn. "When I get where I'm going, I'll send someone back for you—if you're not dead by then."

The whirl of a blade was his only warning as a small dagger flew toward him, catching him in the thigh. The axeman was dragging himself toward the fallen crossbow that lay an arm's length away in the snow. Jonmarc lunged forward, catching his attacker through the chest with his sword just as the man rolled with the loaded crossbow leveled at Jonmarc's heart. The bow fell from the man's hands as his body spasmed and he retched up blood. Jonmarc pulled his sword free and the movement nearly sent him sprawling. He staggered toward his horse, and leaned against it long enough to jerk the dagger from his thigh. He could feel warm blood seeping underneath his clothing from his battle wounds, and knew that it would be a race to reach Wolvenskorn before predators picked up his scent.

Jonmarc dragged himself up into his saddle, leaning forward to clutch the horse's mane, fighting to stay astride as the drug made his head reel. He gave a sharp kick to the horse's side with his heel, gritting his teeth against the pain as the horse began to move, urging him faster in the places where the wind had blown the snow from the frozen dirt of the road. Behind him, the injured *vyrkin* whimpered with the jarring beat of the horse's movement.

"Hang on," Jonmarc murmured, as much to himself as to Yestin. More than once he'd ridden back from battle more dead than alive, but this time, it was the drug's assault on his senses that endangered him even more than pain or blood loss. He clung to the horse's mane white-knuckled as the horse navigated the treacherous roads. Once, he glanced to his side and saw that blood stains trailed them in the snow.

Every hit of the horse's hooves sent a wave of pain through him, enough to keep his battered body fighting off the tranquilizing drug. He turned the horse down the shadowed lane toward Wolvenskorn. Out of the corner of his eye, he caught a glimpse of movement among the trees. *They'd better be vyrkin instead of real wolves or I'm screwed.*

Jonmarc tensed, waiting for predators to spring from cover, expecting the snap of fangs against his thigh. He was slipping in and out of consciousness, jarred back by the pain. In the distance, he could make out the shadowed form of Wolvenskorn. He remembered hearing the wolves howl before the darkness closed in around him and he fell.

Nothing existed but a vortex of pain and shadow. Dreams and memories swirled around Jonmarc. Nightmare images loomed before him, perfect in sight, sound and scent. Fifteen once more, he could smell the fires as his village burned, waking to find himself beneath the dead body of his neighbor. Blood covered him—his own and that of others. Sharp pain lanced through his side where the raider's sword had sliced into him. Jonmarc pushed the body off of him and felt the sticky, warm wetness of his own blood. He staggered to his feet, bracing for the swing of a sword that would finish him off. Silence was the only sound. The village was a ruin of burned cottages and corpses. He stumbled home. The roof of the forge was gone, and the thatched roof of their home had burned. Jonmarc climbed over the rubble, calling for his mother and brothers. He remembered too well seeing his father fall at the village gates. Silence answered him. Near the forge, he found two of his brothers nearly cleaved in two by the strike of the raiders' axes. He shouted for his mother and his youngest brother, but the shouts echoed without reply. Near the hearth, he spotted his mother's body, face down. Struggling against grief to breathe, Jonmarc turned her over. The same sword strike that had run her through had also pierced the small child she had tried to shelter with her body. Both lay cold and staring. Gone.

Memories shifted, but the smell of burning wood remained. Gray-skinned beasts stalked the night. Jonmarc set about himself with his blade, just a few years older than when his family had been slaughtered but already a promising swordsman. He could hear the shouts and screams of the other men in this village as they attacked the magicked monsters with hoes and axes. Across the green, Jonmarc glimpsed the village butcher, cleavers in both hands, charging at the beasts.

Jonmarc turned at the sound of a snarl, barely in time to fend off one of the lantern-jawed beasts before its fangs snapped on his shoulder. His blade cut it through the chest, almost severing its head. As it flailed, one of its razor-sharp claws raked across the left side of his head, opening a gash from ear to shoulder and bathing him in his own blood.

Wounded and near exhaustion, Jonmarc realized that the square around him had grown still. He had no idea how much time had passed since the monsters appeared from nowhere, but he was certain the red-robed mage was involved, the mage who sent him into the tombs for the amulet that hung on a strap around his neck.

Jonmarc stumbled back toward the cottage behind the forge. He'd told Shanna to bar the door behind him, but the door was ripped from its hinges. Shouting her name, Jonmarc threw aside the splintered wood. The inside of the one-room cottage was completely destroyed. Claw marks left long stripes down the walls. Shanna lay in a pool of blood near the bed. Her hands were clutched to her belly, where one of the beasts had slashed her deeply enough that the child she carried spilled out onto the floor beside her. They were as cold as the winter's night. He heard himself screaming...

"Jonmarc."

The voice didn't belong here, not in the time and place of these memories, although something about it was familiar.

"Jonmarc."

The voice was a lifeline out of this nightmare place, and Jonmarc clung to the sound of it. The voice grew stronger, and as the fog of memories cleared, Jonmarc could see the image of the *vyrkin* shaman in his mind.

"Hang on to my voice. It's going to get worse before it gets better. The drug they used is powerful. Before it wears off, you'll wish they'd killed you. I'm sorry."

The memories receded, but pain returned as Jonmarc became aware of his body once more. His vision was still too blurred to see, and his head hurt too much to open his eyes for long, but a stolen glimpse by firelight told him that he was probably inside Wolvenskorn, in a windowless bedroom. He was drenched in sweat, then racked with chills. Without warning, a sharp pain in his belly doubled him up. Sure he had been run through, he felt for blood but found only the spasming tightness of his own abdomen. Strong hands pushed him back into the bed as convulsions made his body buck and jerk violently enough that he felt muscles strain. Someone pressed a towel between his teeth.

The pain lessened, only to come back with a vengeance moments later. Alternately freezing and roasting, wet with sweat and parched with thirst, Jonmarc lost all track of time. His shoulder throbbed where the quarrel had pierced him.

"When will it end?" The voice was Gabriel's.

"I don't know. He's strong. I've only seen this once before. One of the *vyrkin* managed to shift before the drug took him. He didn't regain consciousness for two days."

"Can't you help him?"

"I've done all I can. The flesh wounds are healed. He broke his collar bone when he fell from the horse. It's mended, but only barely, and if he keeps thrashing like this, it may break again. The drug isn't meant for humans. It's to bring down dangerous animals. They aren't meant to survive it, so the aftermath isn't usually an issue."

"Will he live?"

"Oh, yes. But he'll be sore."

Jonmarc stopped counting the cycles of painful muscle contractions. Finally, when the fire on the hearth had burned low, his vision cleared. His head throbbed, and every muscle in his body ached as if he'd been beaten. He waited for the agonizing spasms to continue, but as the moments passed without pain, he gave himself over to utter fatigue.

Sleep. I will guard your dreams.

Too tired to fight, Jonmarc gave himself up to the darkness.

"How long?" Jonmarc's voice was a painful rasp as he forced his dry throat to speak. The *vyrkin* shaman helped him sit forward and sip water from a cup.

"Twelve candlemarks."

"Malesh—"

"You're in no shape to worry about Malesh. Gabriel doesn't think he'll make his move on the Lady's temple until tomorrow night—Candles Night. Rest now." The shaman let Jonmarc lay back, and wiped his forehead with a cool, wet cloth. "You've had a bad day."

"Yestin?"

The shaman's expression darkened. "He'll live. I gather that the ones who attacked him did this to you?"

"Locals gone hunting for *vyrkin* and *vayash moru*."

"Thank you for what you did. I know protecting us sets you against many of your own people."

Jonmarc managed a harsh, sharp laugh. "My own people have been trying to kill me for years. Nothing new about that."

Jonmarc heard a door swing open, and sensed, more than heard, someone else enter the room. He guessed it was a *vayash moru* even before Gabriel spoke. "He's awake?"

"Only just," the shaman replied.

Gabriel moved to stand at the side of Jonmarc's bed. He looked more worried than Jonmarc had ever seen him. "Good to see that you're still with us. How do you feel?"

"Ass-kicked."

"I sent scouts back along the road you traveled. They found the bodies. Six to one. No one can say you've lost your edge."

Jonmarc managed a tight-lipped smile. "After Laisren, mortals move slowly."

"True." Gabriel paused. "I thought you'd want to know that Kolin was here the night before last. Carina's awake."

Jonmarc attempted to sit up. The shaman gently pressed him back down. "She's alive? How is she?"

"Weakening. She's subsisting on a mixture of blood and milk that can't sustain her for long. Kolin said that Carina and Taru have tried to tap into the Flow to heal her, but it hasn't worked."

"She's running out of time."

"Kolin says that Royster thinks there may be a solution. Carina believes the Flow is calling to her. It wants her to heal it. Once healed, it may be able to restore her."

"She tried to heal the Flow once. You were there. She nearly died."

"This time, she's counting on Tris Drayke to anchor her soul."

Jonmarc looked at Gabriel as if the other had lost his mind. "Tris is at war near Trevath."

"They've sent a letter with *vayash moru* couriers to Tris. Kolin said they know Tris can't leave the war, but they're betting that with the way the Flow is tearing itself apart, it's making it difficult for him to fight. The letter asks him to unite his magic with the Flow at the seventh bells tomorrow evening, Candles Night, to anchor Carina's soul while she enters the Flow."

Jonmarc struggled to quell his fear. "She'll die."

Gabriel's expression showed that he shared Jonmarc's pain. "She's dying now. Kolin says that if she can't be healed, she wants to die for a purpose." He paused. "She knows you made the Bargain."

Jonmarc met Gabriel's eyes. "The Magistrate doesn't believe in the Bargain. He said to ask you about the Lady and Her chosen champions."

A moment's hesitation flickered in Gabriel's eyes. "Just before Haunts a year ago, the Lady came to me in a dream. She warned of a great darkness to come." A self-deprecating smile touched the corners of his mouth. "In life, I was something of a scholar. After death, my thirst to understand those mysteries became even stronger. I pledged myself to the service of the Lady lifetimes ago." He looked at the fire for a few moments, as if remembering something from long ago.

"The Lady sent me to make sure that you encountered Tris Drayke. That happened without my help, so I waited until you needed a hand before I introduced myself."

Jonmarc remembered. He'd gone into town to find out how close Jared's men were on their heels, only to be ambushed in an alley by someone with an old score to settle. Without Gabriel's help, Jonmarc was quite sure he would have died that night. "So it was a set-up—the whole thing about my agreeing to guide Tris?"

Gabriel shook his head. "No. The choice was always yours, to stay or to go. I was never to force your hand. I was merely back-up."

Back-up with an uncanny knowledge of exactly when to appear. No, Gabriel had never forced any of them to do anything, he'd just made the way they chose easier to navigate. "Is that why you offered to come with me to Dark Haven?"

Gabriel looked at him for a moment before answering. His gaze strayed to the mark of the Lady inked on Jonmarc's chest above his heart. "In part. Putting Tris Drayke on Margolan's throne didn't solve everything."

"I've noticed."

"I believe there's a greater darkness yet to come—whether it lies in this war or some threat we have yet to see. I've sought the counsel of the Lady, and the answer is always the same. 'Protect my champion.'"

"Do I get a say in any of this?"

"It's entirely up to you."

"What if I decide I'm through getting my ass kicked?"

"Events will take their course."

"How do you know I won't just walk out of here?"

Gabriel's eyes met his. "You won't."

It was the same answer Tris had given Jonmarc in Westmarch, and in his heart, Jonmarc knew it was true. Fool that he was, he could no more walk away from what was going on and refuse to fight than he could fly. Not even when it cost him everything he loved.

"For the record, I hate this 'champion' business."

A flicker of understanding glimmered in Gabriel's eyes. "That's why I didn't tell you. Would it have made a difference, even if I had?"

"No. Not really." What Gabriel called "choice" Jonmarc had seen as a series of practical steps, each following from the one before it. Tris's quest to retake the throne not only offered Jonmarc long overdue vengeance, but more importantly, the chance to end the suffering that Jared's reign caused to Jonmarc's homeland. In spite of everything he'd been through and the bounties on his head, he couldn't turn his back on Margolan. Staden's gift of Dark Haven had been the chance to turn his life around Jonmarc hadn't realized he'd craved until it was placed in front of him. It had been his opportunity to pursue Carina as an equal instead of an outlaw, the chance to take back his life from fate. He'd dared to dream of a future—until Malesh's strike on Westormere pitched the world he knew into chaos.

An awful thought chilled him. "How long have I been Her chosen?" *The raiders that murdered my family. The beasts that followed Arontala to the next village, the ones that killed Shanna and the baby. Chauvrenne. Nargi. Have I been nothing but a pawn?*

Gabriel looked at him as if he could guess his thoughts. "We're not puppets, Jonmarc.

What you've endured has made you who you are. Always, it was your choice. I've seen men who suffered less destroy themselves or become someone else's nightmare."

If only you knew—

"You would have been someone's champion. It's in your blood. Once in a generation a fighter with your skill and intelligence comes along." He managed a bitter smile. "Think of it as recruitment, not conscription. The Lady believes you're the one."

"That's what you meant, the night I made Istra's Bargain, when you told me it wasn't necessary, that I was already Her chosen."

Gabriel nodded. "It's a funny thing, when one accepts the hand of the Lady. Time is different for Her. The soul you swore to Her was already claimed. The vengeance you bargained was already moving forward. You belonged to Her before you made the Bargain. And She will claim what's Hers in Her own time. So was it fate, or did She know what your heart would choose before you did?"

Jonmarc closed his eyes. "My head hurts too much to figure that out. Kiara once told Tris they were like the hounds of the Goddess, going where they were bid and coming when they were called. By the Whore, I hate that thought."

"Then consider a *vyrkin* instead of a hound, obligated by nothing except loyalty and honor."

That was too close for comfort, and Jonmarc let it pass without comment. "If what Kolin says is right, about Carina and Tris and the Flow, then we've got to stall Malesh tomorrow until seventh bells. They deserve that chance."

"You're not in any shape—"

"Try to stop me."

THE TENTH BELLS were ringing when Jonmarc hauled himself out of bed. A servant had brought up a plate of venison and a bottle of brandy for supper, and after several candlemarks of sleep, Jonmarc was hungry. He found clean clothing set out for him, and wasn't surprised that it fit perfectly. He slipped on his boots and buckled his sword belt. Although he knew he was safe inside Wolvenskorn, it made him feel better to feel his sword at his hip. His short sword and the single arrow launcher lay on the bedside table along with his baldric and knives and his crossbow. His body protested as he moved, but he ignored the aches that remained.

Any *vayash moru* would be downstairs, in the common room, Jonmarc knew. Over the last few days, Wolvenskorn had become the headquarters for those who opposed the breaking of the truce. He was surprised that the sounds of heated conversation carried to him, a sign that Wolvenskorn had more guests than usual.

A word with a passing servant confirmed Jonmarc's destination. He paused at the door of a room down the hall from his, then knocked gently. Yestin's voice answered. "Come in."

Yestin lay in bed, his ribs bound with cloth and his arm and thigh bandaged. Yestin's face was haggard, and his eyes haunted. Jonmarc guessed that he'd also fought off the same drug. "Glad you're still breathing."

"Thanks to you."

Jonmarc shrugged, and winced as his recently-healed shoulder twinged. "I wouldn't have placed bets on either of us, tell you the truth. Took one of those damned darts in the neck myself. How do you feel?"

"Like I was dragged by a wagon. You?"

"Yeah. A wagon with low clearance on a rocky road." Jonmarc paused. "Did you find anything out about the hunters who ambushed you?"

Yestin shook his head. "Not really. This kind of thing happens when humans and *vayash moru* fight. My kind—all the *werekin*—get caught in the middle. But I heard that Kolin got attacked on his way back to Dark Haven. Someone set a fire trap for him."

"Damn." Jonmarc could barely look at Yestin without feeling ashamed at what other mortals had done. He remembered the look on Gabriel's and Laisren's faces when they saw the carnage Malesh left behind at Westormere. Now, he understood their shame and horror.

"Don't."

Jonmarc looked up, puzzled.

"You're thinking you need to apologize. Don't. You're not responsible for what other mortals do. We make our own choices."

Jonmarc swallowed and nodded. "Can I get you anything?"

"No. I'll be all right." He met Jonmarc's eyes. "I understand why you swore Istra's Bargain."

The loss Jonmarc saw in Yestin's eyes made him look away. There was nothing to say.

"I'll be on my feet for the fight tomorrow night," Yestin added. "Gabriel says the house and grounds are filled with *vyrkin* and *vayash moru* from across Principality—maybe further. It's going to be one hell of a fight."

If Malesh's side were gathering in equal numbers, Jonmarc didn't doubt that at all. "Then you'd better rest."

"Aren't you the one who says, I'll rest when I'm dead?"

"Yeah. And maybe I finally will."

CHAPTER SEVENTEEN

CARINA SET DOWN her quill and sprinkled sand across the parchment to dry the ink. Carefully, she shifted the paper to let the sand that blotted her ink run off before she folded the letter and sealed it with wax. She pressed her signet ring into it, the ring Jonmarc commissioned for her. It bore the same symbol as the *shevir* bracelet he had given her: the combination of his old river mark as a smuggler and his crest as Lord of Dark Haven.

"What are you doing?"

Carina jumped as Taru entered the bedroom. She sighed, knowing better than to evade the mage's question. "Writing letters. I didn't want to leave Kiara and Cam without saying goodbye." She'd written a third letter, one she feared would go unread. She stared at it, at

Jonmarc's name written on the outside of the folded parchment. In case he returned. She knew better. He had sworn the Bargain. She was past the point of being afraid, but not too numb to grieve.

"You don't have to do this."

Carina looked at Taru. "Yes, I do. The Flow has been reaching out to me to heal it. The way the magic is failing, it's got to be affecting Tris and the war in Margolan. If he can't win against Jared's loyalists, Kiara and their baby will never be safe. Isencroft won't be safe—and neither will Cam and Donelan. I've lost Jonmarc. I won't lose the rest of them—not when I might be able to do something about it."

"You don't know that Jonmarc is lost."

"He's not coming back."

Taru came to sit beside her. "I know you saw men swear Istra's Bargain when you were with the mercs. And a vow to the Goddess is always binding. But did you ever consider this—it's up to the Goddess when she claims his soul?"

"What do you mean?"

"Time doesn't work the same way for immortals the way it does for humans. A day, a year, a decade---a lifetime—when you don't have a lifespan, they stop holding any meaning." Taru met her eyes. "If the Goddess accepts Jonmarc's vow, all it means is that he's sworn his soul to Her. She's not obligated to take it until She pleases. You said that Gabriel called Jonmarc the Lady's Chosen. What if he was right? Does the Goddess really need a champion to swat down a *vayash moru* who's barely a century old?" Taru shook her head. "He's sworn fealty to Her, much like he made a vow to Staden when he received the title to Dark Haven. I wouldn't count Jonmarc out of the game, Carina. Not yet."

Carina looked at Taru and felt the first stirring of hope she'd felt since she found the ink and stylus in the chapel. "I hope you're right."

Lisette came into the room to draw the draperies. Dawn was only minutes away. "You should eat before you rest," Lisette said, sounding motherly. "You'll need your strength for tomorrow night."

Carina sighed. "I know. Raen came to remind me, just before Taru and I started talking." The ghost girl glimmered in the shadows, and Carina knew that the ghost had probably heard everything. Raen's spirit might be over two hundred years old, but in other ways, she was still a teenager.

Carina steeled herself and took the glass of milk and blood Lisette offered her. Whenever her nerve began to fail her about stepping into the Flow, Carina just had to think about feeding like this and her determination returned. Lisette and Taru pretended not to see her grimace as she forced herself to swallow the awful mixture. Carina knew she would have to fight with herself for several minutes to keep from bringing it up—and having to drink another glass.

The sounds of shouting in the distance nearly made Carina drop the empty glass. Out of reflex, she moved toward the window, but Taru stopped her. Making sure the others were far enough away to avoid being burned by the daylight, Taru slipped between the heavy draperies, letting them close over her to leave the room in shadow.

"Sweet Chenne. I don't believe it." Taru moved carefully from behind the drapes to rejoin them. "Dark Haven is under attack."

The rap at the door startled all of them. Lisette opened it, to find Neirin in the doorway. The grounds manager's worry was clear in his face. "Neirin, what's going on?" Carina asked.

Neirin motioned for them to follow him. "Come quickly, m'lady. I want to get you and the others into the inner rooms where you'll be safest. I've already sent for Royster to be brought. Please hurry."

"Who's out there? What's going on?" Carina didn't budge. "I'm not moving until you tell me who's attacking us. It can't be Malesh's brood. The sun's up."

Neirin shook his head. "It's not. They're mortal. They want the *vayash moru* who've been given sanctuary here."

Carina gasped. "Does Riqua know?"

"I know." They turned to see Riqua in the hall. "It's because of Malesh they're here. Neirin and I have been seeing to the refugees all night."

"Refugees?"

Neirin winced. "I didn't want to bother you, m'lady. I know what a burden you're already carrying. The people you healed who held the vigil for you were afraid to return home. Since Kolin was attacked, we've had a steady stream of refugees coming to the back gate. We haven't had very many *vayash moru*—they seem to have taken sides and gone to fight. But their mortal kin are afraid. They've always been safe in Dark Haven. Now, they fear that their neighbors might come after them to draw out the *vayash moru*." Carina could hear the pain in Neirin's voice. "*Vyrkin* are coming, too. The females with young and those too old to fight."

"Why?"

Neirin's eyes were sad. "Because the same people who are attacking the *vyrkin* and burning out day crypts are going after the mortals who defend them. The night guard found five bodies, with the nooses still around their necks, dumped near the front gates. Someone had carved '*rethirnis*' into their skin across their chests."

"What does that mean?" Lisette said, and Carina could hear fear in her voice.

Carina shivered. "I haven't heard that word in a long time." She looked up defiantly. "It means to betray your blood. Not just kingdom or family, but everything, your essence." Carina met Neirin's eyes. "Take me to the refugees."

"M'lady, you need to save your strength," Neirin protested.

"He's right Carina. If they need a healer, I can go. Rest." Taru stepped forward.

A bitter smile twitched at Carina's lip. "As Jonmarc is fond of saying, I'll rest when I'm dead. I may not be able to heal, but I can serve. I'm part of the reason all this has happened. I can't rest, knowing that, without trying to help."

"I'll keep working with Royster to make sure everything is ready for tomorrow night," Riqua said. "I need only a few candlemarks' rest."

Carina and Taru followed Neirin downstairs. All the way down the stairs, the two healers listed off items they would need. Carina was expecting there to be a crowd like the ones that had come for healing before the attack at Westormere. She caught her breath as they reached the inner rooms that were protected from the daylight. The large, windowless common rooms were filled to capacity with people who had barely enough space to sit. In the torchlight, Carina saw that the majority of the crowd were women, children and elders. Most of them were wounded; how badly, she couldn't tell without a closer look. They sat quietly, as if they were too exhausted or too much in shock to do more than whisper.

"It's like this in the courtyard and in the rooms where daylight reaches, m'lady," Neirin said quietly. "I don't know what we'll do if they keep coming. There's only so much room—and so much food."

Carina nodded. "Inventory what we've got. Tell the cook to make the food stretch as far as she can. If it means we all eat gruel, then at least we all eat." She managed a lopsided grin. "Cam and I survived many a winter on gruel when the mercs were between jobs. Builds character."

Neirin smiled. "You have a most colorful background for the lady of the manor."

Carina chuckled. "Not nearly so much as the lord."

Taru recruited two of the mortal chambermaids to help her in the outer rooms, while Carina and Lisette began to make the rounds of the inner rooms. The silence unnerved her. With so many people pressed together, Carina would have expected noise. Instead, the crowd was eerily quiet, as if so stunned to find themselves in hiding as to be beyond conversation.

"Let's sort out the ones who'll need Taru's help from those we can fix up with some potions and bandages," Carina said, grateful that Lisette's experience in all the weeks of tending to the holding's sick and injured would make this task a little easier.

"I know it's been dangerous and difficult for you to come here," Carina said, raising her voice. The people in the torch lit room looked up, and she looked out over their fearful faces. "We'll do our best to get you what you need. Right now, I want to find out who's injured. If you don't need a healer, come to the left side of the room." She waited while the people shuffled past each other in the crowded room to comply. Most of the room's occupants stayed where they were, making the uninjured the clear minority.

"Lisette and I will take care of minor injuries. Sister Taru will handle the deep healing. Then we'll see about getting everyone fed."

Carina knelt next to the first patient. A young man cradled a woman in her mid twenties. Her arm was wrapped with a strip of rags, and Carina could see the blood seeping through the cloth. "Please hurry," the young man said. "She's lost a lot of blood." Carina looked up, and realized that the young man was *vayash moru*, and guessed that decades, not months, separated him in age from the woman in his arms. "She's my granddaughter," the *vayash moru* said, and as Carina looked at him more closely, she saw that the skin on his back was charred.

"What's your name?"

"Gwill."

Carina and Lisette busied themselves tending to the deep gash on the woman's arm. Carina cleaned the wound and treated it with an herbal tincture that elicited a groan from the woman. "What happened?" Carina asked as she worked to close the wound and bind it to stop the bleeding.

"My family's lived for generations in a small farming community," Gwill said. "Several of us who were *vayash moru* remained to help work the land. We've kept to ourselves and never bothered the neighboring farms. We feed from our own goats and mind our business. But yesterday, the raiders came before sunset, while I and the others were at rest. They came to burn our day crypts, and when our families tried to defend us, the raiders killed them." Gwill's grief was clear in his face, denied tears by the Dark Gift.

Carina looked at the woman's arm. She guessed the deep slice had been made by a scythe or a harvesting knife. Farmers' weapons, but no less lethal than a sword or war axe.

"They hoped to lure us out into the daylight, and when we heard the screams of our families, we came." Gwill shook his head. "There were only a few of us left. The rest went to fight for Lord Vahanian and Lord Gabriel. But we were afraid to leave the farms unguarded. We never meant to be their undoing."

"How did you get away?" Carina had finished binding up the woman's arm, and she spooned a little of a bright green elixir into the woman's mouth.

"They set a trap for us. As soon as we came out of our day crypts, the raiders set our village ablaze and waited for us with torches and flaming arrows. My brother and I are both *vayash moru*. He tried to hold back the raiders while I took the others into the caves for safety. As we reached the forest, I heard him scream. I saw him catch fire, as we ran into the forest."

"How many did you take to the caves?"

From Gwill's tortured expression, she knew that he believed his efforts to be a failure. "Six. But there had been thirty of us."

"What happened to your back?"

He grimaced. "Even the raiders don't dare pursue us by night. Down in the caves, there were a few others of our kind, also trying to help their families escape. And some of the *vyrkin* women with their pups. We moved through the caves to travel as safely as we could, knowing that one entrance comes up in the forest not far from the gates of Dark Haven." He gave a bitter laugh. "'Not far' depends on whether you can outrun the rising sun. There were raiders posted in the forest's edge, watching for us to seek sanctuary. They began to fire on us as we ran across the field toward the gates. The guards of Dark Haven tried to protect us, but even they couldn't hold back the sun." A flash of pain crossed his face. "We nearly made it before the first light. I'm lucky that the full rays didn't strike me, or I'd be cindered. I'm young in the Dark Gift. As it is, the early dawn burns."

Carina looked to Lisette. "What can I do to help him?"

Lisette shook her head. "He'll heal—in time. We heal more slowly when we're younger."

"Is there something that will ease the pain?"

"We don't heal the way mortals do. Herbs and poultices don't work the same." Lisette paused. "I've seen Laisren come back badly wounded, and he's never let me doctor him. But he's older in the Dark Gift."

Carina made a mental note to see what Royster knew of *vayash moru* medicine. "I'll see what I can find," she said to Gwill. "And I'll make sure Taru checks on your granddaughter."

Carina looked out across the room. Women and small children huddled together. An elderly man held an equally elderly woman in his arms, and Carina could see that they were both bleeding. *Malesh doesn't need the vayash moru to do his killing for him. All he had to do was set us on each other.*

Midday, Lisette finally got Carina to stop and rest. They went into Dark Haven's pantry, one of the few rooms not overrun with refugees. Lisette gave Carina another glass of the noxious milk and blood mixture and watched as Carina choked it down. Carina was grateful for a few moments to sit down.

"You're deep in thought, m'lady."

Carina nodded. "Just thinking about Gwill." She looked at Lisette. "The *vayash moru* can survive injuries that would kill a mortal. I knew you healed quickly, but I didn't realize that there was still pain."

Lisette looked away. "Aye."

"Is it different from what you felt as a mortal?"

Lisette did not meet her eyes. "No. All that differs is that we endure it. And that very little can be done about it, since neither potions nor whiskey blunt it."

Carina remembered the charred skin on Gabriel's back the night Tris won back the throne from Jared, and the way Gabriel had taken the brunt of the glass shards that exploded across the room when the Orb shattered. He'd fetched her to heal Tris, never giving a hint that his own injuries were agonizing. Lisette seemed to guess her thoughts.

"It's a matter of opinion whether ours is a gift or a curse," Lisette said. "The pain lessens as you grow more accustomed to bearing it."

Carina thought of the scars that covered Jonmarc's body. *Wounds heal, but not memory,* she thought. She'd hoped to change that by becoming a mind healer, but now, time was rapidly running out. "We're only halfway through the room," she said, drawing a deep breath and rising. "And Neirin says there are more rooms full of refugees. Let's go."

Two of the mortal servants came to offer them the opportunity to rest for a few candlemarks, but Carina declined. Neirin came to lead Carina into another of the inner rooms. Carina looked around with a combination of wonder and horror. The room's occupants appeared to be all *vyrkin*. Some were too badly injured to change back to human form without assistance, with blood matting their fur. Others appeared fully human, with only the violet eyes to give them away. As Neirin had warned her, most were females with suckling pups, or with children too young to fight.

"I need more herbs, and some hot water for potions. *Vyrkin* are more like mortals—most of my poultices should work," Carina told Neirin. "And bandages. I need whatever Taru isn't going to use."

"Understood, m'lady."

Carina knelt next to a woman who had two small children in her lap. From what little Carina had learned about the *vyrkin* from Yestin and Eiria, she guessed the children were just barely old enough to shapeshift, but not old enough to hunt for themselves. "How long has it been since you've eaten?" Carina asked the woman.

"Not since yesterday." The young mother's face was drawn. "There were five sets of mothers and pups hiding in the caves. Our mates left us there for safety when they went to Wolvenskorn, to answer Lord Gabriel's call. We had been taking turns hunting so that someone was always left to watch the pups—children. But yesterday, Cadi didn't return. Nia went to look for her, and she didn't come back, either." The woman swallowed hard. "A few candlemarks later, I ventured out. I was one of the best trackers of our group. Almost from the time I left the cave, I could smell blood. *Vyrkin* blood." She glanced down at her two small children. "Do you speak Margolense?" she asked abruptly.

Carina nodded.

The woman switched into Margolense from Common. "I found their bodies in the woods, m'lady. They had been butchered like animals, slaughtered and skinned and their heads taken for trophies. I know it was them. I could tell by their scent." She began to shake with grief. "Nia was my sister. Cadi was my brother's wife. We birthed our pups together. I swear, m'lady, neither we nor our mates ever harmed a mortal." Carina took her in her arms and held her as the woman began to sob. Her children pulled at her sleeves, too young to understand but aware that something was wrong. "I also recognized the scent of her hunters," the woman sobbed. "They were neighbors of ours. We lived beside them in peace for years. Never once did we steal any of their chickens or sheep. Never." She pulled back from Carina and wiped her eyes with her sleeve.

"We didn't know where else to come for shelter," she said raggedly, fighting for control. "My mate is cousin to Yestin. Yestin had told us of his trust in Lord Vahanian. We heard that Lord Vahanian went with Lord Gabriel to stop Uri's brood from killing mortals. But I swear to you, m'lady, no *vyrkin* ever helped Uri or Malesh. So why do the mortals kill us?"

Carina's heart ached as she reached out to comfort the little girl who clung fiercely to the woman's arm. "It's not all of the mortals," she said quietly. "Please believe me. Just like it's only a few of the *vayash moru* who've followed Malesh." Her words sounded hollow. *Wars have started over less, between enemies equally mortal. First Jared burned the vayash moru. Now this. How much can anyone take, before they strike back?*

Carina met the woman's eyes. "I give you my word as Lady of the Manor. So long as the walls of Dark Haven stand, you and your children will be safe here." She managed a tired smile as she looked down at the two children. "Let me talk with the kitchen. We need to see about some meat and milk for all of you."

Carina stood and stumbled. Elen, one of the servants, caught her, and Carina managed to steady herself. She could feel her knees buckle and Elen helped her out of the room and into a chair. Before Carina could stop her, Elen ran to bring Taru.

"You've pushed yourself too far, Carina," Taru chided gently.

"But there are so many of them. They're hungry and they're hurt and I can't even heal them the way I used to." Carina's voice showed her exhaustion and frustration.

"I've already spoken to Neirin about special food for the *vyrkin*," Taru said. "And thanks to the healing you and Lisette did before you were injured, there are several of the servants who are handy with the basics of cleaning and binding up injuries. But there's no one who can step into the Flow except you."

Reluctantly, Carina nodded. "Point taken." She looked up at Taru. "I'm running out of time. I know it. I want what's left to count." She thought she saw tears start in Taru's eyes.

"Rest assured, Carina. What you're doing counts. For all of us."

CHAPTER EIGHTEEN

TRIS DRAYKE ROSE from a restless night. He could see by the light against his campaign tent that the sun was already up, and guessed that once again, Coalan had let him sleep. With a groan, he sat up on his cot. Although he'd slept fully clothed, he shivered as the heavy blankets fell away. Southern Margolan was bitterly cold this time of year.

"You're up!" Coalan said cheerily. Tris had no idea how the young man managed to dredge up his seemingly endless enthusiasm, but it was one of the few things that made the war bearable. Coalan set a cup of steaming hot *kerif* on the table, adding the second, and possibly only, other item on the list of bearable things. Tris drank the hot, dark liquid, feeling it burn down his throat.

"Where's Ban?"

Coalan chuckled. "Are you asking as his friend or as the king?"

Tris looked at him warily. "Why?"

"Because he's out trying to see if we can round up enough sheep for a mutton stew for Candles Night tomorrow evening, to raise the men's spirits. Now his friend Tris might like the sound of that, since he was always partial to mutton as I recall. But King Martris ordered Uncle Ban to take it easy. So who's asking?'

Tris had to smile despite himself. "His friend, Tris. Although of late, that person comes around so seldom I don't recognize him anymore." Coalan was one of the few family friends to survive Jared's reign, and Tris treasured that friendship. Coalan, Carroway, Harrtuck, Soterius and Zachar were some of the very few who knew him from before the coup and still treated him as "Tris" instead of "King Martris," at least in private. They were a link to memories of a time that was gone forever, and loved ones who would never return. And while Tris knew he did not have the luxury of dwelling in the past, those friendships at least gave him a way to keep the memories from fading.

"Good. Because he'd probably thrash me if I got him in trouble with the king." Coalan smiled broadly. "Breakfast will be here in just a moment. It's gruel again, but it's hot gruel."

"I spent the Birth Month in Principality last

year, telling myself that Margolan's winters were so much milder," Tris said, holding the cup of *kerif* between his hands for warmth. "I can't believe I'm just as cold!"

Coalan nodded, and Tris knew the young man was wearing every piece of clothing he owned as well as a few he'd scrounged. "That's the Lady's truth, all right. Maybe it won't be much longer before we can all be home in our own beds."

Tris knew that Coalan had overheard enough of the battle planning to realize how unlikely that was, and to realize that many of the soldiers milling about in the camp beyond the tent would take their final rest here, on the wide open Margolan plains, before the battle was over. "I hope so," he said, pushing aside his own gloomy turn of thought.

Outside, the cook's bell rang and Coalan sprang to his feet. "That's the signal. I'll be right back with that gruel."

When he left, Tris set his *kerif* aside and walked to where a light covering of ash dusted the tent's packed dirt floor near an iron brazier. He squatted down and began to draw in the ash, trying to recall what he had seen in his dream. He traced a long, wide blade that ended in an ornate hilt. But what set this knife apart from others he had seen was the markings on the steel of its blade. In the dream, he had clearly seen a pattern of lines, as if the steel had been folded over on itself countless times, making a swirling design.

"Problem with the fire?" It was Ban Soterius, who stopped at the tent's doorway to brush off the snow that clung to his cloak.

Tris straightened hurriedly. "Just adding some coals." He managed a smile. "Coalan told me you were up early."

"Damn. That boy can't keep a secret." Soterius shrugged. "Since it looks as if we'll be going to battle tomorrow, I just thought keeping Candles Night might cheer up the troops. Not to mention that a little bit more meat, if the cook can manage it, wouldn't hurt. We've been feeding them mostly beans, roots and potatoes for weeks now."

"Excuse me." Coalan stepped around Soterius. He had the serious look he adopted when anyone else was present. "There's a messenger with a packet from Shekerishet." At Tris's nod, Coalan motioned for the messenger to enter. The young man bowed low, and then opened his bag for a large pouch sealed with the seneschal's mark.

Tris frowned as he took the pouch. "Did Crevan say anything when he gave you this?"

"No, Your Majesty."

"How long ago did you leave from Shekerishet?"

"Four days, Your Majesty. M'lord Crevan told me to ride hard, and I rode my horse as long as I dared."

Tris's sense of foreboding grew deeper. "That will be all," he said, waiting until Coalan and the messenger had left them to break the seal. He was aware that his heartbeat had quickened, and he feared that Kiara or the baby had come to harm. Inside the pouch was a single sealed letter, and Tris's fear and disappointment grew when he realized that the handwriting did not belong to Kiara.

"Is Kiara all right?" Soterius asked. "Do you want me to leave?"

Tris shook his head. "Stay, please." He moved to where the light was better and unfolded the letter.

Your Majesty.

It is with great trepidation that I write this, having postponed it as long as I dare, hoping that circumstances would right themselves and the matter would no longer merit your regard. Unfortunately, that is not the case.

There is no delicate way for me to break this most unpleasant news, and I apologize deeply in advance for the necessity of it. Rumors are thick at court that Master Bard Carroway and the Queen have engaged in an unseemly relationship. At first, I dismissed it as nattering. But over the last few days, it has become so widely spoken of as to attract even the attention of the Council of Nobles. I myself have witnessed nothing, but there have been those among the servants who have claimed to witness Carroway departing from the Queen's chambers at unusual hours, always alone and often looking as if he wished not to be seen. Since Carroway's reputation with the ladies is quite well known, such things have led to a level of discussion that has led the Council to meet today. I am not privy to their conversation, but word reached me that they are gravely worried about damage to the honor of the Queen, and by extension, to the Crown.

Your Majesty, it pains me greatly to write of these things and I wish it were not necessary to be the bearer of such dark news. To protect the honor of the Queen, I am taking the extraordinary measure to banish Bard Carroway from the palace until your return. Moreover, he is not, on pain of death, to be in the presence of the Queen.

I know that the temper of the Lady governs how quickly your battle concludes, but I pray you, please do not delay your return longer than is necessary. While there can be no doubt as to the father of the child the Queen carries, much has been said about the Queen's allegiance, and I do not know if we have already passed the point at which it may be repaired.

Ever your faithful servant, Crevan

Tris re-read the letter, feeling his heart pound. He crumpled it in his fist, trying to breathe.

Beyral warned me that I would be betrayed again, by someone very close to me. Sweet Lady! This can't possibly be true.

"Tris?" It was Soterius's voice, and from his tone, it was clear that he had called for Tris before without answer. "Are Kiara and the baby all right?"

Not trusting himself to speak, Tris thrust the crumpled paper at Soterius and turned away, struggling for composure. He heard Soterius's sharp intake of breath a moment later as he read the damning letter.

"Crevan's mistaken. You know that, right? This whole thing is a lie."

Tris shrugged, struggling with the anger and pain that welled up inside him with an intensity he did not expect. "I don't know what to believe."

Soterius took a step toward him. "It's got to be Lady Nadine and her friends again. They never forgave Bricen for banishing her. What a way to take revenge!"

"Kiara hasn't written to me once since I left for the war," Tris said in a voice just above a whisper. "Not once."

"Maybe she hasn't been well. You said her mother had a difficult time of it when she was pregnant."

Another shrug. "Crevan's said nothing about that in any of his letters. The packets come weekly. Surely there was one week when Kiara felt well enough to send a note." Tris knew that Soterius could hear the hurt in his voice. Leaving a new bride behind and going to war was a miserable proposition. But to hear nothing in almost three full months…

"There has to be a reason," Soterius persisted. "Kiara and Carroway both nearly died to help you win back the throne. You told me that when you fought the Obsidian King you shared your life force with Kiara. You made a ritual wedding. Surely with your power you could see into her soul."

I thought I had. "I'm new at this—remember?"

"Kiara risked everything for you. And Carroway has been your best friend since we were kids."

"You know the old tales as well as I do. These things happen." Tris knew Margolan's legends far too well to dismiss such a possibility. Too many of the downfalls of the kings of old came because of the treachery of a friend and the unfaithfulness of a queen.

"You can't be serious."

Tris turned around to face him, and he knew Soterius could see the pain in his face. "I really don't know what to believe, Ban," he said raggedly. "I've sent letters to her with every messenger. I've begged her for word like a schoolboy. No reply. What should I make of that?"

Soterius's glance fell to the drawing Tris had scratched in the ashes. "What's that?"

Tris gave a sharp, hard laugh. "That's what I see in my dreams. That's why I don't sleep. For the last two nights, I've seen that knife. I don't know who's holding it, but every night, I see someone attacking Kiara with that knife and driving it into her belly." He closed his eyes and let out a breath. "I just sent a letter with yesterday's messenger, warning Crevan to increase security. As if there isn't enough to worry about with this war and the plague, I've been worried sick about Kiara." He ran a hand back through his hair, beginning to pace. "And now? I don't know what to think."

"Tris, it's Carroway we're talking about. After what happened with Lady Nadine, you know he didn't even touch another woman for two years. And after that ended badly, he went off by himself again—until he brought Macaria to court." Soterius shook his head. "Goddess! He watched her like a smitten puppy and never laid a hand on her, because didn't want to do to her what Nadine did to him. How many ballads did he write for her at Staden's palace? Did you ever once see a spark of anything but friendship between him and Kiara? Once?"

Tris sighed and shook his head. "No. I didn't. But if everything's all right, why hasn't Kiara written?"

"I don't know. But whoever's spreading these rumors could do as much damage as anything Curane does. If Donelan gets wind of it, he'd be within his rights to avenge Kiara's honor. And when you get back—"

"I know." When he returned, the rumors assured that the joyous reunion he'd sustained himself by envisioning since he left for war would not occur. At best, he'd become the arbiter, trying to salvage the reputation of his foreign queen. At worst, he would have to stand in judgment, condemning his best friend to death or banishment. And he'd be forced to confront Kiara. Tris had the power as a spirit mage to read her soul and know the truth of it. He did not know if he dared. Even if the rumors were true, there was no way for him to set aside his marriage to Kiara without declaring war on Isencroft. Neither kingdom would survive such a conflict. And in his heart, Tris doubted that he could ever set her aside. He was well aware that for him as a Summoner, "soul bonded" was exactly that.

"Can you summon the ghosts from the palace? Surely they'd know what was going on."

Tris shook his head. "Even I can't compel them from so far away. Like most ghosts, they're bound to the place they haunt. I tried." He did not need to add that with the Flow's volatile swings, such magic was even less likely to work now than before.

Soterius swore and handed the parchment back to Tris. Tris tossed it into the brazier, wordlessly watching it burn. "Isn't there anything your magic could do to help?"

Tris closed his eyes and shook his head, looking up to keep from shedding the tears that welled up. "Not that I know of. You heard Beyral cast the runes. She warned me that I'd be betrayed again, by someone very close to me."

"Not to be morbid, but there are several thousand men who are 'very close to you' if you want to take what she said literally," Soterius argued. "And I'd be more willing to bet on one of them as the likely culprit than either Kiara or Carroway."

"I hope you're right." Tris drew a deep breath. "And we've still got a battle to plan."

Soterius nodded. "Senne and Rallan are still trying to get more of those flaming arrow launcher contraptions up and running. And while I've been doing my best to follow your orders and take it easy, I've made the rounds of the camp. Esme has a count on the number down with the pox or plague or whatever we're calling it. We're down more than a third of our men between the sickness and battle dead. That should still give us more soldiers than Curane has left on their feet, but we haven't breached the walls yet, and if his mages are as desperate as they probably are, we may be in for some nasty surprises."

"Agreed. When does Senne think we'll be ready to strike again?"

"He told me that he doesn't want to wait any longer than tomorrow evening. He's afraid to give

Curane any more time to regroup, but, by the Whore! We couldn't move before then, even if our lives depended on it, not at full strength anyhow. We took a pounding the last time out." He paused and looked meaningfully at Tris. "So did you."

"I'm back on my feet."

Soterius was skeptical. "So am I. But hardly mended. And I know you don't heal any faster than I do, magic or not."

That much was true. Tris still felt the effects of the last battle despite Esme's healing. "I don't think either side has enough left for more than one battle. This next fight is going to finish it— one way or the other."

"Shall I call the generals together?"

Tris nodded. "Fallon and the mages, too. And Trefor for the *vayash moru*. If this is our last stand, we need to make sure we've covered everything. There won't be another chance."

As morning became afternoon and then early evening, Tris threw himself into the battle planning, grateful for the distraction it provided. Focusing on the preparations for war kept him from dwelling on Crevan's letter, and the analysis of battle plans let him slip into cold logic. By the time the supper fires were lit, the plans were in place.

"It's as good a strategy as we'll get, Your Majesty," Senne said as he moved for the tent flap. Tris clapped him on the shoulder with a heartiness he did not feel.

"It's sound, and bold enough to force Curane's hand. And when he strikes, Fallon and I will be ready for him."

"I have no doubt, Your Majesty."

As the last of his guests left, Tris could hear Coalan bustling behind him, clearing the maps from the work table and taking away the empty goblets. Without a word, Coalan appeared at his side, and pressed a glass of brandy into his hand.

Tris glanced up, and Coalan met his eyes. "Thought you might want a nip. It's cold outside."

From the look in Coalan's eyes, Tris was quite sure Coalan had overheard enough of his conversation with Soterius to know what was going on, and he was grateful for the young man's gesture. "Thank you," he said, accepting the glass.

"The cook's shorthanded tonight—two of his helpers took sick. With your permission, I thought I might lend a hand—get us all fed faster that way," Coalan said with a twinkle in his eye.

"I'm cold enough that even stew would taste good tonight," Tris replied.

Coalan made a rude noise. "Stew's all we've had since we camped, isn't it? Probably best, as the meat doesn't bear looking at closely. Still, it's better than cold rations and I'm hungry."

Despite his mood, Tris chuckled. "You're always hungry."

330 Dark Lady's Chosen

"Then consider me your court taster," Coalan teased. "After all, if cook's stew doesn't poison me, little else will!" Coalan slipped from the tent, leaving Tris alone.

Tris swirled the brandy in his glass and pulled his chair closer to the brazier, hungry for its heat. Without the distraction of conversation, his mind replayed Crevan's letter word for word. He closed his eyes, squeezing them shut against the pain that welled up inside him. As second-in-line to the throne, jealousy was new to him. Before Bricen's death, had Tris wanted to pursue the young women at court, his title and status guaranteed that he would have triumphed over other suitors. The few brief romances he had before the coup ended badly, but he had not lost out to a rival. Rather, it had become glaringly apparent that the girls he favored cared only about becoming a princess and were indifferent regarding which prince made them so.

Nobody knew that better than Carroway. Before the coup, Soterius had reveled in being one of the court's most eligible bachelors. But there had been many evenings when Tris and Carroway had escaped from the constant swirl of court parties, Tris with his books and Carroway with his music. It was always clear that Carroway favored women who loved music as much as he did. And Tris had doubted he would ever find someone who spoke to his heart—until he met Kiara. Now he wondered if his real rival was not a man, but a kingdom, and duty.

I was sure when our souls bonded that she loved me. But she will always love Isencroft first. Was it love, or just affection that I sensed? Although I released her from the old covenant, Isencroft's situation left her no real alternative. And if she wed me for duty's sake, then I still don't hold her heart, even if her body remains faithful.

"I thought I'd find you brooding in here." Tris glanced up as Soterius entered, holding two trenchers of stew. "Coalan's busy helping the cook, so I figured I'd best bring this myself if we wanted to eat before daybreak." Soterius glanced at the half-empty glass of brandy. "You know how the court takes a small lie and makes a huge scandal out of nothing. Why should this be any different?"

"I've let Kiara down," Tris said, accepting the steaming trencher. "I left her alone too soon, and I should have known what the court was like. Whatever's happened, it's my fault. With the pregnancy, she's more vulnerable than ever." He sighed. "She's carrying my child. Beyral says it's a son. He's the heir to both kingdoms. Even if her feelings have changed, we don't have the option of walking away from this. But maybe I can win her back. I love her, Ban. And I won't let her go without a fight."

Whatever Soterius was going to say was interrupted as one of Tris's guards leaned into the tent. "M'lord. Trefor is here with a visitor— and he says it's urgent."

Tris nodded, and Trefor entered. With him was a *vayash moru* Tris didn't recognize. Trefor made a perfunctory bow. "Your Majesty. This is Yent, one of Lady Riqua's brood. He bears a most urgent message from Dark Haven."

Tris exchanged glances with Soterius as he rose. "Dark Haven?"

Yent nodded. "We've ridden in relays, human and *vayash moru*, for three days straight. Lady Riqua said it was of the utmost importance. The fate of the Winter Kingdoms and the lives of Lord and Lady Vahanian depend on it." He withdrew a sealed letter from the pouch beneath his cloak and handed it to Tris.

Tris recognized Carina's handwriting immediately. His magic could feel the emotional residue of the writer, and he sensed fear, sorrow and a resignation to death that chilled him. There was a touch of magic, Taru's signature and seal. He broke the wax and read down through Carina's careful, small writing. His breath caught as she recounted the attack at Westormere and Jonmarc's vow. He swallowed hard, reading on through the failed attempts to harness the Flow and Jonmarc's battle to stop Malesh, even as the Truce shattered. He handed the letter to Soterius, and watched the other's expression register the same horror and sadness he felt.

"Sweet Mother and Childe," Soterius swore as he lowered the paper. "I never figured Jonmarc to swear the Bargain, and I didn't think, after all we went through to stop Jared from killing *vayash moru*, that one of their own would start a war like this."

Both Trefor and Yent looked down in shame. "M'lord, most of my people are grief stricken over these attacks. And they're terrified, because the mortals have begun the burnings again in retribution," Yent murmured.

"Carina thinks she might be able to heal the Flow. If she can, it might not just save her life. It could also turn the war."

"Can you do what she's asking?" Soterius questioned. "Anchor her soul through the Flow at this distance?"

"I don't know."

Soterius's eyes flashed a warning. "As Jonmarc was fond of saying last year, if you get your royal ass fried, the rest of us hang. I've seen how the Flow chewed you up the last time you tried to draw on it. What's to keep it from killing you if you try to access it now?"

Tris met his gaze. "What's to keep it from killing all of us if I don't? Blood magic is stronger because the Flow is damaged. If Carina can heal the Flow, our side might just have the edge we need to defeat Curane." He turned away. "I owe Carina—and Jonmarc—my life more times than I can count. I have to try."

"Will it save Carina?"

Tris knew Soterius could read the pain in his expression. "I don't know. From her letter, she doesn't think so, although I take it Royster and Taru disagree. If Carina is right and the Flow really is sentient, if it's been seeking her out— that changes so much of what we thought we understood about it. If it can do that, then what's to say that the Flow couldn't heal her?"

"That doesn't help Jonmarc."

"No, it doesn't." Tris looked to Trefor and Yent. "Thank you," he said, barely trusting his voice. "I can't imagine what it took to bring word over that distance so quickly. The camp is hardly luxurious, but whatever comfort we can offer you, I'm in your debt."

Trefor and Yent bowed and left them alone. Tris spoke a word to the guard outside to summon Fallon. He took the letter back from Soterius and re-read it. Carina had kept nothing back, and he knew her well enough to know how desperate she must be to seek his help against all odds. Tris struggled against his own emotions for control. *Once again, my world is coming apart, the people I love are being hurt, and there's so little I can do to help. Damn! What's the use of being a king and a mage if I can't save the people I care about?*

Fallon ducked into the tent just a few minutes

later, shaking the snow from her cloak. "What's wrong? The guard said there'd been an urgent message from Dark Haven."

Tris handed her Carina's letter, and watched as Fallon's expression registered its implications. "By the Crone," she whispered, lowering the letter. "You know this stands as much chance of killing you as it does of saving Carina or healing the Flow."

"I know."

"And you've already made up your mind."

"Yes."

"Then we'd best let Senne and Rallan know how this changes the plans for battle tomorrow. If you're to be anchoring Carina at seventh bells tomorrow night, you'll need me to shield you and pick up the pieces afterward. That takes two of us away from the assault. They'll need to factor that in."

Tris nodded. "The good news is that if it works, we may be able to completely preempt anything Curane's blood mages had in store for us."

Fallon's gaze was sharp. "And the bad news is, if you go 'poof,' Curane wins anyhow." She glanced at the floor by Tris's feet. "What's that?"

Tris stepped aside from the drawing of the dagger he had made earlier. "Something I saw in a dream. Do you recognize it?"

Fallon nodded, and moved closer, bending

down to look at the drawing. "You're sure this is exactly what you saw? The dragon hilt, the lines in the blade?"

"As well as I can draw it in dirt. Why?"

Fallon sat back on her heels. "Tell me what you saw."

Fallon's frown grew deeper as she listened to Tris recount his dream. "That's not good," she said, straightening. "Especially not now."

"What are you talking about?"

Fallon looked from Tris to Soterius. "Tomorrow is Candles Night."

Tris felt as if everyone around him had suddenly started to speak in code. "So? Bonfires and roast mutton. What does that have to do with anything?"

Fallon shook her head. "Long ago, Candles Night was much more than it is now. A dagger like the one you saw in your dream, a *damashqi* dagger, is a ceremonial knife that was used in the Candles Night celebrations. Back then, it wasn't a ewe that was slaughtered. It was the pregnant wife of a rival chieftain. Her blood was said to make the ground fertile for the spring planting. But more than that, the sacrifice worked a powerful blood magic that was controlled by the winning rival."

Sweet Chenne. Kiara. "So you think the dreams are a warning? That Curane means to strike at Kiara while the army is tied up here with the war?"

"It would appear so."

"It's a four to five day ride back to the palace if we're not moving the whole army," Tris said, beginning to pace. Fear welled up in his throat. "A man riding hard might make it in four days, if he changed horses and barely slept—assuming the roads are passable."

"Could you send Trefor to Mikhail, warn him?" Soterius said.

Outside, tenth bells tolled. "There are only eight candlemarks until dawn. He'll never get far enough. And even if he could get a mortal to ride by day, at best the rider will only be half-way by night. There's no way to warn them."

"It could be a false sending. There's been no record of anyone trying to work the old blood magic in centuries. All of the kingdoms made it punishable by death." Fallon's tone was steady, but Tris knew from her eyes that she was not convinced of her own words.

Tris felt his breath leave him as the horror of the possibilities unfolded in his mind. "Curane's intended this as a two-front war all along. He planted someone at court to raise the old scandal about Carroway, hoping to discredit Kiara and isolate her. He's turned the court against her, spreading the story that she's betrayed me. No one remembers the old ritual for Candles Night. If Kiara's murdered after being suspected of adultery—"

"They'll think you had her killed." Soterius finished grimly. "Your heir will be dead.

Isencroft will attack. And Curane gets to sit back and wait for the dust to settle to put Jared's bastard on the throne."

They were silent as the possibilities sank in. "Then we'd better settle this war soon," Fallon said. "Because you have another one to fight when you get home."

CHAPTER NINETEEN

KIARA STOOD AT the window of the hunting lodge, watching the snow fall. It drifted deep around the lodge, and the light from the windows stretched out across the unmarred snow, across the kitchen garden, toward the forest. She had been watching out the window for some time, and just beyond the edge of the light, Kiara could swear she saw shapes moving that had nothing to do with wind or snow.

Kiara jumped as Cerise laid a hand on her shoulder. "Sorry, dear. I didn't mean to startle you. What do you see out there?"

"My eyes must be playing tricks on me. I've been watching just at the edge of the light. I could swear I see figures out there, as if there are ghosts moving back and forth."

Cerise peered into the darkness. "I don't have

your keen eyes. But earlier, before it snowed, Macaria and Alle placed warding runes in a circle around the lodge. They're supposed to keep ghosts and spirits at bay. It might have disturbed some of the local haunts, and they're trying to figure out where to go." She smiled. "Or maybe you're just tired."

Kiara let Cerise lead her away from the window toward the fireplace, where two freshly poured cups of tea awaited. "Where are Alle and Macaria?" When Cerise did not answer, Kiara looked askance at her long-time confidant. "Cerise, what aren't you telling me?"

Cerise sighed. "Macaria's having a difficult time of it. She's trying to be brave for your sake, and she knows her duty lies in protecting you, but she's frightened out of her wits for Carroway's safety. Sometimes it gets the best of her. Alle went to comfort her. Please, don't say anything to her. I'm afraid that would just make it worse."

Kiara nodded. "She and I are about the same age. I know how I feel, worried sick about Tris. I can only imagine how Macaria feels." She gave a wan smile. "After all, I did have all of last year to get used to seeing Tris nearly get killed time and time again."

"And it doesn't get easier, does it?"

Kiara shook her head. "No." She grew quiet, staring into the amber liquid of her tea.

"There's more on your mind, my dear, isn't there?"

Kiara shrugged. "I'm scared, Cerise. Queens aren't supposed to admit that. But I am. The regent magic has failed me so often I shouldn't believe my dreams, but they're dark. Last night, I dreamed of Tris in the middle of a great storm, lightning striking down all around him. At first, I thought he was controlling the storm, but as it grew worse, I realized that it was completely out of control. I saw him disappear into a sheet of flames." Her voice broke, and she covered her face with one hand, waving off Cerise's attempts to comfort her as she struggled for control.

"I've had nightmares about everyone I love. I dreamed about Cam, alone in a dark place. I don't dare tell Alle, but I dreamed that I saw Soterius stabbed in the back. Carina, Jonmarc— I've had dreams about all of them, but the dreams aren't good. What's happening, Cerise? I knew that pregnancy affects the humours of the body, but by the Whore! I didn't expect to lose my mind!"

Cerise put an arm around her shoulders. "These are difficult times, Kiara. They would try the most seasoned monarch. You and Tris have shouldered the burden of the crown at a most unfortunate time. I know from being your mother's confidant that it's never easy. But there are times when it's much harder."

"I know."

They sat in silence for several minutes. Finally, Kiara turned to Cerise. "Do you think Crevan's told Tris… about the rumors? If I could just hear from him, I'd know, but Tris hasn't sent any word at all. I thought he'd want to know about the baby, how I was doing, but there's been nothing." She was sure that Cerise could hear the hurt beneath her worry. *What if Tris believes the rumors? I can't stand by and let him destroy Carroway, but anything I do to intervene will only make it worse. And if he thinks I've betrayed him, what's left to us?*

"If he believes the rumors, he still won't be able to set our vows aside. We made a ritual wedding, and even if we hadn't, something like that would invite war with Isencroft. Margolan couldn't survive a war like that—and neither would Isencroft. But what's to become of us, Cerise? I had been counting the days until he could come home. Now I'm dreading his return. I'm afraid for Carroway. And I'm so afraid that even though Tris can't renounce me in public, he'll have already renounced me in his heart. All the battle training in the world hasn't taught me how to fight something like that."

Cerise drew her close and let Kiara rest her head against her shoulder. "You've always been a good judge of character, my dear. Now, all you can do is hold fast to what you saw in Tris when you made the decision to marry him. And if he's the man you believe him to be, he'll find a way through this. Don't lose heart yet."

Kiara managed to smile and sat up. "Thank

you, Cerise." She began to stand, but before she reached her feet, a blinding pain lanced through her head. Kiara cried out, clutching her temples, and staggered. Cerise shouted for help as she reached to break Kiara's fall. Kiara tumbled, landing on the floor as Alle and Macaria came running.

"What happened?" Alle asked breathlessly.

Kiara groaned and curled into a ball. "Where does it hurt?" Cerise asked, as Macaria ran to get the healer's bag from the other room.

Kiara ran her right hand up over her ribs. "There," she said, panting from the pain.

Alle held Kiara's hand as Cerise mixed together the ingredients Macaria brought to her. Kiara's hand was clammy, and her face was ashen. Alle managed to get Kiara to sit up enough to sip at the elixir Cerise mixed, only to have Kiara roll to the side and retch.

"She's not bleeding, thank the Lady!" Cerise said, giving Kiara a thorough going-over. "Kiara, how do you feel?"

"Dizzy. Sick. My head is pounding. Everything looks blurry." Kiara's voice had lost the timbre of a few minutes ago. Now, she sounded drained and weak.

"What's wrong?" Alle asked.

Cerise reached for a pillow to prop underneath Kiara's head. Macaria ran to grab a blanket from the bed, and returned with it along with her flute. As Cerise and Alle mixed tinctures and poultices, Macaria stepped back to give them room, and began to play a calm, beautiful song infused with magic that brought a peacefulness into the room and helped quell Kiara's fear.

"I haven't seen this often, but it can happen with pregnancy. The internal humours haven't sorted themselves out, and when they struggle among themselves in the womb, it upsets the balance of the body," Cerise said as she made a paste of herbs and water and a strong-smelling liquid from a vial in her bag. "If the humours war against themselves too strongly, they can cause the baby to be expelled before its time."

"This is feverfew and lemon balm. They may help." Cerise gentled Kiara's gown up to expose her belly, and spread a thick mixture of the poultice across her abdomen. Sliding her skirts back into place, Cerise laid one hand on Kiara's forehead and the other on her wrist. Cerise closed her eyes and murmured a chant to herself, rocking back and forth. Kiara felt her heartbeat slow, and the pain over her ribs gradually decreased. She had no idea how long Cerise chanted, but Kiara could sense the healing magic filling her, drawing down the pressure that made her head feel as if it might burst. Finally, Cerise sat back and helped Kiara lie flat on the floor.

"Don't move just yet," Cerise cautioned. "There's no hurry. When you're ready, we'll get you into bed."

"What happened? Am I going to lose the baby?"

Cerise touched Kiara's cheek. "I don't think so. I'll have a word with the cook about your food. And there is a special tea you'll need to drink. The stress isn't good for you—though, Lady bless, I don't know how you're to avoid it, given the state of things. It reminds me of your mother's difficulties when she was pregnant with you. You're going to need to be very careful."

Macaria lowered her flute and came to join them, sitting on the floor beside Kiara. Kiara managed a weak smile. "Thank you. Your playing helped."

"Glad to be of use, m'lady," Macaria said. Kiara could tell from Macaria's eyes that the episode had scared her badly.

"Cerise—is the baby going to be all right?"

Cerise's eyes were uncertain. "I hope so. I can sense the life. The heartbeat is strong. And the energies have sorted themselves. It's a boy."

Kiara felt herself tear up. *A son. That will make the succession so much easier. I wish Tris were here.* "That's wonderful," she murmured. "Can you tell... will he be a mage like Tris?"

Cerise smiled. "Too early to tell. We may not know that until long after he's born. After all, Tris didn't realize his power for quite some time."

Please be a green-eyed, blond mage like Tris, Kiara thought. *Let there be absolutely no question about who your father is. In anyone's mind—the court, or Tris.*

RIORDAN CARROWAY WATCHED the street below his window at the Dragon's Rage Inn. It was already well past tenth bells, and his impatience for the minstrels to visit was starting to become worry. And while he knew they would come to the back door of the inn to avoid being seen, he couldn't sit still. The street was quiet. Earlier, plenty of carts and people struggled through the snow on the eve of Candles Night. It might be a minor holiday, but it broke the tedium of dark winter nights, and this year in particular, Margolan's people needed something to lift their spirits.

Carroway turned as the guard outside his room opened the door. Paiva, Bandele, Halik and Tadghe spilled into the room, faces flushed with the cold. One of the guards nodded in thanks for the bottle of rum Halik withdrew from beneath his cloak, the price of admission. Carroway received their hugs and backslaps with a tense smile. "How goes it at court?" he asked as his guests settled in, draping their snow-wet cloaks near the fireplace to dry out.

Tadghe pulled a bottle of brandy from the ample sleeve of his heavy great cloak and thumped it down on the table, pouring liberal draughts for everyone while Paiva and Bandele unwrapped the stash of food they brought from the palace kitchen. "Drink first," Tadghe suggested, pressing a goblet that was more full than usual into Carroway's hand. With misgivings, Carroway tossed it back, letting it burn down his throat.

"All right. What have you learned?"

Halik turned a chair around and straddled it, taking a long sip of his own brandy. "The court's buzzing about the Queen's decision to go to the lodge. Not that their gossip wasn't the cause for it," he said, disdain thick in his voice. "Some are saying that the King sent orders to move her there, placing her under house arrest. Others are sure she means to flee to Isencroft before the baby's born to conceal the parentage."

Carroway paled. "Sweet Chenne."

Halik met his eyes. "Pray the child takes after King Martris, and Queen Serae's side of the family," he said with a level gaze. "If he's dark-featured, like Jared was—"

"They'll conveniently forget Bricen's coloring and blame it on me," Carroway finished the sentence. He turned away from them with an oath and ran a hand back through his hair. "Does it get worse?"

"I'm afraid it does," Tadghe said quietly. "Count Suphie and Lord Guarov claim to have their own intelligence from the war front. They say the war is going badly, and that the troops are being squandered against an opponent that's too well fortified to destroy. There are even claims that plague has broken out—a mage-sent plague. Guarov says it's probably something King Martris and his mages cooked up to use against Curane that backfired on him—"

"Tris would never do such a thing!"

Tadghe shrugged. "Unfortunately, at least some of what Suphie and Guarov are saying does seem to be true. I've been down to the barracks—have a few friends down there from the rebellion. They're the couriers who take Crevan's packs back and forth to the king. Their stories don't sound good. One man said he saw a cairn as tall as a house. Another said he wasn't permitted to come inside the camp because the King didn't want him carrying plague back to Shekerishet. He was ordered to drop his pouch outside the gate, and another pouch was waiting for him there."

Carroway shook his head. "Tris left with four thousand soldiers. I wouldn't be surprised if others joined up along the way. Curane couldn't have that many men at arms. I knew minstrels who played at Lochlanimar. It's not as large at Shekerishet, and I don't think you could billet four thousand men or close to it at the manor." He started to pace. "Senne and Palinn were experienced generals. Ban knew a thing or two about war as well. And while I never liked Tarq or Rallan, no one ever accused them of incompetence."

"Just insufferable arrogance," Tadghe muttered under his breath.

"It's the magic," Bandele replied. "Even the hedge witches are talking about it. They say there's a magic river of power that all mages draw from, and it's gone mad, for want of a better word." She met Carroway's eyes. "There have been rumors about Curane taking in Arontala's blood mages since the rebellion. If the magic really isn't working right, that would work against the King."

"What else is being said at court?"

Halik and Tadghe exchanged glances. "There's talk of a *vayash moru* uprising."

"I thought we ended that nonsense when Jared lost the throne."

Halik shook his head. "When the King left for war, the *vayash moru* stopped coming to court—except for Mikhail. You said at the time they weren't sure of their welcome without the King. But from what I hear, it's gone beyond court. I have friends in the village whose 'extended family' include *vayash moru*. They've gone missing, and rather suddenly. No one knows where or why."

"That doesn't mean they're planning an attack. Damn, I don't know," Carroway said, leaning back against the wall. He rubbed his forehead, trying to dispel the headache that was rapidly gaining strength. "It's not like the *vayash moru* talk about their customs when they're with mortals. Maybe there's a religious celebration. It could be anything."

"You know the court," Bandele replied. "They'll never take a simple explanation if a conspiracy can be concocted. But people are afraid. The King's gone to war. The Queen's under suspicion of treason. Lord Acton and Lord Dravan are two of the sane voices at court, but the panic is starting to feed on itself. Eadoin might have been able to sway people, but…"

Carroway swallowed hard. "How is Eadoin?"

Bandele's eyes filled with tears. "The only word we've had came when Brynne and Seren rode out to Brightmoor. Guards stopped them before they reached the gates. They had to shout to their friends inside the manor. It's bad. Eadoin refused to leave when the fever first broke out. She didn't want to bring it to court and risk harming the Queen. Now she's fallen ill herself. It's a killing fever," Bandele said, her voice dropping. "About half who come down with it die. And Eadoin's not a young woman."

Carroway closed his eyes, fighting back grief.

"I'm sorry," Bandele said, reaching out to take Carroway's hand. She held it tightly and rested her cheek against it. "I'm so sorry."

After a moment, Carroway found his voice. "What of Crevan?"

Paiva leaned forward. "Bian's niece took me with her to the public house in the town where the kitchen girls like to go. I spent a night drinking with them, and got them talking. Seems Crevan's taken an interest in the cooking since Bian got locked up. Crevan hired her replacement himself. She's a fearsome old hag. The girls call her a witch, but they don't mean magic. They are afraid to speak of it near the palace, but I got them drunk enough to say what was on their minds," Paiva said with a satisfied smile. Her tale reminded Carroway that Macaria had told him Paiva made nearly as much picking pockets as she did with her music before Macaria had brought her to the palace.

"This new cook of Crevan's brings her own ingredients and won't let anyone else touch them. But one day, one of the girls snuck into the pantry on a dare. She found tansy, rue and pennyroyal, plus hellebore, ground up fine as flour."

Carroway looked mystified. "I don't understand."

Paiva rolled her eyes and sniffed derisively. "Men. The girls knew immediately what it meant—and they were scared witless over it." At the blank stares Carroway, Halik and Tadghe gave her, Paiva slapped her palms on the table. "Have you never heard it said that a wench 'takes a flower to bed' with her if she doesn't want to end up with child?"

"They're all herbs to prevent pregnancy," Bandele said quietly. "Worse—they're the herbs women take to be rid of an inconvenient babe. It's more than old wives' tales. Taken at high enough doses, they bring miscarriage."

From the other men's stunned expressions, Carroway knew he was not the only one floored by the news. "Dear Goddess. Wouldn't Cerise be able to tell? Kiara's had Jae testing her food since Malae was poisoned."

Bandele shrugged. "Since it's not technically poison—in that it won't kill the person eating it—Jae probably wouldn't notice. As for Cerise—the girl said the herbs were ground up to dust. If the cook was careful, she might use just enough to do damage without affecting the taste or making Cerise suspicious."

"Can we prove Crevan is behind it?"

"Not unless we can show that he paid for the herbs and knew what they were," Tadghe said roughly.

"Macaria said Alle hand-picked the servants for the lodge," Carroway said, feeling panic begin to rise. "We can hope she saw to the provisioning herself, too. Do you know how much a woman has to eat before she loses the child?"

Paiva shrugged. "Most of the women I knew were so desperate, they figured more was better. I think it depends on the woman."

"Kiara has had a difficult time from the start," Carroway said, sitting down as shock overtook him. "She told us that her mother had nearly died bearing her. But if Crevan intended this, no wonder he wanted Bian out of the kitchen." He looked to Halik. "Can the boy who spies for you find out anything more?"

Halik looked away. "He's gone missing. No one's seen him all day, and he didn't come home last night. Someone said there was a fresh hole in the ice on the lake." He bit his lip. "I never thought he'd be in danger. I wouldn't have asked him to help if I'd ever dreamed Crevan was this thick into it."

"We still don't have enough to accuse Crevan," Carroway fretted. "But I know who will listen." He looked from Halik to Tadghe. "I need you to ride out and find Harrtuck. Surely whatever rioting Crevan sent him to quell has been resolved by now. He may even be on his way back. We need his authority to do anything. He'll believe you, and he'll know what to do next."

Halik and Tadghe nodded. "We'll leave in the morning. With the Queen gone, there's less call for music so it's not as if we'll be leaving brokenhearted patrons behind."

"What about us?" Bandele asked. "What can we do?"

"Stay away from Crevan. We don't need anything happening to you, and he's bound to suspect if you're underfoot. Find out what you can, but don't put yourselves or anyone else at risk. If he is behind the boy's disappearance, he won't hesitate to hurt you if he thinks he's being found out. Promise me you'll be careful."

Bandele and Paiva nodded solemnly. "We'll be careful. We're no use to you or the Queen if

Crevan bans us from the palace."

Carroway managed a smile he didn't feel. "That's my girls. While Halik and Tadghe are gone, play when you can for the court and see what you hear. Tris and Kiara are going to need all the friends they can get if they're going to hang on to the throne."

CHAPTER TWENTY

A MAN'S AGONIZED scream cut through the silence at the old fuller's mill. There was a thud as a body hit the wall hard. The wall that separated Cam's prison in an old wool room from the main mill area shuddered.

"We know you're Donelan's spy," Cam heard Ruggs shout through the wall at his captive. "What I want to know is—what have you told Donelan?"

Another thud, and the man screamed again. In his prison, Cam dragged himself painfully toward the wall. His broken leg was swollen to nearly double its size, and he knew he could not stand without the wall's support. But he couldn't sit by while Ruggs tortured someone. Not without trying to help.

"I'm not a patient man," Ruggs said in a

deadly tone. "Tell me what you know, and I'll stop the pain. Toy with me and I'll still have my answers... even if I have to drag them out of you along with your guts."

Cam winced at the sound of boots connecting hard with flesh. The prisoner groaned and retched. Cam inched his way along the wall. His injured leg sent flashes of pain streaking through his body. His left arm was worse. The wound where Ruggs had severed his finger had gone bad; Cam knew that by the smell. His left hand was hot and swollen, and as the days passed, the infection had gradually made its way up his arm. Now, his whole body was feverish. A few more days and Ruggs's hope for a captive to use for leverage against Donelan would be dashed. Cam was quite sure the fever or the poison from the festering wound would take him before long. Still, he inched on, until he found a break between boards big enough to see through.

Ruggs's captive wore the bloodied uniform of the Isencroft army. He was young, probably not yet twenty. From what Cam could see, Ruggs and his men had already worked the spy over before they got to the mill. The man's uniform was torn and covered with blood, and his face was swollen and bruised. Blood trickled from the soldier's nose and mouth. Ruggs gave the prisoner a vicious kick. "What does Donelan know?"

The prisoner moaned. Cam had to lean closer to the break in the boards to make out his words.

"The men we caught in town sing sweetly," he managed. "Donelan has them all—"

"Liar!" Ruggs bent down and dragged the soldier to his feet. He pinned the prisoner to the wall not far from where Cam watched helplessly and slammed his fist into the soldier's stomach, doubling the young man over. A vicious backhand snapped the prisoner's head back up, slamming it hard enough against the wall that Cam was amazed the soldier didn't lose consciousness.

A bitter smile crept over the young man's split lips. "It's too late. I was the bait. When I don't return, they'll know for sure you're here. You don't have much time left."

Ruggs gave a howl of rage and Cam saw a glint of light as a knife turned in Ruggs's hand an instant before he plunged it hilt-deep into the soldier's belly. The point jammed into the wall, and for a moment, Ruggs let the prisoner hang suspended by the dagger beneath his ribs. The soldier groaned in pain and Ruggs could not restrain himself from landing another punch before he pulled his knife free and let the dying soldier slump to the ground.

"Throw him in with the other one. We have work to do."

Enraged, Cam shuffled closer to the door. Fighting or escaping was beyond reach, but he could at least use his bulk to attack whoever came through the opening. The door opened, and with a roar, Cam threw himself at the two divisionists who dragged the battered soldier between them. His leg gave out on him, and he missed the first man, but he landed hard on the second and clamped his uninjured hand around the man's thin neck, squeezing with all his strength.

"Whore-spawned bastard!" he shouted as he sank his fingers into the man's neck.

The pommel of a sword came down hard on the side of Cam's head, making him see stars. Three men dragged him from the downed rebel and broke his grip on the man's neck. The divisionists gathered their downed comrade and Cam looked up to see Ruggs framed in the doorway.

"The men Donelan's captured won't stop us," Ruggs said as Cam raised his head to glare at him. "The army's on their way. We have some surprises waiting for them. We'll make it clear that some Isencroft men refuse to sell our souls to a foreign king." He gave a cold smile. "Make peace with whatever Aspect you honor. When the king's troops come into sight, I plan to hang both of you from the outer wall as a welcome banner." Ruggs slammed the door shut behind him and Cam heard the bolt slide into place.

Cam dragged himself over to where the battered soldier lay. There was just enough light making its way into the storage room from the late afternoon sun for him to see how bad the young man's wounds were. Cam had seen enough of battle to recognize a mortal wound, and the jagged tear left by Ruggs's knife would have challenged even so fine a healer as Carina.

The soldier turned his head slightly. "Don't move," Cam said quietly, drawing himself up into a sitting position with his good arm and gritting his teeth against the pain as he jarred his broken leg. "I'm nothing much to look at anyhow."

"Cam of Cairnrach?" The soldier's voice was muffled through swollen lips.

"Yes."

"The king thanks you for your warning."

Cam looked at him in astonishment. "Rhistiart made it through with my message?"

"And my mission was to tell you that help is on the way."

"Please don't tell me that you meant to let them capture you."

The soldier gave a weak laugh and sputtered blood. "I was to tell you to watch sharp tomorrow night. That's when they're set to attack." He struggled for breath. "I thought they might want to trade us. Seems they're not much for exchanging prisoners. Live ones, anyway."

As the young man spoke, Cam did his best to staunch the bleeding, but the warm blood drenched his hands. "Lie still."

"Thank you for what you tried to do, there at the door."

"My sister always said I was the size of an ox. Figured falling on someone could do some damage. I'm afraid that's the best I could manage."

"I was proud to serve the king." The young man's voice was faint, and even in the waning light, Cam could see the pallor in the soldier's face.

"You've served well," Cam said, fighting the lump in his throat. With his good hand, he clasped the soldier's hand tightly as the man began to shiver. "Hang on. I won't let go."

"Say a prayer for my soul," the soldier murmured. "There's no family to mourn me."

"What's your name?

"Siarl."

"I promise, Siarl." Cam said. He could feel the other's grip growing slack. The soldier drew a long, ragged breath and was still. Cam bowed his head. He had never been observant about the Lady. Carina had made offerings for the both of them, and Cam guessed that his sister also said whatever prayers he might have overlooked. But any man who soldiered more than a few battles knew the prayer for the dead. The words came to him now, and with them, the faces of so many friends who lay beneath the battlefields.

"Let the sword be sheathed, and the helm shuttered. Prepare a feast in the hall of your fallen heroes. Siarl of Isencroft died with valor.

Make his passage swift and his journey easy, until his soul rests in the arms of the Lady." His voice broke. Gently, Cam let go of Siarl's hand to make the sign of the Lady over his body. He closed the young man's eyes and laid his hands atop his chest, covering the savage wound.

Cam drew a deep breath. He had no illusions about the likelihood of rescue. But he would honor Siarl's sacrifice. His hand went to the flint and steel in his pocket. Donelan would have his warning beacon. Siarl would have a pyre worthy of a hero. And Cam of Cairnrach would have his vengeance.

DAY 5

CHAPTER TWENTY-ONE

IT WAS PAST noon when Jonmarc awoke. His body still ached from the attack, but his head was clear and the pain was manageable. He pulled back the covers and shuddered as the cold air struck him. The fire was banked, and its heat did little to warm the room. Jonmarc dressed quickly. He crossed to the heavy drapes that blocked the sunlight and pulled them back.

Pristine snow-covered hills stretched out around Wolvenskorn, down to the thick forest. Above it all, a bright blue sky was cloudless. A good day for battle. Tonight, one way or the other, the war with Malesh would end.

This was supposed to be our wedding day. He stared out across the snow toward the horizon, and his fists balled tightly as he struggled for control. Come dawn, both he and Carina were likely to be dead.

He turned away from the window and belted on his sword. He strapped on the single arrow launcher, fastening it to his left forearm and fitting it with a fresh arrow. He left his baldric and daggers on the bed, along with his second sword and crossbow. There would be time enough to arm himself later, when they were ready to ride.

A cold breakfast waited on the nightstand, and a pot of *kerif* simmered on the coals in the fireplace. Jonmarc finished his food and drank down the *kerif* greedily, looking to clear the last traces of the attackers' drugs from his system. When no one came to fetch him, Jonmarc let himself into the hallway and followed the sound of voices. The *vayash moru* would be at rest while the sun was high in the sky, so he assumed that it was *vyrkin* that he heard.

Yestin and Vigulf the shaman were the only two Jonmarc recognized as he entered the great room. Twenty-five men looked up as Jonmarc walked in. Yestin and Vigulf greeted him and welcomed him to the table. Platters of roasted venison looked well picked over as Jonmarc waved off offers of food.

"I see we've gotten reinforcements," he said to Yestin.

"I know it doesn't seem like many. But we are fewer than mortals guess. They've sent the women and pups into hiding. These are all the *vyrkin* males within a two-day's ride of Wolvenskorn. I can give you my word that none of my people have sided with Malesh." Jonmarc could see the fierce pride in Yestin's eyes, even as he noted that the shapeshifter moved with a slight limp, evidence that he was not fully recovered from his injuries. Jonmarc knew better than to comment. Like Yestin, he had no intention of allowing his half-healed wounds to keep him from battle.

"And the *vayash moru*?"

Vigulf answered him. "Nearly thirty *vayash moru* sleep in the crypts below. Word of the uprising has spread quickly. They've come from across Principality and even some from Margolan. We've promised them we will stand guard."

Fifty-five *vayash moru* and *vyrkin*, and one lone mortal. The Lady had a morbid sense of humor when it came to picking champions. "No idea how many have gone over to Malesh's side?"

Yestin shook his head. "Gabriel doesn't know where some of the *vayash moru* have gone, especially those who belong to Rafe and Astasia. We don't know whether they'll watch from the sidelines, or whether they've sided with Malesh."

"Anyone hazard a guess on how many fledges Uri's made—for argument's sake? And how many *might* turn out against us if Rafe and Astasia back Malesh? It's an old habit—I like to have some idea of how big the enemy's forces are."

The *vyrkin* shaman gave the barest of smiles. "I, too, like to know such things. For argument's sake. If they were all to turn against us, we may face a roughly equal number, but they will all be *vayash moru*."

"Meaning 'equal' isn't really equal at all."

"They have some advantages. So do we."

An awful thought occurred to Jonmarc. "Are there other *vayash moru* broods, aside from the Blood Council?"

Vigulf nodded. "There are minor families. Some are indirect fledges, while others owe allegiance to less powerful sires. I don't think they'll enter the fight—at least, not yet."

Jonmarc looked at him skeptically. "Why not?"

Vigulf folded his arms across his chest. "*Vayash moru*, like *vyrkin*, respect an order of dominance. Right now, this is a Blood Council issue. The others will wait on the sidelines until they see a clear winner before they risk themselves. Malesh may have recruited from the other Blood Council broods, but he would not think to ask help from what he would consider to be inferior bloodlines."

"Yeah, well I'm living proof that street curs are more dangerous than pure bloods."

"Indeed."

While the *vyrkin* were up and about during daylight, Jonmarc noticed that the heavy draperies in the great room remained drawn.

Torches lit the room, making it difficult to gauge the passage of time. Jonmarc sat at the huge table between Yestin and Vigulf as the *vyrkin* worked out their strategy for the fight.

"We have to hold Malesh off until seventh bells," Jonmarc said. "We owe Carina that chance. After that, he's mine."

The shaman smiled coldly. "We are agreed to contain Malesh without destroying him, and to keep him from entering the Temple of the Lady. Those who fight beside him," Vigulf said, his elongated eye teeth plain, "can fall at any time and not affect Carina. We will make this a costly lesson."

Jonmarc looked to Yestin. "You've been quiet. Thoughts?"

Yestin smiled tightly. "That today is a good day to die."

Jonmarc snorted. "I was thinking that it's a good day to kill the fucking bastard who started this."

Since the *vyrkin* could move about before sunset, they made ready to leave before the *vayash moru* arose. Even Gabriel had no idea where Malesh had gone to ground, and Jonmarc and Yestin wanted to be in position at the temple before Malesh could have a chance of reaching his objective.

Just before fourth bells, servants brought flagons of goats' blood in preparation for the *vayash moru* to rise. Jonmarc went to retrieve his remaining weapons from his room. He touched the amulet at his throat that Carina had given him and closed his eyes. It had never been his way to pray before a battle. Until he met Tris, Jonmarc had stopped believing that the Lady was anything but a myth told by those too desperate to accept the fact that they were on their own. A year with a Summoner convinced him that the Lady existed, but he found it impossible to believe such a being could give a damn about the petitions of mere mortals. He'd made Istra's Bargain out of desperation, and despite what Gabriel said, part of him deeply doubted anyone was listening. But just in case, he had one last favor to ask.

"If you must take Carina, let her passage be gentle," he murmured. He took a deep breath and opened his eyes. Nothing in the room gave any indication that his words had been heard by anyone other than himself. He took up his cloak and fastened it around his shoulders. It was time to fight.

THE SKY WAS still a clear, soft blue as the group left Wolvenskorn. The sun was low in the sky, but Jonmarc knew he was the only one who needed the light. Vyrkin loped effortlessly alongside his horse, able to see as well as wolves in the night. Once it was dark, Jonmarc knew the *vayash moru*'s keen senses would recognize a threat long before his sight or hearing registered danger. And by the same token, their enemies would have ample warning that they were on their way.

They reached the Temple of the Lady well before sunset. The sky turned a deep golden-red as the shadows lengthened. Jonmarc and Yestin took up position outside the entrance to the temple. Vigulf stationed the others around the building, and scouts kept watch. Moments after the sun sank beneath the horizon, Jonmarc saw shadows begin to move toward them.

"They're coming."

The group of *vayash moru* seemed to appear in the blink of an eye. Thirty of the undead fighters stood facing them, their clothes and hair whipped by the night wind. At the fore stood a tall, blond man who might have been in his late twenties had he been mortal. He wore a long black coat that flared back from his body in the wind, exposing a wicked sword at his belt.

"Where's Malesh—or didn't he have the stomach for a fight?" Jonmarc shouted.

The blond man's eyes narrowed. "He'll come. He's looking forward to seeing you again."

"Likewise."

The blond man surveyed the line of *vyrkin* that surrounded the temple in wolf form. The large wolves stood with hackles raised and teeth bared, warning the others not to approach. "Is this the best you can do? Did Gabriel desert you?"

"You wish." Gabriel's voice carried across the snow, and Jonmarc watched as Laisren and the other *vayash moru* stepped into position in the cordon around the temple. At the same time, more *vayash moru* walked out of the shadows to join ranks behind the blond man, making their number easily equal to the defenders of the temple.

Like a sudden gust of wind, Malesh's force attacked, moving so swiftly that the snow swirled around them. Half of the *vayash moru* rose from the ground intending to attack from above only to be met by Gabriel's fighters, who forced the action back to the snowy plain.

Jonmarc was ready with a sword in each hand. Laisren stepped up to stand beside him. Five *vayash moru* closed on them. Out of the corner of his eye, Jonmarc could see the battle beginning all around him. Yestin snarled and launched himself at one of their attackers, dodging the *vayash moru*'s blade and snapping at his neck. Two of the fighters closed on Jonmarc, while the others ran at Laisren, swords flashing in the moonlight.

The cold night air was filled with the clang of weapons and the guttural howls of the *vyrkin*. Jonmarc was grateful for his training with Laisren as his attackers came at him with full *vayash moru* speed and strength. None of the attackers were familiar to Jonmarc; he had no idea from which of the Blood Council houses they came, nor whether they were Malesh's fledges or older. The blond man who had hailed them at the start circled Jonmarc. A glint in his blue eyes said that he relished the fight. Jonmarc parried as the second *vayash moru* swung hard, nearly scoring on his shoulder. The blow made Jonmarc's arm throb but he held his sword, wheeling to meet the blond *vayash moru*'s strike between his own crossed blades.

The pair came at him again, and Jonmarc pivoted to miss the worst of the strike, cursing as one of the blades opened a cut on his shoulder. With a cry, he ran at the second man, pounding a furious offense that drove the *vayash moru* back a pace. Remembering everything Laisren had drilled into him, Jonmarc pressed his advantage, knowing the blond man would strike at any instant. His sword slid against his attacker's blade and slipped free, driving deep into the *vayash moru*'s chest. The fighter's eyes widened in the instant before he slumped to the ground and his body began to deteriorate.

"The traitors taught you well." The blond man came at him at full speed, knocking Jonmarc backward. He regained his balance just in time to stop a swing that was powerful enough to take off a limb.

"Malesh betrayed the Truce. You're the traitors here."

The blond man laughed. His reaction sent a wave of anger through Jonmarc that energized him to charge back through the snow, ready to knock the arrogance from his attacker. The blond man tried to sidestep, but Jonmarc anticipated the move, blocking his enemy's strike and scoring a deep gash on his attacker's upper arm. With a hiss, the man lunged at him, driving him back with a relentless press. Laisren was holding his own against three attackers; help was unlikely from that quarter. Yestin harried another *vayash moru* a few paces away, dodging the man's blur-fast sword strikes with audacity.

The blond man's sword slashed down, opening a cut on Jonmarc's forearm as he barely managed to hold off the worst of the strike. A cold smile crossed the man's pale features and he pressed his advantage, forcing Jonmarc back another step. Jonmarc pivoted sharply and dove into a low kick, taking the *vayash moru* down to the ground. He skidded toward the downed attacker, sword ready, and drove his blade in from the side, slipping between the ribs. Black ichor began to ooze from the corner of the *vayash moru*'s mouth, but his body did not disintegrate.

Cursing, Jonmarc withdrew a dagger from his belt and slashed the blond man's throat, loosing a fountain of ichor as the head rolled free. With a grimace, Jonmarc wiped his blade clean on the snow and withdrew his sword barely a moment before two new attackers closed on him.

Malesh isn't old enough to have fledges that can resist a blade through the heart. Damn. That means more outsiders. No wonder that fighter was so good. Malesh is getting help from the other houses, and some of the Old Ones are siding against us.

The sharp cry of a wounded *vyrkin* snapped Jonmarc's attention from the two *vayash moru* who were fast approaching, swords ready. Yestin was bleeding from a gash in his shoulder, but he had launched himself at his *vayash moru* attacker and clamped his wolf-bite hard on the sword arm of his foe. Jonmarc ducked low, scything his blade just above the snow to take Yestin's opponent down at the ankles. He rose just in time to meet the new threat of two fresh *vayash moru* fighters.

Barely a candlemark into the fight, Jonmarc was sure of Malesh's strategy. He'd anticipated their defense, and now he was sending in his lieutenants to wear them down before making his own appearance. If Gabriel was correct, Malesh would attempt to work his blood magic at eighth bells, a nod to the Faces of the Lady. Jonmarc knew he had a tight window of time. He needed to hold Malesh off until after seventh bells to give Carina a chance to heal the Flow. But too close to the next candlemark, and it might not be possible to stop Malesh's working. No movement stirred beyond the moonlit circle around the Lady's Temple, nothing at all to indicate anyone else dreamed that so much hung in the balance on this night's battle.

"Jonmarc, on your right!" Laisren's warning registered an instant before the blade whistled past Jonmarc's ear. Jonmarc parried, sliding in the snow. One attacker pressed forward with a bone-crushing series of blows that drove Jonmarc back on his heels. The other rose off the ground, and then flew downward, sword angled to take Jonmarc through the chest.

Jonmarc deflected the first *vayash moru*'s sword strikes and threw himself to the ground, dropping the sword in his left hand and grabbing for a throwing knife from his baldric. He threw the knife at the *vayash moru* that was streaking toward him from the night sky and rolled through the snow, grabbing up his fallen sword and curling into a tight ball. The *vayash moru*'s sword struck the ground so close that it tore his cloak, ripping free a hand's breadth of the thick wool.

Seizing the instant's advantage as his attacker pulled his blade free of the frozen ground, Jonmarc brought his twin swords up in a single, fluid movement, impaling the *vayash moru* through the gut so that the bloodied points thrust out through the back of his long coat. The *vayash moru* gurgled ichor and shook violently, slipping down Jonmarc's blades until Jonmarc bucked, kicking with both feet to throw the attacker's body clear. It began to decompose before it hit the trampled snow, and the remaining *vayash moru* closed on Jonmarc with a growl.

Jonmarc was an instant too slow in blocking the sword that came at him, and it sliced into his arm. Blood warmed his skin and Jonmarc saw hunger and satisfaction on his attacker's face as the *vayash moru* delivered a pounding, two-handed strike. Jonmarc deflected it, but he lost his footing and went down hard as the attacker raised his sword for a killing blow.

The whistle of an unseen blade sang through the cold night air, slicing cleanly through the *vayash moru*'s neck. The headless body stood for a moment, and then keeled to the right, following its severed head. Laisren stood behind the dead *vayash moru*, ichor dripping from his sword.

Jonmarc regained his feet but there was no time for thanks. More *vayash moru* came toward them, swords at the ready. Around them, the temple grounds had become a battlefield and in the moonlight the snow was dark with blood and ichor. A glance told Jonmarc that the fighting was going hard on both sides. Still, the line held. The clang of swords rang through the night as the fight raged on. The temple bells sounded six times, and Jonmarc scanned the faces of the *vayash moru* once again for Malesh.

"He's not here," Jonmarc said to Laisren as they regrouped after the latest foray.

"He'll come. He's likely as anxious to finish you off as you are to kill him."

"Not by half."

As quickly as they came, the attackers withdrew. Up and down the cordon, the defenders watched for movement in the moonlight. "Hold your positions!" Jonmarc shouted. With a pause in the fighting, the toll of the battle became more apparent. Several of the *vyrkin* lay dead on the ground. Dark patches in the snow marked where *vayash moru* had decomposed after a fatal strike. From the spacing of the line on the side of the temple he could see, Jonmarc guessed they had lost about a third of their force.

Gabriel's blond hair shone in the moonlight, making it easy to spot him at the far end of the temple. Vigulf was in his place, notable by his sheer size and the unique brown markings on his pelt. Yestin was still on his feet, although his fur was matted with blood in several places. Jonmarc had taken at least half a dozen wounds in the melee. Gashes bled on his arms and upper thighs where his foes had made good their strikes. He glanced at Laisren. The *vayash moru*'s cloak was cut in a score of places, and he had a nasty slash across one cheek. Jonmarc knew that although his undead companion could heal faster than a mortal, the injuries were no less painful. They waited in the silence for the next assault, and Jonmarc scanned the shadows for any hint of movement.

From the darkness, a glimpse of firelight and the twang of bowstrings was the only warning. A hail of flaming arrows arched through the night sky toward the base of the temple. For the *vayash moru* defenders to hold their positions would be suicide, exposed without cover and trapped against the temple walls.

Jonmarc looked to Yestin. "Take out the archers!" he cried, making for the tell-tale glow at a dead run. The *vyrkin* ran alongside him, darting and weaving to draw off the arrows that rained fire down from the darkness.

The arrows are concentrated around the door. We're being herded.

"Watch your backs! It's a trap!" Jonmarc shouted back to the others just as a new wave of attackers swarmed toward the temple's rear wall. He dodged an arrow that flew past him close enough to warm his skin as he and the *vyrkin* closed on the line of archers.

Jonmarc dropped to one knee and sheathed his swords, grabbing the crossbow that hung at his back. Staying low to the ground, his quarrels felled three of the bowmen in short succession as the *vyrkin* stalked their prey and sprang for the kill too close for the bows to be of use.

"Jonmarc—the door!"

Firing off one more shot, Jonmarc turned to see Malesh moving toward the temple doorway.

Go! Vigulf's voice sounded in Jonmarc's mind.

With a glance to make sure the *vyrkin* could hold their own against the rapidly decreasing number of archers, Jonmarc slung his crossbow over his shoulder and sprinted back through the snow, sword in hand. Heavy fighting at the rear corner of the temple had drawn off the cordon. Just as Jonmarc neared the doorway, a dark shape blocked his way.

"Going somewhere?" The dark-featured *vayash moru* was one Jonmarc had never seen before, but it was clear from the man's expression that he was quite aware of who Jonmarc was. His first sword strike was a blur of movement, but Jonmarc blocked it, watching as Malesh neared the temple doors.

A snarl sounded behind Jonmarc an instant before a large wolf leaped into the air, heedless of the *vayash moru*'s sword. The wolf's weight carried the *vayash moru* to the ground, and Jonmarc recognized Yestin. The wolf paused only long enough to give a sharp bark and a toss of its head toward the temple, indicating for Jonmarc to run. Hoping Yestin could hold off the *vayash moru* on his own, Jonmarc headed for the doorway at a dead run just as Malesh cleared the threshold.

Jonmarc entered the temple. Malesh was nowhere to be seen. Too late, Jonmarc spun around, realizing Malesh was behind him. Malesh slammed into him at full *vayash moru* speed, knocking Jonmarc halfway across the temple's open court.

Jonmarc had only an instant to get his bearings. The Temple of the Dark Lady was long and narrow. Banks of candles and scores of torches lined the walls. A shallow reflecting pool lay in the center, warmed by magic in the bitter cold. There were no windows or skylights, yet the floor was cast in rich hues of red and gold from a large stained glass image of Istra that hung suspended from the vaulted temple ceiling, backlit by huge torches. Beneath the glass image stood a large statue of the Dark Lady. Both depictions were the same: a sad-eyed Istra, fangs bared, stood with her arms partially outstretched. She was wrapped in a richly-patterned cloak and, in its shadows, cringing multitudes huddled near her for protection.

Jonmarc heard heavy wooden doors slam shut and the crosspiece fall into place. He scrambled to his feet, sword ready. Outside, he could hear the sounds of battle and the cries of *vyrkin* and *vayash moru*. Inside, there was only the sound of Malesh's footsteps as he slowly circled Jonmarc.

"It seems you're the only guest to witness my ascendance to consort," Malesh said. It was obvious that he had not taken any part in the battle thus far. He looked as if he might have just left court.

"That's what this is about? You want to be a god?"

Malesh smiled, making his eye teeth plain. "Not a god. A consort. One who will rule with the Lady as we were meant to rule. Openly. Taking our rightful place as the top predator."

"Not if I can help it."

"All that remains is to best Her champion. That won't be difficult."

Outside, the temple bells began to ring the seventh hour.

Malesh rushed at Jonmarc. Jonmarc was ready for the attack, expecting Malesh to strike with his sword. At the last instant, Malesh altered his course, streaking upward toward the high ceiling and landing behind Jonmarc. Jonmarc stabbed backward with his short sword, burying it deep into Malesh's thigh.

Malesh grabbed Jonmarc from behind and flung him against the stone wall. With a growl, he pulled the short sword from his leg and threw it in the opposite direction. Dazed, Jonmarc struggled to his feet as Malesh closed again. He swung hard with his broadsword, connecting with Malesh's blade. Malesh slid his own blade down to lock Jonmarc's grip, and tore the weapon from his hand. The sword skittered across the marble floor and Malesh landed a blow to Jonmarc's ribs with his fist that cracked bone. Before Jonmarc could catch his breath, Malesh grabbed him by the shoulders and slammed him hard against the wall.

All I've got to do is stay alive long enough to buy time for Carina. Jonmarc fingered the release for the arm quiver. *Not yet. Not yet.*

"I knew you weren't much of a swordsman," Jonmarc baited. "You know you can't win a fair fight."

He managed to duck the next blow, and twisted beneath Malesh's grip, diving and rolling although the pain of his broken ribs made him gasp. He came up halfway across the marble court, near the base of the reflecting pool, and grabbed his fallen broadsword.

Malesh streaked toward him and Jonmarc spun his sword, gritting his teeth against the pain. The tip of his sword caught Malesh's shoulder and Malesh growled as he parried with a blow that nearly snapped Jonmarc's blade.

"How long before you tire?" Malesh taunted as he returned Jonmarc's parry. "What a fool Gabriel was to think that a mortal champion could ever best one of us. Although I do have a use for you. Your blood will seal the magic." He fingered an amulet at his throat. "I'll make sure to leave enough to work the charm."

Without warning, Malesh attacked again. His blows were calculated for speed and strength, raining down in a pounding fury that forced Jonmarc to stretch to the limits of his training to defend himself. The attack came so fast and with enough of an advantage in strength that what Malesh lacked in sword skill or salle form was meaningless for the sheer brutality of his press. After having already endured several candlemarks of relentless fighting, Jonmarc knew that he could not hold out long against the savagery of Malesh's attacks before he was disarmed or dismembered. The glint in Malesh's eyes said that his opponent knew it, too.

Jonmarc gripped his sword two-handed, needing all his waning strength and concentration to parry Malesh's blade. Jonmarc met Malesh's strikes blow for blow. He felt the strength of the sword strikes jolt painfully through his bones, making his teeth rattle and his head throb. With every moment that passed, the likelihood of rescue and the hope of success grew dimmer.

With a snarl, Malesh wheeled, bringing his full strength and the motion of his turn against Jonmarc's sword. The blade bent and snapped, sending the useless shards clattering to the floor. Jonmarc threw the pommel at Malesh and ran, but Malesh grabbed his shoulder with a grip that threatened to rip his arm from its socket. Momentarily stunned by the pain, Jonmarc gasped as Malesh grabbed him by the throat with his other hand.

"I've watched you fight. Learned how you move. You deserve your reputation as a fighter. And now, I will deserve mine as the one who destroyed you."

Jonmarc spat in his face. He twisted in Malesh's grip, still too far away to launch his arrow from its hidden quiver.

"I took your woman as the first sacrifice," Malesh said, tightening his grip enough that

Jonmarc could barely breathe. "She fought me. Her blood was hot and sweet and she moaned like a whore in my arms when I drank her."

Jonmarc lashed out with his foot, landing a blow with the knife in his boot against Malesh's side that would have felled a mortal. Malesh smiled. "I could easily beat you to death. But that hardly befits such a worthy opponent." He drew back his lips. "I gain the strength of my enemy when I devour him. And I want to taste the fear in your blood as I drain your life."

Malesh brought his arm down until Jonmarc's boots touched the floor and drew him closer. With his free hand, Malesh ripped open Jonmarc's shirt and great cloak, exposing his neck and shoulder.

Wait for it. Only one chance. Wait for it.

In one swift movement, Malesh bared his fangs and sank them into Jonmarc's shoulder at the base of his neck.

Jonmarc stiffened at the sudden pain as the teeth tore into his flesh. Struggling to keep his head clear, Jonmarc brought his left arm up so that his palm was against Malesh's chest above his heart and squeezed the trigger.

Malesh tore loose from Jonmarc's neck as the arrow embedded itself, quills deep, in his chest. With a shriek, Malesh staggered backward as Jonmarc fell to his knees. A warm stream of blood flowed from the open gash in Jonmarc's neck. He could hear his heart beating in his ears, and sensed it slowing as blood soaked his shirt and dripped onto the floor.

Malesh's heel caught the edge of the reflecting pool as he tore at the arrow that protruded from his shirt. He careened into the bank of candles, ripping it and the torch above it from the wall. There was a flash of fire and Malesh screamed again, engulfed in flame.

The fledgling dies the maker's death.

Jonmarc watched in horror as Malesh flailed while the flames consumed him and a black, acrid smoke rose from his charring skin.

Behind him, the door gave way with a crash. *I failed,* Jonmarc thought as the room began to spin. It was hard to breathe. He fell backward onto the cold marble floor, staring into the amber eyes of the stained glass Lady. *I destroyed Malesh but I failed Carina.*

Strong hands gripped his shoulders. "Get the shaman!" It was Gabriel's voice, but with an edge of panic Jonmarc had never heard before.

"Let me die."

"You know I can't do that."

"No choice…"

The temple around him faded into darkness. Gradually, blackness gave way to a gray dawn, and Jonmarc realized that he stood at the edge of an endless sea. The cold surf lapped at his bare feet and the wind whipped at his hair. A lone figure walked toward him at the water's edge, and as it drew nearer, Jonmarc recognized the same face that had stared down at him from the stained glass in the temple. Istra was even more beautiful than any of Her statues. Wild, dark hair framed dusky features and She moved with a predator's grace. Something innate within him warned him that he should kneel in the presence of the Goddess. Ignoring it, Jonmarc remained on his feet, daring to meet Her amber eyes.

"I kept my bargain. Let me die."

"There is a greater darkness coming." Istra's voice seemed to sound inside his mind.

"I've done my part. Let me rest."

The amber eyes sparked with inner fire, depthless and sorrowful. "Not yet. I need a champion."

"Find someone else."

"There is only one champion in a generation. There is no other."

He shook his head. "If you didn't notice, all your 'children' are out there killing each other. How can you watch that and not want rid of the lot of us?"

"See what I see." Her voice echoed in his mind as She raised Her arms, revealing what lay beneath the intricate, moving patterns of Her cloak. In the shadows, Jonmarc glimpsed writhing souls, stripped of their pretense and masks, laid bare in fear and pain. For an instant, he could hear their cries of utter anguish and terror and knew that he glimpsed the world as She saw it. He met Her gaze levelly.

"I'm just a blacksmith's son from the backside of nowhere. You've taken everything from me. How can it matter if I die?"

Istra's expression changed as if She were listening to far-off voices, and Her eyes seemed to see into the distance. "Without you, the currents change. Martris Drayke will die before his time. His heir will fall to an assassin's blade. Margolan will be consumed by her enemies within a generation and the Winter Kingdoms will be carved up as spoils among the legions of its attackers."

Jonmarc swallowed hard. "And if I go back, that will change? You swear it?"

Her features softened. "The future is always in motion. I cannot guarantee it. But if you return, there is a chance. Without you, there is none."

Jonmarc closed his eyes. The pain of his battle wounds was gone. He could make good his final vow and find Carina in the Plains of Spirit. *But at what cost?*

Knowing what he had to do, he opened his eyes. "All right. I'll do it."

Istra reached out Her hand toward him, laying Her palm over his bare chest above the symbol he had traced in ink. Jonmarc gasped as Her palm became hot, searing his skin. When She withdrew Her hand, the symbol was branded into his flesh.

"Let there be no doubt," Her voice echoed in his mind. "You are mine. Now, return. Your work is not yet finished."

JONMARC'S WHOLE BODY shuddered as he strained for air.

"I've got him." The shaman's voice sounded close by. Jonmarc felt a hand pressed against his skin where Malesh's fangs had laid open his shoulder. The pain of his wounds returned in a single breath, enough to make his heart skip a beat.

"Will he live?" It was Gabriel, still as worried as before.

"He's lost a lot of blood. I'll do what I can to heal him, but I can only do so much to replace blood." Vigulf opened what remained of Jonmarc's shirt to lay a hand on his newly healed—and newly re-broken—ribs. "Look," he said sharply to Gabriel, and Jonmarc knew without opening his eyes that it was the symbol of the Lady that caught Vigulf's attention.

"You were right when you sensed Her presence just now. I felt it, too."

"Then he truly is Her champion."

Vigulf's laugh was sharp. "You doubted?"

"Only a fool never doubts."

"Are you going to take him back to Wolvenskorn?"

"Not tonight. I don't think either of us is up to it. There's a pilgrim's chamber just off this courtyard. I'll stay with him. The battle's over. And there are others who still need your help."

"Aye. I've done all I can tonight for him. Let me see how many of the others I can help, and

I'll come back for the both of you at sunset tomorrow."

Jonmarc faded in and out of consciousness as Gabriel carried him to the marble slab that was the only resting place in the pilgrim's chamber. When he was finally able to open his eyes, he saw Gabriel slouched against the wall, seated on the floor of the small room, guarding the door. Gabriel's cloak was torn and darkened with ichor, the same dark substance that matted the blond hair on one side of his head and that marked a gash across his right cheek. His left hand was blistered and the skin was peeling from a bad burn that extended up his arm where flames had burned away the sleeve of his cloak.

"You actually look worse than I feel," Jonmarc managed in a whisper.

"I'm sorry that I couldn't get to you faster. Malesh planned his counterstrike well."

"How bad was it?"

"Yestin is dead. Laisren will recover, but he had to be carried back to Wolvenskorn. We lost all but a third of our forces."

"And theirs?"

"Annihilated."

The enormity of the loss weighed on Jonmarc's heart. So many destroyed out of what was already a small number of Those Who Walk The Night. But the image that would not leave his memory was of Malesh engulfed in flames.

He knew Carina felt Malesh's torment. Jonmarc turned his face to the wall and wept silently for her. Istra may have given him no real choice about his service, but Jonmarc grieved for the lost reunion with Carina's spirit. And though he knew Carina would never have wanted him to pay so high a price, he ached knowing that it might be years before Istra would let him take the final rest he sought.

CHAPTER TWENTY-TWO

CARINA STOOD IN front of the large wardrobe in her room at Dark Haven. She fingered the smooth satin of the burgundy wedding dress that should have been hers to wear this day. The same rich color as the wine and blood for which Dark Haven was best known, it was in the traditional color and style common in Principality. Carina bowed her head and closed her eyes tightly against tears she could not cry. Carefully, she smoothed the dress back into place and closed the armoire doors.

It was early evening. Lisette and Riqua had just arisen, and they were making preparations with Royster for tonight's working. Carina had insisted on remaining awake today, hidden from the sun in Dark Haven's windowless inner circle of rooms or behind its heavy draperies.

She turned and took a small candle from a holder, lighting it from a larger lamp. Carina crossed to the shrine in the corner of her room where candles burned to small ivory images of the Lady in Her Aspects of Mother and Childe. Although Isencroft was partial to the warrior aspect of Chenne, Carina had always sought comfort from the Mother and Childe. Earlier, Carina had made her offering for good measure in Istra's chapel beneath Dark Haven.

Now, she poured dark mead into a goblet and set it in front of the ornately carved figurines. She removed a napkin from over a honey cake and laid the cake next to the mead, and then she made the sign of the Lady and whispered the Prayer for the Dead. She had often murmured those words on the battlefield, over the war dead she could not save. Now, she said it for Jonmarc and for herself, hoping that tonight they might be reunited in the arms of the Lady.

"I'm sorry, Carina." Taru stood in the doorway, and the expression on her face made Carina sure that Taru had seen her putting the dress away.

Carina swallowed hard. "Jonmarc and I made a handfasting. That's all most people do. I guess married is married, even without a ritual ceremony."

"You should be resting to save your strength for tonight."

Carina gave a wan smile. "If this is my last day, I'd really rather be awake for it. Besides,

I needed to meet with Neirin. I know Jonmarc hasn't been Lord of Dark Haven for long, but he and Gabriel made so much progress that I don't want it all to fall to ruin again." Carina knew that Taru understood what she left unsaid: Jonmarc was as unlikely to live through this day as she was.

"Promise me something, Taru."

"If it's within my power, you know I'll do anything I can."

Carina met Taru's eyes. "Promise me that if I die, you'll find a healer to replace me. The need here is so great. I understand why it's uncomfortable for a healer here. Getting used to the empty feeling around *vayash moru* takes a while. But the humans and the *vyrkin* here need a healer." She sighed. "I had hoped to become a mind healer. Lisette thought that with mind healing, I might be of help to the *vayash moru,* since I was able to ease Raen's suffering. Immortality is more painful than I ever expected! And I wanted to experiment with healing magic and potions to see if I could come up with something that would ease the *vayash moru*'s pain when they're injured." She shook her head. "It's all ending too soon, Taru. There's too much left undone."

Taru put her arms around Carina and drew her close. "I know. And it's scant comfort to know that if you do heal the Flow tonight, you may be able to end a lot of other suffering. I wanted this to work out differently for you."

Carina stood back and clasped Taru's hands. "So did I. But maybe this will still count for something. I just hope the messengers reached Tris in time. Otherwise, this may be a very short healing."

Taru winced at the thought. "Riqua believed they could. Will you have any way to sense Tris's presence before you step into the Flow?"

Carina shrugged. "I don't know. We'll see when we get there."

Taru indicated the glass on the table filled with the noxious blood and milk mixture. "You should eat. You'll need your strength."

Carina wrinkled her nose. "Perhaps I've found one good thing about tonight after all. I won't have to drink this awful stuff again!"

When Taru left, Carina let herself into Jonmarc's rooms and lit a torch. Although Jonmarc had been gone for days, the servants kept the fire banked in his room, awaiting his return. Carina sat down in the leather chair near the hearth. A shirt lay discarded across the back of the chair. She pulled it to her and caught a breath of his scent. She buried her face in the linen, wishing she could cry.

SINCE LATE MORNING, the sounds of battle rang across the plain as the Margolan army resumed its siege of Lochlanimar. Despite a bitter wind that swept down from the mountains, Tris's remaining soldiers held their positions, battering at the stronghold's crumbling outer walls. For most of the day, Tris stayed at the forefront of the battle, taking the active role Soterius was not yet well enough to play. By agreement, he let the remaining mages take turns striking Lochlanimar with magic to preserve his own power for the night's working. He was grateful that the constantly shifting battle kept his mind focused in the moment, leaving no time to worry about either Kiara or the Flow.

Come nightfall, the *vayash moru* surged forward to help their mortal comrades. And as the evening of Candles Night approached, Tris felt his own sense of dread grow. Finally he heard the sound of a gong, and wheeled his horse and rode for the relative shelter of the rear lines. The guards parted for him to enter. Fallon waited for him inside his tent.

"Ready?" she asked.

"Hardly. Is there a choice?"

"No. But I still don't understand how you think I can help."

"I need you to shield me. I have no idea what Curane's mages can read from the Flow, but I'm betting they'll realize we're up to something pretty big. With my attention on anchoring Carina, I'll be vulnerable. They could blindside me—assuming that I even *could* pull free from what I'm doing without causing a catastrophe. I need you to watch my back," he said with a nervous half-smile as he removed his cloak.

"Is that all?" Fallon replied, her eyes softening the retort.

"Yeah, and drink a glass of brandy in my honor if I go up in a puff of smoke," Tris cracked. He wondered if Fallon had any idea of how nervous the night's working made him.

"I've brought the things you asked for." Coalan stood in the tent's doorway. He held out a flat, intricately worked metal plate the size of a man's palm, a labyrinth to help Tris center his thoughts. A scabbard hung over his shoulder, with the hilt of a sword protruding. A braided rug made of wizard's cords hung over his arm.

"That's not just any rug," Fallon observed as Tris spread the small, circular rug out on the tent floor.

Tris managed a nervous smile. "It was my grandmother's. I don't know what made me bring it with me. It was her workspace in her room. I learned my first magic there as a boy. I don't know if you can feel it, but I can still sense Grandmother's power in the cords."

Fallon nodded. "Great power leaves a signature, like a residue. I've encountered that same feeling before, in other magical items that belonged to Bava K'aa. And it's also in that sword." She glanced at the sword Coalan held out to Tris, a different weapon than the heavy broadsword Tris had carried with him into battle. "That's the sword Taru gave you at your coronation, isn't it? Bava K'aa's sword."

Tris took the sword and drew it from its worn scabbard. It was beautifully forged but without ornamentation, save for the faint tracery of runes inscribed on the blade. Now, the runes were almost invisible, but when he had first been presented with the sword, they had blazed with fire. "Another one of those things I threw into my trunk without knowing why. I've been leery of carrying it into battle until I had a better idea of its power. But for this working, I'll take all the help I can get." He glanced at Fallon. "Taru was cryptic about it when she gave it to me. Can you shed any light on what it can do?"

Fallon frowned and closed her eyes, letting her hand skim just above the sword, palm down as she extended her magic. "There is a trace of your grandmother's power. I can feel it, like a signature. Beyond that… its magic won't speak to me. I wouldn't be surprised if it requires a Summoner's power to activate it." She opened her eyes. "I'd warn you that it's risky to use a magic object if you don't know its power, but considering what you're about to try, the danger seems small by comparison."

Fallon, Tris and Coalan arranged a workspace in the center of the tent with a pillar candle on a small flat board and the labyrinth in front of it. Coalan took a place blocking the tent doorway, with his own sword in hand. Fallon glanced at the notched candle on the desk that measured the time. It was burned down nearly to the nineteenth notch. "Nearly seventh bells. We'd better get into position," she said.

Tris nodded, fighting back his own nervousness. What Carina's letter suggested had never been tried before—at least not to Fallon's considerable knowledge. The idea that he could send his magic across the Flow to anchor Carina's soul all the way in Dark Haven seemed absurd. But at the same time, the damaged Flow was making it nearly impossible to harness magic for this night's battle. "If I'm going to burst into flames, better here than on the battlefield," he said with a cheerfulness he didn't feel. He stepped onto the braided rug and raised his sword as his athame.

Tris walked the circle of the braided rug as his grandmother had taught him long ago. He spoke the invocation of the quarters as he focused his concentration on the tip of the blade. Around him, the warding flared in a dome of blue-white power. Once his warding was in place, Fallon walked the same circle in the opposite direction, adding a golden dome of power to reinforce the warding. Looking out toward Coalan and Fallon, Tris saw their images distorted as if through rising waves of heat on a scorching summer's day as the wardings surrounded him.

Tris knelt on the rug and laid his sword at his knees. He focused first on the pure flame of the candle, slowing his breathing as Bava K'aa had taught him until the roar of the battle beyond the thin canvas walls of the tent faded and only the flame remained. Centered, he turned his focus to the silver labyrinth. He lifted it reverently into his left hand, holding it in his palm as his right index finger began to slowly trace its intricate pattern. Chanting to himself, he felt his heartbeat and breathing slow further as he entered into a trance.

Slipping onto the Plains of Spirit, Tris saw himself walking the complex labyrinth that appeared before him, carved into the gray stone at his feet. In the Nether, Tris felt his focus shift fully from where his mortal body knelt to a place in his consciousness where only spirit and magic existed. In this place between the living and the dead, Tris reached out his power to touch the Flow.

CARINA HEARD FOOTSTEPS in the doorway to the sitting room.

"It's nearly time," Taru said quietly.

Carina rose and put Jonmarc's shirt aside. She straightened her healer's robes and squared her shoulders. With a confidence she did not feel, she walked with Taru down the long corridor toward the stairway to the ruined vaults beneath Dark Haven. Royster, Riqua and Lisette waited for them at the top of the stairs, and Carina could see Raen's ghostly shape glowing in the shadows.

"I took the liberty of asking Neirin to secure anything that might shake loose and to keep the servants and the refugees well away from this end of the manor," Royster said, clearing his throat. "Just in case."

Carina took his meaning clearly. The last person to tamper directly with the Flow had been Foor Arontala, when he had torn loose the orb that imprisoned the soul of the Obsidian King. The resulting burst of unharnessed power had collapsed part of the manor house, killed the last lord and wounded the Flow. "You shouldn't come with me. It's too dangerous."

"And miss history in the making?" Royster protested. Carina saw a scroll, quill and bottle of ink bulged from one of Royster's pouches.

"We will see this through," Riqua said in a voice that let Carina know the matter was settled.

Carina managed a half smile, grateful for their courage. "Let's go."

They made their way down the stone stairway, picking through the rubble. Raen led the way, followed by Riqua and then Royster, carrying a torch to light the way for the others. The lower they descended the colder it became, until Carina could see Taru's breath and Royster was shivering despite his woolen robes. The frigid air was still, and as they reached the bottom step, they heard the tower bells chime the seventh hour.

"Hurry. I doubt Tris can hold on for long," Carina said, picking up her skirts to move more quickly.

Beyond the archway, Carina could see the coruscating lights of the Flow. Like the Spirit Lights of the far north, the colors of the Flow flashed across the reflective crystals of the cave walls. Even without touching the powerful energy, Carina could sense that it was more damaged than when she visited before. But this time, she sensed something else: within the pulse of the Flow's wild energy, Carina felt Tris Drayke's magic.

Carina took a step toward the Flow as if approaching a wounded beast. The chamber flared with light as the energy river acknowledged her presence. Carina moved closer, one halting step at a time. She struggled to quell her own fear, searching for a place of inner calm. Holding her breath, Carina stepped into the power of the Flow.

Light surrounded her. Carina felt as if she were completely surrounded by the glittering ice crystals of a sudden snow squall. The Flow enveloped her, filled her, becoming the essence of her blood and bones. At the same time, she felt a comforting and familiar presence. Tris's magic found her and anchored her to his power.

A TORRENT OF pain and primal anger washed over Tris. He kept chanting. The violence of the Flow's contact slammed into him, but the chant and the labyrinth kept him anchored. In the Nether, Tris could see the Flow in all its brilliance, a radiant ribbon of light and color. Its sheer beauty took his breath away as it undulated, glistening like powdered diamonds. He stretched out his mage sense further, seeking Carina. He felt nothing but the turmoil of the Flow and forced despair from his thoughts, struggling to hold the trance.

Suddenly, he felt the Flow shift. The patterns of the colors changed. Tris pictured Carina, sought her through the Flow, throwing out tendrils of power on the wild currents of magic. Willing his power along the course of the Flow, he felt Carina's presence like a flutter against his skin.

Tris doubled his effort, sending the full power of his magic along the link to her, searching for the blue glow of Carina's life thread. Carina's thread faltered and flickered, buffeted by the power of the Flow. *Sweet Chenne, she's dying,* Tris thought as he connected his power to her. Tris slipped deeper into the trance until his sole focus became Carina's life thread. He willed his power to strengthen the thread, anchoring it to his own life energy.

The Flow began to convulse and Tris could now feel Carina's healing magic streaming out into the damaged river of energy. Tris poured his magic into the link, letting the power flow through him. The pounding of his heart seemed to shake his whole body, and the sound of his breath was deafening. Every fiber of his being tuned to the pulse of the Flow. He felt its pain. Images of the Soulcatcher orb being torn from the Flow flashed in his mind, and caught up in the Flow's magic, Tris felt the rending as if he were being torn on the rack and disemboweled. His body arched in agony and he screamed, but no sound came. Wave after wave of pain shuddered through him, too intense for him to black out.

HESITANTLY, CARINA REACHED out toward the Flow with her healing magic. She felt the pain of the long-ago rending and the imbalance in the Flow's energies as if it were torn muscle and sinew. Acting on instinct, Carina began to will all of her healing essence into mending the broken places and soothing the pain. She could feel the draw of the Flow depleting her, weakening her life force, and she knew that without Tris's support, soon she would be lost to the currents of energy that pulled her under in the torrent.

Carina willed herself to ride the waves of the Flow, focused completely on its pain. She let the pain wash through her, cleansing the energy. As the Flow calmed, she no longer sensed the boundaries between herself and the river of energy. Carina felt strength returning, and she could sense her connection to Tris, knew he was supporting her with his magic and his life force.

Suddenly, Carina's view shifted and she saw a dimly lit temple with soaring gray stone walls. Banks of candles and torches in sconces flared along the temple walls, and a glowing stained glass image of Istra hung from the buttressed ceiling. A man lay slumped against one of the temple pillars, and as he struggled to his feet, battered and covered with blood, Carina recognized Jonmarc.

Carina fought down panic. Bound to her energy, the Flow flared brilliantly in angry shades of red. Carina saw Jonmarc's sword snap in two and watched as Malesh pulled him in for the kill.

Jonmarc loosed his hidden quarrel, and Carina felt Malesh's pain as it tore through the *vayash moru*'s heart. Carina's screams echoed in the rock chamber as the wild energy of the Flow whipped around her. Fire engulfed Malesh, and Carina felt her skin burn and blister.

IT TOOK ALL of Tris's will to focus on the blue glow of Carina's life thread. Just when he thought the pain would overcome him, he felt Carina's healing magic as a cooling presence along the pathways of power. The chaos of the Flow was beginning to coalesce, and the inchoate energies torn asunder by Arontala's betrayal were weaving together into a seamless whole. Tris watched in awe as the strands of power blended together and the pain gradually subsided. Power from the healing river of energy surged into him, giving him the energy to sustain the link.

Suddenly, Tris felt as if his chest had been pierced by a sword. Panic overcame reason and he fought for control. Gasping for breath, he realized that he felt Carina's pain. Linked to her life force, Tris tried to blunt the worst of it, taking what he could onto himself until he cried out and every muscle strained. A searing wave of fire engulfed them. Tris could feel it consuming Carina, hear her screaming. Carina's life thread flickered wildly, slipping away. Tris wrapped his power around the dimming thread, drawing heavily from his own life energy until he felt both of their threads weaken.

The Flow roiled. Power beyond his imagining surged around them, lifting them up like an ocean wave. Tris redoubled his grasp on Carina's life thread and felt the Flow shift. Like a storm surge, the Flow rushed back, and Tris felt his whole body burn with wild magic as the Flow channeled its power through him, making their life threads glow brilliantly.

THE FLOW HAD become a maelstrom, howling like a blizzard wind. Carina felt her life force flicker wildly. Then she felt Tris wrap his power around her, supporting her with his magic and his own life energy. She knew Tris was tiring quickly, and she drew on Tris's power in the hope of sending one final burst of healing energy into the Flow.

Time meant nothing suspended in the infinite currents of the Flow's power. Gradually, the violent reds and oranges faded to more subdued hues of yellow and pink, and then calmed to the blue-green of the clearest ocean. The energy drew back from Carina and Tris. The Flow swirled around them as powerful as the tides. As the tempest subsided and the currents of the Flow became quiet, Carina felt Tris gently withdraw his power. The Flow became a sparkling curtain of light once more, and Carina realized she was lying on the floor of the shattered vault as the world grew dark around her.

In the darkness, she could still feel the Flow sustain her. An ethereal music called her back from unconsciousness, and Carina could feel the Flow all around her. Gone was the raging storm. The energy that pulsed around her was soothing and gentle. The magic of the Flow suffused her body, warming her. Gradually, the music faded. Carina drew a deep breath and opened her eyes.

She was in her own bedchamber, surrounded by her friends. Taru sat on the edge of her bed holding her hand as the others looked on with worried expressions. Raen glowed dimly in the corner, and at the edge of her senses, Carina could hear the ghost girl singing nervously to herself.

Tears glistened in Taru's eyes as she smoothed back the hair from Carina's face. "It worked," she said. "The Flow is healed—and so are you."

The memory of what she had witnessed through Malesh's eyes returned to Carina vividly enough to take her breath away and she began to sob. "He's dead. I saw him die."

Taru took her by the shoulders. "What are you talking about?"

Carina looked up, struggling to breathe through the tears. "Did you see when the light flared?"

"Yes, but—"

"The bond Riqua said was between Malesh and me, the bond between maker and fledgling, it was real. All of a sudden, I saw through Malesh's eyes. He was in a temple, with candles all around and a stained glass image of the Dark Lady. He and Jonmarc were fighting, and I saw Malesh sink his teeth into Jonmarc's neck. I *felt* it. And then, Jonmarc struck Malesh through the heart and I felt that, too. Malesh fell against the candles and he burned, and—Goddess help me!—I burned with him."

Taru and Riqua exchanged glances as Lisette gasped. Royster paled at the description and ran to thumb through a worn book on the desk. "What happened then?" Taru asked quietly as Carina struggled for control.

"Tris hung on to me and supported me with his magic. And then the Flow surged. It seemed to know... know what was happening." Carina turned to look at Riqua. "You were right about the bond."

Riqua's expression softened. "I am so sorry."

"The Flow is healed," Carina murmured. "Maybe now, Tris can win the war." She looked back to Riqua. "I saw a temple to Istra. It had a large stained glass portrait of the Dark Lady. Do you know where that temple is?"

Soberly, Riqua nodded. "In the hills, several candlemarks' ride from here. It's a sacred place for the *vayash moru*, for all who worship the Dark Lady. For Malesh to desecrate it with battle means that he really did mean to make the offering to Shanthadura. He thought the old legends were true, that he could become the consort of the Goddess. And for him to get that far means Gabriel and the *vyrkin* could not protect the temple. I'm afraid this evening's victory comes at a tremendous cost."

Carina bit back tears. "We don't dare send Kolin to Wolvenskorn after what happened last time, not with the mob at the gates and no idea where Malesh's fighters are. At dawn, I'll have Neirin see if two mortal guards can slip through and find out what's happened." She paused until she found her voice. "At least... perhaps they can bring back the bodies."

CHAPTER TWENTY-THREE

A PANOPLY OF colors and images that defied description danced through Tris's mind as he remained locked in the connection with Carina and the Flow. Time and place became meaningless as the cosmos seemed to bend around him. Gradually, the brilliant display faded and along with it the light that shone from Carina's thread. The Flow was whole, and Carina's life energy was stable. Completely weary, Tris withdrew his magic, following his own glowing life strand back to consciousness. He came to himself with a start. The candle in front of him burned steadily, barely lower than when he had begun the working, but the runes on the sword at his knees were blazing with cold fire.

Shaking from the exertion, Tris climbed to his feet and raised the sword, dismissing the wardings. He could hear Fallon chanting as she, too, released her warding. Only then did Tris realize that Coalan was also chanting, and he smiled tiredly as he recognized the words to a prayer very young children learned to banish shadows from under their beds. Coalan stopped suddenly, as if he only then realized they could hear him.

"What? It's the only chant I know," Coalan said defensively as Fallon helped Tris to a seat.

"Did it work?" Fallon asked anxiously. Tris could feel her magic wash over him, assuring her that he was undamaged. "Something happened, that's for sure."

Coalan pressed a glass of brandy into Tris's hand, and Tris downed it to steady his nerves as the aftermath of the powerful working gave him the shakes. After a moment, he found his voice and told them as best he could what had happened, finding that words were insufficient to fully describe the experience. "Thank you both," he said, setting the empty glass aside. "But Fallon and I had best get back to the fight."

"Are you up to it? A working like that should have you flat on your back."

Tris managed a wan smile. "Thank the Flow. I could feel it healing Carina—and it seemed to know that I was fading, too. It healed both of us. To tell you the truth, other than being a bit shaken, I feel better than I have in weeks." He sobered. "Which is a good thing. Once Curane's mages realize that the Flow is healed, I'm afraid they'll make a final strike with everything they've got left. We breached the wall in several more places. Their line can't hold much longer. One way or another, this ends tonight."

BEFORE HALF A candlemark had passed, Tris and Fallon rode back to the front lines. In the torchlight, Tris could see the pounding Lochlanimar had taken. Two more sections of the outer wall had fallen, and the Margolan forces now held a position closer to the fortification than before. The night smelled of pitch and smoke as the trebuchets lobbed large, tarred bundles of straw into the air which archers set afire in flight with flaming arrows. They streaked across the clear winter night sky like comets, landing between the inner and outer walls.

Around them, teams of men maneuvered catapults over the frozen ground for a better shot at the inner walls through the gaps in the outer fortifications. Once those inner walls were breached, Senne's soldiers were ready to storm through, along with the remaining *vayash moru* and the legion of ghost soldiers that were Margolan's own battle dead.

Tris sent out his magic to touch Tabok. *Are you in position?*

Aye, Tris heard the ghost's reply. *Mohr's been tearing the place apart, throwing whatever he*

*can move. He drove soldiers out of one wing
of the castle by hurling pots and pans at them.
And he flooded the cellar with wine and ale by
popping the corks and splitting the barrels.*

*I don't know when I'll need you, so be ready
for the signal.*

As you wish, my king.

The spirits from the necropolis beneath
Lochlanimar did not speak in words, but the
images they sent as their restless energies swept
through the the walled keep told Tris that they,
too, were committed to ending the battle this
night. Fallon, Vira and Beyral, the remaining
mages, were ready to join their magic with
Tris's for a last salvo. Tris looked up as a horse
and rider came up beside him and he recognized
Soterius.

"You're not supposed to be out of bed."

Soterius gave a harsh laugh. "Neither are
you."

"Shows how well we listen."

"Is everything in place?"

Tris nodded. At ninth bells, the final full press
to take Lochlanimar would begin. Tris knew
how badly his own forces were stretched, and
the ghosts within the stronghold had informed
him that Curane's resources were even thinner.
Whichever side survived this night would take
the victory, and Tris could only guess how high
the cost in blood would be.

"Where do you need me?"

Tris met Soterius's eyes, and knew that his friend was well aware of how much was at stake this night. "Senne's covered the front press. Rallan has the rear and west. The mages and I will also be at the front—the ghosts say it's closest to the mages' workshop, and we'll make the best strike against them from that angle. That leaves the east without a senior officer. We've got several catapults in place, lobbing whatever we can burn over the walls."

Soterius smiled tightly. "Then that's where I'll go." He paused. "Be careful, Tris. Out of all of us, you're the one who has to make it home in one piece."

Tris clasped his forearm. "I intend to bring as many home with me as I can. Watch your back." Soterius nodded, and rode off.

A sense of foreboding washed over Tris as the candlemarks passed. Curane's response to their attacks had been muted at best, without the all-out counteroffensive Tris expected. There could be only one reason: Curane was saving his waning resources for a final strike. And knowing Curane, Tris feared that the traitor lord would not hesitate to sacrifice his own people in a doomsday maneuver.

The winter night was filled with the squeal of trebuchet wheels and the shouts of soldiers. Torchlight and bonfires cast dancing shadows across snow fouled with soot and blood. The hard-frozen ground allowed them to move the huge war machines with relative ease, although heavy snow made it slow going. At the gates of Lochlanimar, a new battering ram swung from its frame, beating a steady, pounding rhythm that seemed to reverberate in Tris's bones. Hewn from the largest tree to be found within two days' ride, it was plated with as much scrap iron as could be spared, and a metal roof cobbled together of leather and steel shielded the soldiers beneath it from a rain of flaming arrows and boiling water.

In the distance, Tris heard the camp gong strike nine times. Just as he wheeled his horse to confer with Fallon and Beyral, he felt a pulse in the currents of magic. It didn't come from the direction of Lochlanimar, and it didn't come from the Flow. Images filled his mind, brief flashes that were there and gone, and Tris knew with cold certainty that they touched the part of his mind that had made a bond with Kiara.

Tris glimpsed Bricen's hunting lodge. He felt Kiara's fear and glimpsed the same *damashqi* blade that he had seen in his dreams, only this time, it was stained with blood. An instant of vertigo washed over him, as if his magic were pushed beyond reach by wormroot. He heard Kiara scream and saw her fall backward. Instinctively, he reached for her, but his power dissipated in the Nether. The image winked out, leaving Tris gripping the reins of his horse white-knuckled, as his vision returned and only the battlefield lay before him.

"Are you all right?" Fallon had ridden up beside him.

Tris turned toward her, ashen. "Kiara's in trouble. I felt it in the soulbond we made. If my power can reach Dark Haven, why can't it reach Shekerishet?"

"The Flow doesn't run beneath Shekerishet as it does beneath Dark Haven. Its power spreads wide, but it is strongest in its course, like a river. The next nearest energy river runs through Isencroft and down into the Southlands through the far west corner of Trevath. Shekerishet's site was chosen for defense, not for magic. Even the Flow has its limits," Fallon said.

Tris struggled to gain control of the panic that roiled within him, fear that had nothing to do with the battle. *I don't care what Crevan says. I don't care if the rumors are true. She's my wife and she's carrying my child—and I love her. I swore I would defend her and I've failed.* The vision eluded his attempts to see more. He stared bleakly down at the rebel stronghold. *I may save my kingdom and my crown tonight, but if Kiara dies, I don't know if I have the will to carry on. Goddess help me! The crown drains everything, and gives nothing in return.*

"Look there!" Fallon's cry shook Tris from his brooding. Just outside the front gate of Lochlanimar, a whirlwind of fire began to coalesce, growing quickly from swirling sparks into a howling vortex.

"Fire Elemental," Tris breathed. He could hear Senne and Rallan shouting for retreat above the panic of men and horses already stampeding toward the rear, fleeing an enemy no courage could stand against. Tris met Fallon's eyes.

"No," Fallon said, wide-eyed. "Even you can't hold that off alone."

"We have no choice. See if you and Beyral can conjure up some kind of barrier to shield the men. Although, if it reaches the camp, it will have already gotten past me, so—" The rest went unspoken. If it reached that far, a rout was certain.

"The Lady's hand be upon you," Fallon said, raising her hand in blessing. Tris dug his heels into his horse's side and urged his mount forward at a gallop as his soldiers ran past him for their lives.

The Elemental was moving slowly but gathering power. It had more than doubled in size since it appeared, and Tris could feel the blood magic that conjured it even at a distance. When his panicked horse would take him no further, Tris dismounted and let it run. On the blackened and trampled plain of battle, Tris stood alone and awaited the firestorm.

It was easier than he thought to silence his emotions. Battle coldness filled him, focused on his mission, indifferent to his own survival. Tris raised the sword he brought with him from his earlier working, the sword once wielded by

Bava K'aa. It thrummed in his grip, resonating with his magic. The runes along its blade flowed with inner fire as Tris began to chant a warding. Elementals were difficult to conjure and draining to maintain. The longer he could keep the Elemental from destroying his troops, the greater the strain on the mages sustaining it. He hoped he had the strength to outlast Curane's mages.

Tris raised a double warding, one layer of protection around himself and another curtain of power to keep the Elemental from moving past him toward the camp. Though invisible to others, he could see the shimmer of power in the cold winter air. It seemed thin protection against the rapidly growing wall of fire that was rushing across the battlefield. The Elemental moved relentlessly, its flames so hot that the wagons and war machines exploded. The Elemental moved through a haze of steam, vaporizing the snow with a loud hiss as it scorched the ground beneath it.

Tris felt his heart pound as the wall of flame grew closer. His training had been admittedly lopsided; skewed toward defeating a single powerful opponent. Now, he was painfully aware of the gaps in his magical education. He braced himself and focused all of his will and his magic on his wardings as the fire engulfed him.

Flames licked at the blue-white dome of his shielding, crackling against his power. Tris had to avert his eyes as the ball of fire became both sky and horizon. Despite his protections, the temperature within his warded dome began rising quickly. The Elemental's fury pounded at his protections, requiring all of his concentration to hold the magic in place. Raw, unreasoning power battered his defenses, and Tris remembered what Soterius had told him about the air Elemental he had once faced. Nothing, not even the Sisterhood, could turn an Elemental until it was recalled by the mage who sent it.

Sweat dripped from Tris's face and he loosened his cloak, letting it fall from his shoulders. His shirt was soaked, and his mouth was dry. He might die from the heat within his own wardings before the flames could take him, Tris thought, struggling to keep hold of the magic. The Elemental was straining his wardings, and Tris knew he could not hold them indefinitely. His head ached from both the heat and the stress of magic. He gritted his teeth and drew from his life force, doubling the effort. If his defenses failed, the Margolan army would be completely destroyed, overtaken by the unyielding flames before they had a chance to flee.

The sword thrummed in his hands, and Tris shielded his eyes, looking down at the blade. Amid the maelstrom of magic, the runes on its blade flared brighter than ever, and Tris remembered the words Taru had spoken when she gave it to him at his coronation. *This was the sword of Bava K'aa. You may find it harbors a vestige of her power, as well as her memory.* Wary of the sword's unknown abilities, Tris had not carried it into battle before this. Its runes had eluded even Royster's attempts to translate. But now, as he felt his strength fading, Tris grasped the sword tightly, and let his power course through it. As he did so, the runes seemed to rearrange themselves until the fiery writing appeared as Margolense, written in fine script.

"I am Nexus. Bound by blood and wrought by will, the spirit remains to conquer."

And in that same moment, his power touched something within the blade that flared to his sight in the Plains of Spirit and he saw a ghostly image of his grandmother. *The blade remembers magic,* he heard her voice in his mind. *But beware. The price is a breath from your soul.* An image formed in his mind of the blade making a cut across his palm.

Well aware that his wardings were weakening fast, Tris took a deep breath and drew Nexus across the open palm of his right hand. The blade glowed white for an instant, and Tris felt a shift in his soul. Nexus now appeared in his hand as he saw his essence on the Plains of Spirit.

Tris focused on the gleaming sword blade and let his magic call out to the Flow. No longer wild and damaged, the river of power undulated in his mage sight like the Spirit Lights. Using Nexus, Tris drew the Flow toward him, twining his own power with that of the river of energy, concentrated into a blue-white stream of magic that erupted from the tip of Nexus' blade as Tris's inner warding shattered.

The heat of the fire Elemental seared his lungs and blistered his skin. An instant later, the combined power of the sword and the Flow's energy created a shield wall that enabled Tris to stagger to his feet. And while he was holding the Elemental at bay, Tris knew that the cost of channeling the Flow through his body was burning him out quickly.

One desperate idea formed in his mind. He remembered Soterius's recount of defeating the air Elemental by distracting the mage who called it. Tris's head ached so badly that it was becoming difficult to form his thoughts, but he called out to the ghost Mohr within Lochlanimar.

Can you find the mages who called the Elemental?

At first, only silence answered him. Finally, he felt Mohr's spirit. *Aye.*

Throw something at them. Anything. Break their concentration. Do it now!

Power unlike anything he had wielded before coursed through him and found its vent in Nexus until Tris felt as if his entire being had ceased to be flesh and bone and existed only as raw, pure magic. Without the newly-healed Flow, Tris knew he would have been consumed by that untamed power, but the glistening energy of the Flow sustained him, though he felt the effort draining him badly.

A sudden flash of white light over Lochlanimar lit the cold night air. The Elemental flared blindingly bright, and then rushed back like a storm tide toward the embattled keep with a deafening roar. The wall of flames hit Lochlanimar all at once, sending its energies the length of the walled fortress and lancing high into the night sky like a beacon.

A wave of unbearable pain forced Tris to his knees as the last of his warding shattered. From the burning wreckage of Lochlanimar, Tris could feel the souls burn loose from their cindered bodies as the fiery cataclysm reduced every living thing within the fortress's walls to ash. Wrenched with them onto the Plains of Spirit, Tris saw the souls stream into the Nether bearing the charred flesh and the blackened skin of their death wounds; men, women, children and elders. As flames consumed Lochlanimar, Tris despaired at the hundreds of lives claimed by the Elemental as it returned to its place of sending.

Their blood is on my hands, Tris thought as the innocent dead fixed him in their baleful glare. *Goddess help me. There was no other way.*

No longer certain whether he was alive or dead himself, Tris did the only thing that remained within his power as Summoner to do; he began to speak the passing over ritual. In the distance, he could hear the faint strains of the Lady's soulsong. As his power opened up the gateways to the Aspects, the dead began to drift away toward their rest. Yet of the mages, Cadoc and Dirmed, there was no trace, nor did Tris sense the presence of Curane's soul. For the first time, his own spirit feared the judgment of the Goddess. He tensed, awaiting the Dark Aspects, but soon the Plains of Spirit were empty and the sweet soulsong faded into nothing.

Conscience is its own inquisitor. Tris heard a voice say in his mind, and he knew that the terror and pain he felt from the murdered residents of Lochlanimar would haunt his dreams for the rest of his life.

Just as suddenly as he had shifted onto the Plains of Spirit, Tris felt himself return to his own body. Nexus fell from his hand, and the supporting magic of the Flow swept away from him. Tris crumpled to the scorched ground, completely drained.

CHAPTER TWENTY-FOUR

CARROWAY LISTENED TO the city bells chime as he paced in his room above the Dragon's Rage Inn. He had tried—and abandoned—several distractions. Neither music nor books could still his restlessness or dispel the sense of foreboding that filled him. The smell of roasting mutton filled the air from the kitchen below as the inn filled with patrons for Candles Night. And although Carroway was certain the innkeeper would reserve a plate of the evening's fare for him, even the delectable smells could not overcome the knot in his stomach.

When the door to the passageway opened unexpectedly, he spun to face it. Paiva's eyes widened as she and Bandele closed the door behind them. "Sweet Mother and Childe,

Carroway! You're jumpier than an old hen."

"You're early," he said, ignoring her comment. "Does that mean you have news?"

Paiva smiled conspiratorially and gestured for them to move to the corner farthest from the guards' post outside the door. She set the basket of food she had brought on the table. "I broke into Crevan's office."

Carroway felt the blood drain from his face. "You did what?"

Paiva shushed him. "Keep your voice down. Bandele watched the corridor while I picked the lock." She shrugged at his sideways glance. "I was on my own for quite a while before Macaria brought me to the palace. You learn things. Anyhow, we knew Crevan would be tied up down in the kitchen seeing to Candles Night. So it was the best chance we were going to get."

"And?"

Paiva withdrew two stacks of sealed parchments from beneath the food in her basket, each tied with twine. She handed them to Carroway, who felt his hands begin to shake as he recognized the writing on the first stack. "That's Tris's handwriting," he whispered. "And the other stack is in Kiara's hand. I don't understand."

"You know how Kiara has been pining because she hasn't received a letter from the king since he left for battle?" Bandele said, her eyes flashing. "Turns out, that's not exactly true.

Count the letters in that stack—all sealed with the king's signet and addressed to her. There's one there for each week. Only they never got further than Crevan's office."

Paiva lifted the other stack. "These are the queen's letters—but they never got put in the packets that went to the king. I found them in a false bottom beneath the trunk he keeps in his office." She looked rather proud of herself. "Still have the touch," she said, dusting off her hands as she returned the unopened letters to Carroway.

"Want to bet Crevan didn't want the king to know what's really going on here—the attacks on Kiara, locking up you and Mikhail and Bian? Zachar and Malae dead. Kiara would have mentioned all of that and Crevan couldn't take the chance," Bandele added.

Carroway nodded slowly. "I can see that. But what of Tris's letters for Kiara?"

Bandele met his eyes. "What better way to make her feel completely alone than to make her think her new husband can't be bothered to write to her? Besides, Crevan couldn't take the chance that Tris might say something in one of his own letters that made it clear he wasn't getting Kiara's letters."

"That's not all," Paiva said smugly. "I found something else in Crevan's desk." She reached into her pocket to withdraw a small item wrapped in rags. An oddly-shaped metal implement spilled out onto the table. It had two sharpened conical points attached to a ring big enough to fit over a man's two fingers.

"What's that?" Carroway said, reaching out to touch it before Paiva smacked his hand clear.

"Watch out! They're sharp. Take another look at them." She picked up a stale roll from the table and slipped the metal ring over her two fingers, then stabbed the points into the roll. "Look like anything to you?"

Carroway swallowed hard. "Puncture marks. Like a *vayash moru* might leave in a victim's neck."

Paiva nodded. "Mikhail said the marks didn't look right. But at first glance, if the shape and spacing was about right, who's going to look harder? People see what they want to see." Her face darkened. "There was one other thing, but I couldn't bring it. I found it in a locked box in Crevan's drawer. Managed to get the lock opened, but even I could tell the thing inside had some kind of curse on it, and I've got no magic in my bones at all. I'm not scared of much, but you couldn't have paid me enough gold to set my hand on that awful thing!"

"What was it?"

"A dagger, the likes of which I've never seen. Had a handle made from what looked like human bone. But it was the blade that caught my eye. The steel had lines in it, wavy and folded, as if someone had made a design in it. The lines seemed to blur and move when I looked hard at them, and I could swear when I listened closely, I could hear voices in the distance." She shivered. "I couldn't tell what they were saying, and I didn't want to know. I was scared to death. Never put anything back where I found it so quickly in all my life."

Carroway walked across the room to pull down a book from the shelf near his bed. He flipped through the yellowed pages until he came to the drawing he sought. "Did it look like this?" he asked, pointing.

Paiva nodded. "That's it. Good as its twin, it is."

Carroway's hands were shaking as he set the book aside. "Was Crevan still at Shekerishet when you left?"

Paiva and Bandele exchanged puzzled glances. "Yes, but he was just getting ready to leave. He was going up to the hunting lodge to take the feast night dinner to the queen." Carroway gave a low groan and they looked at him in alarm.

"He's going to use that dagger to kill Kiara tonight. The evil you sensed from the blade must be blood magic." Glancing nervously toward the door, Carroway read them the passage from the book in a low tone. Bandele covered her mouth with her hand to stifle her exclamation.

"What can we do? Halik and Tadghe haven't returned yet with Harrtuck. No one will believe us—and that goes double for you," Paiva said, gripping Carroway's arm.

Carroway shut the book and set it aside. "I've got to stop him."

"You can't! You go anywhere near the queen and the guards have orders to kill you on sight," Bandele whispered.

"There's no one else to do it. How can I stay here, knowing what's going to happen? That would be a true betrayal." He shook his head. "If Crevan hasn't left yet, I just might make it in time to warn Kiara and Macaria before he arrives. I might be able to slip past the guards so that no one sees me except Kiara. If they're warned they can defend themselves. I can be safely back here before anyone knows I'm gone."

Bandele cleared her throat. "Nice plan, except for the guards at the door. They're friendly enough, but I doubt they'll let you out of here, even with a story like that one."

"Then again…" They turned to look at Paiva, who had a guilty expression on her face. She reached beneath her cloak into her bodice, drawing a small vial of indigo liquid from between her breasts. "It's sleeping potion. I got it from the hedge witch when I was asking around about the herbs we found in the kitchen. Thought it might be handy to have on hand, just in case."

"Just in case of a jail break?" Bandele hissed.

Paiva unwrapped the food in the basket she had brought from the palace. Inside was a warm meat pasty, fresh pastries with cheese and a bottle of aged Cartelasian brandy. "Nicked the bottle on the way out of the kitchen. Figured the guards might have some good food from the inn given the feast night, but no one pours a brandy like this for the help."

"Did you have anything in mind after you put the guards to sleep?" Bandele asked with an edge to her voice.

"I figured Carroway could improvise something."

Carroway grinned at Paiva's audacity. "All right. Here goes. I tie the two of you up, so that if this goes wrong you can say I overpowered you. Then I take Bandele's cloak—she's tall enough that it should cover most of me. With the feast crowd, no one should give me a second look if I hunch over and keep the hood up. I'll slip down the back stairs and steal a horse. I should be at the lodge within a candlemark."

Bandele looked appalled. "They hang horse thieves in Margolan, you know."

Carroway fixed her with a sideways glare. "If I get caught, I'll have an arrow through my chest or a knife in my back. Hanging's the least of my worries." He fetched two mugs for Paiva and watched as she poured a liberal draught into each one and then emptied half of the vial into the cups in turn.

She gave each a swirl and looked up with a guileless smile. "Shall we give the boys their feast day treat?"

Carroway and Bandele hung well back from the door as Paiva fixed a plate for the guards to go with the brandy. She tugged at her dress to make the bodice scandalously revealing, flirting coyly with the guards as she teased and joked before giving them their drugged repast. She closed the door and leaned against it, all coquettishness gone from her manner. Paiva put a finger to her lips and kept her ear to the door. Before long, there were two heavy thuds from the other side.

"You're dangerous," Bandele said, only partially joking. She stripped off her heavy woolen cloak as Carroway looked around the room for a belt and a sash to tie them with. He dug into the trunk that held his things to find the daggers that were hidden in the lining, and slipped them into his belt. Within a few minutes, he had bound and loosely gagged both of his friends and wrapped himself in Bandele's cloak.

"Hurry," Paiva said, her voice muffled through the cloth. "Get out of here before the innkeeper decides to bring up your supper."

"Wish me luck," Carroway whispered with more certainty than he felt as he slipped from the room, locking the door behind him.

"THAT'S THE SIXTH hand of *tarle* you've won tonight!" Macaria exclaimed. Kiara set her cards down triumphantly. "Honestly, if you weren't queen you could earn a living as a card sharp!"

Kiara, Macaria and Cerise sat around a low table near the fire in the great room of Bricen's hunting lodge. Compared with Shekerishet, the room was closer to the size of a parlor, sufficient for a hunting party to feast on the spoils of their hunt. Kiara grinned at Macaria.

"I spent a large part of the winter cooped up in a library in Principality last year," she said. "While Tris trained, all the rest of us had was salle practice and card games to pass the time." She laughed. "And if you think I play a bloodthirsty game of cards, don't ever make a bet with Berwyn of Principality. She actually beat Jonmarc a few times."

When the laughter subsided, Macaria stretched and sniffed the air. "I don't know what Alle has the cook making for dinner, but it smells wonderful." As if on cue, the mastiff that sprawled at Macaria's feet stretched and stood, wagging its tail. He padded to the door, and the two wolfhounds followed him, heading in the direction of the kitchen. On the hearth, Jae lifted his head and looked around, then curled back up and went to sleep.

Kiara sighed. "Candles Night was a minor holiday in Isencroft, but it was still an excuse for jousting and bonfires."

"Name one holiday in Isencroft that *isn't* an excuse for jousting and bonfires," Cerise replied drolly. "Now that I've heard more about how the other kingdoms celebrate, I've started to think that Isencroft is ever-so-slightly less than creative."

"You're probably right. Between the jousts and the legends of the warriors of yore, we do seem a bit focused on things military."

"Really? Hadn't noticed," Cerise deadpanned.

"On the other hand," Kiara said, enjoying the harmless sparring, "I haven't seen quite so good a joust since I left Isencroft. Maybe all that practice makes perfect."

"I don't miss freezing my rump off watching grown men beat at each other with sticks," Cerise rejoined. "But I've been hungry for the mincemeat pie and for Cook's mutton roasted in ale since the snow began to fall."

Kiara leaned back in her chair. "If I'm going to have mutton, I like the little balls Cook made with dates and cloves and currants in them. It covered up the mutton taste!"

Outside, the bells in the distance chimed the eighth hour. "I thought Crevan said he'd be out with some of the palace goodies," Macaria said. She stood and moved away from the fire, walking to the window and pulling back the heavy draperies. "He's quite late. I thought he'd ride out before nightfall."

Kiara shrugged. "He probably got detained taking care of one issue or another. Honestly, with the feast going on, I'm surprised he planned to come at all."

Just then, Alle came to the door with a pleased

expression on her face. "Ladies," she said with a flourish, "dinner is served."

Alle joined them and they took their places at the table as the cook and her assistant began to bring out the food. A platter of crispels in honey and pokerounce with a thick spread of dates was served with mugs of warm watered wine, followed by an almond egg custard and spicy stuffed eggs. Two steaming crocks followed, one of peas porridge and the other of stewed cabbage and onions. Finally, the cook presented a platter of roasted lamb seasoned with wine and currants and Kiara and the others gave a round of applause. When the cook reappeared a few moments later with ramekins of warm almond rice milk with cinnamon and fig pies basted in spiced honey, Kiara and the others exchanged glances at the bounty.

"A magnificent groaning board!" Kiara pronounced, and the cook beamed at the praise. "But surely, you didn't expect four women to eat all this?"

"You're eating for the young prince as well, m'lady," the cook said with a glance to Kiara's belly.

"Fair enough," she laughed. "But there's only one in there, not a hungry legion! You've done yourself proud. I promise there will be more than enough for you and the guards to feast as well."

"Thank you, m'lady," the cook said, smiling broadly at the praise. "Now please, enjoy while it's hot. There'll be a round of wassail to drink with the desserts."

Alle and Macaria made certain that Kiara's plate was heaping full. They laughed and talked, remarking on the ingenuity of the cook to put so fine a meal together without the resources of the full castle kitchen.

Finally, when they could eat no more, Kiara pushed back from the table. "Goddess true! I feel like I should spend the next week in the salle working off a dinner like this one. I'll need a stouter horse to carry me back to Shekerishet if you feed me like this too often!"

Alle chuckled and set aside her napkin. "I'll give the cook your regards," she said, rising. "And if Jae wants to come with me, I dare say the cook will have some leavings for him—that's where those greedy dogs are, I wager." She reached for Jae and the little gyregon flapped his leathery wings once, then settled down and let her gently pick him up. "Let me go check on something." Alle grinned. "I asked Cook to make one of my favorites—little cakes with a charm inside for good luck. I brought the charms with me from Aunt Eadoin's. It's said that you may know your fortune for the month by the charm in your cake." She excused herself and went toward the kitchen, which was in a separate building just outside the main lodge.

"This may be the best time to get some herbs from the cellar," Cerise said, standing. "If I wait much longer, I'll be too full to move and as wonderful as this feast was, I'd rather not find my way to the bottom of those steps in the dead of night if your stomach decides to disagree with you!"

Kiara and Macaria sat in silence, staring at the ample food that remained on the table. "I was just thinking of how many nights we ate salt pork and hard biscuits on the road outrunning Jared's troops," Kiara said, shifting in her chair to find a more comfortable position. "I don't think I'll ever take a meal like this for granted again after that."

Macaria laughed. "When we minstrels fled the palace, we played for our supper in taverns far enough from the palace to avoid the king's eye. Many a night the meat didn't bear too close a look, and you didn't want to scrape away the sauce to see what was underneath. Those times make a good tale, but they weren't something I'd like to repeat."

Outside, Tris's dogs began barking loudly. Kiara moved to the window. "Funny," she said. "I don't see anything out there."

"Come back by the fire," Macaria urged. "They've probably spotted a stag in the woods." After a few moments, the barking subsided and Kiara took a chair by the hearth. Macaria went to the corner of the room to fetch her lute. Just as she returned, footsteps in the doorway made them turn. Crevan entered, his face flushed with the outside cold and his eyes bright.

"We'd just about given up on you making it tonight," Kiara greeted him. "Late for you to come all this way."

"It's Candles Night," Crevan replied, still warming his hands in the pockets of his cloak. "I wouldn't have missed it."

"Come over by the fire and tell us the news from Shekerishet," Kiara said, motioning toward a chair. "The good news, at least."

"I can't stay long," Crevan said as he joined them. Macaria's head was bent over her lute as she tuned it, but something in Crevan's voice made Kiara pause.

"Is there a problem?"

Crevan gave a tight-lipped smile. "Not after tonight." Moving more quickly than she had ever seen the seneschal move, Crevan stabbed a dart into Kiara's shoulder. As Kiara gasped, Crevan wheeled, grabbing a pewter pitcher and slamming it against Macaria's temple. Macaria went down hard, landing on her lute which splintered into pieces beneath her.

Crevan backed away a few steps as Kiara groped for the dart in her shoulder and came away with bloodied fingers. The room was beginning to spin around her and she felt sick. Her entire body felt by turns cold and hot. Kiara tried to rise from her chair but her body refused to obey her thoughts.

"I didn't know the true extent of your regent magic, but that dose of wormroot should be sufficient to stop even a mage like the king," Crevan said as he watched her struggle. "It's a kinder poison than what I gave to the guards—and to those troublesome dogs. Don't expect the others to barge in and save you. The healer is locked in the cellar, and the others are locked in the kitchen. They won't be going anywhere for a while."

Kiara struggled for words against the drugs that dulled her senses. "Why?"

"Because Isencroft must be free." From the folds of his cloak, Crevan withdrew an ornate dagger with a strange, patterned blade. "Your father thought I was the perfect spy. And I was—for Curane and the divisionists. With you out of the way, we can go back to the natural order of things. No heir, no joint kingdom. As it should be."

Crevan raised the knife and it glittered in the firelight. "The blade eliminates the threat to Isencroft, while your blood shed this night seals the magic that will defeat King Martris." He smiled, moving forward. "Don't move, and I'll make this quick."

The whirr of a blade was the only warning as a throwing knife arced across the room and struck Crevan between the shoulders. Kiara's eyes widened as the blade bounced harmlessly aside, making a cut in his cloak that revealed a cuirass beneath Crevan's shirt. With a growl, Crevan turned. Carroway stood in the doorway. He looked more frightened than Kiara had ever seen him, but his blue eyes were resolute.

"Get away from her, Crevan. I'll have no conscience over killing you."

Crevan began to laugh. "This is better than I expected. I didn't see a way for me to avoid the blame, but now you've given me an alibi. The spurned lover, come to take his vengeance. A struggle, and you both die. What a pity that I arrive too late to stop it from happening."

Carroway ran at Crevan with a shout, his own dagger raised to strike. With unexpected agility, Crevan dodged the blow and knocked Carroway off balance. As Carroway reached for the table to steady himself, Crevan stabbed down with the blade, pinning Carroway's left hand to the heavy oak table. Carroway twisted in pain, trying to free his hand from the knife that was sunk deep into the hard wood. Crevan took up a carving knife from beside the mutton roast and stepped over Macaria to move closer to Kiara.

"Crevan, no!" Carroway shouted as Crevan lurched forward, stabbing down toward Kiara's belly as she tried to throw herself out of his way. There was a rustle from the floor, and a blur of motion. Crevan stiffened, eyes wide, as blood gurgled from his lips. The shattered neck of a wooden lute protruded from his throat, and he crumpled to the floor. Macaria staggered, bleeding on one side of her head, her hand covered with Crevan's blood. In the distance, the bells tolled nine times.

Carroway gripped the hilt of the dagger in his right hand and wrested it from the table with a cry. His freed hand was bleeding badly and he wrapped it in a discarded napkin from the table as Macaria knelt next to Kiara. Blood stained the side of her gown, and Kiara's eyes were wide and her pupils large.

"Is she—"

Macaria knelt next to Kiara and gingerly pulled the carving knife free. "He sliced through her gown and there's a gash in her side that's bleeding pretty badly, but the blade went into the back of the chair, thank the Lady."

Pounding bootsteps behind them made Carroway and Macaria turn. Both of them stepped protectively in front of Kiara.

"Hold it right there."

Five Margolan guardsmen, crossbows notched and ready, filled the room. Carroway and Macaria raised their hands in surrender and Carroway saw two of the bowmen train their weapons on his heart. "Our orders were to shoot on sight," the bowman said, raising his hand for the signal.

"Belay that!" A stout man shouldered past the guards, sword in hand. Harrtuck pushed his way into the room. "I'll have the skin of anyone who fires on them. Weapons down!"

"Sir?"

"Are you hard of hearing? Put down your weapons."

"You've got to find Cerise," Carroway said, daring to take a step so that Harrtuck could see where Kiara lay slumped in the chair. "Kiara's hurt badly."

"She's locked in the cellar," Macaria said, reaching to steady herself as she eased into a chair. Carroway stepped aside, cradling his wounded hand close to his body as the soldiers rushed in to take over the scene and two men left to free Cerise and the others. Harrtuck walked over to him, shaking his head.

"What a mess."

"I take it Halik and Tadghe reached you?"

Harrtuck rubbed his beard. "Aye. I had a feeling in my bones we shouldn't have left the queen when Crevan sent us out to put down that uprising. And I was right. It was hardly more than a feast day riot. We turned around to come back as quickly as we locked up the handful of troublemakers, and we were only a day's ride out from the city when your two friends came riding like the Crone Herself was chasing them." He chuckled. "Believe me when I say that it's the first time I've had bards ride down a guard squadron. I took half the group and rode for the lodge, and sent the other half to the palace, just in case." He shook his head, stepping back to make way for Cerise to reach Kiara. "I'm only sorry we didn't get here sooner."

"Thanks for not shooting me."

Harrtuck's expression sobered. "I can't lift Crevan's order of banishment, although I can explain why we didn't follow his directions to the letter. But I'm afraid I'll have to take you back to the palace and put you under arrest until Tris comes back."

Carroway swallowed hard and nodded. His hand throbbed, making it difficult to think clearly, and blood was soaking through the napkin he had wadded against the wound. The slightest motion of his fingers sent excruciating pain up his arm.

He watched as Cerise felt for Kiara's pulse and called for a guard to bring her healer's bag from her room. "Will she be all right?" Harrtuck asked as Cerise ripped a large enough hole in the side of Kiara's gown to treat the wound.

"It's a deep cut, but the point of the blade went into the chair. She'll be sore, but it's not the gash that worries me. She's not reacting right."

"Crevan drugged her with wormroot," Macaria said. She held a cloth against her bleeding temple and was pale enough that Carroway thought she might pass out. "He hit me with the pitcher, and it stunned me. It's good I have a hard head."

"You're luckier than the guards," Harrtuck

said, his voice roughened from the weather. "They're both dead in the guardhouse—poisoned. One of the dogs is dead and the other two looked mighty ill. I'm betting Crevan brought them poisoned meat to shut them up."

"Crevan said he'd locked Alle and the servants in the kitchen," Carroway said, not taking his eyes from where Cerise labored over Kiara. Harrtuck barked an order to one of the guards, who left immediately to free the others. Alle joined them in a few minutes, with Jae perched on her shoulder. The little gyregon gave a shrill cry and flew to perch on the top of Kiara's chair. Alle took one look at Macaria and Carroway and left the room, only to return with a bowl of water and strips of cloth for binding. Carroway motioned for her to take care of Macaria first.

"Looks like you'll have a goose egg tomorrow, but it's not as bad as it could be," Alle said, wiping the blood from Macaria's temple and giving her a cool wet cloth to hold against the injury.

Alle grimaced as she glanced at Carroway's hand. "That's beyond my skill. When I patched up bar fights with the Resistance, I left the bad stuff for the healers. But I can get you something for the pain." She went to a cabinet at the far side of the room and returned with a bottle of whiskey. Carroway bit back a curse as she gingerly daubed the wound with water to clean it and then splashed it with whiskey. She poured an ample amount of the amber liquid into a cup and pressed it into his good hand. "Drink this before we have to carry you out, too."

Cerise straightened and stood. They grew silent and looked at her, fearful of what she might say. "Kiara's life isn't in danger, but the wormroot dose he gave her was massive. She's drugged to a stupor, and I have no idea what that will do to the baby." She looked to Harrtuck. "There's no point in keeping her here, since Crevan was the danger. It would be best to get her back to the palace."

"There's a wagon in the barn," Alle said. "We can leave in the morning if there's no hurry. We're not in much shape to meet up with wolves on the way back by night."

Cerise nodded. "Agreed. And in the meantime," she said, "I'll see to the two of you as best I can," she said with a look to Macaria and Carroway.

Harrtuck gave terse orders to his men. He turned back to Carroway and the others. "I'm sorry we didn't get here earlier." He looked down at Crevan's body. "We'll get that out of your way and take it back with us." Harrtuck gave an apologetic look to Carroway. "And I know it doesn't make any sense, but technically, I need to put you under arrest."

Macaria looked up sharply, her eyes worried. Carroway gave a slight shake of his head. "I understand," he said, wishing the whiskey did more for the pain.

"Surely you can leave him with me long enough for healing," Cerise said, glancing at Harrtuck from where she knelt next to Macaria.

"For my money, I'd leave him free on his own judgment. But I can't undo the seneschal's edict, and I don't want to make it any worse on him than it already is," Harrtuck muttered.

Carroway found himself holding his breath as Cerise turned her attention to his hand. She said nothing, and even her gentle touch was agonizing. His hand curled protectively around the gash through his palm, and straightening out his fingers to let her see the wound made him cry out through gritted teeth. Cerise was silent as she applied a poultice, and Carroway felt her healer's magic closing skin and knitting together tissue. Gradually, the worst of the pain subsided, although the slightest movement of his fingers made his whole hand throb.

"I've healed the flesh and sinew, but a hand is a delicate thing," Cerise said. Carroway felt his heart thud in his throat. "I don't know how that will affect motion."

"Can I play again?" Carroway asked in a strangled voice, looking at the pieces of Macaria's lute that littered the floor.

Cerise met his eyes. "I don't know. We'll have to see how it goes. I'm sorry I can't do more."

Carroway couldn't bear the look in Macaria's eyes as she gasped at Cerise's words. Macaria reached out to take his uninjured hand, and he knew that she understood just how great a loss it was to him. She pressed his hand against her cheek and brushed her lips against it.

"I'm glad you're all right," he said quietly, giving her hand a squeeze. She returned a wan smile, and he knew she realized how thin his control was right now.

Harrtuck laid a hand on his shoulder. "C'mon, lad. Let's get some sleep. We'll put your arm in a sling tomorrow, so you can handle the reins with the other hand. Don't fret. I've busted up my fingers plenty of times, and I still grip a tankard of ale just fine."

CHAPTER TWENTY-FIVE

WHEN THE DIVISIONISTS didn't bother to push a bowl of gruel and a cup of water into his makeshift cell, Cam took the meaning of the sign immediately. No use feeding someone who was going to die.

It had taken Cam most of a candlemark to wrestle Siarl's body onto the bales of wool that packed most of their prison room. Now, he waited, watching as the pale rays of winter sun moved across the floor of his cell through the gaps between the boards.

Outside, he heard Leather John and Ruggs. "The men aren't happy about this," Leather John said. "You've let the king trap us here like rats. So much for your 'glorious' rebellion if we all die."

"*Your* men have less spine than a gaggle of milk maids. *My* men understand that we've drawn the king into a trap. You heard what the runner said—we're in place to make the valley expensive for Donelan."

"Unless your friend Curane wins his war, that does nothing to free Isencroft. The traitor princess is still married to the king of Margolan. Whether she's here or in Margolan makes no difference. What matters is that the crown of Isencroft remains in Isencroft," Leather John argued.

"I received a message Crevan sent by pigeon just yesterday. By now, he's eliminated both the princess and the heir. Donelan will have no choice except to declare war on Margolan and nullify the union pact."

"And if Donelan dies in battle?"

Cam could hear the cold humor in Ruggs's voice. "Then Isencroft is ours to remake. We seize the crown and place a king we control on the throne."

"Who, you?" Derision was clear in Leather John's voice.

Ruggs snorted. "I prefer to work from behind the throne. Let some other patch wear the motley and be the target."

"Then who?" Leather John demanded.

"Alvior of Brunnfen comes to mind," Ruggs replied. "After his father fell through the ice last winter—an *unfortunate* accident—Alvior has been most supportive of our cause. He's got royal blood—distant, but confirmed. He's the one who maneuvered Crevan into Donelan's sights as a spy. Meanwhile, he's been quietly arming our side. He's had a grudge against Donelan ever since the king gave protection to the twins his father banished. Good reason, too. They both helped put Martris Drayke on Margolan's throne."

Cam felt as if he'd been gut-punched. His head reeled. Alvior of Brunnfen, his oldest brother. And although he hadn't seen any of his family in the eleven years since he and Carina were exiled, he'd never expected Alvior to side against the king. His chest tightened. Ruggs's words suggested that Alvior had something to do with their father's death. And while Cam had long ago renounced the father who sent him away, the depths of Alvior's treachery made his face flush with shame and anger.

Unbidden, memories rushed back. Cam and Carina had been barely fourteen years old when their father Asmarr had discovered Carina's healing magic. In the harsh lands of Isencroft's northern reaches, their father had presided over Brunnfen with an iron hand. A distant cousin to the royal family, Asmarr had no patience for the niceties of court. He was as hard as the climate of his lands and as relentless as the cold Northern Sea. For Asmarr, healing only had a place on the battlefield, something to be done for warriors by a warrior-priest. To do more "weakened the herd," as he said.

Shamed by the birth of twins, Asmarr had submitted to the pleadings of his wife to keep Cam and Carina despite the ill omen. But when Carina's magic manifested, neither the cries of his wife nor the begging of their youngest brother, Renn, would change his mind. Cam and Carina had been banished.

Ruggs's statement shook Cam. Asmarr was a hard man, but he was never disloyal to the king. Alvior, on the other hand, Cam thought with disgust, had ever only served his own interests. It had been Alvior who discovered the healing Carina practiced in secret and betrayed her to their father. Cam still remembered Alvior standing with Asmarr as the gates of Brunnfen closed behind him and Carina. Alvior had been as expressionless as his father, his eyes utterly lacking in compassion.

"Won't your patron take exception to us hanging his brother over the wall like a deer from the hunt?"

Ruggs's laugh was cold. "Mind? I expect he'll reward us. He's been looking for a way to finish what his father started. They're a superstitious lot up north. Swears that Brunnfen's poor harvests have been because his father let the twins live." Cam could hear the malice in Ruggs's voice. "The woman is out of our reach. She's gone to Dark Haven, under the protection of its brigand lord. But if I give Alvior a chance for the crown and his brother's head, it's certain to fix a place for me at his right hand."

"And the rest of us?"

"Loyalty is always rewarded."

Cam swallowed hard. If Ruggs was correct, then Crevan had already attempted—or succeeded—in killing Kiara and the child she carried. Ruggs seemed confident that Curane had the means to destroy the Margolan army, and Tris along with it. He recalled all too well what Margolan had looked like under Jared's iron hand, and had no illusions that it would be any better when Curane put Jared's bastard son on the throne. *All that we fought for, for naught.*

Grief hardened his resolve for the job he had to do this night. There was only one bright spot. *The woman's out of our reach*, Ruggs had said of Carina. Cam was grateful that Carina was far away in Dark Haven. *Jonmarc will keep her safe*, Cam thought. That gave him a sense of peace. *Maybe I can reclaim some honor for our family, to temper what Alvior has done.*

He could see by the position of the sun that the day was far spent. With his good hand, Cam withdrew the flint and steel Rhistiart had given him from his pocket. He dragged himself closer to the bales of dry wool. Long ago, he had seen a fuller's mill go up in flames when stray sparks from a lantern lit the dust and dung fumes. It had exploded with a boom that shattered the glass in the windows of houses. With any luck, Cam hoped to recreate that spectacle.

He made a bed of kindling-dry wool near the pile of bales and wedged the flint under his good knee as he struck at it with the steel until sparks lit the dirty fluff. Cam repeated the effort down the length of the bales, painfully dragging himself along until he reached the outer wall. He looked back with satisfaction as the bales quickly caught fire. Before the smoke had grown thick enough to alert Ruggs and the others, the filthy wool caught like dry wood, until the flames roared toward the ceiling, engulfing Siarl's body in a proper pyre.

Ruggs opened the door with a curse, and the flames rushed toward the fresh air, forcing Ruggs and the others back. Cam flattened himself against the furthest corner, against the cold outer wall and waited to die.

All at once, the air around him seemed to glisten like fire. The dusty air exploded with a bang, blowing a hole through the rickety old wall. Deafened from the blast and burned from the fiery bits that rained down on him, Cam crawled with all his might toward the hole as a second explosion lifted the floor beneath him. The gases from the dung pits erupted, and the force threw Cam through the air. He was burning and freezing at the same time. The old mill was a conflagration, sending a pillar of fire high into the frigid night air. Cam laughed through his pain. He landed hard in the deep white snow and surrendered himself to darkness.

DAY 6

DAY 6

CHAPTER TWENTY-SIX

"**D**ON'T MOVE."

JONMARC roused from an uneasy rest to find himself staring at the business end of a notched crossbow. The bowman was a *vayash moru* Jonmarc didn't recognize. Three of his fellows crowded into the pilgrim's chamber, and two of the others held their bows trained on Gabriel.

"The quarrel might not kill you," the bowman said to Gabriel, who had not moved from where he leaned against the wall, "but it will him," he added with a jerk of his head toward Jonmarc. "So I suggest cooperating."

Outside, the bells tolled the third hour of the morning. Although the *vyrkin* shaman had healed Jonmarc's injuries that were life threatening, too many other wounded fighters had needed his assistance for him to bother with the rest of Jonmarc's wounds, intending to heal them later. Exhausted and injured from the battle, stiff from the beating Malesh had inflicted, Jonmarc knew he was not up to another fight. Gabriel's burned and blistered skin had hardly begun to heal, and Jonmarc took that as an indicator that the *vayash moru* had sustained vital internal damage that was not apparent. Gabriel looked ragged. The odds were against them winning this battle, especially when Jonmarc spotted four more *vayash moru* armed with swords waiting in the ruined temple.

"Malesh was destroyed," Gabriel snapped. "The war is over."

The dark haired man whose bow was pointed at Jonmarc shook his head. "We were sent by the Blood Council. You're to be brought before them for trial."

"The Blood Council?" Jonmarc started to sit up, then thought better of it as the bowman calibrated his aim.

"What nonsense is this?" Gabriel's voice was thick with disgust. "The Council dissolved."

"Lord Rafe issued the order for your arrest. You're both to be brought to answer to the Council for your actions. The charge is treason."

"Treason!" Gabriel snarled. "By whose measure?"

The dark haired man's face was stony. "You betrayed the Blood to side with the mortals against *vayash moru*." He met Jonmarc's glare. "And you betrayed your sacred oath as Lord of Dark Haven when you made war against our kind."

"I have a few things to say to Lord Rafe," Gabriel said.

The dark haired man signaled for the other *vayash moru* to enter. "Bind them. We'll carry them to the carriage on the road so that there are no tracks to follow."

A crossbow fired. Jonmarc flinched, expecting to feel the razor-sharp point lancing through his skin. Instead, he saw Gabriel stiffen, his face tight with pain, eyes wide. The bolt pierced his heart.

"That will make sure he doesn't attempt anything heroic," the dark haired man said, meeting Jonmarc's gaze. "He'll recover. The Council's only requirement was that you be alive to stand trial. They didn't specify in what condition."

Jonmarc gritted his teeth as a *vayash moru* came forward to bind his wrists and jerked him to his feet. Another *vayash moru* lifted Gabriel as if he were weightless and carried him from the room. Jonmarc looked around the temple at the wreckage from the battle. Where Malesh had fallen lay a pile of charred clothing. Jonmarc winced at the sight of the large bloodstain that marked where he had gone down before Gabriel reached him.

Outside, the snow was trampled and dark
with ash and blood. Just as the bitter wind
struck him, a *vayash moru* grabbed him hard
from behind, squeezing his cracked ribs in an
iron grip. Jonmarc fought back a cry of pain
as they lifted off from the ground, traveling in
a rush of air and snow to touch back down on
a rutted road a few minutes later. An expensive
black carriage waited for him. The team of four
black stallions snuffled and pawed at the snow
impatiently. His captors trundled him none too
gently into the carriage, thrusting Gabriel in
behind him like a piece of luggage, and locked
the carriage door.

Jonmarc struggled to lift Gabriel as gently as
he could without putting any pressure on the
arrow that pierced his chest. He managed to
get Gabriel onto the carriage seat, where he
slumped to the side and sat unmoving. Only his
eyes moved, and Jonmarc clearly read pain in
Gabriel's gaze.

"Lovely end to a perfect day," Jonmarc
muttered, sitting down on the seat facing
Gabriel. The carriage bumped and jostled
roughly as the horses raced through the night.
After more than a candlemark, the carriage
slowed. Out the frosted window, Jonmarc could
see the silhouette of a manor house.

Where Wolvenskorn was notable for its
great age and Dark Haven for its austerity,
this grand home was much newer, in the style

of King Staden's palace. Made from brick and granite, the three-story structure was topped with a carved stone railing. Gargoyles and grotesques looked down on the entrance, which was flanked by two equally large wings of the building. Candles glittered in every window as if the grand home awaited guests for a ball. Jonmarc felt his gut tighten. Too tasteful to be Uri's home at Scothnaran, not ascetic enough to be Rafe's country villa, this had to be Astasia's manor. That alone did not bode well.

Guards came to unlock the carriage door. Jonmarc, wrists still bound, was escorted by four *vayash moru*, two of whom carried crossbows loaded and aimed at his back. He resisted the urge to smile at the threat his captors perceived him to be, even bound and bloodied. *Let them wonder*, he thought, though he was acutely aware of the fact that he was hardly ready to hold his own against mortals, let alone *vayash moru*. Behind Jonmarc, another *vayash moru* carried Gabriel, who hung limply in his arms like a corpse. They walked up the broad stone steps and into a front hall that glittered with gold and crystal reflected from mirrored walls and a gleaming white marble floor.

The guards hustled them past the finery to a room at the end of a long corridor. The lead guard opened a door to a small, windowless room that appeared to be an unused pantry. It was bare and lit only by a single overhead lamp. "You'll wait here," he instructed curtly. He drew a knife from his belt and advanced on Jonmarc, who eyed him warily, but the guard slit the cord that bound his wrists and sheathed his knife. Jonmarc's guards prodded him inside, while the man who carried Gabriel set him down hard on the bare floor. With one swift move, he jerked the arrow from Gabriel's chest and stepped back as Gabriel groaned and fell backward. When the door locked behind their captors, Jonmarc edged closer.

"Gabriel?" He kept some distance between them, having no idea how lucid Gabriel might be. "Are you all right?"

"That depends on your definition."

"Where are we?"

"Airenngeir. Astasia's manor."

"Does the Blood Council usually meet here?"

"No."

Jonmarc cursed. "This just keeps getting better." He paused. "Is there anything I can do for you?"

"Short of feeding me the idiot who shot me with that arrow, nothing I can think of." Gabriel groaned and pulled himself up to sit against the wall. His shirt was stained dark with ichor. He grimaced and let out an uncharacteristic expletive.

"I thought you could heal just about anything."

"Heal, yes. But not immediately. The greater the damage, the longer it takes. If you hadn't noticed, I'd seen better days before I got shot. Chest wounds are particularly slow to heal and they hurt like hell."

"Yeah, well, for the record--getting bitten in the neck doesn't feel great either."

Gabriel glanced at him. "It can be nearly painless. Malesh wanted you to suffer."

Jonmarc was silent for a few moments. "Why didn't he try to turn me?"

"Malesh knew that you'd never accept him as a master. He probably didn't doubt that you'd kill him the first chance you got, even if it destroyed you as well. He knows first-hand how a fledgling can turn against his maker. And if he ever tried to influence your thoughts, he would have realized you have a certain... natural resistance. You have no idea how much effort it took for my compulsion to break through your shielding at Westormere."

Again, they sat in silence for a while. "What now? We both know the trial's a farce."

Gabriel shifted and gritted his teeth against the pain. "Astasia and Uri may have clamored for it, but Rafe is usually a fair man, if rule-driven. The question is whether or not they've included Riqua. She's not in here with us, which is a good sign. On the other hand, they must know she's at Dark Haven. That would make her less than impartial."

"Wouldn't they consider her just as guilty of betraying the Blood?"

Gabriel shook his head slowly. "I don't think so. She was bloodsworn against Uri's brood, but she herself never battled either mortals or *vayash moru*. Depending on how this goes, there may be repercussions against those in her brood who fought alongside us. By logic, the Council can't rule for our destruction without condemning more than half of the *vayash moru* in Principality. And they should have no hold over you at all. This is an internal matter."

Jonmarc could hear the pain in Gabriel's voice. He'd never seen Gabriel vulnerable before, and it made him more uneasy than he cared to admit. Jonmarc assessed his own injuries from practice born of far too many fights. The wound at his throat was healed. With a healer's help, he'd be back to fighting strength in just a day or two. On his own, it might take several weeks. He remembered times when he'd felt like Gabriel looked, and how long and painful the recovery had been.

It was close enough to dawn when they arrived that Jonmarc guessed their trial would wait until sundown. As the candlemarks passed without anyone coming for them, his surmise appeared to be correct. Both he and Gabriel dozed. Having one of them sit sentry when they were captives in a locked room seemed pointless.

After a long time, Jonmarc heard a key move in the lock and he tensed as the door swung open. "The Council demands your presence," a guard announced.

Gabriel refused the guard's offer to help him to his feet, baring his long eye teeth in warning. Jonmarc managed to stand on his own, although he couldn't hide a limp. Under armed escort, they made their way into a paneled library that was as cold as the winter night outside. The huge fireplace was dark and empty, and the room was lit by a massive central chandelier. A space had been cleared in the center of the room facing a long heavy wooden table. Seated behind the table were Rafe, Astasia and Uri.

Rafe rose to read the charges against them. "Gabriel, Lord of Wolvenskorn. You are charged with betraying the Blood and violating the Truce. You have made war against our own kind, enabled mortals to burn day crypts, and incited the *vyrkin* against *vayash moru*. How do you plead?"

Jonmarc had never seen the anger that burned in Gabriel's eyes. "One hundred percent guilty— and you know why I did it." His voice was scathing. "Talk to Uri about violating the Truce. I sought to finish what Malesh started before he brought the king's wrath and the vengeance of every mortal in Principality down on us."

"You understand that the penalty for betrayal is destruction."

"So is the penalty for cowardice," Gabriel snapped. "You saw what Malesh was doing, and you and Astasia chose to do nothing. How many villages did you think he could destroy before the mortals came to burn us all? It's already started. And while you're here making a mockery of what's left of the Council, you've imprisoned the only man who has a chance of stopping the mortals," he said with a glance toward Jonmarc.

Rafe turned toward Jonmarc. "Jonmarc Vahanian, Lord of Dark Haven. You are charged with—"

"Destroying the murdering bastard who killed my wife and annihilated three mortal villages," Jonmarc interrupted. "And no, I'm not sorry."

"You swore an oath to protect the residents of Dark Haven," Rafe countered.

"*All* the residents—mortal and undead," Jonmarc countered. "How long did you think Malesh could go on before Staden decided to ride in here with an army and put an end to it? Malesh broke the Truce. Once Malesh started slaughtering villagers, that oath gave me no choice. But the Truce went both ways. When Malesh decided that mortals were fair game, the *vayash moru* lost their protection, too. Don't tell me about 'betraying Blood.' I cut down six mortals who were hunting *vyrkin*. And assuming I live through tonight, I'll stand between the mortals and the *vayash moru* to protect your kind, just as I fought them to protect my own."

"If the Council finds you guilty, the penalty is destruction," Rafe replied.

"You have no jurisdiction over him." Gabriel stepped forward, and Jonmarc could only guess how much willpower it was taking him to move as though he weren't in pain. "The Lord of Dark Haven's authority comes from King Staden, not from the Blood Council." He fixed Rafe with a lethal glare. "And to strike the king's liegeman is to declare war against the king himself."

"We do, however, have jurisdiction over our own." Astasia's voice was like ice. Jonmarc had no idea what prompted the hatred he saw in her eyes. Beside her, Uri appeared to be watching the proceedings with amusement.

"In other words, you're not going to be satisfied unless someone bleeds," Jonmarc said, feeling his temper rise. "Fine. If you need blood, take mine. Everything Gabriel did was to protect me. He believed he was fulfilling a vow to the Dark Lady. I burned the day crypts. I led the attack at the Caliggan Crossroads, and I led the mortals against the *vayash moru* at Mead's Ferry. I destroyed Malesh at Istra's Temple. You want a blood sacrifice? Here I am."

"You would die to protect one of the Blood?"

Jonmarc strained for control. "What part of this whole discussion didn't you get? Malesh put the lot of you in danger. Do you really think the *vayash moru* can stand against the armies of the king and the mobs of villagers if it comes to that? Riqua knew better. She remembers the burnings before the Truce. Malesh had to be stopped. Either Gabriel and I stopped him, while this was still a 'family matter,' or there'd be no ending the vengeance until every *vayash moru* in Principality went down in flames."

"Will you raise your hand against the Dark Lady's chosen?" Gabriel's voice cut through the conversation like a cold knife. "Look at the brand of the Dark Lady and the wound that healed on his throat. Malesh desecrated Istra's temple to become the consort of Shanthadura. He started the war not to make our kind ascendant, but to make himself a god. To do that, he had to challenge and defeat the Dark Lady's champion. He failed. But when Vigulf, the *vyrkin* shaman, healed Jonmarc, we both sensed Istra's presence in the temple." Gabriel looked at Jonmarc. "He hasn't spoken of this to me. But I'm certain that She appeared to him."

"Is this true?" Rafe's voice had lost some of its edge as an inquisitor, and Jonmarc recalled that Rafe was once a scholar.

"It's true."

"We have nothing but their word for it," Astasia protested. "Men will say anything to avoid destruction."

Rafe glared at Astasia to silence her. "Are there any other questions for the accused?"

Uri leaned forward. "I wish to know exactly how Malesh died."

Jonmarc met Uri's dark eyes. "I put a quarrel through his heart when he sank his teeth into my neck. He fell backward into the candles and burned."

"Yet you live."

"Not by choice."

Uri seemed to ponder that for a moment. "Why didn't you burn me, when you found me in the day crypt? Lady knows, we're hardly friends."

"Because as much as I would have enjoyed it, you didn't lead the revolt. Malesh did. And while your bluster gave him the words to recruit his helpers, you promised Riqua and Gabriel that you'd try to stop him. It kills me to admit it, but you kept your word. I've never killed someone who couldn't fight back. Not even you."

Rafe cleared his throat. "If there are no other questions, it is time for a vote. Both of the accused freely admit their guilt. Shall the Council rule for their destruction?"

Jonmarc found that anger overrode fear. Gabriel's eyes gave no clue to his thoughts. The next few moments seemed to last forever.

Finally, Rafe spoke. "No."

Astasia looked up with fury in her eyes. "Yes."

They turned toward Uri, who seemed to relish the suspense. "My answer is... no." He met Jonmarc's eyes. "Don't mistake me. I still don't like you, nor do I like having a mortal lord at Dark Haven. But Malesh was my mistake. He got badly out of hand. And unlike Astasia, I am old enough to recall the burnings. I have no wish to see those days return."

Rafe stood. "The Council has ruled." He looked to Jonmarc. "Lord Vahanian. I would not recommend that you ride alone in your condition by night. You are welcome to spend the night and leave in the morning." As if he expected a retort, he raised a hand to forestall a reply. "I will personally guarantee your safety. In the morning, you'll find a horse and provisions for the ride. Your weapons will be returned to you." He met Jonmarc's eyes. "We will honor the Truce."

Jonmarc regarded him warily. "And Gabriel?"

Rafe nodded. "Lord Gabriel returns to his position on the Blood Council and to his manor at Wolvenskorn without prejudice. Whether he returns to Dark Haven is up to him."

Gabriel gave Jonmarc a reassuring nod. "I'll see you in Dark Haven once I settle a few things at Wolvenskorn." He glanced toward the Council. "And I'll make sure you have better accommodations here," he said in a tone that warned Astasia that he expected her to comply. Gabriel gave a curt bow toward the others. "Until later."

Jonmarc did not speak until they were alone in one of the upstairs rooms. "That's it? They haul us in here trussed up like thieves, put a stake through your heart, threaten to burn you and kill me, and then it's over with nothing more than a 'by your leave'?"

To his surprise, Gabriel chuckled. "After several hundred years, sometimes the form matters more than the function. They feel they've been heard. Rules have been observed. Order is restored. Astasia had her say, Rafe can feel that he's satisfied the regulations and Uri got to be magnanimous. And we remain."

They fell silent. "Thank you," Jonmarc said finally.

Gabriel shrugged. "Likewise. You didn't have to defend me to the Council. It was a rather foolhardy thing to do, given the circumstances."

Jonmarc shrugged. "I owe you."

Gabriel met his eyes. "I don't know what you saw, there in the temple. But in all the years I've existed, I have only believed one other person to be the Dark Lady's chosen."

"Who was that?"

"Bava K'aa, Tris's grandmother."

"I didn't want this."

"I know."

Jonmarc turned away and felt the room begin to reel. Gabriel caught him before he fell and helped him to a chair. "I'll make sure someone brings you food. And while there's no healer here, I can probably find something for the pain." Jonmarc nodded, leaning back in the chair and closing his eyes as Gabriel slipped from the room.

Every time I turn around, there's someone new in line to kill me. Just like old times. And as soon as Donelan finds out what happened to Carina, he'll make good on his threat. He'll send the bounty hunters after me with a price so high even Gabriel won't be able to protect me if I set foot outside the manor house. So much for being anyone's champion. Before long, a servant delivered a meal of hard sausage, cheese and bread, along with a bottle of dark Trevath whiskey. Jonmarc ate his fill, finishing off half of the whiskey until he could no longer feel his battle wounds. But even the whiskey could not dull the dread he felt over returning to Dark Haven, and despite the strong drink, his dreams were troubled.

CHAPTER TWENTY-SEVEN

B Y THE TOLLING of the bells in the courtyard, Carina knew it was the sixth hour of the morning. Still sore and weary from her encounter with the Flow, she climbed out of bed and made her way to the heavy draperies that completely obscured her windows. Holding her breath, she drew them back and waited for the faint rays of dawn to burn her skin. Cautiously, she opened her eyes. A slash of red and orange lit the eastern sky along the horizon as heavy gray clouds obscured the moon, but the cold, pale light did not burn. It was true. She was fully mortal once more.

Heedless of the hunger that gnawed in her stomach, Carina slipped into a shift and her healer's robes. She knew that Neirin would already be at his desk. She made her way through Dark Haven's upper corridors without meeting anyone, and stopped at the door to Neirin's office. Steeling herself, she knocked. At Neirin's response, she opened the door.

Neirin looked up. He registered first shock and then genuine relief. "M'lady. It's good to see you about once more in the light of day. I'm so glad the healing was successful."

Carina nodded, and Neirin sobered. "I fear that you did not come to catch up on news."

"We need to send guards to Istra's temple in the hills," Carina said. "I saw a vision in the Flow that I believe was a true sending. There may be no survivors. But we owe the dead the honor of a proper burial."

"The mob begins forming at the front gates once it's fully light, and it won't leave until the sun begins to set," he said. "I can slip two men out if we move quickly. Getting them back in may be more of a challenge. It will take them most of the day to journey there and back again, but if they leave within the candlemark, they should be able to return before sundown if they ride hard."

"Thank you." Carina paused. "In Isencroft, it's the custom to fly a gray flag of mourning when there are deaths within a household. Is such a thing done in Dark Haven?"

Neirin nodded. "Yes, m'lady. I'll take care of it this morning. We've not done so at Dark Haven for ten years, not since the last lord died."

Carina drew a deep breath. "Thank you." She met his eyes. "How does Dark Haven mourn its dead?"

Neirin gestured her toward a chair and drew a pot of hot water from the coals in the small fireplace that warmed his office. He poured her a cup of tea, which she accepted gratefully. "The custom is the same whether it's a mortal who dies or a *vayash moru* who is destroyed. There are eight days of mourning, one for each Aspect. The first four days honor the Dark Aspects. Those who mourn fast from dawn to dusk, and eat an evening meal of cold food without seasoning. No music is played. The mourners light candles and make offerings to the Lady for the safe passage of the souls of the dead. A hedge witch preserves the body so that all may pay respects.

"On the fifth day, the fast is broken. The last four days honor the Light Aspects. A great party is held in honor of the dead, with feasting and much wine. Stories are shared about those who have died, and they grow larger by the telling. Wenching is encouraged among single mourners to bring new life to replace that which was lost. Most families in Dark Haven have a shared crypt where the mortals are buried and the *vayash moru* seek shelter during the day. If the dead was mortal, the body is interred in the family crypt. If *vayash moru*, no body remains, and so a suit of the dead person's clothing is taken to the crypt instead." He paused.

"M'lady, I am afraid to ask. But your questions bode ill for the return of Lord Jonmarc."

Carina swallowed hard as her throat tightened. "He's not coming back, Neirin. And I'm afraid he won't be the only one."

Neirin drew a deep breath and made the symbol of the Lady. "Dark Haven grieves with you, m'lady. We will begin the fast today."

Carina nodded. "Thank you." She gestured to her clothing. "I assume there is something special I'm supposed to wear?"

"I'll secure what you need and send it to your rooms." He met her eyes. "When the days of mourning are completed, will you return to Isencroft?"

She had wrestled with that question all night. Carina shook her head. "Jonmarc put too much of himself into rebuilding Dark Haven for me to walk away from it. And there are so many people who need a healer. I'll stay... until another lord is chosen."

Neirin's eyes told her that he recognized how difficult that choice had been. "This is your home, m'lady, so long as you choose it to be. The staff will honor your wishes with the same faithfulness with which they served Lord Jonmarc."

She bowed her head as she struggled for control, and finally looked up, knowing that Neirin could clearly see her grief. "Thank you."

TARU WAS WAITING for her when Carina returned to her room. "I was beginning to worry," Taru said. She had a plate of biscuits with honey and a cup of dried berries along with a fresh pot of tea. "Now that you're healed, you need to eat to keep up your strength." When Carina hesitated, Taru laid a gentle hand on her arm. "I guessed that you were talking to Neirin about making the Passage Fast. Before it begins, you must eat. It serves no purpose for you to collapse."

Carina nodded, but she found that, hungry as she was, the food had no appeal. The vision she had glimpsed in the Flow haunted her, and any elation she might have felt over the healing was bittersweet at the cost.

"Riqua and Lisette are worried about you," Taru said quietly as Carina picked at her food. "And if you hadn't noticed, Raen hasn't left your room." Even now, Carina could glimpse the ghost girl in the shadows. "We'll stay with you for as long as you need us. Certainly we'll mark the fast and feast with you."

"I told Neirin I'd be staying," Carina said. She looked up as if she expected Taru to argue with her. "At least, until another lord is chosen. I want to carry on what Jonmarc's started. And there's so much healing left to do."

Taru nodded. "I thought you might. But given that ten years passed between the death of the last lord and Jonmarc's choosing, there may come a time when you change your mind."

Carina sighed. "The world is changing, Taru. The last letter I got from Cam made it sound as if Isencroft is on the brink of revolution. We have no idea whether healing the Flow gave Tris his victory. Either way, it'll be a struggle to secure Margolan. And even though Jonmarc destroyed Malesh, there's no guarantee that will stop the fighting here. There's still a mob at the gates, demanding that we turn over the *vayash moru* to them. You know what happened to Kolin. The courtyard is full of refugees. How will we know when it's safe for them to go home? Once the madness starts, how do you contain it?"

Taru looked down. "I don't know the answer to that, Carina. No one does. But having you here at Dark Haven makes a difference. That's all any of us can do—take the step we see, and do what we can."

Carina finished the last of her breakfast and drained her cup. "Let's go down to where the refugees are camped. It will take Neirin's scouts most of the day to get back. And although I'm in no hurry for confirmation, anything is better than watching the candle burn down."

It was nearly sunset when Neirin came to the great room where Carina and Taru were tending the refugees. At Neirin's summons, they left their work and followed him to a small parlor where two guards waited. "Tell me what you found," Carina said, taking a seat. Taru laid a hand on her shoulder in support.

The guard who spoke was a blond man who looked to be close to Jonmarc's age. The other was one of the manor's best trackers. It was the guard who spoke. He had the manner of a seasoned soldier, but his expression was shaken. "There was a great battle at the temple, m'lady. Outside, the snow was dark with *vyrkin* blood and the dust that remains when a *vayash moru* is destroyed."

"You're certain the blood was *vyrkin*?"

The tracker nodded. "Absolutely, m'lady."

The guard continued. "It was clear that the battle continued into the temple. The door was smashed in, and the banks of candles along one wall had been knocked to the ground. Inside, we found the remains of a *vayash moru*." He withdrew a signet ring from his pocket, and Carina recognized it from Malesh's hand the night of the attack on Westormere.

"Did you find anything else?"

The guard hesitated, and then spoke. "We found a pool of blood. Human blood. And this." He opened the sack that lay at his feet and withdrew the pommel of a broken sword.

Carina gasped as she recognized Jonmarc's sword and fought back tears. "Did you find a body?"

"No, m'lady. No bodies. And no tracks leading away from the temple. That's the strange part. The *vayash moru* can fly, but the *vyrkin* can't. Though I imagine someone could magic away the tracks if they wanted. Not knowing what happened, we didn't think it wise to ride to Wolvenskorn. Weren't sure what our reception would be, barging in without an invitation."

"Thank you." Carina's voice was barely more than a whisper. Neirin motioned for the two scouts to leave, and they filed out behind him in silence, leaving Carina alone with Taru. When the door shut behind them, Carina's resolve broke. Taru folded her into her arms, letting her sob.

"It's just as I saw it, Taru," Carina said in a strangled voice. "He's gone."

CHAPTER TWENTY-EIGHT

TRIS WAS ALREADY staggering to his feet as Fallon and two of his guards rushed toward him. He was surprised to be alive, and even more astounded that he had remained conscious. The pain that throbbed in his head and seemed to ache through his bones reminded him that one benefit of losing consciousness was a temporary reprieve from pain. In the distance, he could hear the tolling of the midnight bells from the camp.

"Are you all right?" Fallon asked, and Tris knew that she extended her healing magic to assure herself even before he spoke.

"That depends on what you're expecting," Tris replied. It was taking all of his concentration to remain standing. "I'm not dead. That's something." He looked toward Lochlanimar. The explosive force of the Elemental had blown out huge parts of both the battered outer wall and the thick inner wall, but the flames that raged inside would preclude any search for survivors for quite a while.

"There's no way our men can search the castle until the fires burn out," Fallon said, as if she guessed his thoughts. "Curane might have had an underground escape tunnel. We know there are caves beneath Lochlanimar. But it'll be late tomorrow before we dare go close enough to find out."

As sore as Tris's body was, the channels of magic were worse. Just thinking about harnessing his power hurt, and as he tried to concentrate, it felt as if the pathways of magic had been blasted raw. With an effort of will, he stretched out his magic toward the burning ruins. He could sense the old dead, the ghosts from the necropolis beneath Lochlanimar. He could sense the stirring of Tabok, Mohr and their companions. They were heading back toward his camp to make their report. And Tris could sense their own battle dead, both those newly torn from their bodies in the night's battle and those who had gathered to be a part of the final stand against Curane. But inside the fireswept castle, Tris could not sense any souls other than the dead.

He met Fallon's eyes. "If there are survivors, they're beyond my reach."

"Given what you've been through, I'm not

surprised. We need to get you back to camp," she said archly.

They looked up to see Soterius riding hard toward them. He dismounted and dropped his reins, running to meet them. "Are you all right?" he asked, looking at Tris with concern.

Tris and Fallon exchanged glances. "Since I'm not dead, I guess the answer is 'yes'," Tris replied.

Soterius gave him a look that took in his singed hair and burned clothing, and the new blisters on his hands and arms from the scorching heat of the Elemental. "Senne and Rallan sent a runner to find me. They're regrouping so that we can place a watch around Lochlanimar. No one's expecting there to be a lot of survivors, but on the chance a few try to slip out, we'll round them up and bring them back until we can figure out who's who."

Tris nodded, and winced at the way it made his head ache. "Make sure you keep them well away from the rest of the camp. We know Curane loosed a plague in there; we don't know for certain whether it's the same fever that Esme is dealing with among the soldiers. The last thing we need is for it to spread."

They turned to head back toward the camp, and Tris staggered. He would have fallen if Soterius hadn't steadied him, getting under Tris's arm and supporting his weight. "You need to lie down," Soterius growled under his breath. "There's no way you can ride right now. It's going to be a long walk back to camp—unless you've got the good sense to pass out, in which case we can toss you into the back of a wagon without damaging your dignity."

Tris meant to answer with a snide retort. Instead, his knees buckled and he slid through Soterius's grip to land in the snow. Everything was slipping away from him, receding into a gray void. "I was kidding," he heard Soterius say as if from a great distance as the world around him disappeared into darkness.

Tris awoke to find himself in his own tent, flat on his back on his cot. Someone had treated and bandaged the worst of his burns, and the headache was now just a dull throb behind his temples. As soon as he opened his eyes, Coalan bent over him.

"Fallon said I'm to give you this," the young man said, in a tone that told him the healer had vested Tris's squire with the authority to enforce her wishes. "She says it will help with the pain and speed the healing." Coalan slid another pillow behind Tris, helping him to sit enough to drink the warm elixir.

"How long have I been out?"

Coalan shrugged. "Almost seven candlemarks. It's nearly dawn. After Esme and Fallon took care of you, they went to handle the casualties. We have a lot of men down. Not everyone got out of the way of whatever that thing was."

"An Elemental," Tris murmured.

"If that's what you call it, then I hope to the Lady that I never see one again," Coalan said fervently. "Thought we were all good as roasted, until you turned it."

Tris ignored Coalan's protests as he swung his legs down and sat up, stifling a groan. "I need to see what's going on."

"Beggin' your royal pardon, but you don't look like you can make it out of the tent on your own. Tell me what you want and I'll be your eyes," Coalan volunteered. "Please, Tris. Be sensible for once. The battle's over and you're the hero. But nothing's served if you push yourself until you collapse again."

Tris tried to stand and fell back to the cot. His legs refused to hold him and as soon as he was upright, his headache returned with a vengeance. "All right," he said hoarsely, lying back down. "But only for a few more candlemarks. Then I'm going out there even if I have to prop myself up on crutches."

Coalan gave a lopsided smile. "And you would, too. How about this? I'll be your spy for now, and while I'm out there, I'll give Fallon an update on how you're doing. You rest, and by midday, if you still need them, I'll fetch the crutches for you myself."

Tris managed a weak grin. "Agreed." He closed his eyes. "I want to know how soon Senne thinks we can get a reconnaissance team into what's left of Lochlanimar. If there are survivors, we need to find them. And if anything remains of Curane and his mages, we need to know that, too."

"Done, m'lord," Coalan promised, grabbing for his cloak. "And I'll bring lunch, too, when I come back. Can't wage war on an empty stomach," he said before he disappeared through the tent door.

Tris lay back and closed his eyes. He knew better than any of them how unlikely it was for there to be survivors in the wreckage of Lochlanimar. Drifting between sleep and drugged unconsciousness, he opened the channels of his power, beckoning to the ghosts to give their report. The temperature in the tent plummeted as the spirits surrounded him. Tris did not have the strength to give them form, but he saw them clearly on the Plains of Spirit.

Tabok and Mohr appeared before him and saluted. "All is done as you bid us, Your Majesty," Tabok said. "Mohr broke the concentration of the dark mages who called the Elemental. When it returned to the workshop, it consumed everything. Nothing remains. Cadoc, Dirmed and Curane burned to ash in its fury and along with them, everything in that cursed workshop. All but these." Tabok gestured to three small orbs that lay on the table, hurled from the wreckage by Mohr, the poltergeist. "You recognize this magic?"

Tris nodded. "Spirit orbs. Cadoc, Dirmed and Curane didn't leave. Their souls are right there, in those orbs. And before we're through, they'll account for what they've done."

The spirits from the necropolis moved forward. "We've searched the caves and tunnels beneath the castle," their leader reported. He wore the spectral remains of a style of armor several hundred years old. "There are no survivors in the passageways. We saw no one alive anywhere inside the ruins." He paused. "It would not be wise to send living men into the tunnels. The fire that swept the castle has weakened parts of the tunnel roof. It isn't safe for those who wish to remain alive."

Next came the report from the spirits of the fallen Margolan soldiers, both those who returned to fight and those newly dead in the latest battle. Tris recognized Pell and Tabb among the ghosts, two men who had fought beside Soterius in the rebellion and who had been betrayed to their deaths by Tarq. He beckoned for them to come forward. "What report would you make?" he asked.

"We spirits held our positions when the firestorm came," Pell replied. "It had no power to harm us. We saw ghosts aplenty rise from the ruins after the explosion, but no living man, woman or child escaped the walls."

Standing before them on the Plains of Spirit, Tris nodded. "Very well. How many of our own have we lost?"

From the ranks of the dead, he could hear the count begin. On and on it went, and his heart grew heavier with each number. "There are sixteen hundred and eighty-nine of us, Your Majesty, including those who fell with fever," Pell reported. "And to a man, we were honored to lay down our lives to keep Jared's bastard off the throne."

Tris swallowed hard at the enormity of the sacrifice. "Margolan honors your memory," Tris replied. "As do I." He paused. "Would you go to your rest?"

Pell looked back to the ranks of the dead, toward the shadowed men who stood in somber silence. Tris recognized many of the fallen as *Scirranish*, those who had lost families to Jared's brutality. He saw in their faces quiet resignation, the completion of duty, and a weariness that he was beginning to understand. Pell turned to him and nodded. "Yes, m'lord. We would be grateful if you would make the passage for us."

On the Plains of Spirit, Tris stretched out his hands in blessing toward the spirits who desired rest. "Let the sword be sheathed, and the helm shuttered. Prepare a feast in the hall of your fallen heroes. These men have died with valor. Make their passage swift and their journey easy, until their souls rest in the arms of the Lady," he said, closing his eyes as he felt the power of the Goddess at the very edges of his senses.

He was not surprised that it was Chenne, Aspect of the warrior, who came for them, wearing a golden helm and wielding a sword of flame. Tris extended his power, easing the passage for the soldiers as they turned to follow the soulsong that they heard. He grieved to see Vira, Ana and Latt from the Sisterhood among the dead. They nodded in farewell as they followed the gray paths toward the Lady's rest. Soon, the spirit plain was empty except for him. Not until he was certain he was alone did he dare to seek the one spirit he did not wish to heed his call.

"Kiara?" he asked, hearing the fear in his voice that she would answer. "Kiara?"

There was no answer. Exhausted and heartsick, Tris slipped from the Plains of Spirit and returned to himself. He felt stretched thin as fog, and if it weren't for the feel of the stiff cot beneath him, he might have doubted that he was more than a shade himself.

"Tris?" It was Coalan's voice, close to his ear. "Are you awake? Uncle Ban is here to see you. He has a report from Senne and Rallan."

Tris groaned and opened his eyes. "Send him in." He struggled to sit up, knowing that Soterius would not be fooled into thinking that he was functional.

"Goddess! You look awful," Soterius said as he entered. "Lie down. I promise not to tell anyone." He gave a tired smile. "After seeing you turn that Elemental, half of the men think you're a god. And the other half just don't ever want to get on your bad side."

"How long before the army can go home?"

Soterius pulled a chair up alongside Tris's cot. "Senne doesn't think we can even get into the ruins for a couple of days. Most of the village and the manor are still on fire. We took more wounded on this battle, largely from the ones who didn't outrun the Elemental. I just saw Esme. She says we have about three hundred men who won't be able to travel for at least a week, maybe longer, even with healing.

"And there are probably five hundred down with fever who never even made it into the last battle. They shouldn't move at all, not unless we want to take this bloody plague back with us." He shook his head. "Esme says that about half of those who get the fever die of it. And it's not a peaceful way to go. They're bleeding from their ears and noses, they've got bloody flux and they're burning up despite how cold it's been. I don't have a death count yet—"

"One thousand, six hundred and eighty nine," Tris murmured.

"How do you know that?"

"They told me."

"Esme and Fallon?"

"No. The dead."

"Damn."

Tris met Soterius's eyes. "As soon as I can ride, I'm going back to Shekerishet. Something's happened to Kiara. And I've got to deal with the rumors before it gets completely out of control."

"You're in no condition to make the trip, Tris," Soterius said with concern. "You'd have to push hard to make it in less than five days, and the snow's deep. Plus we have no idea how many of Curane's supporters are out there. There've been incidents with the supply wagons, snipers in the forest—"

"Then send twenty men with me. I have to go."

"I'm going with you." Tris looked up to see Coalan standing just inside the tent door, hands on hips. "You're going to need me."

Soterius took a deep breath and finally nodded. "As you wish. It'll take a couple of days to provision you, and you'll need that time to square away the clean-up plans with Senne and Rallan." He paused. "And if there are survivors from Lochlanimar…"

"There aren't. The ghosts from the necropolis said that no one survived. I made the passage for the soldiers and villagers myself."

Soterius's expression darkened. "None? Curane really had no idea what he was playing at with that Elemental, did he?" Tris could see the shadows of memory in Soterius's eyes that told him that the other remembered all too well from his own experience the fury of an Elemental unleashed against villagers trapped within a walled citadel.

"Apparently not." Tris sighed. "And we've got to keep the army from bringing the plague back with them. Esme and Fallon will have to make a ruling on each man before he can leave the ranks. That includes me and everyone who rides with me. You know how many volunteers we had, from the villages, the *Scirranish*. We can't let them scatter to the winds and take the fever with them. Father once had to keep two divisions in the field for forty days until a fever spent itself."

Soterius leaned back in his chair and shook his head. "That's going to be tough. We're barely feeding them as it is. Wintering them for another month won't be easy, even if it's just a few hundred men. We're already having some problems with the volunteers. They're not regular soldiers. It was their fear of Curane seizing the throne that kept them here, but we don't have enough soldiers to police them all if they decide to slip off. If they think you're leaving them here to die, they'll riot."

"You know that's not what I mean," Tris snapped. He was feeling the headache and the bone weariness and it made him short tempered. "But I've no desire to rule over the land of the dead, and that's what Margolan will be if the plague spreads. If they panic and run, they could spread it to Dhasson and Isencroft. We won't be able to contain it if we let it get away from us here."

Soterius nodded. "I understand. But most of these soldiers are farmers and workmen. There are some already wondering if it's the Crone's judgment on us for one thing or another. Bound to be talk like that. It'll get worse if the plague spreads. People don't blame things like plague on ill humours for long. After a while, they want someone to sacrifice."

"All the more reason we've got to keep this from spreading," Tris said. "We've had enough bloodshed in Margolan. Enough death." He knew Soterius could read his feelings clearly in his eyes. "It has to end."

Soterius was silent for a moment. "When you get back to Shekerishet, then what?"

Tris looked away. "I deal with the situation."

"You know, I realized that since we've been gone, I've only gotten a couple of letters from Alle. One of them was mangled so badly I couldn't read most of it. One of them had gotten wet and the ink ran. The two that got through without damage had loose seals. From what they said, I wondered whether she'd even read my letters." He met Tris's eyes. "What if someone's made sure we didn't hear from Kiara and Alle—and that they didn't hear from us? Someone who might have a stake in sabotaging Kiara."

"You have someone in mind?"

Soterius shrugged. "No. But I don't like coincidences and there are too many for me to let this go. Because I don't believe for a moment that either Kiara or Carroway betrayed you."

Tris closed his eyes. "When I get back to Shekerishet, I have a choice to make. I can take their word—or I can read their souls. My power could remove all doubt—or damn them both without reprieve. Do I trust, and always wonder? Or do I know for certain and risk destroying everything?"

"My mother would have said to follow your heart."

Tris opened his eyes and looked at him. "I love her, Ban. Even if the rumors are true. But the court—"

Soterius laid a hand on his shoulder. "One catastrophe at a time, huh? Clean up here. I'll find twenty men I trust with my life to ride with you. Anything can happen between now and when you get back to the palace. The answers may be clear by then."

"That's what I'm afraid of, Ban," Tris said quietly, meeting his eyes. "That's what I'm afraid of."

CHAPTER TWENTY-NINE

CARROWAY PACED HIS new prison, measuring the same steps. After the relative ease with which he slipped his guards at the Dragon's Rage Inn, it didn't surprise him that Harrtuck felt obliged to move him to a more secure cell in the guardhouse tower of Shekerishet's bailey. It was a cell made for prisoners of noble blood, and Carroway knew the legends of its former residents well. None of those imprisoned in this room had ever gone free, save at the end of a hangman's rope.

Harrtuck had been apologetic about returning him to custody, but they both understood the stakes. His belongings had been transported from the inn and thoroughly searched. He'd feared that they would find the evidence Paiva had stolen from Crevan and the book with the drawing of the blade in it among his things, sealing the case against him. To his relief, the letters, the book and the odd metal ring had disappeared.

A lack of evidence did not dissuade the mob that gathered by nightfall outside the tower. Led by one of Count Suphie's men, they had tried to storm the tower and take him by force to hang him for the attack on Kiara. Only Harrtuck's stalwart refusal to yield had prevented his murder. Grudgingly, the crowd had dispersed at swords' point.

Now, Carroway looked out the thin slit of a window that was one of only two openings besides the locked door. The winter night was cold and still, and the clear sky shone with stars. The frigid air kept all but the duty-bound or the most intrepid indoors. He looked down at his crabbed left hand, still wrapped in the bandages.

Hanging would be a mercy, he thought. *I can't play with a hand like this. Singing will earn me a pittance of what a good musician can beg. And those who fancied my face more than my music won't take a scarred lover to their beds. Banishment's as good as a death sentence. Harrtuck should have offered me up to the mob. It would have saved Tris the heartache and solved the problem. Kiara could save herself by saying that I forced myself on her. There's no future for me—here, or anywhere.*

He tensed when he heard the heavy bolts draw back on the door, and steeled himself for the worst. *Maybe Harrtuck's realized that sacrificing me is the best solution after all. If I'm to hang tonight, just please make sure someone knows how to tie a proper noose. I'd rather snap than strangle.*

To his astonishment, Macaria slipped inside. The door slammed shut behind her and the bolts clanked into place. "How did you get in?" he asked, crossing to take her in his arms. The bruise on the side of her head where Crevan had hit her with the pitcher had faded, and the swelling had gone down considerably.

Macaria looked down, avoiding his eyes. "I lied to Harrtuck. Please forgive me."

"What did you tell him?"

"I told him we'd made a secret handfasting, and I claimed a wife's right to visit." She lifted her head defiantly. "They have to allow it. It's old law. Even the condemned—" She broke off suddenly, as Carroway began to laugh.

"Forgive you? I'm only sorry that it's not the truth. I didn't think I'd see you again—this side of my hanging, anyhow."

She cringed. "Don't say that."

He sighed and held her to him. "Came a heartbeat away from swinging a few candlemarks ago. Won't be surprised if the mob returns. Maybe it's for the best."

She pushed away and stared at him, aghast. "The best? You risked everything to save Kiara's life. You're innocent. How could that possibly be best?"

Carroway lifted his bandaged hand. "Innocent or guilty, there's no life for me without my music, and there's no music without my hand."

Macaria put her hands on her hips and fixed him with a glare. "Riordan Carroway! You have a voice like one of the Lady's consorts. You write the best ballads in the Winter Kingdoms, and you have invitations from four kingdoms to arrange their next holiday feasts. Cerise said the hand may heal—"

"And it may not," he finished for her. "I can't move it without terrible pain. I'm no use to anyone, Macaria."

Her eyes relented and she wrapped her arms around him. "I disagree, but I didn't come to fight with you. I figured you'd want to know how Kiara is doing."

"And?"

"She's in and out of consciousness. She hasn't lost the baby, but she's not well. Cerise said it's the wormroot. Even if Kiara and the baby survive, Cerise has no idea what that high a dose of wormroot might do. It's possible the baby could live and not be right."

Carroway bowed his head. "I'm so sorry. If I'd just been faster—"

"That you got there at all was amazing," Macaria interrupted him. "You're all that stopped Crevan from killing her—and probably the rest of us, too."

"Harrtuck said that's going to be hard to

prove," Carroway said quietly. "When you look at it from what Harrtuck and his men saw, what's to say I didn't barge in there intending to kill Kiara and Crevan died trying to stop me?"

Macaria looked away. "Dame Nuray has already been spreading that version of the story."

"Have you seen Paiva and Bandele?"

Macaria shook her head. "They're probably lying low, waiting for some of this to blow over."

"If it comes to trial, they have the evidence against Crevan," Carroway said in a low voice only she could hear. "That's how I knew to come after him. They brought it to show me, and they must have smuggled it out of my room at the inn after I left. Without it, there's no reason why I would pick last night to escape or why Crevan intended to kill her on Candles Night." He paused. "What about Alle and the others? How are they?"

Macaria shrugged. "Alle, the cook and the scullery maid are fine. Jae, too. Cerise was able to save two of the king's dogs, but the mastiff must have eaten the largest share of poisoned meat. He was already dead."

"What a mess," Carroway said. He leaned his cheek against the top of her head and breathed in the scent of her hair, wanting to remember how it felt to have her arms around him. "I can't believe you told Harrtuck we were handfasted."

"Are you angry with me?"

Carroway chuckled. "Angry? Not at all. But I don't want my shame to taint you."

Macaria stretched up on tiptoe to kiss him. "I don't care what anyone thinks." She took the heavy woolen scarf from around her neck and clasped his right hand with hers, winding the scarf around their wrists. "There. It's hardly official, but now it's not a lie. It's as fasted as my parents ever were. Will you have me, Riordan Carroway?"

He looked at her, astonished. "For all my days, however long or short that is. But why would you bind yourself to me now? I'm as good as dead."

"No one knows how many days are left. My dad didn't mean to drown in the river, and my mum didn't set out to die of pox. I'll take these days, however many there are, and be glad for them," Macaria replied, meeting his eyes. "No regrets."

He bent down to kiss her. "None at all."

CHAPTER THIRTY

CAM OF CAIRNRACH waited to die. The explosion at the fuller's mill had tossed him into the cold winter air and hurled him into a snow bank; no small feat considering his bulk. Scorched and bleeding, he lay in the snow amid the rain of wreckage. He could still see the flames that danced high into the night sky and despite his pain, he laughed.

Abruptly he stopped, and coughed up blood.

"Let the sword be sheathed, and the helm shuttered," he murmured. "Prepare a feast in the hall of your fallen heroes. Cam of Cairnrach was stupid enough to be captured and blew his own ass sky high. Overlook that, please, and make his passage swift and his journey easy, until his soul rests in the arms of the Lady."

Jonmarc was probably right. Nobody's

listening. And if the Goddess was, she'd be laughing. What a ridiculous way to die, half burned and half frozen and spattered with fuller's muck.

"Cam! Cam of Cairnrach!" The voice came from a distance. The accent was odd and managed to mangle "rach" into "reech." Cam listened, certain he was hallucinating.

"Cam! Cam of Cairnrach!" Cam tried to respond and managed to nearly choke on his own blood. *You can't answer a vision. Dying men hear strange things. Most of them hear their mothers. It figures I'd be called to my eternal rest by a vision that can't even pronounce my name right.* Unable to move, he looked about but saw no one. Then he spotted a battered tin pot lying where it had fallen in the explosion, hanging from a piece of splintered wood. With his good hand, Cam squashed a handful of snow until it became a hard pellet of ice. He threw it against the pot, sending it clattering into the wreckage.

"I heard something. Over here!" *With my luck, he'll be a divisionist with a sharp knife.*

To his utter amazement, Rhistiart appeared out of the smoke. "I found him!"

Rhistiart dropped to his knees beside Cam and motioned for two men to follow. Cam recognized one of the men as Trygve, Donelan's personal battle healer. The other man held a sword and remained standing, taking up a position that let him ward away any unwanted newcomers.

"You got through," Cam rasped.

Rhistiart grinned. "Aye. For once in my gods-forsaken life, I did something right. And the king promised me a pardon if I could lead them to you. So here I am!"

"Lie still and don't talk," Trygve commanded sternly. Cam wanted to tell him that neither one was a stretch, but instead, he turned his head and spat blood.

"Your sister will have my hide if this doesn't work," Trygve murmured. "And you don't want a healer like her mad at you. So I'll have to do my best to heal you, and you're going to have to do your best not to die. Do we have an understanding?"

Cam gave the barest of nods.

"Good. Let's get started."

The snow chilled him through, dulling the pain as Trygve began the healing. Overhead, the moon crossed the sky as the candlemarks passed. And when Trygve reached to Rhistiart for help with the healing, to Cam's surprise, the fugitive silversmith agreed. From the look on Rhistiart's face, Cam guessed that this had become the greatest adventure of the man's life.

"No, Donelan didn't come himself," Trygve answered Cam's unspoken question. "But he sent the Veigonn, with a direct order to execute the men who captured you and to do it slowly if you were dead."

Cam's surprise must have registered on his face despite his pain. "Yeah, I know. The Veigonn doesn't go after just anyone," Trygve continued. The Veigonn were the king's personal protectors, an elite squad committed to protect the royal family. That Donelan would send them for him was a high honor.

Trygve gave a harsh laugh. "Then again, from the ransom they demanded, the divisionists must have thought you were really worth your weight in gold." Cam groaned as Trygve pressed his hands against his abdomen. "Hush. You're hurt worse where it doesn't show than where it does—and that's saying something. I've got to stop the bleeding."

"Will this help?" Rhistiart unfastened a flask from his belt, and Cam knew from the smell when it was uncapped that it held river rum.

"That will do just fine. Give it to him a bit at a time so he doesn't choke. He'll need all you can spare; he's tore up bad. But maybe not too bad to fix, if the Lady smiles on me today," Trygve said.

Cam drifted in and out of consciousness as Trygve worked. Although it seemed to Cam as if every bit of his body ached or bled, Trygve seemed most worried about the injuries no one could see, followed by the festering wound on his hand where his finger had been severed. Finally, when Cam wondered if they were all going to freeze to death, Trygve sat back on his heels.

"It should be safe to move you, though Lady knows, I'm not done yet. But at least the wagon ride back to Aberponte won't kill you."

Trygve made it as comfortable as possible, wrapping him in horse blankets and filling the wagon with straw to keep him warm. Even so, the wind was bitterly cold. To Cam's continuing surprise, Rhistiart rode with him in the back of the wagon. Rhistiart snuggled down in his heavy cloak, huddled against the wind.

"I heard Trygve talking with the leader of the Veigonn," Rhistiart said, keeping up a one-sided conversation although his teeth were chattering. "They weren't sure how they'd find you. You certainly solved that problem."

"One of my many talents," Cam murmured.

"I never thought I'd see Aberponte from the inside. At least, not unless they took me to the dungeons to hang," Rhistiart went on. "I said my piece to the first guards I came to, just like you told me to. They took me to another set of guards, and then they took me to a different set until, before I knew it, they were marching me into the palace to see the king."

He leaned forward conspiratorially. "He's taller than I thought, but then again, I've only ever seen his face on a gold piece. Anyhow, the king made me say what you told me, and then tell him everything I knew. He's a fearsome man when he's angry. Seems he's had his men out searching for you since the traitors sent him your finger. They sent me out of the room, but I could hear them arguing after I left about whether or not the king should ride out with the guards tonight. 'Tis not an easy thing to tell the king no."

"Especially Donelan."

Cam coughed and Rhistiart looked alarmed. "No, no. Don't you dare die on me. Do you hear, Cam of Cairnrach?" His breath fogged in the cold. "I'll have to sing."

"Are you trying to kill me?"

In response, Rhistiart launched into an off-key tavern tune that made the carriage driver wince and glance over his shoulder. Rhistiart's awful singing and the beat of the horses' hooves marked the time until the wagon passed through the city gates and made its way up the approach to Aberponte.

It took four men on each side to gentle Cam onto several stout boards in order to carry him into the palace. Donelan himself stood in the doorway, a dark, imposing shadow. As Cam was carried toward the upper rooms of the palace, he heard Donelan demanding a briefing from the head of the Veigonn. Rhistiart stayed beside Cam, although his singing ended abruptly as soon as the lights of the palace came into view.

Cam groaned as the men transferred him into a bed. Allestyr, Donelan's seneschal, had the room ready. It was well lit with candles and reflectors, and Cam could hear a kettle of water whistling as it boiled on the hearth. Rhistiart seemed to shrink into the shadows as the door swung open and Donelan strode into the room with Trygve.

"Well?"

"I was able to do enough at the battle site to keep him from dying," Trygve said. "This will take a while. If he weren't so well padded he'd have been dead from the explosion alone. The wound where they took his finger has soured. And his knee is shattered. I don't know how long those will take to fix—if I can fix them at all."

"I need to warn you," Cam rasped.

Donelan turned and moved to stand beside his bed. He laid a hand on Cam's shoulder, and withdrew it quickly when Cam groaned at the touch. "Rest. It will wait."

"No. Listen. Alvior betrayed you."

Donelan's eyes widened. "Alvior?"

"Ruggs… told Leather John. Alvior gave them money. He wanted the throne. I'm ashamed."

Donelan cursed. "The shame is Alvior's, not yours. Though I disapproved of what your father did to you and Carina, he always served me loyally."

"Alvior murdered him."

Donelan's eyes flashed and he strode to the door, bellowing for the leader of the Veigonn. When the man appeared, Donelan recounted Cam's report. "Send the Veigonn to Brunnfen.

Bring me Alvior in shackles. He has an account to make for himself to me."

"As you wish, m'lord."

With a backward glance toward Cam, Donelan left the room as Trygve returned through a side door with a bottle of elixir. Trygve gestured for Rhistiart to move forward from the shadows. "He'll need someone to sit with him until he's through the worst of it."

"I'll do it."

Trygve nodded. "I thought you might. The king is grateful for your service."

"You wouldn't happen to need another silversmith around the palace, would you?"

Trygve chuckled. "We might yet, before all is settled." He turned to Cam. "I need to work on your knee, and lance the poison from your hand. To spare you pain, I'm going to put you into a very deep sleep. You won't wake for several days. Your body will handle the shock better that way. Do you understand?"

Cam nodded. "Do it."

Trygve laid a hand on Cam's forehead. "Sleep, now. Find a place where there is no pain, where you feel no hurt, where there is neither fever nor cold. Sleep, while your body heals. Do not awaken until I call for you."

As Trygve spoke, Cam felt a deep calm settle over him. His eyes became too heavy to remain open, and his limbs were too leaden to move. Trygve's voice sounded as if he were moving backward, away from Cam, growing fainter and fainter until nothing remained except blessed darkness.

DAY 7

CHAPTER THIRTY-ONE

Tris Drayke looked out over the ruins of Lochlanimar. Wisps of smoke still rose from heaps of rubble, but most of the wreckage lay cold and silent. The ghosts of the necropolis and the spirits of the village dead who had not accepted Tris's offer of passage had returned to their resting places. Those soldiers who were still uninjured worked in teams headed by Soterius, Senne and Rallan to sift through the broken remains of the manor house and its bailey. On Tris's orders, they had already cordoned off the lower sections of the manor village where the plague had spread. The search progressed more quickly than expected, since so little was left standing. Still, Tris could not wait to leave the ruins.

Soterius rode up to him. "We've finished the

quadrant. It's as the ghosts said. No survivors. Not much left, aside from ash." He looked shaken. "I remember how little the air Elemental left when I fought it during the rebellion. I can't imagine that power coupled with fire."

Tris nodded. "I felt them die," he said quietly. "I heard them scream. They had no chance, no chance at all."

Soterius reined in his restless horse and looked at Tris. "I'm staying in my saddle due to sheer cussedness, and I haven't been through half of what you have. By rights, you should be flat on your back."

Tris shrugged. Though Fallon and Esme had done their best, Tris knew he was far from up to his full strength, either physically or magically. "You're probably right. But the men need to see me. I'd feel like I wasn't honoring their sacrifice if I lay abed in my tent while they're soldiering on." He grimaced. "And besides, both Esme and Fallon threatened to knock me out if I so much as moved to ride back to Shekerishet before tomorrow."

Soterius grinned. "Good for them." He sobered. "You can soothe your conscience by tending to the souls of the new casualties. We're still losing some of the battle-wounded as well as the ones with fever." He dropped his voice. "I came here prepared to lose men in battle. I didn't count on plague. We've ended the battle. But can we contain the fever?"

"In truth, I can't leave without knowing for certain that Curane and his blood mages are dead," Tris replied. "This is why I never wanted the crown. The king is duty-bound to stay. But my heart wants to set out for home tonight."

"Have there been more dreams?"

Tris shook his head. "None. That's worse. There's been nothing since Candles Night. She doesn't answer when I call for her on the Plains of Spirit." He met Soterius's eyes, and knew that the other understood the implication.

"But then again, neither did Bricen," Soterius said quietly.

Bricen's ghost had never come to Tris because Jared murdered him with a dagger that destroyed the soul. The thought that Kiara might have been taken from him forever filled Tris with the greatest fear he had ever felt. As a Summoner, he could transcend death. But even he could not bring back a soul that had been utterly destroyed.

I don't care what's happened while I've been gone. I don't care if the rumors are true. I'll win her back, or I'll stand beside her, regardless. Only please, let Kiara and the baby live.

"Can you tell from the Flow whether Carina was successful?"

Tris nodded. "The Flow is healed—and it restored my power instead of draining me. I believe it did the same for Carina. I hope so."

"Have you called for Jonmarc?" Soterius

asked quietly. "You said he'd sworn the Bargain."

Tris let himself slip into the Plains of Spirit. The paths of power were still raw and sore. He cast his magic, calling for Jonmarc. To his relief, there was no reply. He came back to himself, and shook his head. "He doesn't answer."

"That's good. It would be too quiet without him."

Tris managed a smile. "Coming from you, that says a lot."

Soterius shrugged. "He grows on you. Like fungus."

"Did you choose the men who'll ride back to Shekerishet with me?"

"They're already provisioned. They'll be ready when you are. And if you don't mind, I'd like to send Coalan with you."

Tris nodded. "He'll be a help. Fallon and I think we've figured out how to use magic to make sure the plague doesn't cling to us. The last thing we need is to carry it home. Once we're gone, she and Esme and Beyral will start releasing the healthy ones as quickly as they can. The others will have to stay here until they recover."

Or die. Tris didn't have to say it, but he knew Soterius took his meaning. And every day that it took to pack up the camp carried with it the risk of infection for those who had, so far, evaded death. There was a reason, Tris thought, that war, famine and pestilence were so frequently mentioned together by the legends. It would be Margolan's bitter fate for their shadow to cross over the land, and nothing in Tris's power as king or sorcerer could stop it.

LATER THAT EVENING, a trumpet heralded the convening of a military tribunal. Senne, Rallan, Soterius, Fallon and Beyral filed into seats along one side of the parade ground in the camp. The three highest ranking senior officers joined them, making a jury of eight in honor of the faces of the Lady. The rest of the open space was packed with soldiers curious to watch their Summoner-king try the spirits of the dead. Along with the soldiers were those ghosts who had not chosen to go to their rest: spirits of fallen Margolan soldiers, ghosts from the necropolis and the wights of the murdered villagers who had elected to remain. At the very back stood the *vayash moru*, and Tris grieved to see how their number had been reduced.

"There's no reason this can't wait," Esme scolded as she helped Tris get ready for the working. "You're not back to your full strength, even with the Flow's help. You were lucky to live through the Elemental. And you have no idea whether this is one last trap Curane's left for us."

Tris sighed. "You're probably right about everything. But I have to do this. The men

520 *Dark Lady's Chosen*

deserve to see Curane stand trial for what he's done. The ghosts deserve vindication. And, Goddess forgive me, I want to see them called to account for the harm they've caused."

Esme nodded. "I understand. Just be careful, Tris, please. Especially if you plan to start the trip back to Shekerishet tomorrow."

"That's another reason why this has to be done. I need to know whether Curane's got something to do with the rumors and my dreams about the knife. I need to know, Esme."

"As you wish, m'lord."

The orbs lay on a small table toward the front of the clearing. They pulsed with inner fire that sent streaks of red, orange and yellow through their misty interiors. Tris walked toward them, already raising a shielding between the orbs and the onlookers, mindful of how dangerous it had been to splinter the orb of the Obsidian King. The winter wind snapped Tris's hair around his face. Compared to facing down the Elemental, summoning Curane's spirit was a less powerful working, though no less fraught with potential dangers.

When his inner and outer shieldings were in place Tris raised his hands and gathered his power. In the battle for the throne, he had inadvertently gained experience in shattering magical orbs, a painful and dangerous lesson. Drawing on the Flow as well as his own magic, Tris sent a blast of power toward the orbs, a blue-white arc so bright that onlookers gasped and turned away. At the same time, Tris reached out with his Summoner's magic to grasp the souls hidden inside and wrest them free. The orbs exploded with a hail of broken glass that bounced harmlessly against his wardings and fell like ice shards into the trampled snow. When the explosion was gone, three spirits stood inside the inner wardings. Lord Curane, Tris recognized from court. One of the mages was a thin man with red hair close-cropped enough to resemble a skull cap. The other was a sullen-eyed man with lank black hair and stooped shoulders.

Tris smiled coldly and focused his power again. One more soul still needed to give full account for his treachery. Tris reached out onto the Plains of Spirit and found a soul that shrank away from his power but feared the crossing over.

Tarq. Tris felt his power make contact and closed his hand, wrapping the balky spirit in his magic to drag him back to stand trial. The audience gasped as Tarq's spirit became visible in the center warding.

"You have been summoned here to stand trial for your crimes against the crown of Margolan, the Margolan army and the villagers of Lochlanimar," Tris said, hoping his voice sounded more impartial than he felt. It would be so easy for him to be judge, jury and executioner. Just a tightening of his power, a sudden twist, and he could snuff out their souls, deny them even eternal torment and condemn them to oblivion.

I won't make Lemuel's mistake.

Setting his jaw, Tris faced the ghosts. "Curane, Lord of Lochlanimar. You are charged with treason against the throne of Margolan and conspiracy. General Tarq, you betrayed the men under your command and actively aided the enemy." He looked to the two mages. "You have invoked blood magic and caused the deaths of your own people, as well as creating a plague which may well reach beyond this battlefield. For these crimes, you stand trial before this assembly. How do you plead?"

"Unsuccessful, and unrepentant," Curane spat. "You'll never be half the king your brother was. You're weak like your father, and like Donelan. The divisionists were too stupid to know my men were behind them, using them to weaken Donelan until the Isencroft crown fell. With Jared's son on the Margolan throne, Margolan would have ruled Isencroft and soon, the Winter Kingdoms." He gave a cold smile. "Enjoy your trial. Crevan's betrayed both you and Donelan. He's carried out his orders by now. Your outland queen is dead, and with her, your heir."

Although Tris had steeled himself to remain emotionless, Curane seemed to see what he wanted in Tris's eyes. "Let the plague run its course. It will make it all the easier for Trevath to pick up the pieces. My grandson is safe inside Trevath. Your heir is dead. I may not have lived to see my victory, but while you may have won this battle, I have won the war."

Every fiber of Tris's being warred with his conscience. *I want vengeance. I want to avenge Kiara, the baby, all the soldiers and villagers whose lives have been squandered. I want to make him pay for what he's done. I want to destroy him myself. Goddess help me! And if I do, I become what Lemuel was, a monster worse than anything he destroyed. I make a mockery of everything we've fought for. Forgive me, Kiara. I won't do that, even if I forfeit my right to avenge you.*

Tris knew that Soterius and Fallon were watching him closely. He could see in their eyes that they guessed at his struggle. Forcing down his emotions, Tris turned to the ghosts of Tarq and the two mages. "Have you anything to say for yourselves?"

Tarq smirked as he glanced from Tris to Soterius. "My only regret is that I didn't have better aim."

The red-haired mage drew himself up to his full height. "I was privileged to serve my lord," he replied, meeting Tris's gaze. "And I served him to the best of my ability."

The second mage did not look up, avoiding Tris's eyes with a sullen look. "I have no regrets.

I serve the memory of King Jared, Margolan's rightful king."

Tris turned to the jury. "You've heard them speak for themselves. What is your ruling?"

Senne's eyes were hard. "Judgment."

Soterius looked at Tarq and Curane with loathing. "Judgment."

Fallon glanced at the remaining jurors, who slowly nodded. "We rule for judgment."

Tris found that he felt nothing as he looked back to the four condemned spirits. No triumph, no vindication, not even satisfaction. Just an eerie coldness that seemed to permeate every corner of his soul. "The jury has spoken. We give you over to the judgment of the Lady. May you answer to Her for your crimes for eternity."

On the Plains of Spirit, Tris felt a shift that signaled the presence of the Goddess. His soul cringed as he recognized the Aspect that came for the condemned men. It was Nameless, the Formless One, a dark and faceless presence. Tris had no idea how much the living audience could sense, but the spirits in the audience fled before the Formless One as her bleak aura filled the space. Tris held his ground, although everything in him wanted to flee. Nameless passed by him like a frigid wind, covering the four cringing spirits with her shroud-like wings. Tris could hear the screams of their spirits as Nameless drew them into the Void.

Dirmed's spirit fell to his knees, sobbing and rocking. "You're not real," he murmured over and over, until the darkness that was Nameless began to draw off strips of soul that unwound like ghostly entrails until there was nothing left.

Cadoc screamed and tried to flee, but Tris's power held him in his place. Frozen with fear, the red-haired mage began to chant, calling on his magic and the names of the ancient gods to save him. Nameless's shadow passed through his ghost like obsidian slivers as he screamed and begged for mercy, his cries echoing until, like the tattered bits of his soul, his voice faded to nothing.

Tarq shrank back against the warding, screaming in terror. The darkness pulled at him from all directions, shredding his form as if he were being flayed, drawn and quartered. He shrieked until the tendrils of darkness had pulled his form limb from limb, leaving it until last to smash in his head as the whips of his soul dissipated.

Curane stood rigidly, his face betraying no emotion. He did not try to run, and he did not grovel. Eyes clear, chin lifted, Curane stared into the darkness, resolute. Only when the night swallowed him completely did a strangled scream escape the enveloping shadow.

Abruptly, there was silence. Tris felt himself shaking as he carefully lowered the wardings. From the ashen faces and terrified looks of the jury and audience, he knew that, even though they lacked his power as a Summoner, they had sensed something of Nameless's terrible presence.

"Believe that you are fully avenged," Tris said quietly. He felt utterly spent, but he stayed on his feet and was steady enough to refuse Esme's help. Fallon, Esme and Soterius walked back with him to his tent. His control lasted until they were safely inside. Coalan moved silently to bring them each a warm mug of brandy. Tris sank into a chair and covered his face with his hands.

"How could I have been so blind? Curane's had a man at the very heart of things all this time. Crevan was Curane's man, and I left Kiara and the baby defenseless." The loss he felt was overwhelming, making it difficult to breathe.

"We're a long way from Shekerishet," Soterius said quietly. "Curane has no way to know that Crevan was successful. He knows even less what's going on in Isencroft. That's cause for hope."

Tris said nothing. Fallon laid a hand on his shoulder, and Tris felt her magic join with his, helping to bear the burden of his grief. Esme knelt next to him. "I'll do everything in my power to make sure you're as fully healed as possible so you can ride with the first light," she said quietly. "There's nothing left to do here that requires the king's presence. After Curane's confession, the men know what may be at stake at Shekerishet. No one will begrudge you your leave."

"Thank you," Tris said raggedly. He drew his sleeve across his eyes. "It's hardly the homecoming I envisioned." He dared not let himself think about what lay ahead if Curane was right. *Donelan would be within his rights to declare war—assuming he's held his throne against the divisionists. Both our kingdoms will be destroyed if it comes to that. Margolan will be without a legitimate heir. And I—*He could not bring himself to finish the sentence. Without Kiara, he would be forced into a political alliance just to secure the succession. That thought chilled him more than any fear for his own safety. *I will have lost everything.*

CHAPTER THIRTY-TWO

THE STEADY POUNDING of hammers echoed within Carroway's tower cell. Below in the bailey, workmen built a gallows within sight of his window. After the first night, the mob had subsided, making him apprehensive about Guarov's next move.

He did not have long to wait. Before the noon bells rang, the door to his cell opened. Harrtuck entered first, with a scowl that made his mood plain. Behind him was Lord Guarov. "M'lord," Carroway said cautiously. He glanced to Harrtuck for some kind of signal, but Harrtuck looked away.

"How do you like my new construction?" Guarov asked, watching Carroway closely.

Carroway did his best to give away nothing in his expression. "It looks to be sturdy, m'lord."

Guarov looked around. "I guess you're entitled to this chamber, as your family was noble, but if it were up to me, I'd have you in shackles in the lower level."

"It isn't," Harrtuck growled.

Guarov ignored Harrtuck. "The queen has not yet awakened. As it stands, your treachery is a hanging offense. But if she and the heir die, the Council of Nobles will have no choice but to charge you with treason, conspiracy against the king and regicide." Guarov's dark eyes narrowed, and the muscles of his jaw tightened. "The penalty for which is to be hanged, drawn and quartered."

Carroway blanched. He tried to keep his face emotionless, but his heart raced and one hand balled into a fist. "I understand."

"Are you familiar with the process?" Guarov pressed. "They hang you until you're nearly dead, and a healer revives you. Then you're broken on the wheel until your bones snap and your joints are sundered, and finally, they take four large horses—"

"For the love of the gods, enough!" Harrtuck said.

"You forget your place, *Captain* Harrtuck."

Harrtuck's expression made his feelings clear, but he fell silent.

"I am familiar." Carroway drew on all of his acting skill to keep his voice steady.

A cold smile touched the corners of Guarov's

face. "There is an alternative. If you were to make a full confession of your crimes before the court, I might be able to get the executioner to shorten your pain. But it would need to be a full confession: that you forced the queen to your bed, and that you went to the king's lodge in a jealous rage to strike her down, killing Crevan as he tried to protect her."

Carroway's jaw was tight. "I understand."

Guarov met his eyes. "It's unfortunate about the girl. As an accomplice, she'll be banished under interdiction, along with any bastard she bears to you." His eyes gleamed as he saw Carroway flinch. "Do you know what interdiction is? She'll be anathema, by writ of the king. No noble house or legitimate inn may give her shelter without incurring royal penalty."

He paused. "Still, I can be merciful. If she were to renounce you publicly, tell the court that you abused your patronage to take advantage of her and that she feared for her life to go against you, I could be persuaded to lessen her sentence to banishment only. She might find work in a tavern instead of a bawdy house."

Carroway's fist tightened until his nails dug into his palm. "Let her renounce me. I'll be dead."

Guarov's eyes shone. "The king may be in the field for months with the army. If the queen dies, this matter cannot be allowed to fester.

Listen for the death knell. I'll see you hang that same night."

Guarov turned with a flourish of his heavy cape. "See that his door is secured and doubly guarded," he commanded Harrtuck as he left the room. "We can't afford another escape."

When Guarov was gone, Harrtuck looked to Carroway. "I'm sorry, Carroway. I have authority over a mob, but I can't act against the Council."

"What have you heard? Is Kiara dying?"

Harrtuck shrugged. "Cerise is worried. Kiara hasn't awakened. It may be the wormroot. Cerise still doesn't know how it may affect the baby. Goddess knows what a mess it made of Tris last year! And unfortunately, we have no idea when Tris and the army will return."

Carroway turned away, walking a few steps to stand before the fire. "Is there anything you can do to protect Macaria?"

Harrtuck snorted. "I've got my hands full protecting you. But it may not be quite as dire as Guarov makes it sound. Alle told me that some of the Council are livid about the way he's been threatening you. She says Acton practically had a stroke when he heard about the gallows, he was so angry. Lord Dravan nearly came to blows with Guarov over it. He's taking this personally, since he was a friend of your father's. And according to Alle, Eadoin's gotten wind of it and informed the Council that she will join them in person before the week is through if she has to wake from the dead."

"I'm grateful. But if Kiara dies, the court will need someone to blame. Crevan's already dead. I'm convenient."

Harrtuck nodded. "Aye. And all too few seem to remember Guarov's ties to Lady Nadine to see that he's finally taking her vengeance." He paused. "I hope it doesn't come to this, but I won't see you suffer." He took a dagger from his belt and handed it, hilt first, to Carroway. Harrtuck met his eyes. "I've only seen one man drawn and quartered. I haven't the stomach to see another—least of all a friend. Many a soldier's turned his blade on his own wrists rather than give his enemy that satisfaction. 'Tis a quick and honorable way to seek the Lady, if there's no other choice."

Carroway swallowed hard and took the blade, concealing it in his doublet. "Thank you."

Harrtuck laid a hand on his shoulder. "I'll see that the guards bring you brandy by mistake tonight. Take comfort where you can."

CHAPTER THIRTY-THREE

JONMARC VAHANIAN ROSE just after dawn. His room at Airenngeir, Astasia's manor house, was opulent, furnished almost as lavishly as King Staden's palace. A cold breakfast waited on a side table, along with his weapons and a new sword to replace the one broken in the battle at the Lady's temple. A note in Gabriel's handwriting drew a rough map to show him the way back to the main road. The house was silent, giving Jonmarc to believe that few, if any, mortal servants assisted Astasia and her brood.

He ate quickly and buckled on his weapons, trying the new sword in his hand. It was perfectly balanced and beautifully made: Jonmarc was certain Gabriel had a hand in its choosing. His body ached as he moved. Vigulf's healing had cured only the wounds that were life-threatening. Other damage, such as his cracked ribs and the gashes from the battle, still throbbed. Jonmarc bandaged them as best he could, resigned to a painful ride home.

I'm afraid of what I'll find when I get back to Dark Haven. I saw Malesh burn. I know what that had to have done to Carina. I have to return. People are depending on me. But Dark Haven without her will never be home.

He descended the broad staircase without encountering another person, living or dead. The manor house was deserted, its undead occupants safely resting in hidden chambers below. Jonmarc found a horse tethered outside for him, its saddlebags already provisioned for the ride. Without a backward glance, he swung up to the saddle.

The road was deep with snow but passable. He saw few other travelers, and those he passed gave him wary glances. Knowing how he must look, Jonmarc couldn't blame them. His leather great cloak was cut and torn from the battle, stained with blood and ichor. He was dirty with grime and sweat and sported a week's growth of beard. His tunic was torn open at the neck, dark and stiff with his own blood. *I look like a brigand, or worse. I'll be lucky if I don't have to outride guardsmen to get home.*

The day was bitterly cold. Jonmarc did his best to keep his thoughts focused on scanning the road for threats. As for what would happen when he returned to Dark Haven, he kept his mind blank. Time enough for that when he arrived. He ate a cold lunch as he rode, unwilling to chance causing a scene at a tavern. Candlemarks slipped by, marked only by the crunch of his horse's hooves.

Maybe Gabriel was right. Maybe Riqua and Taru were able to heal Carina, protect her from what happened to Malesh. Part of him clung to that thought as he rode.

Mid-afternoon, he reached a rise in the road. In the distance, Jonmarc could see Dark Haven against the snow-covered mountains, and all hope died. From its tower flew a flag of mourning.

Jonmarc stopped in his tracks. High winds whipped the gray flag. His throat tightened. *I can't do this. I can't bury her.* He would find where they had laid Carina's body to say goodbye, and then find oblivion in a bottle of brandy.

A new sound carried on the winter wind. In the distance, he heard the clash of steel.

Dark Haven was under attack.

Grief became rage as Jonmarc urged his horse for as much speed as he could muster in the rutted snow. As he neared the gates, he saw his guards engaged against a mob armed with sickles, scythes and axes. With a roar, Jonmarc stood in his stirrups, brandishing swords in both hands. The mob heard him and turned as the beleaguered guards raised a cry in greeting.

"Drop your weapons and go home," Jonmarc shouted to the mob. "The war is over."

Three men charged at him. One swung a sickle, while the others were armed with farm axes. Jonmarc's swords glinted in the sun. The sickle man fell back with a scream as the sickle and the hand holding it fell into the snow. The two axemen closed, but Jonmarc's horse reared, kicking its huge front hooves to fell one of the men as Jonmarc's sword finished the other. He stared down the remaining mob.

"Go home. The war is over. The Truce will stand. Leave now, or by the Crone, they'll carry you home in pieces."

Caught between the emboldened guards and Jonmarc's swords, the mob grumbled, and then man by man, began to disperse, straggling off in all directions.

Jonmarc rode through the cheering guards as the manor's gates opened for him. He slid from his saddle and absently handed his reins to the groomsman who ran to assist him. Neirin was striding toward him.

"Where is she?"

Neirin pointed, and Jonmarc turned, frowning against the glare of the sun on the snow. A cloaked figure was running down Dark Haven's broad steps. The hood fell back as the figure reached him, and Carina threw her arms around him.

Jonmarc gritted his teeth against the pain of his broken ribs as he caught her, stunned. It took a few seconds for it to register that she stood in full daylight and that her lips were warm. He could feel the warmth of her breath and the beating of her heart as she kissed him.

"How?" he whispered in a strangled voice as the crowd in the bailey began to cheer.

Carina stepped back far enough to meet his eyes. "It's a long story. I didn't think you'd make it back." She seemed to take in his grimy cloak and the bloody tunic, as well as the newly healed punctures on the side of his neck. Her expression changed, and Jonmarc knew she had extended her healer's magic. "You're hurt."

"Nothing that won't heal. Now." He took her hand, amazed at its warmth, too overcome by this sudden reversal to think straight.

It suddenly registered with him that the courtyard was full of strangers. "Who are all these people and how did they get here?"

"They're refugees. Every spare room is full of them. They got caught in the crossfire of Malesh's war, or they came here because their neighbors were trying to kill them. Humans, *vayash moru, vyrkin.*"

"And the flag?" He could see sorrow in Carina's eyes as she turned away.

"We thought we'd lost you. So many are dead. Not just the guards who went to fight for you, but the *vyrkin* and the villagers. And the families of the refugees." She shook her head. "I don't know how we'll know when it's safe to send the refugees home."

Jonmarc took her hand. "We'll figure that out tomorrow. I want to know everything that happened," he said as she walked with him into the manor house. "But first, I had better clean up or you'll put me out with the pigs." He gave her a wicked look. "And I have no intention of missing another night with you. Ever."

CARINA CALLED A servant to draw a hot bath for Jonmarc. She saw him wince as he shouldered out of his great cloak and she put a hand against his arm to gently press him into a chair.

"What are you doing? I've been in battle for a week. I smell."

Carina wrinkled her nose. "No worse than all those times we hid in barns and cellars for weeks at a time last year. Or did you forget?"

"At the time, we all smelled equally bad. Now, I suspect you'd notice."

"I do. But it bothers me more that you're in pain."

"It's not so bad."

Carina gave Jonmarc a look that let him know she knew he was lying. She swallowed hard when she looked at his blood-soaked tunic, remembering her vision of Malesh's attack. She touched him with her magic, moving her palm to the gashes and deep bruises of the battle, making them whole. The ribs would take longer, but she sped their healing, easing his pain. She lifted away his tunic, and caught her breath at the sight of the branded mark over his heart. Carina could feel a shadow of the Lady's touch. She had healed enough times with Tris to recognize it.

"How did you make the Bargain and live?"

Jonmarc met her eyes. "The Lady owns my soul. Maybe She always did. It seems I'm the Winter Kingdoms' best bet against some big, nasty badass we don't even know is out there. Poor Winter Kingdoms. I guess even the Lady has to make do."

Carina let her magic fill her, healing the torn ligaments and pulled muscles that were evidence of a vicious battle. Enhanced by her encounter with the Flow, her magic went deeper than before, and Carina felt a raw wound that had nothing to do with blood or sinew. She gasped as she touched the pain and realized it was mind and not body. Jonmarc reached out to steady her, a confused look on his face. His emotions overwhelmed her: grief, rage, vengeance and finally, in the Lady's temple, resignation. Carina felt the horror of the last days wash over her and she marshaled her nascent mind healing gift to blunt that pain, not erasing it but making it recede to a manageable memory.

"How did you do that?" Jonmarc asked raggedly as she bowed her head.

Carina looked up to meet his eyes. "Thank the Flow. I was in the middle of healing it when you and Malesh fought. Without the Flow and without Tris anchoring me, I probably wouldn't have survived. I healed the Flow. And since then, my magic is... different. Stronger. I can mind heal. Taru doesn't have an explanation, but she has a theory. She thinks the Flow gave me the power to mind heal out of gratitude."

"Gratitude? It thinks?"

"Something like that." She reached out to touch his cheek. "There's so much to tell you. But there's time."

Just then, a servant opened the door from the sitting room. "M'lord, your bath is drawn."

Jonmarc grinned. "There are only two things I want right now: you, and a bath. But I'd better take the bath first."

Carina was waiting for him when he toweled off from his bath, and from the way she drew him to her, Jonmarc knew Carina had missed him as intensely as he had longed for her. They made love with a ferocity that rocked him to the core of his being, and Carina let her magic slip against his mind, twining their thoughts. Afterward, they lay tangled together, and he ran his fingers through her short, dark hair, breathing in her scent. "I didn't think I'd see you again," he confessed. "Not this side of the Gray Sea."

She gently touched the newly healed puncture wounds on his throat. "I saw this," she said in a voice barely above a whisper. "I saw you fall. I felt him burn."

"It's not fair," Jonmarc said, kissing her forehead. "You can heal my memories, but I can't do the same for you."

Carina snuggled into his shoulder. "Taru can. Maybe I'll ask. But not today." She drew his arm around her. "You're here. That's enough to keep the bad dreams away."

A knock at the door startled them. "M'lord?" It was Neirin's voice. "I'm sorry for the interruption, but it's not something that can wait."

Jonmarc frowned and disentangled himself from Carina with a quick kiss. He sat up, pulled on his clothes and belted on his sword as Carina reluctantly dressed in a shift and her healer's robes. Jonmarc was quite sure Neirin could guess what he'd interrupted, although his grounds manager was discreet enough to pretend otherwise.

"This had better be important."

"There's a regiment of the king's guards at the gate."

Jonmarc followed Neirin downstairs and across the courtyard with Carina a few steps behind them. He gestured for the guards to open the sentry's door, leaving the massive gates barred. Outside, he found one hundred mounted soldiers in King Staden's livery armed for battle.

Carina and Neirin remained inside the walls. With his hand well away from his sword, Jonmarc stopped a few paces outside Dark Haven's walls in front of the ranking officer's horse and looked up at the captain. He was a large man a decade or so older than Jonmarc, his hair short-cropped beneath his helm and enough scars visible on his cheek and forearms to convince Jonmarc the man was a seasoned fighter.

"What brings you and your men to Dark Haven, Captain?"

"I'm Captain Gellyr, commander of the king's force at Jannistorp," the man replied. Jonmarc knew the place. It was an outpost at the edge of Dark Haven's lands, on one of the major roads leading to Principality City. "In the last two days, we've been overrun with villagers asking for protection. Something about a war between *vayash moru* and mortals. You know anything about that?" He glanced up at the gray flag that snapped in the night wind.

Jonmarc motioned for the captain to come with him. With a nod to his men, the captain dismounted and gave his reins to one of Jonmarc's guards. He followed Jonmarc into the guardhouse, where Jonmarc offered him a chair and a tankard of ale. Gellyr sat down and waved off the ale.

"You may change your mind after you've heard the story," Jonmarc warned. The captain accepted the tankard. Grimly, Jonmarc told the captain about Malesh's attacks and the battles that had followed, omitting only his Bargain with the Lady and Carina's healing of the Flow.

"You're certain Malesh is dead?"

"Quite." Both Jonmarc and Carina answered in unison.

The captain set down his tankard and bit his lip as he thought. "So you've got a keep full of refugees?"

Jonmarc nodded. "I don't have enough guards to assure a safe return to their villages. The battle took a toll on the *vayash moru* and the *vyrkin* who fought to preserve the Truce. They're in no shape to protect their families, and they could be in danger themselves if they return. It's not a *vayash moru* attack I'm worried about now. It's the mortals, out for vengeance." He grimaced. "I fought off some on the road, and I stared down a mob at the gates, but frankly, captain, I've been at war for seven days and I'm tired."

"I dare say we can help with that." Captain Gellyr grinned. "You're liegeman to King Staden, which makes your problems his problems. My men and I are posted out here to keep the king from having problems. Without being heavy-handed about it, I'm betting things would cool down really quickly if my soldiers were to patrol the roads, make ourselves very visible in the villages and let it be known that *all* of Dark Haven's residents—living or dead—are under the king's protection." He leaned forward. "For the record, Staden absolutely hates raiders, whether they're home-grown or outlanders. I'd say the mobs you've faced down qualify, so this duty is well within my charter." He held out his hand. "Pleased to be of service, Lord Vahanian. A few weeks of seeing my men keep the peace, and I'll bet money your troublemakers will think twice and fade away."

Jonmarc shook the captain's hand and watched as Gellyr returned to his soldiers. Carina slipped an arm around Jonmarc's waist as they made their way back across the snowy courtyard toward the manor house. "Do you think it will work?" she asked.

"If there aren't any new incidents, maybe. We'll have to do our best to make sure the refugees don't go looking for vengeance or we'll have a whole new war on our hands." He turned as they climbed the broad front steps and looked at the shadowed mountains. "Gabriel and Riqua will have their hands full seeing to the *vayash moru*. Their broods have lost a lot of good people. As for Uri, he's scared more than repentant, but I think even he will keep his mouth shut—for a while."

Jonmarc and Carina walked back into Dark Haven, closing the heavy door behind them. "Now I have a question," Jonmarc said. "How long does the mourning last?"

"Eight days, starting yesterday. Why?"

In answer, Jonmarc took her in his arms. "I made a vow at Winterstide that we'd make a ritual wedding. And I have no intention of letting little things like a war, the Goddess or the Flow get in the way."

DAY 14

CHAPTER THIRTY-FOUR

CAM OF CAIRNRACH stirred as consciousness returned. His mouth tasted of old vomit, and he doubted he had the strength to lift himself from his bed. When he opened his eyes, it took a moment to recognize the room as his own. He was back inside Aberponte, and he was alive.

"He's waking up."

The voice came from somewhere near his left shoulder. Cam managed to turn his head far enough to see Rhistiart's broad grin.

"Glad to see you, sleepy head," the silversmith teased. "You've given us a right scare."

Trygve came into Cam's field of view. "Good to have you back with us," the healer said. "Get your bearings, and we'll bring up some food. We've managed to get some broth into you, but if you don't eat, you won't keep up your battle weight, that's for sure." Something in Trygve's eyes told Cam that the teasing covered serious concern.

Cam heard Trygve speak a few muffled words to the guards outside his door. After a while, he heard bootsteps in the hallway and the door swung open again.

"He's awake? By the Lady! That's good news. Let's see him." King Donelan strode into the room, and Rhistiart scrambled out of the way. Donelan bent over Cam and grinned broadly. "Good to see you, m'boy. You've given us all a scare."

"Good to be here," Cam croaked, his throat dry.

"Trygve says he's patched you up as best he can," Donelan continued. "But as soon as the roads are passable and you're up to the journey, we'll send you to Dark Haven, where Carina can fix what's left. Do you some good to get away from here for a while, I wager."

"What of Alvior?"

Donelan cursed. "Seems your brother caught wind that my men were on their way. He disappeared across the Northern Sea on a ship with markings no one seems to recognize. Found your younger brother, Renn, locked in the basement. By the look of him, he and Alvior had disagreed." Donelan stroked his beard. "With Alvior a fugitive and wanted for treason, the title and lands would go to you as the next oldest heir."

Cam's head spun at the thought of it. "What about Renn?"

Donelan shrugged. "Everything my men uncovered says he opposed what Alvior was doing, and Alvior nearly killed him for it. He's not the baby brother you left behind. Renn's a grown man, the same age as Tris Drayke. He asked after you and Carina, and he sent this back with the guards for you." Donelan reached into his doublet and withdrew a sealed parchment letter. He laid it on the bed next to Cam.

"And the divisionists?" It was taking all of Cam's will to maintain the conversation, and from the look on Trygve's face, the healer disapproved.

"With Ruggs and Leather John dead, the rest folded with little more than a whimper," Donelan said with a predator's smile. "Hell of a thing you did there, blowing yourself up. Remind me to give you a medal once you're up and around." He cleared his throat. "Which reminds me. The brewer's daughter has refused to leave the grounds without seeing you. She arrived the night we brought you back. Bit of a firecat, that one," he said with a wink.

"Rhosyn?"

Donelan shrugged. "That might be the name. Looks like a healthy lass. Shall I let Trygve clean you up and then give permission for them to let her in?"

"I'd be grateful."

Donelan chuckled. "Figured you'd end up with a girl who could keep you in ale. Maybe she'll be good for you." He nodded toward Cam's injured leg, still immobilized in a splint. "It's going to take a bit to get you up and around." Donelan looked to Trygve. "Send down for the girl when you're ready. And keep me posted on how Cam's doing. I want to be the first to know when he hauls his sorry rump out of bed." With that, Donelan turned and strode from the room.

Trygve cleared his throat. "Well, then. Where were we?"

"How about telling me whether I'll ever walk again, for starters. And whether my left hand is still attached."

Trygve took a long breath. "Ah, about that. Yes. You haven't lost either the leg or the hand, but it was close as a whisker. I may not be quite the healer Carina is, but I wager that any less magic would have lost you both. What do you remember?"

"Freezing my ass off in the snow outside the fuller's mill," Cam replied. "Waking up here. You said you were going to make me sleep."

"That I did. You slept for three days, and then I brought you up to consciousness long enough to sip some water—most of which you spat back at me—and a bit of broth. You've been down for another three days, and I don't dare keep you under longer or you'll starve. You're not fixed up yet."

As he awakened more fully, Cam became aware of a dull ache in his left arm. His broken knee throbbed despite Trygve's efforts to blunt the pain. "I feel like my head's full of wool."

Trygve chuckled. "That's because of the drugs you've had for the pain. You needed more than my magic could do for you. The potions are hard on the stomach, but they're far better than the alternative."

"Will I heal?" Cam was sure Trygve could hear the apprehension in his question. *I've seen soldiers banged up like this. Most of them never were any use for soldiering again. I can fight with a bum left hand, but if I can't walk, my fighting days are over.*

"Heal? Yes. And before you ask, I think you'll be able to walk, tho' I won't guarantee you won't have a limp. Your knee looked like a smashed piece of crockery. Took me several days just for that working, not counting the mess they made of your hand. That's why I asked Donelan to send you to Carina once you can travel. I'm nearing the limit of what I can do, but I'm certain someone with her skill can do more." Trygve grinned. "Besides, if you're in Dark Haven, you won't be tempted to sneak back on duty before you're ready for it."

Cam gestured with his good hand to the letter Donelan left behind. "Please. Read it," he requested as two servants came to change his clothes and sponge off his face and the parts of his body not covered in bandages.

Trygve frowned in thought as he picked up

the letter and broke the wax seal. "How long has it been since you heard from your brother?"

"Eleven years."

Trygve drew a deep breath and paused to make out the cramped writing. "Dear Cam and Carina. With father dead and Alvior gone missing (may he rot in the Crone's belly), I'm finally free to write to you. For years, I didn't know where you'd gone. We only learned you were with the king a few years ago. I tried once to get a letter through, but Alvior found out and told father, and he beat me for the effort.

"I know your last memories of Brunnfen weren't pleasant. Mother never forgave father for sending you and Carina away. She took fever and died shortly afterward; I always thought she lost the will to live.

"I wanted you to know that the nobles who had such a fit about you being twins are long dead, and the issue about magic was mostly in father's head. What I'm trying to say is that you'd be welcome here if you're of a mind to come back, seeing as how you're the eldest living son and the title is vacant.

"I'm taller by half than when you left, with more than a passing resemblance to Carina. I'd had a farmer's tan from helping in the fields (it kept me out of Alvior's way), but when he found out that I suspected he had ties to the divisionists, Alvior locked me in the basement. Now I'm pale as the *vayash moru*, and likely to stay so until spring.

"The last few seasons have been hard on Brunnfen. As with most of Isencroft, the harvest has been middling and the wheat got blight. It's no real prize, but the house is sturdy (though still as cold as I wager you remember it). Until you make up your mind, I'll do my best to keep the servants directed and start the planting as soon as the snows melt.

"Whether you choose to stay or not, I would give anything to see you and Carina again. If you don't want to return to Brunnfen, then send for me and I'll make the journey to Aberponte.

"I trust this finds you and Carina in good health. May the Lady's hand be upon you," Trygve concluded. "It's signed, 'Renn'."

Cam was silent for a moment. "All these years, and I never imagined a time when Brunnfen would be open to Carina and me again. And now... I don't know what to think."

"There's no rush. It could well be summer before you're back from Dark Haven."

"I don't know what Carina will say. She half raised Renn. I know she'll be grieved to know about mother's passing." Cam sighed. "It's a bit much, all at once."

"Perhaps you'd like to see your visitor now," Trygve suggested. At Cam's nod, he spoke a word to Rhistiart, who went downstairs. Before long, a knock came at the door. Trygve opened the door to admit a plump young woman. She looked decidedly uncomfortable amid the palace's finery, but the glint in her eye was resolute. She spotted Cam in the bed and rushed forward, covering her mouth with her hands to stifle a cry.

"I'll leave you two alone," Trygve said with a wink to Cam. He turned to the woman. "Mind that you can't stay long," he warned. "He's only just awakened. I wouldn't have called for you this quickly under most circumstances."

The young woman nodded. Trygve closed the door behind him. "Cam?" she asked hesitantly.

Cam managed a wan smile. "Hello, Rhosyn."

Rhosyn moved closer, and gasped as she got a good look at Cam's injuries. "Does it hurt?"

"Some. Though I think Trygve's given me enough drugs to fell a cow."

Rhosyn dared to touch his right arm, a rare spot between bandages. "I heard that you'd been captured," she said quietly. "There were guardsmen at the ale house talking about it. Then Dav, the boy who slops the pigs, saw the wagon when they brought you back. I came to see you, but they wouldn't let me in. The girls in the kitchen gave me a place to stay. I asked after you every day." She looked down. "I hope you don't mind."

"Trygve says I may walk, but he won't promise I can soldier," Cam said, fighting against the drugs that slurred the edges of his words. "Wants me to go to Carina and see what she can do." He tried to put on a brave face.

"May be that I'll need Dav's job slopping hogs if they can't put me right."

Rhosyn squared her shoulders. "Don't you say that, Cam. How many times did father tell you that if you get tired of the palace he'd take you for a partner in the brewery? Besides being his best customer, you make a fine mash when the hops are in."

"You deserve better than a lamed old war horse like me."

"Are you deaf? Have you not heard a word I've been sayin'? You must take us for the vintners, making wine with our feet. You've a good head on your shoulders, Cam of Cairnrach. You can taste things in the brew others can't. Doesn't take a sturdy back to brew ale, but it needs a nose and a tongue that's above average." She gave him a sideways glance. "And you're smarter than you look, which could get you a good bargain with the growers."

"I don't know how long it will take before they think I'm up to the trip to Dark Haven, or how long I'll be there," Cam warned. Part of him wished desperately that he could take her in his arms, and the rest feared that she would eventually change her mind when she fully realized what a mess Ruggs had made of him.

"Then I'll wait. I've got my dad's stubborn streak. Unless you're wantin' to be rid of me." She phrased it teasingly, but Cam glimpsed uncertainty in her eyes.

"What I want is you beside me, to warm me up. By the Crone! I don't think I'll ever be warm again. As for what else I want... well, between the drugs and the way Trygve's got me bandaged up, anything else will have to wait."

Rhosyn blushed. "Mind your manners, Cam. If father heard you talk like that, he'd go to the king to save my honor, and you'd find yourself handfasted at sword's point."

"Truly a fate worse than death."

"If you hadn't been thrashed within a breath of seeing the Crone, I'd smack you for that! Seeing how you are, I'll blame the drugs." She gave him a broad grin. "There's nothing to stop me from helping you recuperate until they send you away. Might even smuggle you in a pint or two if you're nice to me."

Cam felt himself fading. "That's what I thought about, when they had me locked up. You and your daddy's ale."

"I guess that's romantic, in a strange, backhanded sort of way," she replied. "The question is, which did you miss more?"

Before Cam could answer, the door opened and Trygve returned. "He really needs to rest," the healer told Rhosyn. He glanced from her to Cam and back again. "Perhaps you'd do me a favor," he said. "Could you visit again, in a day or two? This great ox is going to need some incentive to finish his healing, and it won't be easy. Having a visitor might be the tonic he needs."

Rhosyn pretended to think about it for a moment. "Agreed." She looked at Trygve slyly. "And I can guarantee you an open tab at the brewery if you let me visit regularly."

"That's bribery!" Cam protested half-heartedly.

"Damn right it is," Trygve replied. "You have a deal," he said to Rhosyn. She blew a kiss to Cam before she turned to follow a servant from the room.

Trygve moved to stand beside Cam's bed as Rhistiart let himself back into the room. Trygve helped Cam sit and Rhistiart brought over a tray with soup, custard and a cup of watered wine. "I'm glad you've got a reason to live," Trygve said, "because the next stage in your healing may have you wishing Ruggs had finished you off. I'll have to lance the last of the poison from the blood in your arm, and after I make a few more healings to that knee, you'll need to start trying to bend it or it will freeze that way and you really won't walk again."

"I'll be ready," Cam promised, losing his battle to keep Rhistiart from feeding him. "Only next time, can you ask the cook to send up brandy?"

CHAPTER THIRTY-FIVE

"Sorry for the delay, Your Majesty," the young lieutenant apologized. "But the snow's drifted too deep for the horses up ahead. I've sent two men to clear a way through."

Tris Drayke nodded. The winter wind tore at his heavy cloak, whipping the new snow with blinding ferocity. A snowstorm had frustrated his efforts to travel quickly, dropping snow so heavily that they had been forced to take shelter one whole day. Now, just a day's ride from Shekerishet, their progress was maddeningly slow.

They trudged on, with four men clearing the way as the others carefully picked a path through the deep snow. But as they rounded the bend near where the old Lamb's Eye Inn stood, Tris felt a shift in the temperature that had nothing to do with the foreboding clouds overhead. He held up a hand for the party to stop.

"What is it, m'lord?" the captain asked.

Tris extended his power to make clear to them what he already saw on the Plains of Spirit. A score of ghosts glided toward them, unencumbered by the snow. Tris dismounted and walked to meet them. Several he recognized as the palace ghosts, Comar Hassad, Ula the nursemaid and Seanna. His eyes widened as he saw the newly dead spirits of Zachar, Malae, Bian the cook, Kiara's guards Ammond and Hothan and several of the palace help.

Zachar's spirit moved to the front, and he gave a courteous bow. "Your Majesty," he said. "We must speak with you before you reach the palace."

At Tris's signal, the soldiers circled their horses to provide as much shelter from the wind as possible. Tris gestured for the captain and the lieutenant to join him. Unbidden, Coalan followed them. "What happened?" Tris asked, appalled to find his old friend and loyal seneschal among the dead.

"Crevan betrayed all of us," Zachar replied. Tris listened as Zachar recounted Crevan's treachery and told of the murders. Tris felt his temper rise as Zachar told about the attacks on Kiara, Carroway's imprisonment and Guarov's use of the Council of Nobles. "We can vouch for the queen's honor, and for Carroway's as well," Zachar finished. "But what Crevan started, Lord Guarov seems intent to finish. It's the old scandal, given wings with new accusations. We know Crevan kept your letters from reaching Kiara, and hers from you. We feared for the queen and for Carroway, unless you knew the truth of what's happened since you went to war."

"Thank you, Zachar," Tris said quietly, letting the enormity of Crevan's betrayal sink in. "Once again, you've served with honor, all of you."

"Ride with haste, m'lord," Zachar cautioned. "Your lady and your friend depend on it."

Tris let the images of the ghosts fade and turned to the twenty hand-picked soldiers who rode with him. "You heard them," he said. "We have to reach Shekerishet before nightfall."

Snow was drifted deep as a man's waist against the outer walls of Shekerishet when Tris and his soldiers arrived. A cold sunset of yellow and orange silhouetted the bare trees against the horizon.

Tris pushed back his hood to reveal his face as they reached the gate, as if the guards required more identification than the king's colors on the horses' livery or the crest on Tris's shield. "Open the gates!" he commanded, chafing at the delay as the massive doors to the outer bailey creaked open. Tris and his soldiers thundered through, stirring up a cloud of snow behind them.

Tris jumped down from his horse as groomsmen ran to take his reins. He set out at a run for the palace doors, with three of the guards hard pressed to keep up with him. A stocky figure ran toward them from the guards' tower, and Tris recognized Harrtuck, even at a distance. Tris's eyes narrowed as he spotted the new gallows in the bailey yard.

"Tov, where's Kiara?"

Tov Harrtuck bowed as deeply as he could as he caught his breath in the freezing air. "Thank the Lady you're back! The queen is in her rooms. But there's something I need to tell you—"

Tris met Harrtuck's gaze. "The palace ghosts found us a day's ride out. Don't worry. I know what's going on."

With that, Tris sprinted up the steps. He dashed past the servants who stopped to stare and took the stairs two at a time. When he reached the door to Kiara's chamber he slowed, and signaled for the guards to stand back.

Now that he was finally here, his heart was in his throat. Part of him feared for the safety of Kiara and the baby, and part of him dreaded the reunion, despite the testimony of the palace ghosts. He of anyone knew that ghosts were not omniscient. While he did not doubt Crevan's treachery or Guarov's vindictiveness, his stomach tightened at the thought that the rumors might have their root in truth.

Squaring his shoulders, Tris opened the door slowly. Cerise, Alle and Macaria were in the outer sitting room. They rose as he entered, and dipped to a hurried curtsey. Cerise was the first to recover from the surprise.

"Welcome back, Your Majesty."

Tris cast aside his sodden cloak on a chair near the fire. "Where's Kiara? Is she awake? Is she all right? What of the baby?"

Alle and Macaria stepped aside as Cerise beckoned for Tris to follow her. "She slipped in and out of wakefulness for a few days, while we tried to get the wormroot out of her system." Tris listened with a growing feeling of dread as Cerise told him about the danger at Shekerishet, the decision to move to the safety of the lodge, and the near-fatal attack. "She hasn't lost the baby, although it's been close a few times. As for how the wormroot affected him—I'm afraid we may not know until after the birth."

Tris swallowed hard. "I understand." He looked past Cerise to where Kiara lay in her bed. "Will she wake if I go to her?"

Cerise nodded. "She's been alert for the last two days, although she's weak." She paused. "If I may speak boldly?"

"Please."

"She feared for your safety when you went to war. Of late, she's feared your return." Cerise's eyes met his with a fiercely determined stare. "She's been totally faithful to you, m'lord, and so has Carroway. I'll swear it on any relic. What you decide to do about the rumors is between the two of you. But please, if you mean to send her away, don't tell her just yet."

Tris moved quietly toward Kiara's bedroom, and closed the door softly behind him. Her long auburn hair was tied back in a braid, and her face looked drawn and pale against the pillow. Beneath the bedclothes, Tris could see the gently rounded curve of her belly. For a moment, he watched her breathe, gathering the courage to speak.

"Kiara?"

She stirred, and turned her head toward his voice as he closed the steps between them. Her expression ran the gamut of surprise to joy to apprehension and finally, he saw a glint of fear. "Tris? Is that really you?"

"I'm no ghost, though I feel stretched thin as one," Tris said as lightly as he could. He took her hand. "Cerise said you were doing much better. She told me what happened at the lodge."

He was unprepared for how fiercely Kiara gripped his hand. "Read my soul," she said, meeting his eyes. "I know you can."

Tris felt his heart begin to thud. "I don't have to, Kiara. I love you and I believe you. The palace ghosts told me—"

Her grip tightened. "Read my soul. It's the only way you'll know for sure. The only way you'll ever trust me—and the only reason you'll ever be certain about Carroway."

Tris's gaze held steady. "I had already resolved to stay with you, regardless."

"I don't want this between us. Don't make me beg."

Tris nodded, and reached out to lay his hand lightly over her heart. He felt the shift on the Plains of Spirit and he saw the glowing pulse that was Kiara's soul. He let his power and his consciousness slip against it, and for an instant, they were one. In that moment, he saw her memories, her fears, her thoughts. And he knew, beyond a shadow of a doubt, that she had never been unfaithful. He let her see his heart, the horror of the siege, the loneliness and worry, and the reckoning. The strength of her love for him washed across the bond, healing the ache of their separation. Tris knew that his feelings were equally clear to her, and he saw the reassurance ease the strain in her face.

Only then did he realize that he had been holding his breath. Tris relaxed as he gently disengaged, drawing back on his power. When he came back to himself, he saw that Kiara's eyes were shining with tears.

"You know?"

He nodded. "I know. And I love you" He leaned over and kissed her, laying a hand gently on her belly. "Rest. I'll take care of everything."

Tris had barely closed the door behind him before Alle stepped toward him. She held out a box. "Carroway's friends found this when they broke into Crevan's office."

Tris took the box and opened it carefully, catching his breath as he realized what it held. "The letters," he murmured.

"Yours and hers," Alle said quietly. "She wrote you every week, and she waited for word from you. Now we know why it never came."

Tris knew that pain all too well. He closed the box and handed it back. "There'll be time for us to read those when Kiara's well. Thank you." He turned toward the door, but Macaria ran to him. To his astonishment, she dropped to her knees and threw herself at his feet. "Your Majesty, please! Don't let Lord Guarov kill Carroway!"

Tris winced, looking at Macaria on the floor. "Please, don't do that." He reached a hand down to help Macaria to her feet. "The ghosts met me on the road. I know all about what happened—and I'm going to do something about it."

"Please, m'lord. Mercy!"

Tris's eyes hardened. "It's time for the court to hear from Crevan."

Two CANDLEMARKS LATER, Tris adjusted the collar of his satin tunic and fastened on a heavy cloak of velvet edged in ermine. A hot bath had cleaned him up from the road. His blond hair was pulled back in a formal queue, making his newly-grown beard more noticeable. Tris had already decided the beard was worth keeping.

The court would be scrambling to comply with his command to assemble in the throne room with only two candlemarks' notice.

Coalan bustled about, adjusting Tris's cape and fussing over his formal jewelry, then placing the crown carefully on Tris's head. Tris smiled grimly. *Let them wonder about my reason for calling the court together. Just as well they're off guard. And for those who think they know what I'm going to do, they're in for the surprise of their lives.*

Four guards, hand-picked from the men who had ridden back from the siege with him, surrounded Tris as he left his rooms and headed for the throne room. He could hear the buzz of conversation at the top of the stairs, but the voices silenced abruptly as a trumpet heralded the king's arrival. Before he moved into sight, he spoke to one of his guards.

"Go to where Master Bard Carroway is imprisoned. Have him pack his things. When this is over, we'll see about his hand." The guard nodded and left to follow his orders.

The nobles rose to their feet with awkward suddenness as Tris made his way to the dais at the front where his throne awaited. Always before, he'd eschewed the show of power a slow entrance made. Now, he understood the usefulness of increasing his audience's anxiety. The less sure they were of him, the more likely they were to reveal themselves. Two footmen removed his cape and laid it to the side, revealing the sword he wore. For this purpose, Tris brought Nexus. His grandmother's warning did not deter him, even if the sword stole another breath of his soul. *This matter will be settled, once and for all.*

A large space separated Tris from the crowd, an area traditionally reserved for the accused to make their pleas. To his right, in raised seats in the place of honor, sat the Council of Nobles. Acton and Dravan were present, their faces grim. Eadoin sat with them, and while she appeared even more frail than usual, Tris knew better than to underestimate her determination. Lady Casset fidgeted with a string of beads. It was impossible to read Count Suphie. Lord Guarov and Dame Nuray looked composed, even a bit excited.

The herald signaled for the assembled courtiers to sit. "While I have been at war to protect Margolan from loyalists to the Usurper, certain charges have been made against trusted members of the royal household and the royal staff. You are here to see those charges answered and for judgment to be served."

Lord Guarov cleared his throat. "Your Majesty, is it not Margolan custom for the accused to be present at these proceedings?"

"And so they shall." Tris drew Nexus, and the runes on its blade burst into flame as it left his scabbard. With one swift movement, Tris brought the sword down with both hands so that its tip bit into the wooden floor. With a rush of air, a fiery circle swept out from the blade and Tris poured his spirit magic through the sword as an athame. On the Plains of Spirit, he sent the full force of his power seeking for the one soul that had gone to the furthest shadows to flee from him. Crevan.

In the spirit realm, Tris pursued Crevan's soul until he ran it to ground. Heedless of Crevan's pleading, Tris extended his magic and his power moved like ghostly talons, latching onto Crevan's soul and digging into its substance. *Damn the consequences. Damn my soul. I will see you pay, and so will they.*

Tris ripped open the boundary to the Plains of Spirit and flung Crevan's ghost into the warded circle shielded by Nexus's power. A collective gasp went up from the audience, and Guarov paled. Tris struggled to rein in his anger enough to extend a civil invitation to the spirits he invoked as witnesses. One by one, they assembled outside the circle of fire. Malae. Zachar. The three men whom Mikhail was accused of killing. The butcher's son. Ammond and Hothan. Bian, and the others who had gone missing over the last few months. The assembled nobles rose to their feet and the racket grew so great that it required the herald to sound a blast from his trumpet to restore order.

"Let's start with the charge of murder against Mikhail," Tris said. His voice had a deadly note to it, and his eyes were hard. "You three, step forward," he said, addressing the men whose bodies had been found with punctured throats. "Is your killer in this room?"

The three men nodded. "Aye, Your Majesty," said one of the men. "He's right there." He raised his arm to point at Crevan, and the others did the same.

"Tell your story."

The man who had spoken before cleared his throat. "'Twas during the festival, Your Majesty. I was an assistant to the wine master, and I'd gone to fetch more casks from the cellar. On my way back up, I felt a stinging in my back, like I'd been bitten by a fly. It was a dart, poisoned to bring me down like a wild boar. That's when I saw him," he said with a nod toward Crevan. "My body wouldn't move and I couldn't breathe. He pulled out a ring from his pocket and stabbed me in the neck, and caught most of my blood in a basin. When he knew I was dead, he pitched my blood down the garderobe and carried my body to where they found me."

"You're certain this is the man?"

The victim nodded. "You don't forget something like that, m'lord."

The other two men gave stories that followed the same tale. Both had been unlucky enough to be in a deserted part of the castle when Crevan sought his victims. Throughout their testimony, Crevan's ghost remained on his knees as he had fallen, with his head bowed, defiantly refusing to show his face to the king. When Malae and Bian came to tell of the poisoned *kesthrie* cakes, Tris turned his attention for a moment to Crevan.

You need to show the witnesses a little more respect. With a flicker of power, Tris jerked Crevan to his feet and tightened his grip on the man's soul, forcing his head up so that his face was visible. Crevan fixed Tris and the ghosts with a hateful glower, but said nothing.

One by one, the ghosts testified. The court exclaimed in outrage as Bian told of the poisoned cakes and the herbs Crevan's helper in the kitchen mixed into Kiara's food to bring about miscarriage. Their mood turned even uglier as the young son of the butcher recounted how Crevan had chased him with an axe out onto the treacherous ice until he'd fallen through to his death, and as Ammond and Hothan identified their poisoner and told of Carroway's desperate battle to save Kiara. Macaria, Alle and Cerise all willingly recounted Crevan's attempts to kill Kiara, attempts that the other ghosts corroborated.

"I'm the one who got away." The court turned in shock as Lady Eadoin rose to point a trembling finger at Crevan's ghost. "He sent me linens that carried sickness. My healer confirmed it. Half of my household died of the fever, and I came close enough myself to hear the Lady singing for me." She turned toward Lord Guarov, who seemed to shrink in his chair at the intensity of her anger.

"Guarov and Crevan struck a deal. Crevan would remove me from getting in the way, one less protector for the queen, and Guarov would finally have Lady Nadine's revenge on Bard Carroway." A small silver dagger appeared in Eadoin's hand from beneath her sleeve, and before anyone could move, Eadoin had the point of the blade under Guarov's chin. "You started the rumors about the Queen and Carroway, didn't you?" She jabbed him with the blade, and a thin trickle of blood started down along his throat.

"I and my people," Guarov said in a strangled voice, careful not to move against the knife that pressed against his flesh.

"Tell them that it was all lies." Then in a voice only Tris and Guarov could hear, Eadoin added, "I'm an old lady. My hand trembles, see? If it slipped, I could claim palsy."

"The rumors were lies," Guarov said, and repeated it louder as Eadoin prodded him with her blade. "All of it. There was no affair. Neither the Queen nor Carroway betrayed the king."

"Tell them why you did it." Tris's voice was harsh and completely without mercy.

Guarov's fear was visible in his eyes. "Crevan promised me he would restore the contracts I held with King Jared."

Tris's attention returned to Crevan's ghost, standing in the fiery dome. "Time to make your confession," he said quietly. "Make it good."

Crevan fixed Tris with a disdainful glare. "You want my confession, *Your Majesty*? Here it is. I was recruited to be King Donelan's court spy. Don't blame him. He didn't realize that Alvior of Brunnfen had put my name out, knowing my sympathies were with the divisionists. Yes, Curane paid me. He had his own reasons to be rid of an heir to the throne. Want the truth? I don't give a damn what happens to Margolan so long as you keep your hands off Isencroft.

"I couldn't stop the wedding, but killing the Queen would have eliminated the heir to the joint throne, and it might have made Donelan declare war on Margolan. Only she didn't die easily," Crevan sneered. "So I thought I'd let the court see her the way those of us loyal to Isencroft do: like a prize bitch put out to stud for the highest bidder.

"My only regret is that I wasted my dagger on that damn bard instead of skewering the whore and her brat like I intended."

Tris felt himself shaking with anger so overwhelming that his magic coursed through him like lightning at the peak of a storm. With a crack like thunder and a flash of blue-white mage light, Tris's power shot through Nexus until the warded dome became blindingly bright. Torn between the realm of the living and the Plains of Spirit, Tris felt his power rip through Crevan's spirit, burning him from within with a fire that could consume the soul.

An ear-splitting shriek wrenched from Crevan's spirit.

Tris fought for control of his rage. *I... will... not... make... Lemuel's... mistake.*

The light died and the dome became transparent. Crevan's spirit slumped to the floor, released from its torment.

"I don't have to kill you," Tris said raggedly as he struggled for composure. "Did you forget that you invoked the Old Gods when you worked your blood magic? You promised Shanthadura a sacrifice. You'll do."

And with that, Tris stretched out his power, once more completely in control of his magic. Nexus became both athame and shield, guarding him and protecting the others as he opened up the gateway to the Nether. Crevan's spirit screamed in utter terror. What awaited Crevan on the other side bore no relation to the Sacred Lady. Far more ancient, Shanthadura was the roiling chaos in which stars die and from which no light escapes. Tendrils of darkness snaked out from the Nether, stripping Crevan's soul like meat from a carcass. Crevan screamed again, the sound of madness joined with unendurable pain. Shanthadura was in no hurry.

Beyond the wardings, nobles retched and fainted, sliding to the floor from their chairs. No one dared to move. Tris felt the primal terror in his own soul, and knew that even his power was scant protection should Shanthadura turn his way.

Crevan's torment seemed to last forever. No matter how much of his soul Shanthadura consumed, consciousness remained. As the last glowing wisp of Crevan's soul disappeared into the fathomless darkness, Tris's magic confirmed what the others did not know. Within the belly of the monster, Crevan's soul remained conscious.

The gateway to the Nether slammed closed with an abruptness that nearly blacked Tris out. Fighting a sudden, staggering headache, Tris dismissed the wardings and warily returned Nexus to its sheath. With a word of thanks, he dismissed the ghostly witnesses, too spent just now to see them to their rest. Instead, he turned toward the Council of Nobles.

"To those who showed their loyalty to the crown at great risk to themselves, you have my thanks. Dame Nuray and Count Suphie: You are banished from this court and removed from the Council of Nobles. Lord Guarov. For treason against the crown, you are condemned to hang from the gallows you constructed." He looked out over the silenced audience. "Justice is served. This court is adjourned."

CHAPTER THIRTY-SIX

FROM HIS TOWER cell, Carroway watched the king's return with a churning mix of emotions. *Maybe he can save Kiara and the baby. The heir's what matters. A bard's life means nothing to history.*

Candlemarks passed. Carroway found that he was too nervous even to pace. He sat in a chair watching the fire in the fireplace, his stomach knotted. *How will it be? A soldier sent to escort me beyond the city walls, or beyond the kingdom's borders? One of the Sisterhood, to take me into custody? Or maybe a brace of guards to lead me to the gallows.* He could feel the blade of Harrtuck's dagger against the small of his back where he had hidden it in his belt. He looked to the parchment and ink, sent by Lord Guarov for his confession. *If I make the confession Guarov wants, maybe I can save Kiara and Macaria. I won't care what people believe of me after I'm dead. There's still time to cheat the hangman.*

The door opened, and Carroway jumped from his chair, his heart pounding. A lone guardsman entered. "The king sent me. You're to pack your things."

Carroway was shaking so badly he didn't trust his voice for a moment. "So that's to be it, then," he said. It took him less than half a candlemark to gather his belongings and secure his two trunks. He slipped his lute into its leather case and carefully fastened the shoulder strap. "Shall I get my boots and cloak?"

The guard shrugged. "The king didn't say. I'll report that you're ready. Wait here." With that, he was gone.

Carroway sagged against the wall and covered his face with his right hand. Despite a splint he had made to try to straighten out his crippled left hand, the fingers were still stiff and weak, straightening only slowly and not all the way. *I can't grasp a fork with my hand, let alone play. Perhaps if I can get the fingers not to curl up it won't distract a patron from my looks.* But he knew the truth. Without his ability to play and made less desirable by his injury, banishment was only execution postponed.

Two candlemarks later, the door opened again. "Is it time to go?" he asked, and then froze when he saw Tris Drayke in the doorway, looking as if he had just come from high court. Carroway fell to one knee, bowing deeply.

"Your Majesty," he said, feeling his heart thud in his throat. He dared to look up. Tris was watching him with an unreadable expression. In the months since his friend had left Shekerishet for battle, it seemed as if he had aged years. It wasn't the beard, or the half-healed battle scars. Something in Tris's green eyes spoke of pain and loss that could never be mended.

"Kiara never betrayed you. Neither did I. But I will accept whatever you decree to protect the crown."

Tris took a step toward him and laid a hand on his shoulder. "Crevan's spirit made a full confession in front of the entire court. Mikhail is free. You're completely exonerated." He reached out his hand to help Carroway to his feet. "Thank you. For everything."

Slowly, Carroway stood. "But the guard told me to pack my things. I thought—"

"When the ghosts met me on the road, they not only told me about Crevan, they told me about what happened at the lodge, and to your hand." He looked down at Carroway's crabbed hand and winced. "If anyone can fix it, Carina can. Go to Dark Haven. Let her heal you." Tris managed an exhausted smile. "I hope you don't mind, but I asked Macaria to go with you. Stay a few months. By the time you return, the court will have something else to gossip about. Even better: come back married."

"Come back?"

"Whatever happens with your hand, you're still Margolan's Master Bard, for life. And my friend."

"What about the Council of Nobles?"

Tris shrugged and eased into a chair. He looked exhausted, and Carroway wondered if Tris was moving on willpower alone. "Dame Nuray and Count Suphie will never return to court. As for Lord Guarov, Crevan implicated him beyond doubt in the conspiracy. Guarov and any of his retainers who had a hand in this will hang."

Carroway sat down beside him. For a moment, they were silent. "What of the siege?"

Tris drew a deep breath. "Technically, we won."

"Technically?"

"Casualties were high, both from the fighting and an outbreak of plague. Tarq betrayed us. Curane's magic backfired on him, and ended up destroying Lochlanimar and everyone in it."

"There have been worse ends to a siege, if you believe the legends."

"Funny how the legends never really talk about burying the dead."

"Do you think Curane's bunch were the last of the loyalists?"

Tris gave a bitter laugh and shook his head.

"I wish I could, but Crevan proves that wrong. Curane managed to send his granddaughter and Jared's son into Trevath before we ever besieged Lochlanimar. That problem isn't going to go away." He ran a hand through the blond hair that had escaped his queue. "It's going to be impossible to bring the army home without the plague spreading. We know some of the volunteers have already slipped off, and a couple of the nearby villages have been wiped out. Goddess true! As if Margolan hasn't had its share of sorrows."

He looked at Carroway. "Dark Haven may be safer than Margolan, if the plague takes hold. Neither the *vayash moru* nor the *vyrkin* can catch fever." He managed a wan smile. "Maybe your ballads and Royster's chronicles will outlive all of us."

"There have been plagues before. Margolan endured."

"I thought we would have enough problems keeping the peace until the spring planting was done, with food scarce this year. There are still villages where no one's ever returned after Jared's men drove them off. How much can Margolan take before Trevath or Nargi make a move?"

"You know, you're the gloomiest war hero I've ever met."

"Except for Jonmarc and Ban, I'm the only war hero you've ever met."

"As I said." The old banter returned naturally, and Carroway felt a wave of relief.

Tris stood. "You're officially a free man, so you don't have to stay here in the tower. The weather mages say tomorrow will be clear. I'll have a carriage ready for you and Macaria after seventh bells, with a purse to provide for food and lodging from here to Dark Haven. No more sleeping in crypts and cellars."

Carroway chuckled. "You don't know how glad I am to hear that." He sobered, and met Tris's gaze. "Thank you for believing me."

Tris nodded. "Give Jonmarc and Carina my best. Try to forget what happened. After all, bards write history as they choose. In the end, you make or unmake the kings and mages with your stories. Why not write this with an end that pleases you?" He clasped Carroway's arm and drew him into an embrace. "Ride safely, my friend. May the Lady's hand be upon you."

CHAPTER THIRTY-SEVEN

"**Y**OU'RE SURE ABOUT this?" Carina gave Jonmarc a sideways glance.

"I've never been more sure about anything in my life."

Carina gave his hand a squeeze. Lisette stepped closer to place a circlet on Carina's head. It was woven from grapevines and ivy. "You look beautiful, m'lady," Lisette said encouragingly, handing Carina a thick candle which was already lit.

Carina smiled and a blush crept to her cheeks as Jonmarc's gaze added his approval. In a moment, the double doors to the great room would open, and they would walk together to where Sister Taru waited to complete their ritual wedding vows. And while there was nothing Jonmarc wanted more, even that certainty wasn't enough to completely dispel the nervous tightness in his stomach over his own imminent wedding.

As was the custom in Dark Haven, Carina's dress was a deep burgundy, the color of the wine for which the region was noted, and the blood that sustained its best known residents. The dress had a high waist that flared just below the bustline, and was sleeveless on one side. Her left arm was bare, and an intricate, stylized grapevine ink pattern wove from the puncture wounds of Malesh's bite on her left shoulder to a drawing of an oak leaf in the palm of her hand, the symbols of life and ancient power. The *shevir* Jonmarc had given her as a betrothal token glittered at her wrist.

By custom, Jonmarc wore neither a shirt nor a sword. The scars that told the story of his life were plainly visible, as was the mark of the Lady branded above his heart and the two small punctures on his shoulder. A broad red satin sash belted his waist over black pants and boots. There were two reasons why ritual weddings were so rarely performed in Principality. The first was that few people felt confident enough of their choice to make a declaration that joined their souls as well as their lives. And the second was that tradition called for the man to prove both his bravery and his dedication by completing the ceremony without weapons. Jonmarc was not completely unprotected. To his right, Gabriel stood *shevirse*, a combination of groomsman and bodyguard. He carried Jonmarc's sword as well as a sword of his own, although they both knew that Gabriel himself was the deadliest weapon.

Jonmarc and Carina had already made their offerings to the Lady at sunset in Dark Haven's chapel. Now all that remained was the ceremony. Like most things in Dark Haven, the ritual differed here from what they had seen in Margolan or elsewhere, following more ancient sacred ways.

"It's time." Gabriel said solemnly, and leaned forward to open the doors. A crowd awaited, and voices buzzed as the guests turned to watch them enter. Jonmarc took a deep breath and squared his shoulders. He flashed an impudent grin at Carina before sobering and taking his place beside her as they walked to where Taru stood.

Taru wore the brown robes that marked her as one of the Sisterhood mages. In her right hand, she held an oak staff, and she wore a stole of evergreen twigs plaited with strips of oak bark. Together, the icons of immortality and ancient magic were powerful symbols. At Taru's feet was a circle of braided cloth, and in its center, a mat of oak leaves. The mage had requested that Jonmarc and Carina each give her a garment they had recently worn to make the strips that became the braid, making the magic highly personal. Jonmarc had no magic of his own, but he felt a shiver go down his spine as he and Carina stepped into the circle and knelt facing each other.

Chanting in a language Jonmarc did not recognize, Taru struck her staff on the floor behind him, and then turned it in her hands to strike the floor behind Carina with the opposite end. Jonmarc felt a sudden wind sweep along the ground, and by the way Carina's eyes widened, he suspected that her magic gave her the power to see something more dramatic. Turning the staff as she chanted, Taru marked four corners of the warding, one for each of the Light Aspects. When she had returned to her original position, she laid the staff aside and lifted an oaken chalice adorned with a band of silver that wound from the lip to the base. She filled the chalice with red wine, and lifted it to the four corners.

"Blessed be the elements. Wine from the soil." She swirled the cup, and a flame flickered over the chalice. "Fire from the sun." Drops of water fell from her cupped palm into the chalice. "Waters of the oceans." The air over the cup stirred, descending into the wine to form a vortex. "Winds of the sky."

"Do you consent to be bound in life, in death and in the dark places between life and death, joined in body and soul?"

Jonmarc's gaze locked with Carina's. "We do."

Taru took Jonmarc's left hand, turning it palm up. She withdrew a dagger with a moonstone hilt and an obsidian blade from her belt. In one smooth motion, she opened a thin cut to form half of the Lady's symbol on Jonmarc's palm, and flicked droplets of the blood into the chalice. She took Carina's hand and made a cut in the shape of the symbol's matching half, adding her blood to the chalice. Then she pressed their hands together so that their blood combined to form the Lady's mark, and took the mantle from around her neck, wrapping it four times around their wrists.

"Drink."

Jonmarc had spent enough time around mages to recognize the tingle of strong magic. He felt it sear through the joined blood between their palms, even as he felt Carina's presence slip against his mind. She smiled at the secret they shared, that she was a few days pregnant with his child. Then he felt the familiar burn of her magic healing the cut Taru had made, and Carina laced her fingers between his.

"Rejoice," Taru said. "You are joined in the law of the kingdoms and in the presence of the Lady, in life and in death—and beyond." She removed the stole from their wrists, and when they released their clasped hands, the cuts had healed into thin, white scars.

Behind them, the crowd began to clap and cheer as Jonmarc and Carina rose to their feet.

Jonmarc took Carina in his arms and kissed her. The ritual bond heightened his awareness of her, and it felt as if her thoughts and emotions flitted just beyond his grasp. He could only imagine the strength of the bond for those who shared magic as well as love.

"Congratulations." Gabriel handed Jonmarc his shirt as well as his swordbelt and weapons, which Jonmarc accepted with a sense of relief. "May the Lady in all Her Aspects bless you now and always."

The guests crowded around them to wish them well. Riqua and Rafe were present, as were Kolin and Tamaq. Vigulf, the *vyrkin* shaman, added his blessing. Laisren stood arm in arm with Lisette, looking none the worse for the injuries he had sustained in the battle against Malesh. Jonmarc felt the absence of Yestin and Eiria keenly, and although the days of mourning were completed, he knew it would take a long while for the feeling of loss to lessen. Near the wall, Raen swayed to the music with her eyes closed, singing silently. From the cold spots in the room and the inexplicable drafts of air, Jonmarc was certain Raen was not the only one of Dark Haven's ghosts that was present, although she alone was visible. The head of the wine guild and the other town dignitaries were present, along with the *vayash moru* and *vyrkin* who had fought alongside Jonmarc and Gabriel. Even Jonmarc's old friends Maynard

Linton and Jolie had managed to arrive in Dark Haven for the wedding. But as Jonmarc moved among his guests, more than once he heard the others whisper an unfamiliar word, and he turned finally to Gabriel.

"Who are the '*mogorifi*'?"

Gabriel looked at him. "You and Carina. It's an old word. It means 'the changed ones.' There are legends about a few who stand between the living and the undead, who are both and neither. In the legends, the *mogorifi* are guardians." He gave a pointed glance at the puncture scars on Jonmarc's neck. "You returned alive from making Istra's Bargain. Carina returned as a mortal from Malesh's attempt to turn her. Either one would be rare, to say the least. For the two of you together," he shrugged, "it's not unreasonable to view it as highly significant."

The implications of Gabriel's comments were more than Jonmarc wanted to think about.

"Oh, and just so you know," Gabriel continued, "the only ones who aren't aware that Carina is expecting are the mortals. The *vayash moru* and *vyrkin* can sense a shift in the life force like that." He smiled. "Congratulations, to both of you."

Jonmarc slipped his arm around Carina's shoulders as musicians began a round of lively tunes and drew her out on the dance floor for the circle dances, enjoying her laughter as they wove through the complicated steps.

As the dance concluded, a hush fell over the room. Jonmarc turned to see an unfamiliar *vayash moru* in the doorway. He tensed, unsure whether the newcomer was friend or foe.

"That's Alfarr," Gabriel said in a low voice just behind him. "He's the keeper of the torches in the Lady's chapel beneath the manor house. He's kept them lit for hundreds of years, but he rarely ventures out. This is highly unusual."

Had Alfarr been mortal, Jonmarc would have supposed him in his middle years, with dark black hair edged with gray at the temples. He moved with a dignified confidence, and something in his eyes hinted at a burden long carried. Alfarr stopped in front of Jonmarc and Carina and made a low bow.

"Peace and blessings to you both." His voice had an unusual accent, one Jonmarc could not place. Alfarr met Carina's eyes. "Now I can rest, because my vision has come true. Twin daughters will each bear a son. One will wear a crown, and the other will wield a sword, and together they will challenge the abyss."

Carina's eyes widened. "Twins," she whispered.

Daughters. Jonmarc caught his breath and tightened his grip on Carina's hand.

Before he could collect his thoughts to reply, Alfarr was gone.

"What do you suppose that means?" Carina asked, looking toward the empty doorway.

"Visions are strange things," Gabriel said. "They can mean a great deal, or nothing at all. Even if they come true, they can lead to an end that the seer never imagined." Jonmarc met his eyes, and knew that Gabriel's insight came from visions of his own.

Gabriel clapped a hand on Jonmarc's shoulder. "Let the future take care of itself, for once. There'll be time enough for visions. Today, we celebrate."

"That works for me. I'm a one-day-at-a-time kind of guy." Jonmarc pulled Carina into his arms and looked into her eyes. "Twin girls, huh? That'll take some getting used to."

She chuckled. "It's too late for second thoughts."

He kissed the thin pink scar on her palm. "Second thoughts? Never. But even if they're healers like you, expect me to teach them to use a sword."

"We'll see about that."

Jonmarc leaned down to kiss her. As he met her lips and drank in the scent of her hair, he realized that for the first time in half his life, the future was no longer a dark unknown. He heard the crowd around them clinking goblets and cheering for their kiss as Carina leaned against him and returned his kiss with fervor.

Visions be damned.

The Lord of Dark Haven had come home.

ABOUT THE AUTHOR

Gail Z. Martin discovered her passion
for science fiction, fantasy and ghost stories
in elementary school. The first story she
wrote—at age five—was about a vampire. Her
favorite TV show as a preschooler was Dark
Shadows. At age fourteen, she decided to become a
writer. She enjoys attending science fiction/fantasy
conventions, Renaissance fairs and living history
sites. She is married and has three children, a
Himalayan cat and a golden retriever.

You can visit Gail at:-

www.chroniclesofthenecromancer.com

Read her blog:-

blog.myspace.com/chronicleofthenecromancer

And follow her on twitter:-

twitter.com/gailzmartin

SOLARIS BOOKS

Founded in 2007 as an independent imprint, Solaris set out to publish a mix of innovative and traditional science fiction, fantasy and horror, by new and familiar authors alike, and to fill the gap between large-scale mass-market publishers and the small genre press. In two years, we've published gritty, hard-SF and high-octane adventure, creepy horror and swashbuckling fantasy. We've discovered new gems like the hugely successful Gail Z. Martin and snagged old favourites like Brian Lumley and Eric Brown. We've published seven anthologies, including new science fiction and fantasy, steampunk, and stories inspired by H. P. Lovecraft and Edgar Allan Poe, with contributions by some of the best-loved and most recognised names in science fiction. As of 2009, Solaris has been part of Rebellion, and are confident that they can only go from strength to strength in the future.

More than anything, Solaris exists to publish fantastic books by great authors, and to bring to your attention, as a reader, a plethora of exciting new stories and novels.

http://www.solarisbooks.com/

"Attractive characters and an imaginative setting combine
in an excellent, fast-moving quest novel."
— David Drake, author of the Lord of the Isles series

GAIL Z. MARTIN

THE SUMMONER

Book One of the
CHRONICLES OF THE NECROMANCER

UK ISBN: 978 1 844164 68 4 • US ISBN: 978 1 844164 68 4 • £7.99/$7.99

The world of Prince Martris Drayke is thrown into chaos when his brother murders their father and seizes the throne. Forced to flee with only a handful of loyal followers, Martris must seek retribution and restore his father's honour. If the living are arrayed against him, Martris must call on a different set of allies: the living dead.

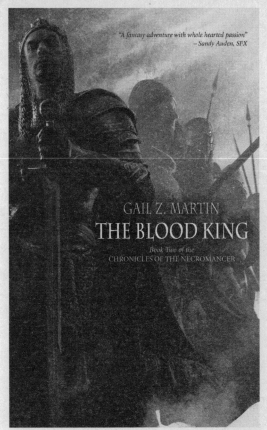

"A fantasy adventure with whole hearted passion"
– Sandy Auden, SFX

GAIL Z. MARTIN

THE BLOOD KING

Book Two of the
CHRONICLES OF THE NECROMANCER

UK ISBN: 978 1 844165 31 5 • US ISBN: 978 1 844165 31 5 • £7.99/$7.99

Having escaped being murdered by his evil brother, Prince Martris Drayke must take control of his ability to summon the dead and gather an army big enough to claim back his dead father's throne. But it isn't merely Jared that Tris must combat. The dark mage, Foor Arontola, plans to cause an imbalance in the currents of magic and raise the Obsidian King...

GAIL Z. MARTIN

DARK HAVEN

Book Three of the
CHRONICLES OF THE NECROMANCER

"A fast-paced tale laced with plenty of action."
— SF Site on *The Summoner*

UK ISBN: 978 1 844167 08 1 • US ISBN: 978 1 844165 98 8 • £7.99/$7.99

The kingdom of Margolan lies in ruin. Martris Drayke, the new king, must rebuild his country in the aftermath of battle, while a new war looms on the horizon. Meanwhile Jonmarc Vahanian is now the Lord of Dark Haven, and there is defiance from the vampires of the Vayash Moru at the prospect of a mortal leader. But can he earn their trust, and at what cost?

 WWW.SOLARISBOOKS.COM

Follow us on Twitter! www.twitter.com/solarisbooks

UK ISBN: 978 1 844166 17 6 • US ISBN: 978 1 844165 84 1 • £7.99/$7.99

When he mysteriously finds himself drawn into a world of his own devising, bumbling writer Rod Everlar is confronted by a shocking truth - he has lost control of his creation to a brooding cabal of evil. In order to save his creation, he must seize control of Falconfar and halt the spread of corruption before it is too late.

 WWW.SOLARISBOOKS.COM

Follow us on Twitter! www.twitter.com/solarisbooks

UK ISBN: 978 1 906735 63 0 • US ISBN: 978 1 844167 64 7 • £7.99/$7.99

Having been drawn into a fantasy world of his own creation, Rod Everlar continues his quest to defeat the corruption he has discovered within. With the ambitious Arlaghaun now dead, he sets off in pursuit of the dark wizard Malraun, only to find that he has raised an army of monsters and mercenaries in order to conquer the world...

 WWW.SOLARISBOOKS.COM

Follow us on Twitter! www.twitter.com/solarisbooks